GOOD BUDDY

a novel

Dori Ann Dupré

For Eric

"His life was gentle; and the elements

So mixed in him, that Nature might stand up

And say to all the world, THIS WAS A MAN!"

— William Shakespeare, *Julius Caesar*

EJD Press

Raleigh, North Carolina

This book is a work of fiction. All names, characters, places, and incidents either are products of the author's imagination or are used in a fictitious manner. Any resemblance to actual persons, living or dead, is purely coincidental.

Dumas, Alexandre, 1802-1870. The Count of Monte Cristo. New York, N.Y., U.S.A.: Penguin Books, 2001.

Whitman, Walt. Walt Whitman's Leaves of Grass: The First (1855) Edition. New York: Penguin Books, 2005. Print.

Printed in the United States of America. First Printing, 2019.

ISBN (Print Edition): 978-1-54396-665-7
ISBN (eBook Edition): 978-1-54396-666-4

Cover Design by Dionne Abouelela / HappyWriting.co

Author Photo by Kelly Walker Photography

Distribution and Printing by Book Baby

CONTENTS

Part I

Part II

PART I

"Who knows? Perhaps your love will make me forget all I wish not to remember."

—Alexandre Dumas,
The Count of Monte Cristo

CHAPTER 1

May 17th, 1975

The Middle of the Night

Light flickered in-and-out and in-and-out in a rhythmic cadence through the dark finger-smudged window. The sound of the road passing underneath the hole in the floor board could have been the beat of a song. But Buddy didn't know which song. He didn't know that many songs.

The car was otherwise quiet, his mother driving with both skin tight, bony hands on the big black steering wheel, street lights whirring by in the night. She made no noise, no movement – even the big dark curls in her hair stayed immobile, paralyzed in space, kind of how he felt in the back seat. He couldn't remember her putting that spray stuff on her hair this morning, and he couldn't remember coughing because of the fumes in the bathroom before he left for school. He was confused as to how she got her curls to stay so still, even with the car moving so fast.

There was no noise around them as she drove along the highway, and he didn't know what time it was. It seemed late. Maybe it was the morning – the dark time of the morning that everyone called "the middle of the night." That never made much sense to Buddy – how it could be both morning and night at the same time.

A thin white sheet covered him. It was full of Snoopy dogs, so he knew that it was from his bed at home. He spread out his body along the back seat with his spine facing the rear of the car. His hands were under his head, a real hand-made pillow. His new Adidas sneakers, a birthday gift from his parents, were still on his feet, and he was wearing the same blue and green striped shirt that he wore to school this morning. Or yesterday morning now, he guessed.

Buddy moved his legs and saw his mother's eyes quickly glance into the rearview mirror.

"You up?" she asked, her voice quiet, breaking the sound of the silence in the car like a mumble in a dream.

"I got to pee," he answered, afraid to move, still feeling like he was suspended in time. The weight of the air was heavy in this car, and he felt like he was in some kind of trouble, like his mother would send him to his room the next chance she had with no ice cream or Lady Fingers cookies for dessert.

She pulled the car off to the side of the highway, put it in park and turned her head. "Son, you run out in the bushes right there and go relieve yourself real quick."

Pushing the Snoopy sheet off, he scooted out the side of the back seat and into the thin grass off the shoulder of the road. There was a light coming up, but not a soul to be found on this road, other than Buddy and his mother. He walked over to the bushes, unzipped his fly and a long overdue stream began the process of killing anything that was still living on that spot. He breathed in the cool early morning air and felt it fill his lungs with fresh life. There was a sudden pause in his heart beat as he heard some rustling in a nearby bush.

Rather than wait to find out what it was, he hopped back into the car again, only this time, he rode shotgun.

"Where we goin'?" Buddy asked his mother, watching her hands again, tighter than ever on the steering wheel, like she was holding on as if her life depended on it.

"Somewhere far away."

He had heard her say that several times before when she had him locked inside of the car and they had been driving for a long while. But this time – unlike those other times – it seemed true. He had no idea where they were, or where they were going, but he knew it was late. Would Kenny be mad at them for not going back home?

"Was today my last at school?" he asked her, already certain of the answer.

"Yes, son."

Buddy sank down into the seat, the vinyl hard, slippery and uncomfortable. His mother lit a cigarette and rolled down her window. He rolled down his window, too. The smoke hurt his nose sometimes, and he wanted to be able to stick his head out with the wind in his face like a dog when the smoke got too bad inside.

In the distance, off to the side of the highway, he could see one of those big metal monsters that go up-and-down, supposedly drilling for oil. They were scary looking, and there were times when he thought that they could pull themselves from their spots and start walking over toward them. They were so big – maybe they would be able to stomp on his mother's car, crushing them both inside. Or maybe his mother would pull him out before it got to them and protect him from their huge metal feet...because that's what mothers do. They protect their sons from monsters.

Looking out at the headlight-lined empty road, Buddy tried to figure out what was going on with his mother. And, in order to put the big oil drilling monsters out of his head, he started to think about yesterday…or maybe the day before…he wasn't sure.

He woke up like normal and got dressed for school. He had Rice Krispies for breakfast that did not snap, crackle or pop for very long at all. Not like the commercial says it does. He watched Bugs Bunny on the little black and white TV on the kitchen counter. Kenny, his stepfather, was sleeping on the couch in the living room, and he could hear him snoring that big deep, loud snore – the one he made when his mother said, "Kenny is sleeping it off."

Kenny was not wearing a shirt or socks, and his jeans hung loose and low on his waist, almost like they were too big for him. His right arm was touching the floor. Buddy's mother was ironing her light pink skirt in her bedroom, and when she heard Buddy shut off the TV, she came out and kissed him goodbye. Buddy had picked up his lunchbox, a small metal one with comics on it that was all scratched up but had managed to last him the whole school year anyway. Then he swung open the screen door, heard it bang shut behind him, walked down the two wooden steps that needed fixing for the whole time they lived in this small house, and then down the sidewalk toward James Street.

He saw Mr. Sogg sitting out front of his house on the steps reading the morning paper.

"Hey, Buddy boy," he grunted at him with a salute.

Buddy waved and replied politely, "Good morning, sir," as he walked by.

Crossing James Street, he took the usual way to school: a path through a back alleyway in between two houses, then ran through an empty field leading all the way to John Morrow Primary School, where Buddy was finishing up the second grade. And other than seeing his best friend Gary ride up to the school playground on his silver Schwinn, his teacher Miss Clemmons taking the roll in her nasal voice – "Daniel Kaspar Junior" – and some kind of light pink blur in front of his eyes, Buddy couldn't remember anything else from the whole entire day. Not lunch or recess or art class or even the spelling test that he knew he must've taken because of how his mother quizzed him on the words the night before.

The last thing Buddy recalled was waking up in his mother's car in the dead of night with the Snoopy sheet over his waist, feeling like the life he had was over…forever.

Buddy's stomach growled. His mother puffed.

"Where are we?" he asked her, breaking the thick fog of quiet. His mother wasn't a real talkative woman even in the daytime, but he could feel something horrible coming from her, all the way through her pores. Her hair wasn't messy or anything, and he didn't remember ever seeing the shirt she was wearing before now. But the light pink skirt she wore while driving was the same one she had been ironing before he went to school.

"Still in Texas," she said.

"Are we leaving Texas?" Buddy asked, slightly confused. He had never been out of Texas before that he could remember.

"Yes," she responded and then flicked her cigarette out of the window, the tiny orange light flying solo onto the black road behind them.

New Mexico

Retta had been driving west on I-20 and then I-10 since Abilene, and she still didn't know where in the world she was going. She had never been west of Killeen. But after driving for more than a day and operating on about two hours of broken, anxiety-ridden sleep while huddled with Buddy in the back corner of a parking lot in a gas station a few hours ago, Retta realized that soon daylight would start to color the sky on their second day of this peculiar liberation. She knew she needed to get off this highway and start taking smaller, less traveled roads. Part of the problem was – to where?

Even though a part of her had planned for this moment for a couple years now, she never realized it would come to fruition. And not like this: sudden and unplanned, sprung on her like the worst kind of surprise party or like a scary, pointy-toothed Jack-in-the-Box clown. She was a planner and not the kind of girl who was good on the fly.

Retta and her sweet son Buddy had nothing with them but this Duster – which she needed to get rid of, the gun in the trunk – which she also needed to get rid of, and $76 left of the $88 she had in her hidden stash – which used to be tucked deep down into her panty drawer and was now stuffed inside of her bra. No clothes, no food, and no clue. She couldn't contact her mother or older brother or even her best friend May Ellen. Buddy and Retta had to disappear and never be found again. That was the only thing she knew for sure.

Whenever she would think about taking Buddy and running away from Kenny, Retta figured she'd go stay with her brother Frank and his wife Nikki in Maryland, just until they got back on their feet. Frank had always told her that she'd have a home with him. He was, after all, the father she never really had.

In her plan, the one that had been percolating inside of her head for quite a while, she'd pack up Buddy's clothes and toys, her clothes and photo albums, and they would go hide out with Frank and Nikki until Kenny got the message that she was done with him and long gone and never coming back.

But this? This was not really something she had thought about before. And now it's four o'clock in the morning, many hours removed from the event that changed everything, and she still hadn't figured out a damn thing. And she needed to. Buddy was relying on her. She was all he had in this world now. And he was all she had, too.

Retta knew that I-10 led into El Paso and that El Paso led into New Mexico, so she figured she'd just get there, stop someplace off the road to get their bearings, maybe attempt to take another nap, and then try to figure out where they'd go next. She didn't know how much time she had before someone would come searching for them. But first, she needed to get rid of the Duster or at least trade license plates with somebody before trying to get rid of it.

Isn't that what the bad guys do on TV? Trade plates with some unsuspecting farmer? Is she a bad guy now? And other than stealing a pack of cigarettes from her best friend Chrissy's house once and some penny gum from Neal's General Store when she was twelve, all on a dare from that ass who lived in the room above her family, Retta Bellinger had never stolen anything in her life.

Looking over at Buddy, who was sitting with his buzzed head resting on the window, she could just make out the subtle moonlight reflecting through the length of his beautiful eyelashes. She thought about the gravity of everything that was going on. What did Buddy know? What did he remember? He'd been sleeping for the past nine hours, and they hadn't talked the entire time since she rushed him out of the house, into the car and down the road. She didn't even know how to break the ice with him. She thought, *My God, my baby boy is only nine years old. What will become of him if I can't get us away from all this?* By marrying Kenny Bellinger, she knew she had unintentionally put him through enough suffering to last him another nine years. But that was ending. Right now.

The flat desolate parts of Texas lent a clarity to the world that she didn't think East Coast people understood. Dry, bare, naked, the end – and yet endless at the same time. Quiet, lonely, desperate – kind of like what death must be. Or what a lot of her life had been so far, except for the brief peaks of relief with normal things like falling in love with Buddy's father, having her firstborn child, and even falling in love again later…with Kenny.

Growing up, Retta's family was desperately poor, and her father had died from a heart attack on her third birthday. She had no specific memory of that day, or even of her father, but she always saw a strong man's hand holding the hand of a small girl within the depths of her dreams.

Since her mother had no employable skills, other than the kind that every woman possesses at even a basic level, she moved Retta and Frank into a room on top of an old tavern sitting in a military town nearby. Apparently, she made a deal with the owner of the tavern: she'd work as a bar maid in exchange for the free room. And the owner would allow her to earn additional money by letting it be known…quietly…that she was available for "entertaining" or "keeping men company." Since soldiers and mill workers were always around, she had no problem finding opportunities to do either.

The day Retta learned that her mother was a prostitute had started out like any other day. Frank, who was three years older than she was but forced to grow up much faster than his peers, woke her up from a deep sleep. He tried to move her along, to get her out of their room before their mother returned from her night out "entertaining" and "keeping men company." Frank knew what his mother did to put food on the table and was embarrassed about it. The other boys at school knew, too, and they would give him a hard time. He even got into a few fist fights in the woods near the school over the things they'd say about her.

"C'mon Retta. Get up. We got to go," Frank was poking her bony side with his fingers. He had her dress spread out on the bed, the one with the puffy sleeves that the lady from the Children's Society gave her, as well as her saddle shoes, all worn out with a big hole in the bottom of the left one, sitting on the floor underneath. Retta figured that if Frank had been a girl, he would've made a good mother someday because he did the kinds of things for her that her friend Chrissy's mother did for Chrissy. But Retta was so sleepy that morning, it took her longer than usual to get up and moving.

"Retta, you got to move it. We can't be late today," Frank moaned at her, sounding desperate. "If you hurry, I'll get you a lollipop from Neal's."

But it was too late. As she pulled the dress over her head, the same dress she had worn for the past two days, her mother walked in the door, her dark brown hair frizzed into a messy nest and her makeup all run down on her face. She stunk of liquor and smoke and was shocked to see them still in the room.

"Dammit Frank, why're you still here?" she shouted at him. He stood taller than his own mother at just twelve years old.

"I'm sorry Mommy, we're just leaving."

"Retta, you're late for school today! How are you ever gonna get out of this town if you're late for school and don't learn nothing?"

Then she stomped into the tiny bathroom attached to their room, turned on the tub water, and shut the door behind her. Retta looked up at Frank, whose buzzed-cut brown hair needed another buzz to it. His olive-skinned face was a shade of red, and he knew he was in big trouble. In that moment, Retta realized that Frank and their mother had an understanding, and he blew it. He held out his hand to his younger sister and said, "Let's go Retta."

She had never seen her mother like that before. Normally when she'd see her, she was working like the other women in the tavern. She'd look pretty and dolled up with her dark curly hair and face makeup and nails painted. Sometimes, she'd paint Retta's nails for her and put red lipstick on her lips. She'd have her kiss the mirror in the bathroom and would always say, "Retta, your lips are the lips of an angel. What kinds of things does God tell you, baby doll?"

Retta would always try to make up a good answer, like, "God told me that today is gonna be sunny out!" or "God told me that we should get a kitten!" One time she shouted, "God told me that Daddy says that he loves us." Her mother smiled that day, like she really believed God told Retta stuff because she had lips like an angel.

"Why did Mommy look like that, Frank?" she asked him, as they walked to school.

"She's been working all night."

"What do you mean? The tavern was closed."

Frank stopped walking and turned to her. He bent down and grabbed her arms. His face got serious and he looked angry. "I'm only gonna say this once, Retta. She don't work at the tavern all night. Our mother is a prostitute. She keeps men company over night and they pay her for it. And if she didn't do it, we'd be living on the streets like the Branson kids and their mother."

Retta thought that what Frank was telling her seemed strange. She knew what "keeping men company" meant because of what Chrissy told her last summer when they were playing school in Chrissy's pale pink bedroom. The dolls and stuffed animals were all sitting in a straight line, like pupils in a classroom. Before Chrissy handed out pencils to her toys, she explained to Retta that "keeping men company" meant that men stuck their peckers into womens' bellybuttons and then the women got pregnant with a baby.

Retta looked at Frank and shook his hands off her arms. "Mommy lets men stick their peckers in her bellybutton?"

Frank's eyes got wide and big, and she could tell that he was trying not to laugh. "Who told you that?"

"Chrissy told me last summer. She said that Mrs. Hassel was keeping company with Mr. Stevens and that her husband didn't know about it. So, when I asked her if they were kissing each other, Chrissy said that it was more than kissing. That Mr. Stevens was putting his pecker in her bellybutton and that she would get pregnant and then not know which man is the real father of the baby!"

Frank looked at Retta stunned, like this is the first time he's heard of such a thing. Because it was. Responding, with a touch of surprise in his voice, "Mr. Stevens was doing that?" He shook his head and looked over his shoulder. "Well what do you know? All that man ever does is talk about the Bible and how our family is going to Hell for living in the tavern."

"I'm not going to Hell, Frank. Mommy said that I have the lips of an angel. Angels don't go to Hell."

Frank smiled at his tiny sister, who looked so much like their mother. There were days it seemed like she had just spit Retta out of her mouth and onto the floor. "Let's go. We're already late for school."

As they walked, Frank reached down and held her hand.

"Frank? You know, brothers of angels don't go to Hell either."

Frank picked up her hand and kissed it.

"You're right about that, Retta."

When Buddy and Retta crossed over the border into New Mexico, she breathed a sigh of relief. Just getting them outside of the Texas border made her feel like she checked off the first item on a list that had been meant to-do for a long, long time. "Out of Texas," check. "Eat something" was next. "Get rid of the Duster" was after that. It took forever to get out of the state; she never realized how big the place was and how often she would have to stop to get gas just so she could leave it altogether.

As the sunrise's blinding rays began to consume the haze of early morning in Las Cuatro, a mid-sized New Mexico border town, she found a busy breakfast kitchen with dusty pickup trucks parked outside. Inside were matching dusty brown-skinned men sitting in booths as they devoured plates of eggs and coffee in small white cups. Buddy and Retta sat on a stool at a bar, and as Buddy looked down at a torn menu, Retta quietly pulled out her cash, eyeing the men around her.

A short and rotund woman with her black hair pulled up and a name tag that read "Lucinda" put a glass of water in front of them both and started speaking to them in Spanish. Buddy looked up at her and uttered, "No habla espangol, ma'am."

She didn't smile, but Retta could see that she had a warmness to her by the way she peered down at Buddy and tilted her head to the side. "Do you want the special?" she asked in heavily accented English.

"Yes ma'am," Buddy responded, clearly not knowing what the special was.

Retta just wanted to get out of there as fast as possible, so she blurted out, "Two specials, please."

Lucinda walked away, and Retta's eyes darted around the dining room. She knew the two of them stood out. The place was full of what seemed to be half of Mexico – hardened, leathery migrant workers sending their meager American earnings back across the border to their families at the end of the week. Buddy and Retta looked nothing like them. Fast Spanish voices filled the air in a muffled tone, and she was starting to become paranoid that these men would say something to them. But as she ate the special, which was two scrambled eggs, bacon, toast, and coffee – pretty much an all-American breakfast served at diners everywhere – no one even seemed to notice them, much less talk to them.

As Lucinda walked by, Retta asked her if she knew of anyone interested in buying a car.

"My uncle buys cars all the time," she answered.

That sounded odd to Retta, but she needed to get rid of this Duster as soon as possible.

"Does he live nearby?" she asked, hoping Lucinda wouldn't ask too many questions.

"He has a car place just up the road, like a mile or more, called "Hector's." The sign is white. It's brand new."

Buddy looked over at his mother as he continued to eat a piece of toast. And as Retta observed her good little boy, she wondered... What did he know? What did he remember? What did he think was going on?

Since she just didn't know what to say to him, she checked "Eat something" off the long and overdue Running Away List, paid for their specials with the ten-dollar bill she pulled out of her shirt and walked out of the restaurant. Then they both got into the Duster, and she drove to Hector's with the intent on checking off the next item: "Get rid of Duster."

The Inn Between

I was looking down at myself lying on kitchen floor. It was kind of weird, like looking into a kaleidoscope and seeing colors go into lines, turning and turning along, only my face staying the same and still within the swirls around me. My face was white with bloody flakes coming up onto my chin. My eyes were closed, and I appeared to be sleeping. Or dead. The rest of my body looked woozy and dream-like, fuzzy and blurry, like I was still drunk from this morning...and the day before...and the day before that.

There was a broken glass next to me on the floor, and as my body became a little clearer, I could see a big crimson stain coming from my chest, soaking my white tee-shirt. My jeans had some blood droppings on my right thigh, and my right hand, covered in blood, lay along the side of my leg on the floor. My head had blood caked on the side of it, my hair strands sticking together like they were dipped in industrial strength glue.

The fridge was behind me, humming rather loudly. There were no lights on inside the house, except for a small one near the oven, and it was pretty dark outside. But for some reason, I could see myself as if there were lights shining everywhere, only it was background or studio lighting, like when you get your portrait taken in the picture studio at Sears...my own real life or real death photo session going on in front of me.

"Hey!" I shouted. I wasn't sure if I was trying to wake myself up or if I was dead or if I was trying to get Retta's attention to come and help me.

"Hey! Retta! I've been shot!" I yelled again.

It was strange. I hollered, but there was no sound. There was nothing, like I was the only person who could hear my voice.

I tried looking around the kitchen to see what could've happened to me. Obviously, I had been shot. Maybe even twice. But there was no gun nearby. I could feel a numbing sensation in my chest but nothing else. Other than the broken glass on the floor, and a frying pan upside-down in the corner, the kitchen was its usual spotless self. Retta was the cleanest housekeeper I ever knew, and even Buddy kept his own mess neat and orderly to please his mama. There were no dishes in the sink or even in the dish drying rack. A small towel was on the counter where Retta would cut up vegetables whenever she made a meal. I could see some of the errant knife blade marks grooved in it. Damn woman, we might get lose our deposit to the landlord if he saw those.

"Retta! Help me!" I shouted into the house. "Buddy!"

Still, nothing. I couldn't move from where I was, even though I felt like I was floating. It's like I drifted up into the air and just hovered there – no floating around allowed, only up. I was acutely aware of my surroundings, so I knew I wasn't drunk anymore. How long had it been since I was last sober?

The phone was on the wall, but I couldn't get to it to call somebody. Maybe one of the neighbors heard the shooting and called the cops. Maybe Retta and Buddy went to get some help. Maybe they were hiding from whoever shot me. Maybe they were in another room, both shot dead on the floor. Maybe the three of us will meet in this floating pool of air...the Inn Between...a surreal home caught in the middle of life and death that I seemed to be wading in right up to my waist. But then again, maybe not. If they can only float up like me, they won't be able to move from where their bodies were lying to tell me that we'll all be together soon.

My mind was busy conjuring up all kinds of scenarios about where Retta and Buddy could be, why I was laying down there like that, and who could've shot me. I know Retta's been mad at me for a good long time now, and she's threatened to leave lots of times. But there wasn't a crazy bone in her tiny little body, so I knew she wouldn't have shot me. I knew she really loved me. I knew I never deserved her.

I realized that my hands were hurting and knew it had to be from wailing on Retta earlier today when she pissed me off with her smart fucking mouth. I hit her hard in the head, and she grabbed a cookie sheet off the counter and put it up to protect herself. When I went to punch her again, I hit the metal pan instead. I could see the bruises on my right knuckles, with dried blood coming around to my wrist.

"Kenny, get up!" I shouted at myself. I didn't move. My arms and legs were as still as could be. I couldn't tell if I was breathing or not. I bled a lot from that hole in my chest, but there was nothing gushing out. And here I was, completely aware of myself and my existence, feeling the pain in my hands and the numbness of my chest and as awake and alive as I'd ever been in all the years since I got back from Vietnam.

CHAPTER 2

August 1996

Jonathan Cordova, Attorney-at-Law

"No, it doesn't work that way," Buddy explained to the lady on the phone.

"But he's just a boy. He didn't do nothin' that bad," Dolly Craig said on the other end of the line.

"Ma'am, in the eyes of the law, he is not just a boy. He has a serious drug problem, and the best deal he is going to get is the one that the DA offered him," he tried to explain to the distraught mother of his client, a drug addicted teenager who he had been trying to get into a treatment program so he wouldn't be sentenced to jail. "You have to trust me on this. He is getting a good deal. And he's lucky to have a mother like you who cares so much about him."

Dolly's voice was bordering on a tremble, and he could tell that she was simply exhausted. Exhausted from all these years of poverty, drugs choking the life out of so many family members, an alcoholic husband who beat her, and the daily misery that defined her life, as she continued to live through one sordid mess after another, always being the one who had to clean up the depravity of those she loved.

She tried. She tried to instill good values in her children, but she was just unsuccessful in combating the ugly forces around her. It was a common theme that accompanied the many sad voices of his clients' family members. They were all the same, really. They were all just simply exhausted.

When Dolly first came to his office last week, he was surprised to learn that she wasn't too much older than he was. Buddy thought she looked like she could've been his mother's age or even older. Tattered hair with more silver than a woman in her late thirties should have. A cratered, yellowing face full of that one roadmap which outlined the pattern of life's unfairness toward certain people. He remembered watching her mouth move, wondering how many cigarettes have sat along her dried, coarse lips, revealing so much of her life-long pain and suffering. He felt for her. He felt for most of his clients and definitely felt for all of his clients' mothers…who have had to answer in some way for so many sins that they didn't commit themselves.

Life is hard for everybody at some point, but the people who Jonathan Cordova, Attorney-at-Law, sees day in and out seem to have it just a bit harder. A lot of times, he sees himself as a little buzzed-cut boy in their sad backstories and what could've become of him if his mother hadn't plucked them both from the maniacal clutches of his mentally ill and alcoholic stepfather in Killeen, Texas so many years ago. Alcoholism, physical abuse, drug addiction, promiscuity, teen pregnancy, poverty, crime, unemployment – it all fuels one another. It all feeds on the souls of the young who start out as promising, well-meaning and curious little creatures, who then morphed into addicts…which then eventually morphed them into criminals.

Maybe, just maybe, if some of his clients had also been fortunate enough to be plucked from their unfortunate circumstances, they would've had a real shot at a decent life, too. Maybe instead of sitting in a cell, waiting for Jonathan Cordova, Attorney-at-Law, to meet with them so they could figure out the best way to answer for their crimes...they'd be practicing law someplace themselves.

After hanging up with Dolly Craig, Buddy got up and stood at his office window. He looked at the clock on his wall. It was a warm and sunny day in Fayetteville, North Carolina. Summer still held on tightly, with its white knuckled grasp, to the slowly shortening days. Since he had been cooped up inside all morning, and because the clock was reading 1:56 PM, Buddy figured it was time to go ahead and take Bo for a quick walk. It was about that time for the daily jogger to go by.

Walking out of his home office and then into the rest of his old echo-filled three-bedroom house, Buddy found Bo lying on his big fluffy bed in the living room with a sun blade cutting through the dusty air resting on his coat. Bo's bed really served as one hell of a pillow when Buddy needed to lie down on the floor to stretch out his back. He picked up Bo's leash off the coffee table, and Bo's huge golden head moved, his eyes looking at his beloved owner. Other than food, this was the most excited Bo would get in his advanced age. A walk – a walk was the best thing in the world next to food.

Bo and Buddy walked out the front door. Jasper the mailman was walking up the sidewalk toward them with a handful of envelopes. Maybe in his younger years, Bo would've gone after the mailman, but these days, all he did was walk up to Jasper and wait for him to rub his head and maybe hand him a treat from the pocket of his long blue shorts.

"Hey there Mr. Cochran," he said, handing Buddy about six letters. "You save anyone from jail today? Did the glove fit?"

Jasper called Buddy "Mr. Cochran" because he's a criminal defense attorney, and apparently Johnnie Cochran from the OJ

Simpson trial is the only criminal defense attorney he knows. And that's a good thing because that means that Jasper has never had need of a criminal defense attorney's services.

Buddy grinned slightly at this affable black man, who he's known for two years, and noticed a huge bandage on his arm just under the cuff of his postal uniform. Jasper leaned over to pet Bo behind the ears.

"Jasper, what have you done to yourself?" Buddy asked him, pointing at the bandage.

He looked at his arm and answered, "Cut it real bad yesterday on my day off. I was working in my shed. Shay had to take me to the hospital for stitches. Blood everywhere."

"What you been working on?" Buddy asked. Jasper was a wood carving master. He made beautiful furniture and artwork and trinkets and sold his creations at the flea market on Sundays, along with his wife Shay, who sold her crocheted crafts and baskets. The two rocking chairs resting on Buddy's front porch were made in Jasper's shed. It was a nice little side business for him, and when he retired from the postal service, he planned to do it full time.

"A crib this time," he said.

"A crib?"

"Yeah, Melanie is expectin'. We just found out."

"Wow, so I guess, 'Congratulations,' is in order," Buddy added. "What is this – your third grandchild?"

"Yes, it is. Shay is just beside herself happy."

Just then, Buddy saw her go by. His jogger. She was running at a decent pace on the side of the street, wearing a plain gray tee-shirt and hunter green runner's shorts. Her blond hair was pulled tightly back into a long ponytail, and it bobbed gently with each touch of her shoes hitting the pavement. His eyes followed her as he remained in a trance. She kept going, steadily, not looking anywhere in particular but directly in front of her feet. She ran by Buddy's house almost every day at this same time. And she was the most beautiful woman he has ever seen.

Jasper stopped talking as he noticed Buddy's vacant stare and turned around to see what he was watching. Then he snickered. "You have it bad, Mr. Cochran. Real bad. Maybe you should stop hiding in your house all day and go say, 'Hey,' to her."

Buddy blushed. His face got hot and sweat beads began to form around his mouth. He just didn't know how to talk to women. If they were his clients, he was fine. If women were answering his questions in the jury box during voir dire, he was fine. If women were checking his groceries out at the Food Lion, he was fine, as long as they weren't too talkative or too pretty. If women were giving him paperwork at the Clerk's Office, he was fine. But that was only because the ladies in the Clerk's Office were closing in on retirement age. If women were serving him a plate of pasta at Ragazzi's Fine Italian Dining down near the Courthouse, he was fine, as long as he only looked at the food. But if they were just women…out and in the world…standing in line next to him or walking on the sidewalk by him or sitting in a church pew around him, his nerves overwhelmed his stomach, his hands got sweaty, and he couldn't speak. The only thing he's mastered in this domain is the ability to look just past their eyes when he absolutely must talk to them. They might think he has something wrong with his vision, but it's the best he can do to manage this awkward situational anxiety inflicted upon him by the mere existence of the fairer sex.

As much as he would like to initiate a conversation with the daily jogger, he didn't know the first thing to say to her.

A couple of weeks ago, Buddy was walking Bo on the sidewalk. He heard the familiar thump-thump of her adorable jogging rhythm coming up behind them. Normally, she was on the side of the road when she went by, but for some reason, she was jogging on the sidewalk.

"On your left," she blurted out to Buddy. She came by him on the left, turned her head toward him and smiled. Her eyes were sky blue. Buddy couldn't respond at all because his vocal chords closed, like he had just swallowed a bee, and it was all he could do not to fall over his own feet or get himself tangled up in Bo's leash. When he could eventually breathe again, he was relieved she was long gone and headed to wherever she ran to each day.

That was the closest he had ever been to her, and the only communication they ever shared up until then. He had watched her jog by for several weeks, like a slightly disturbed voyeur with absolutely no harmful intentions. When she smiled at Buddy, he could smell the faint scent of creams and lotions, the kinds of things that women put on themselves, even when they are going to go work out.

Ever since then, if he's not in court or if he doesn't have somewhere else he needs to be, Buddy is outside with Bo, hoping just to get another whiff of her or another smile sent his way.

Loretta and Joe

Loretta Cordova walked into the cute little crafty knick-knack store on Hillsboro Street, hoping to find something different and interesting for Joe's birthday. What do you buy a man who already has everything he'd ever want or need? Which is just his TV remote, a good book, a comfortable chair...and her?

Wandering through the store, a hippy-ish lady with long gray hair and a colorful dress that looked like she took it off an actor in a Native American history reenactment, asked Loretta if she could help her with anything.

"No thank you," Loretta replied. "It's one of those things where you don't know what you want 'til you see it."

The Hippy nodded, indeed understanding what she was talking about.

Loretta took a gander at the gag gift section, mostly for her own amusement. She loved gag gifts. She thought that if she got to come back for another round of living, she'd like to be someone smart and witty enough to make gag gifts.

Joe was turning sixty-five in two days, and she was putting together a party for him at the homestead. Buddy was going to come up for it, and she was hoping that he might like the new young lady from the Methodist Church she met last week during the eleven o'clock service. She was very pretty, single, and on exchange from a law school up north, spending the semester studying over at the Carolina Law School. Loretta invited the young lady over to the party, hoping that maybe Buddy would break out of his shell, welcome her to the area, and talk to her a bit about practicing law and his own experiences at Carolina.

"Mother, really, you need to stop doing this sort of thing to me," Buddy deep-sighed over the phone when she called him about the party and the young lady.

"You are thirty-years old, and no girl has ever had that big beautiful heart of yours!" Loretta scolded him.

"You're right. No girl but you. It will happen when it's supposed to happen, not when my mother is setting me up!" Buddy stated in frustration. "Now I'm going to feel all stupid talking to her, knowing what you're trying to do. And I would've felt stupid enough as it is without all the added pressure!"

"Well, just talk about the law with her. Talk about the Constitution. Should keep your hands from clamming up and your nerves taking over."

"The Constitution? Really, mother?"

Buddy was the best son a mother could ask for, but the way things were looking, he was never going to fall in love and get married and give Loretta some grandbabies. And she wants some damn grandbabies before she's too old to play with them.

Joe Horton walked down the freshly installed wooden steps, which led from the rickety front porch, up on deck for the 'Honey Do' list. Loretta sure liked her lists. He sat on the bottom step, holding a glass of freshly squeezed lemonade in his hand and wearing his finest khaki slacks and his finest collared polo shirt – which also happened to be his only khaki slacks and only collared polo shirt. Joe grinned at Loretta as she put white plastic table cloths over some eight-foot tables that she borrowed from the church.

"You want some help, sugar?" he asked.

"No, sir. You sit there and sip that lemonade and watch me make this special day happen for you."

Joe Horton was one of the kindest souls Loretta ever had the good fortune to meet in her entire life. Today was his sixty-fifth birthday, and folks from all over this rural small town, the place she called home for about twenty years or so now, were coming over to the two-acre plot of land to celebrate this milestone with them. Joe was already retired from when he sold his longtime family-owned feed store, but now he could collect social security and go on Medicare and sit around out front of the General Store and play cards on Fridays like all the other old people who lived in Welby, North Carolina.

When Loretta congratulated him that morning for officially being "an old man," he pulled her into him, kissed her with more force than he had in quite a while and murmured, "As long as I have you, I'll never be an old man, sugar."

All these years that Loretta knew him, and it wasn't until the past five that he made her feel like a young woman again. She wasn't sure exactly when or how it happened, but one day, love just snuck up on her like a warm blanket, a prize she had been without for so long and was finally able to wrap herself inside and cure the lost deserted feeling of so many cold, dark nights. Her heart would feel fluttery whenever the word "sugar" would drop from his lips. Although he had always called her "sugar," it amazed her that she took so long to get to this point – this point where she'd let herself love a man again. And so completely.

She continued taping down the white plastic cloths over the tables and then started putting out metal chairs, also borrowed from the church. Joe continued to watch her quietly. After several minutes, he said, "Thank you for the birthday gift."

Holding a chair, Loretta turned around and replied, "I haven't given you anything yet, mister."

"Yes, you did," he stated, looking down at the ground, blushing. "This morning. And then there's the fact that you are my gift every single day."

Loretta blushed herself and relished in this feeling of just simply being in love with someone kind and thoughtful…and knowing that she was loved back…probably even more than she knew she deserved.

Loretta had only known this feeling once before in her entire life, and it had been with Buddy's real father. Only that time, it was feverish, fast, hard and so strong. People called it "young love." They had been so consumed with each other, infatuated really, and it was war time, which always had a way to add a certain desperate spice to love affairs.

At barely eighteen years old, then-Retta Scarpelli up and left her poor mother in New Jersey and ran off with Private Danny Kaspar to Fort Hood, Texas. She didn't even take a suitcase with her. It was the first time in her life that she had done something unplanned and on a whim – she had eloped with a young soldier she met at the movie theatre, who had just finished his training at Fort Dix and would eventually head off to Vietnam.

Since Danny, Loretta never knew love quite like that again. But who is that lucky in life after all? To experience such a flood of happiness where you believe that everything you do is right…just because it's with him? They were so young and in a time of difficult circumstances – it seemed like the imminent danger of war in a foreign land, and Retta's own frantic need to get out of her impoverished life and hometown, just added to the mountain of ever-growing feelings for each other.

But Joe Horton, the love that now-Loretta Cordova had for him, was the same as it was with Danny – but different at the same time. It was the same because there was a simmering passion, the kind that bubbles underneath your bones like a pleasant flu most days, and then comes out from time to time in a boiling rage, but a good kind of rage. Danny and Retta had been like that too, after the initial frenzy. Their love had settled into genuine contentment.

Joe and Loretta shared a slow growing and respectful love, one similar to long-term marriages that withstood the test of time and the harshest trials. Joe was widowed himself and had been on his own for a few years by the time Loretta and Buddy were driven up onto his land and into his life.

She knew Joe for twenty years now, and their genuine friendship came long before the rest of it. They built upon the foundation of their relationship in a mature way, an older person way, the way that life's cruel experiences teach you to calm the hell down, begin and grow in life – and then in love – with another person. Be a person first. Then after you got that figured out, and if you meet someone, be friends, companions…and then if you feel it…lovers. And even though Joe was a lot older than Loretta, she had lived the hardened years of a woman well beyond her age.

When Loretta first met Joe, she knew he found her and Buddy to be curious creatures. She could tell soon after their arrival that he was very fond of her, found her to be attractive and probably developed romantic feelings toward her. But he never said anything about it or acted on anything, and he never asked her any intrusive questions. So, she told him no lies. She did not want to compromise Joe and his integrity in any way, and she figured that he never asked her too much about her past because he didn't want to become compromised himself. He was one of those people who accepted that there was a bliss to a certain amount of ignorance.

It was easier for him to just not know about why he was really helping them…and why she was in hiding. Besides, he knew what really mattered about Loretta: she was a good mother and had a good heart and Buddy was a good boy. The rest of her untold story was just an ugly large dead flower print window dressing, and she supposed that just made her more interesting than all the other ladies in town who took a keen interest in Joe after his wife died.

A blue catering van pulled into the long dirt driveway and parked in front of the house. Bobbi and Kelly, the mother-daughter duo caterers who also attended the Methodist Church, began unloading and setting up the good old fashioned North Carolina summertime spread.

Soon after, several guests started to arrive. Joe was up and talking with all the women and their husbands from town, some of whom had known him since he was born. It's funny how a place full of people who never left forget nothing of its town and the people in it. They might forget to turn off the stove when they leave the house or the lights when they leave a room or even their wives' birthdays, but they don't forget what it was like "way back when." They don't forget the time that Don Martin fell into the Haw off his new bike and got bit by a copperhead in 1973. They don't forget the time Misty Wells and Tommy Gibbs ran away from home and got hitched down in South Carolina back in 1949, breaking her mother's heart so bad it sent her into a tizzy and then a deep depression for a year. They don't forget when Billy Ray Day stole Jane Moody away from Gil Tart during the Winter Ball at the high school back in 1956. They are like a cult of sorts. Their secrets, their inside jokes and stories, their own intimate language. Loretta used to be jealous of it, but now she just let it run over her like a warm bath. It's Joe – it's a part of who he is and why he is who he is and another reason Loretta loved him so much.

The Young Lady

Pulling up to his second childhood home, a large off-white farmhouse with a huge wrap-around porch and open windows, Buddy parked his green Pontiac Grand Prix behind Mr. Murray's old rust orange Chevy pickup truck, which held the center space in a line of several other old pickup trucks – the standard for country living here in his adopted North Carolina hometown.

Buddy's mother and Joe had been living in sin for several years now, and while they acted like they still lived in separate quarters, people weren't stupid, even when they have thick country accents and say things like "y'aunt to?" It's almost as if his mother and Joe were afraid to admit to everyone that they were deeply in love and have been having old people sex for a long time. There's still that subtle keeping up appearances thing going on between them. And while all the proper southern people knew the truth, everyone politely pretended otherwise, as proper southern people do.

The last time Buddy was up visiting with them, they went out to eat in downtown Welby. As they sat down in their booth and looked over the menus, Mrs. Cady, a seventy-something year old widow who watched Buddy grow up since he and his mother arrived in the Fall of 1975, asked Loretta if she wanted some lovely curtains for her apartment, a small one-bedroom place which sat neatly on the top of a small barn on Joe's property.

"I just finished them last week for my daughter's spare bedroom, but she already got a set that she's gonna use instead," Mrs. Cady explained.

"No, ma'am, but thank you Mrs. Cady," Loretta said to her, grinning shyly and slightly hiding her embarrassed face behind her menu.

Buddy and his mother lived in that apartment since he was a boy, and while he had no doubt Mrs. Cady knew that his mother and Joe were indeed living in sin, she acted like Loretta Cordova still lived in that small one-bedroom apartment on Joe's property like a proper unmarried woman who sang in the choir at the Methodist Church.

When she walked away with her rather massive hand-sewn purse engulfing her small shoulder and arm, Buddy just started to laugh. His mother kicked him under the table.

"Buddy, stop it. You know I'll still slap your behind no matter how old you are."

Joe has told Buddy several times that he wants his mother to marry him.

"I love your mother very much, and I'd like to make an honest woman of her. It's a bit unnerving for me to share my home with a woman and live like a married couple when we aren't married," Joe explained a few years ago, as they sat on his porch on a chilly Fall evening.

"I'm sorry, Joe, I don't understand her sometimes," was all Buddy could say in response to him.

But he did understand his mother. Too well. She couldn't marry Joe or anyone else. She was too afraid of being found out if she did. If Kenny Bellinger was still alive somewhere out there, then she was still married. It was better to be an independent woman with a lingering mystery. And the longer she stayed in this small town and lived how she had been living, the more a part of the decor and background and the way of life that defined this place she became. No one asks questions when everything is the same as it's always been. People are comfortable with the status quo.

"Well, I wasn't raised to live like this, Buddy. My wife – God rest her soul – is probably rolling over in her grave, wondering what's gotten into me," Joe confided.

"Honestly, I'd bet your wife would be happy that you're happy," Buddy responded. "I'll be real surprised if my mother changes her mind, Joe. But you know she loves you and that she's not going anywhere. Besides, it's the Nineties. It's okay to not be married and just live together instead. Lots of people think marriage is just a piece of paper anymore."

"Well, I don't think that way about marriage. I do know she loves me, son. But just because more time has passed over this old land and all over my face, and just because times have changed in the big city, doesn't make it okay. I'm a traditional man," he said solemnly, rising up into his work boots and walking back into the house with a slight limp.

Bob and Tess McLean greeted Buddy as he walked up to the gathering of people. Buddy went to high school with them, and now they were married with three little kids. Honestly, he felt like he shouldn't be surprised about how many folks were here for this party. Joe himself was this town, the unelected Mayor, he reckoned.

As he grabbed a beer from the cooler, his mother tapped him on the shoulder. He turned around and she presented him with a young, beautiful blond with bouncy curls and a slim figure. She wore a white mini skirt and a tasteful salmon colored summer blouse.

"Buddy, this is Jennifer," she said, introducing him to the young lady. "She's the law student I told you about who has been visiting our church. She's from New York."

Jennifer's face was delicate and fresh, her eyes a soft green, and she beamed at Buddy with an orthodontics-approved smile.

"Hi," she pronounced, putting her hand out for him to shake.

Buddy was prepared – in his head – to have an attractive girl tossed at him by his mother. Driving up from Fayetteville, he gave himself a few pep talks. He would try not to stutter, keep to talking about law school about Carolina and what kind of law she was interested in practicing and maybe talk about the Yankees or something else that was New York-ish. He had even read up on current Broadway plays and watched a few episodes of Friends, as if she were nothing but a cliché from a Nora Ephron film. If he kept himself firmly on a discussion path, he wouldn't pass out onto the grass, needing to be revived with a bucket full of cold water. But, he couldn't look at her while talking either, or he wouldn't be able to continue. Damn all the pretty girls in this world.

Looking just past her porcelain face, Buddy's eyes gazed over her shoulder and into the distance. He took her hand and responded, "Hi. My name's Buddy. Real nice to meet you."

"Oh, my God, I'm so happy to meet you. Your mom has just been going on and on and on about you ever since I visited her church. She is so proud of you," Jennifer yammered.

He thought to himself that maybe he should just let her yammer because that would mean that he wouldn't have to say much, nod once in a while or utter an, "uh huh," or, "yeah," just to show he was listening. But then those awkward pauses started happening, where she expected him to respond like an actual adult man…or a lawyer…and all lawyers talk…a lot…like they really do enjoy hearing themselves…and he couldn't avoid having to open his mouth and speak.

"Um, yeah, she's a typical mother like that, I guess."

"When did you graduate from law school?" she asked.

"Three years ago. I live down in Fayetteville now, have a small criminal practice there. Just trying to get something positive started."

"You didn't want to go to a big firm?"

Still peering just over her shoulder, hoping she was falling for this eye contact system he had mastered over the years, he replied, "No, I wasn't real interested in the big firm life."

"Yeah, lots of work, that's for sure. Billable hours and no time off – I'm lucky I can get into my father's firm easy. I figured if I can just get through those first few years working like a dog as a lowly associate, he'll make me a partner quickly and it would at least be a lot more money."

Jennifer was clearly on the high-priced Manhattan attorney track. As a fairly-priced lawyer who was also on the Court-appointed list, the high-priced way was as far away from Buddy's legal track as could be. He supposed the only way the two of them could be further from each other professionally is if he worked for Legal Aid. Or for the Public Defender's Office. Or pro bono, which he did sometimes.

"Would you like something to drink?" Buddy asked her, feeling a bit more confident and calm now that he realized they would never be a good fit. He knew his mother would be disappointed.

"Yeah, that would be nice," she said, eyeballing him rather aggressively.

Buddy reached into the cooler, pulled out a beer and handed it to her. She caught his gaze, forcing him to look at her. She was smirking a bit, and Buddy realized in that moment that she had come here with actual intentions. On him.

"You're a really good looking guy, Buddy," she started, taking a sip of her beer. Buddy was not accustomed to women being so upfront and forward, at least not toward him. "Your mom said you were very handsome, but all moms say that about their sons. Not all moms are right, though."

Buddy started to feel bashful and overly shy. He could sense his face getting hot, but because he was sure that there was nothing special between them – at least on his end – he contained his rising nerves and forced them to submit into a quiet fester instead. Because while his heart was not moving toward feeling anything about her, it didn't mean that other parts of him were sitting still. Jennifer was drop dead gorgeous. And he was very much a red-blooded American male.

"Do you like it at Carolina?" Buddy asked, trying to change the subject.

"Yeah, I do. Great atmosphere in Chapel Hill. I don't miss the city too much at all, but it's early yet, and New York in the Fall is the best. So, I hate that I'll miss it."

"You'll like North Carolina in the Fall, too. I promise you that," he said, looking around at all the folks talking, drinking and eating. "The best part of the Fall in North Carolina is in the Appalachian Mountains. It's just incredible up there. All the foliage and colors, I try to go once a year."

Jennifer stood a little closer to him and her arm was touching his slightly. "Maybe you can take me up there sometime," she cooed. "I'm still new here, and I hope you'll be my first friend.

CHAPTER 3

May 17th, 1975

Hector

"Are you Hector?" Retta asked a very dark-skinned Mexican man wearing a pin-striped short sleeved dress shirt, untucked, and faded blue jeans. The collar had a ring around it, and the top button remained unbuttoned. He stood behind a counter, which had large books piled on top, and was holding a coffee mug up to his mouth with a bushy mustache appearing to dip slightly inside of it.

He looked up and then peered behind her as Buddy walked in the door.

"Si," he answered.

It was still early, and she was fairly certain that his little car business wasn't even open yet. He seemed surprised by them, startled even. She was afraid that he would only speak to her in Spanish, so she asked him if he spoke English.

He laughed and took another sip of whatever was in his mug.

"We are not open until later, miss," he said slowly, enunciating each word so that it was clear to Retta that he indeed spoke English just fine.

She looked around the inside of the building, which appeared as if it only housed this small and somewhat trashed, busy office room with a bathroom attached. A calendar from 1973 with women dressed in provocative clothing and posing on different colored Corvettes was pressed onto the wall, along with a plain white clock that read it was two o'clock. A chalkboard with all kinds of sloppy writing scratched on it was hanging on the opposite wall, and there seemed to be official papers everywhere, strewn about like a wind blew through the space earlier and no one bothered to clean them up. The floor had books piled in the corners, and there was a desk, a chair and then a blue loveseat with more books piled on top. The guy ran a messy business, and the sight of all the disorder and chaos made Retta cringe.

"Lucinda sent me," Retta stated, hoping that he would understand she needed to talk with him now and not when he was open.

Hector put his mug down on the counter and walked over to his desk. He picked up a ragged brown folder and then looked up at this harried looking mother and son duo.

"Are you wanting to buy a car from me?"

"No, sir. I am looking to sell my car."

"What do you have?"

"A Duster."

"What year is it?"

"1971, I think."

"Is it with you now?"

"It's just outside."

Hector walked past them and out the door. Retta glanced down at Buddy who looked up at her, obviously confused and wondering why they would be getting rid of their car.

"Mother, why do you want to sell our car?" he asked.

Retta looked out the small window on the door and could see Hector walking around the opposite side of the car, ducking down underneath and then looking in the driver's side window.

"Because son, we need to get rid of it so Kenny can never find us. And so no one else can, either."

She opened the door, and they both walked outside and onto the tattered asphalt lot. It was warm for this early in the day, but she was relieved that it seemed like Hector was at least interested in the Duster for the moment. There were several other cars sitting around the outskirts of the parking lot and surrounding the small terra cotta building. Some of the cars had seen better days. The sign by the highway that read "Hector's Cars" looked brand new just as Lucinda said it was, but also out of place with the rest of the business' appearance.

They watched Hector open and close the doors, look under the hood, but when he got to the trunk, Retta stopped him from unlatching the lock. It was an instinct – she couldn't stop herself – but now she was afraid that she spooked him off from considering the Duster. Although, Hector didn't look like the kind of man who could be easily spooked.

He stopped and looked at her directly in her eyes. "Why don't you want me to look in the trunk?"

Retta didn't know what to say, so she blurted, "I just have something in there that I don't want anyone to see."

"We are just north of the Rio Grande and Mexican border. Do you think there are things in trunks that I haven't seen before?"

She was scared now. She didn't want him to see the gun back there. It would make them look like they were running from something – even though they were – and what if he decided to call the police and tell them that there was some woman and little boy with a gun trying to dump a car at his store in New Mexico?

And as if he read her mind, he asked, "Are you running from something?"

Retta didn't answer and was absolutely no good on her feet, even under normal circumstances. Since she never thought she'd be in such a situation, she found herself unsure of how to handle anything at all.

"From Kenny," Buddy divulged, out of the blue, completely honest. Just like a kid.

Retta glared at Buddy. They hadn't talked about anything that happened so far or what exactly they were doing – other than running away, so it was silly for her to be angry at Buddy. He didn't know what was going on. Or maybe he did and figured that he shouldn't lie. After all, that is what she taught him his whole life. If an adult asks you a question, you tell the truth.

"Who's Kenny?" Hector asked.

Buddy looked up at his mother, his face full of trust.

"He's nobody," Retta said, feeling defeated.

Hector walked closer to them and asked her to follow him into the building. "I won't bite, miss. Young man, please stay out here and stand watch over your car."

She followed Hector back into the building and he asked her to take a seat. Looking around, Retta found that suggestion amusing. The floor? That was the only place that seemed like there'd be space to sit.

"Your son is telling the truth. You are running from someone named Kenny, aren't you?" he asked.

She felt like a little girl, caught in a lie by her parents. Hector looked like he was a lot older than Lucinda and probably someone's grandfather. He didn't seem to want to buy her car anymore. And that was okay. Retta just wanted to get out of Las Cuatro now and find another way to dump this car.

"Look, I will buy your Duster from you. I will give you a fair price. I buy many cars like yours and send them over the border where I can make more money on them. So that is not a problem." He stopped and looked out one of the windows toward the highway. "But we have another matter."

"What?"

"Miss, you are running from a man. And I can see why." He stopped, faced her, walked a bit closer and looked at the large finger laden bruises on her arms and the cut above her eye that had long ago shed its makeup. "He beats you and so you are trying to get away with the boy."

Retta nodded. If it were only that simple. But since he was taking in all her surroundings and making his judgments about their situation based upon what he saw in front of him, then she would just let him do it.

"What is in the trunk? A gun? A body? A bag of money?" he asked.

Retta laughed at the suggestion that she'd have a bag of money.

"I have a gun for protection. It's mine and I don't want you to take it," she said.

"I'm not going to take your gun, miss. But what I am going to do is call my cousin who will help you."

Puzzled, she immediately braced her arms around her torso, felt herself toughen up, looked directly into his chocolate brown eyes, with deep, dark wrinkles outlining his entire face. And for the first time, she noticed what it was that he held in his eyes the entire time they had been interacting here. Not intimidation or power or cruelty. But compassion. Kindness.

Hector wasn't just a business man who sold questionable cars across the border. He was a good man with a big heart.

"What do you mean?" she asked, feeling like she had no other option but to put her trust in this stranger.

"My cousin helps women who need to get away from their husbands. She helps them get into a shelter for safety. Helps them get new names and gives them bus tickets. She is a wonderful woman who has helped many ladies just like you."

They stood in silence for a minute.

"Miss, will you let me call her? I am only trying to help you and your boy."

Retta knew that she didn't have many other options. If he bought her car and gave her cash, where were they going to go then? She thought they could buy bus tickets somewhere, maybe to Las Vegas, where she could get work in a casino or maybe in hair and makeup at one of the theatres that puts on the big shows with the pretty dancing girls. But the thought of having a bed to sleep in tonight and a few minutes to sit down and come up with a plan sounded good too.

"Why are you trying to help us?" she asked, drilling right into Hector's eyes, desperately praying inside that what she believed about him was indeed the truth. Her confidence was shaken, so she didn't want to trust the wrong person.

Hector grinned, closed-mouthed, his bushy mustache thinning out along his top lip and sighed. "Because miss, I was like your little boy once. My papi was an angry man. Your boy, he deserves to get away from that, just like you do. Just like I did."

The Underground Railroad

Pilar Rodriguez pulled up to Hector's in a brown Gremlin. When she turned left off the highway, Retta could hear the horn beep. When she and Buddy got into the car with Pilar, she noticed that every time the Gremlin turned left, the horn beeped. So, making a quiet escape into the bowels of Las Cuatro with a bunch of do-gooder Mexican immigrants didn't appear to be a possibility at the moment.

"You are my first gringo in a long while," Pilar stated to Retta as they turned off the highway and onto a side road. Her accent was slight. She must've lived on this side of the border for most of her life, if not all of it.

"First gringo for what?" Retta asked.

"For my underground railroad," Pilar responded, which only made Retta more confused. She studied American history in school. What in the world does the Underground Railroad have to do with her situation?

The morning was fully alive; people were working and focusing on their tasks at hand. Another day, another dollar. As she looked out the window of the moving Gremlin and observed the average day outside, Retta didn't know how to respond to what Pilar said. But she was grateful for this unexpected stroke of luck. She learned that sometimes, the best plan is having no plan at all. If she had a plan, maybe the police would have caught up with them by now, and she and Buddy would be sitting in a jail cell in Texas wondering what number to dial with their one phone call.

They drove up to an old southwestern styled home with an off-peach color stucco siding and a lot of dust. A tall cactus stood sentry outside the front door, almost nodding at them as they walked by. Retta and Buddy followed Pilar inside, each holding their meager belongings like two orphans being sent to a new foster home. Since Hector requested that Retta remove the bullets from her gun, she could feel them crunched down in her skirt pocket. They walked into a hallway and then into a sitting room, where Pilar pointed to a couch.

"Please, sit down. Are you hungry?"

"No, Ma'am, we just ate something."

"Do you need some water?"

"No thank you," Retta said, feeling very much like a child in the Principal's office.

Pilar was a big woman with rich, thick brown skin. She wore a large, burnt-orange, tent shaped dress and flat shoes, with chalky hard creases making their way out of the back of her heels. Her hair was jet black and braided, her face tired but friendly and welcoming. If they didn't know she was Mexican, they would have thought she was an American Indian. Pilar sat down on a chair across from the couch and smiled at Buddy.

"So, Hector says that you are trying to get away from your husband?" she started.

"Yes," Retta replied, still trying not to give away too much information about their plight.

"Hector said that you have a gun with you," Pilar cocked her head sideways.

"Yes, but it's not loaded."

"Well, while you're here, if you want to stay, I need to keep it. You understand, right?" Pilar looked serious, like this was a request she expressed often.

Retta nodded her head. Looking around, she saw a painting of the Madonna on the wall and several unlit candles sitting along a window sill. The floor consisted of wooden slats with no carpets anywhere. The furniture was old and worn, like years of small children had taken the once colorful fabric out to play in the desert for good.

"Is this your home?" Retta asked Pilar, at last feeling a bit more comfortable.

"Yes, it is. I live here with my mother. She is in failing health and sleeping in her room."

Retta sighed, thinking of her own mother, living all alone up in New Jersey with no desire to leave. Who would take care of her when she was old? Frank. Who would tell her that she was gone? Frank. That she would never get to meet her only grandchild in person? Frank.

Buddy shifted in his seat. He was tired and not quite sure he understood everything that was going on around him. This Pilar woman stunk of chicken grease, but she was being real nice to them and might help them find their way to a new place, somewhere far away from Kenny.

"We have a quiet system in place here in the southwest, but it's usually to help Mexican women fleeing their homes and trying to find a better life in the states. We help women who are already over here, too. I have a small place where I house some of them and their children until we can get them some papers and set up with jobs or a plan to go far away and start over."

"What are they fleeing?" Retta asked, her gut already knowing the answer.

Pilar grinned at her. "I think, the same thing as you." She leaned back in her chair, her doughy arms sinking on the arm rest. "My people suffer the same things as your people, only in a different language and culture. Mexico is violent and has more poverty than over on this side of the border. Both of those things together is a dangerous combination for a woman with no options. As you know, it's a man's world – but it's even more of a man's world in some parts of Mexico. Women are merely things to produce children, cook and clean and suffer the whims of her man. And many of the men are not happy, so they take it out on their women. Some men are like Hector. They are kind and do the best they can. But many are not."

The bruises on Retta's arms and forehead hurt, and she could feel the cut on her eye stinging at the mention of battered women.

"He wasn't always like this," she confessed to Pilar, her voice starting to crack. "He was so nice to me at first. It was…later…something changed."

Retta could feel the tears swell up in her eyes, her images of Kenny before the alcohol took hold of him like an anchor around his neck, before the night terrors tormented him throughout his waking days and sleepless nights, before he lost his job because his co-workers complained about his inability to control his temper, before he became obsessed with finding someone named Han.

"You don't have to tell me about it, miss. It was bad enough that you needed to run away and sell your car to Hector."

"He was a mean son of a bitch and I'm glad he's gone," Buddy stated, flatly.

Retta's head jerked toward him. "Buddy, you keep quiet."

Buddy sat back into the couch, his body sinking deep into the cushion. Retta wanted to ask him what he remembered, but she was so scared of what Pilar would think now that he blurted that out loud about Kenny.

"You are both welcome to stay in the place that I have for my women. I have people who help me get papers and will help you get new papers if you want. I can get you set up with a job around here and help put the boy in school or he can stay out of school for a while, until you're settled somewhere. Is there no one else who can help you?"

Retta, with her head down, nodded gently. "We have nowhere to go. We have no family left."

It was a lie, but it was a good lie.

Coma

There was a constant beeping noise and the faint sound of something hissing off in the corner near a window. A woman with honey blond hair pinned up with a clip and wearing a white nurse's uniform kept coming in and out of the room. Sometimes, she had a clipboard in her hands, and other times she had nothing. She would look down at me, scribble something on the piece of paper, read squiggly lines and numbers on the loud machine, and then she'd sigh.

I looked down and could see myself sleeping. It had to be sleep. If I was dead, I would be in a drawer inside of a morgue instead, I figured.

There were tubes coming out of my mouth, a white blanket covered me all the way up to my chin, and I could see my socks poking out from the bottom. They put a white knit cap on my head like I'd be leaving any minute to go downhill skiing up in West Virginia.

All I could figure out is that I had been shot by someone. Not sure how many times. I don't know where Retta and Buddy were. No one I knew had ever come into this hospital room to check on me. I don't know how anyone knew to come inside the house and get me out. I never saw Retta come out of our bedroom, or Buddy either, and no one came into the house and saw me lying on the floor, that I knew of.

I had no idea how long it had been since I was shot and no idea how much time had passed since I was on the floor, my head propped up by the sink cabinet. All I knew was that at some point, three people stormed into the house and took me away in an ambulance. The youngest one, a fresh-faced boy no older than my little brother when he got popped in 'Nam, kept trying to wake me up.

"Kenny! Wake up! Do you hear me?" he would drone over and over and over in a blurry, drowsy southern accent. A couple times, he got rough with my face, but I couldn't feel it. But I knew that I wanted to punch him for getting in my face like that.

I kept hollering at him, "I'm here! I've been shot! Please find my wife and son! Please! See if they're okay!" But he never responded to any of it. He just kept telling me to wake up. The other two worked on the hole in my chest and apparently the one in my head, too, and then carted me out on a gurney.

It's strange watching yourself be lifted and rolled out and then lifted again and then switched to a bed and then stripped of your clothing by an old woman who looked like she could've doubled as Glenda the Good Witch in The Wizard of Oz. It's an odd experience yelling to a room full of people who are performing surgery on you and none of them hear you and you can't feel the scalpel digging into your chest…but you can see it clearly. And you want it all to stop.

Time stands still. I've lost track of it all. I can't go back to before all of this happened and I can't go forward, on to Heaven – or probably in my case, considering what I had done and what I had failed to do as a man – Hell. I'm just stuck, in my own kind of hell, and I've never felt so alone in my life.

"Gee Eye," I heard a small voice say.

It wasn't a voice in the room. It was a voice from somewhere else but still close. Close by me. In me. Near me?

"Gee Eye," it said again. It was quiet but song-like.

"Who's there?" I shouted. "Can you hear me?"

"Gee Eye, you come now," the voice sang, closer, closing in on me like a choking smoke.

I saw nothing else around me. Nothing near my body but the beeping machine. A chair was off alone in the corner, untouched. No one sat in it, no one was keeping watch over me here in this white, clean and sanitized room.

Putting my hands over my ears, I heard the voice again, softly whisper as if it was in my own space, "Gee Eye, come." All I could make out – not in front of me or behind me but almost like within me – was a shadow of a child's head, her hair dark as the starless night and silky smooth. Why was this child telling me to come? Who or what was Gee Eye?

CHAPTER 4

August – October 1996

Joe's Party

Buddy opened his eyes and noticed that it was still dark. There was a touch of moonlight shining through the top of a white curtain rod, which was resting just above his head. Where was he? This was not a familiar place.

He rolled slightly onto his back and felt a body next to his legs. It stirred. He turned his head and saw a huge crop of blond hair sprawled out from a comforter, consuming at least a pillow and a half. And suddenly, the stench of his sins smacked him in the face like a splash of cold water. He had a one-night stand with Jennifer the Carolina Law student, on loan from Columbia? Cornell? Fordham? Buddy couldn't remember. He heard almost nothing she had yammered about for the entire night.

His mother's birthday party for Joe had been loud, considering most of the attendees were either collecting social security or soon approaching it. Maybe it was loud because so many of them couldn't hear on the best of days. Anyway, nothing Jennifer told him seemed all that interesting when he could actually hear her speak. And because she was so pretty and he was so shy, why would he even bother to ask her to repeat herself, or holler about it, or go somewhere private in the house so they could have a real conversation?

The only thing that seemed worth asking her to repeat was when she suggested that he come back to her apartment for some peace and quiet and to get to know each other better. She'd been sending Buddy the "I want you" eyes all night. While Buddy wasn't really all that interested in getting to know her, other than maybe in a Biblical way, women rarely sent him such signals as far as he could tell.

The last time he had an actual sexual encounter, the OJ trial was still going on. It was with a court reporter who had just gone through an awful divorce, and for some reason, started talking to Buddy at the sandwich shop next to the courthouse one afternoon, crying in her Diet Pepsi, and requesting that Buddy rid her of her crippling depression with a passionate roll in the hay. She was in her late thirties, very pretty and knew exactly what she wanted from him. Since he had nothing else going on relationship-wise, he thought maybe he could have some fun and learn a thing or two from her. After all, Buddy had been well advised by a well-meaning client that women approaching forty knew what they want and how to ask for it, unlike the younger women who were still "trying to find themselves."

They had an active physical relationship in her bed for about half a year before she met her "soulmate" – a high ranking officer in the Army who was closer to her age and moving to Germany. So, the fun was over for young Buddy. Court reporter went to Germany. Buddy went home to Bo.

Jennifer was a beautiful girl, well-mannered, well-groomed, and thin. She was young, intelligent, headed for success, and her skin was that tone between too pale and porcelain. But he had never really been the kind of guy who went home with women he just met, and he was certain that he'd never been "picked up" at a party before.

Part of that had to do with the fact that he had no game whatsoever. Part of that had to do with trying to be a gentleman regardless of what his natural instincts wanted. He never had a one night stand before, not even in college, not even in law school, not even with the chubby girl from Canada who hung all over him while he was in Jamaica for Spring Break.

But after he had a few beers, and then after he had that odd tasting drink that Smitty Smith made for him in the kitchen, which included some kind of fruit juice and some kind of soda and some kind of moonshine and some kind of super secret magic potion from Smitty's grandmother's barn, Buddy lightened up a little and started white-man-overbite dancing with Jennifer during the Eighties music portion of the evening. She was holding onto him tightly the whole time, and before he knew it, they were making out in the hallway outside of the downstairs bathroom like two horny felons finally out on parole.

He didn't recall eating some of Joe's birthday cake or the barbecue or even getting back to Jennifer's apartment, but he knew his car still had to be sitting along Joe's driveway. How embarrassing would that be – getting Jennifer to drop him off at his car at his mother's home –like a teenager who had been out all night and got caught? Of course, his mother would probably be standing on the porch, waving, giving him a thumbs-up and maybe even applauding. She might even go as far to invite the high school marching band over to play a fight song for him as he walked up the side of the house toward his car.

Buddy rolled out of Jennifer's bed and stumbled into her bathroom. He turned on the light. It was neat and smelled like fresh fruit, that undeniable scent of high maintenance women with good pedigrees. The shower curtain was pink, and she had a fluffy carpet on the floor with a drawing of a cat on it. Her toothbrush and toothpaste sat in a pink plastic cup on the sink. A pink towel hung on the small rack. Buddy opened her medicine cabinet and took a look at what she had inside. You can tell a lot about a person by what they have in their medicine cabinet.

Aspirin, a box of Band Aids, Chap Stick, and some KY Jelly. A tube of something for women's issues. A small bottle of mouthwash. Cough syrup. Some generic pills for cramps. Ibuprofen. Basically, nothing offensive or secret exposing at all. Jennifer seemed like a normal, nice girl with ambition and a sexy body. So why didn't Buddy like her all that much? And why, if he didn't like her all that much, did he go back to her apartment? Was he really that hard up? Has he turned into that guy now? No. Buddy reckoned that he was indeed that hard up and had been that drunk. Never a good combination.

Since Buddy wasn't the proverbial douche bag, he cleaned himself up and got back into the bed with Jennifer. He figured that when she woke up, he would make her some breakfast and apologize for his behavior. She might not care, but he had to at least explain himself. He didn't want to come across as that guy who gets his piece of ass and then never calls. He was a gentleman, or, at least wanted to behave like one during his one-night stand.

As he slid under the covers, Jennifer rolled a bit to the side and turned her head.

"You're still here?" she asked, voice parched and cracked.

Buddy put his hand on her bare waist and moved himself closer to her, his chest along her side.

"Yeah, did you expect me to be gone?"

She turned her head back around. "No, you're one of the good ones."

Well damn. Buddy knew that this wouldn't be easy. He didn't want to have sex with her and then run away into the night because that would be a shitty thing to do. Lots of guys do stuff like that, and he never wanted to be one of them. But he also wasn't really interested in getting to know her or developing any kind of relationship, no matter how attractive she was.

Which was worse? Cutting and running or pretending to be interested and stringing someone along?

Maybe he wasn't being fair. Maybe she was a great fit and they needed more time to get to know each other. After all, it was a loud party with a bit too much booze and not a normal date where you have adult conversation. Maybe he should ask her out on a real date.

Jennifer turned herself toward Buddy and put her body against his. She started kissing him gently, like you do first thing in the morning, warming up to what could be. Buddy kissed her back, forgetting all the thoughts going through his head, and allowing his guy brain – that thing dangling between his legs – to take over.

They kissed like two new lovers this time, not like two goofy drunks with no inhibitions. There was passion, but quiet and in control, purposeful and explorative, full of the kind of energy two lonely people release onto each other. Jennifer moved along his body with her hands and eventually placed him inside of her, the sun rising to a new day.

Grandfather Mountain

On a beautiful Sunday in early October, Buddy and Jennifer parked the Pontiac and hiked their way up to the top of Grandfather Mountain in Blowing Rock. The plan for the day was to enjoy the spectacular views of the peaking Autumn foliage adorning the Blue

Ridge Parkway as well as the mountain vistas provided by Mother Nature this time of year, have lunch at the Daniel Boone Inn in the charming college town of Boone, and then drive back to Chapel Hill before it got too late. Jennifer had a huge assignment due in her Professional Responsibility class the next day, and she needed to get back at a decent hour to finish the last part of it. The research was completed at the law library on Thursday and Friday nights, and both questions were started; however, the weekend away had been much needed for them both.

Buddy had found that he liked Jennifer enough to see her on a regular basis. Okay, who was he kidding? He saw her just about every day. He referred to her as his girlfriend, even though they never talked about such labels or exclusivity. He wasn't sure yet if it was her specifically he liked – or the promise of so much great sex, as if there were such a thing as bad sex, with a girl who looked like Jennifer.

He never realized that any girl would want to have sex with him so much – he always figured that he didn't offer that much in the good lovin' department. Not because he was incapable of it but more so because he got so nervous around women and never had the right thing to say. And he couldn't fake it like some guys can. He couldn't play it off like some adorable personality trait, endearing himself to the, "Aww, he's so shy and cute," crowd of young females.

He always thought that maybe it would take a special girl to bring out all that he was capable of emotionally. Jennifer wasn't necessarily that girl. To be honest, he liked her enough, but he didn't see himself ever really loving her and knew deep down that this relationship was not going to last forever. But she had brought out things in him that he never knew were there before, and while he'd never admit it to anyone, she taught him a lot. And he enjoyed learning what she knew. He also enjoyed her company, having someone to talk to, and someone to do things with.

Buddy never realized that there were so many ways and places in which a woman could make him feel so good. While he might've been thirty in years, he was more like an inexperienced seventeen-year-old boy sexually and perhaps even a twelve-year-old boy when it came to matters of the heart.

His mother had been so happy to learn that Buddy and Jennifer were seeing each other.

"I knew you would like her!" Loretta hollered at him from the front porch, with a large cup of coffee in her hands, on the morning after Joe's birthday party, as he tried to quietly sneak away in his car without being seen.

Buddy had just thrown his hand up in a quick wave, mortified, and sped out of Welby.

Later the next day, when Loretta called him to see if he and Jennifer would like to come by for some banana cream pie, Buddy decided it would be easier for everyone if he just did what his mother wanted. So, he called Jennifer and they met at Joe's house for some banana cream pie. Then afterward, he followed Jennifer back to her apartment where they proceeded to make love to each other some more until the next morning.

As he drove home on that Monday morning with his man parts in a good kind of pain from overuse – a feeling he never knew before – and a level of exhaustion that he hadn't experienced since those Bar Exam all-nighters, Buddy realized how pissed off Bo would be for leaving him alone overnight. He decided at that point, he was just going to see where this situation with Jennifer would lead him.

However, that nagging feeling underneath his conscience wouldn't go away – the one where he knew he didn't like her enough to be continuing along this path and exploring a relationship, the kind of one that he knew he really wanted to attempt with the daily jogger. The one where he was certain he was choosing to do the wrong thing mostly because the sex was so damn good – and frequent.

When they got to the swinging bridge on Grandfather Mountain, Jennifer pulled out her camera. She walked across the bridge along with all the other lookie-loos also in town, experiencing the wonder of the Appalachians in the Fall. She wore a yellow fleece pullover with her collar up around her beautiful, flawless face. Her long hair fell along the back, shiny and bright in the sun. She took photo after photo, probably going through the whole roll of film in just a few minutes. Buddy walked up behind her on the bridge and wrapped his arms around her waist. He put his mouth on her neck and kissed her. Jennifer didn't respond to it, only walked away with her camera, shooting the endless sea of yellow, orange, red and green specks of natural art spreading out before them.

Jennifer seemed quieter than usual this morning. Buddy noticed that she hadn't been as talkative for the past couple of days, either on the phone or when they were together. They woke up naked this morning in a cozy mountain room in Blowing Rock, and after having a rather extended sexual interlude – the only way to fully wake up properly, Buddy has since decided – she got out of bed and showered. There was no holding and talking, like usual, which Buddy had grown to enjoy during their brief involvement.

Jennifer threw on her clothes and announced to him, as he still laid in bed, "I'm heading down the street to see if I can get some coffee. Do you want some?"

"Okay," Buddy said, a little bewildered. She seemed a little short with him. "Is everything okay?" he asked her, starting to feel concerned. She seemed stressed out. Law school is very stressful, so maybe she was feeling out of sorts.

"Yeah, all good," she said, shutting the door behind her and heading down the sidewalk on Main Street.

As he watched her walk away from him on the swinging bridge, Buddy knew in his gut that she wasn't just stressed out from school. He knew this feeling too well. The few times he had tried to be in relationships, tried to make something be more than what it was, he eventually got kicked to the curb. Because he had always been the "nice guy," he never felt right about kicking any of them to curb first. So, he'd go along, enjoying the benefits, hoping that the elusive magical feeling he's heard about so many times from other people would at last happen to him. Kind of like that feeling he gets when he sees that jogger go by his house every day around two o'clock.

He didn't say anything about his gut feeling to Jennifer as they drove back to Chapel Hill. As she got out of the car, he asked, "Do you want me to come up for a bit?"

She leaned over and kissed his cheek. "Not this time, Buddy. I really got a lot of work to do. But thanks for taking me to the mountains. I can check that off my North Carolina sight-seeing list now."

With that, she got out of his car and walked up the steps to her apartment. She didn't even turn around and wave goodbye to him.

Wife, Interrupted

"Molly?" Julie Saint whispered in sing-song to her little girl who was sleeping soundly in her bed. Not in her own bed – but Julie's bed. For the past year and a half, Molly used her own bright yellow walled bedroom for changing her clothes and housing her rather large and elaborate stuffed animal and ceramic elephant collection…

but not for sleeping. She also had a nice set of books in there for first and second grade readers, even though she was reading at a fifth-grade level.

"I'm glad she's so advanced, but why would you bother reading something like Tuck Everlasting when you're barely seven years old?" Julie asked Mrs. Topper, Molly's first grade teacher, during a parent-teacher conference last April. "Good point," Mrs. Topper responded. "Junie B. Jones and a Little Monkey Business is perfectly fine for her reading log. But maybe the two of you can read something together, something more on her level, just to keep her challenged."

Julie rubbed her daughter's mousy brown hair away from her face, revealing the legion of freckles that smattered along her milky white skin, her head resting peacefully on the pillow. She hated to wake her early on a Saturday, but it was a big day at Frederick Morrison Elementary School. Today was the Fall Festival, the huge annual PTA fundraiser, and they were in charge of the dunk tank from Noon to two o'clock. It was on the warm side of a Carolina October, and even if it hadn't been warm, the school celebrities: Mr. Godwin the Principal, Miss Cole the head lunch lady, Mrs. Paladino the librarian, Mr. Mertyn the lead janitor, and of course the ever-popular (with the ladies) gym teacher, Mr. Holland, would all be on standby for their afternoon of getting dunked by excited students – whether they could hit the target or not – for the bargain price of a dollar donation.

The Fall Festival was always a lot of fun and was turning into quite the annual tradition. For the past four years, Julie taught Kindergarten in the mornings. She split the school day with another teacher, who taught the second half of the day. It worked out for them both because they each had a young child to care for in addition to teaching.

Julie learned rather quickly in life that career choices are always different for mothers, especially when the children are young. But last year, it was a God-send for Julie to have a solid part time job when her husband Gabe died in an Airborne training accident on Post. Julie needed to work – anything to keep herself going from day to day and keep her from not losing her mind. But she needed to grieve, too. She kept her head occupied with work because she had a little girl to raise, but she also needed the afternoons to herself while Molly was still in school. That was when she would be with Gabe, grieve for Gabe, attempt to sort through the range of emotions and heartache that occupy the heart of a woman who has suddenly lost the man she loves, in addition to the life they were building together. Forever.

She ran with Gabe every day, her heart melted with his, quiet step after quiet step, along the sanctuary of working middle class homes in Fayetteville. People here in the towns surrounding Fort Bragg were busy families. They were military. They were transient. They were special. They were their own breed of cautious but hardened – optimism coupled with the indescribable underlying fears that go with being the family members of soldiers on a highly deployable post, even during relative peace time. It was these nuances about this town, sometimes called Fayettenam…that made her stay around…at least for now. She found comfort in having been a part of a military family, and this had been the longest Molly ever lived in one place. She never realized how important some semblance of stability was to her own sanity when their lives had been thrown into chaos by Gabe's untimely exit from this world.

The only time Julie tried a widow's support group, part of an area church's ministry, the women in the group appeared to be in their sixties and older. Julie felt that perhaps she had been pointed to the wrong group of widows for help and healing. After all, how could a woman who got to raise her family, have grandchildren and have her husband for more than thirty-five years possibly understand what she was going through?

But when one of the older widows described her beloved husband's passing as, "an atomic bomb going off in my life," Julie realized that she may have had more than a few things in common with these ladies. So, she stayed for a while, learned a bit about her feelings and the bond they all shared, and then came to terms with the fact that she was simply a different kind of widow. She was, in some ways, lucky to not be locked into one way of life for so long that she had no identity of her own remaining. So many of those women had no recollection of their lives before their marriages. She wasn't too old to have another baby someday. Those women were all post-menopausal grandmothers with grown children who'd invite them over for Christmas dinner. She was still young enough to start over…or at least start again.

Julie had…really…another whole lifetime ahead of her. She was twenty-eight. Some of those women were barely married the first time at twenty-eight.

Julie would remind herself, on those rides home after listening to these women, what kind of mother would she be if curled up into a ball on her bed for the next eleven years until Molly went off to college? No matter how hard it was, she still had a daughter to raise. So, she found her own space in coming to terms with the loss of her husband, apart from the widows of the little Fayetteville basement church group, and instead ran with him. Literally. Every day. And continued to work in her career field. And raise their daughter. Julie decided she would find a way to live. And she knew that was what Gabe would have wanted her to do.

Molly stirred in her sleep, and Julie started to lightly tickle her to get her moving. She opened her eyes and said, "Is today the dunk?"

"Yes, Pudge. Let's go. We need to get ready and you need some breakfast."

Molly rolled out of bed and hopped over to her own bedroom, skinny white freckled legs sticking out from underneath a huge tee shirt – one of Gabe's old ones from when he ran the Army Ten Miler years ago.

Julie put her feet on the wood floor of her bedroom and started to get ready for the day. She pulled on her denim Bermuda shorts and the elementary school's official red and blue tee-shirt. She brushed her thick blond hair into a high ponytail and clipped a red bow in the back. She brushed on some concealer – damn the McVicar Women's curse of early crow's feet – and she dotted some lipstick over her thin lips. Looking down at her wedding photo: she, barefoot, in a simple white dress from Dress Barn and a straw hat with a make-shift veil from a craft store and Gabe in his dress blues carrying her up into his arms over the walkway bridge outside of the Venetian in Las Vegas, Julie rubbed the glass frame with her finger into a heart shape. This was not supposed to be how her life would be.

"I told you not to marry him! That he would only end up hurting you!" Julie could still hear her big-mouthed mother yell at her through the phone, when she called in the worst hour of her life to tell her that Gabe died. How does a person respond to the death of their son-in-law with, "I told you so?" Julie never got to ask her that because she hasn't spoken to her mother since that day.

After a bowl of Captain Crunch for Molly (only allowed on Saturdays) and a piece of toast and coffee for Julie, the "Us Against the World" duo headed off to the school to begin their day of community involvement and fun. There would be vendors and crafters from town set up inside the cafeteria and games and contests going on throughout the school with donated prizes. The silent auction included a three-night stay at a resort in the Bahamas, donated by a friendly dry cleaning businessman in town. Julie wished Gabe was here to bid on that. They sure could've used one last getaway together before he was gone for good.

There were arts and crafts for the children in the art room, balloon making and face painting on the playground with a local clown named Marcie, the Humane Society was coming for dog and cat adoptions, and a few food trucks would be there with hot dogs, sodas, cotton candy, and snow cones. The volunteer fire department was bringing the fire truck with Dallas the Fire Safety Dalmatian. Outside there was a yard sale, with all proceeds going to the PTA. The big blue dunk booth sat ready, full of water, waiting for its first celebrity victim. It was going to be a great day all around. For the first time in quite a while, Julie was feeling on the upbeat and positive side of the mood spectrum. Her heart was singing not quite a happy song...but one of quiet contentment for the moment.

Matt Holland, the adorable twenty-six-year-old PE teacher, walked up to Julie and Molly in his gray Army tee shirt and gray issue Army PT shorts. He was average height but big in personality, with a sweet baby face and a smile that would light up the Crown Convention Center all on its own. His brown hair was cropped high and tight, like he must've had it cut just this morning...and then realized he wasn't in the Army anymore.

"Miz Saint and Good Golly Miz Molly, how are you ladies this fine Saturday?" he asked, with his signature crooked grin, causing all female teachers, staff members, and even the little elementary school-aged girls to swoon.

Julie smiled, wishing she had the level of swoon for Matt that all the others had. It would've made his shy pursuit of her easier to deal with if his feelings were reciprocated. He was cute, the same age as her childhood best friend's younger brother, and she couldn't get passed thinking of him as one of those little brother types of friends. So, the few times he asked her out, she politely turned him down…"Sorry Matt, I'm just not ready to date anyone." He understood, of course. What else was he supposed to say? The benefit of being a young widow was that no one knew quite what to say to her under any circumstances, so she was always right.

Julie wondered what the hell people thought was a proper grieving period when you're widowed so young. Was it so different for twenty-eight year olds than for sixty-eight year olds? Julie thought that maybe it was.

Molly jumped up and down in place and yelled out, through hopping breaths, "Mr. Holland, when are you going to be dunked?"

"I'm first Molly Berry. Are you gonna cheat and press the button when I'm not looking?" he asked, bending down.

"No, I promise," she answered, averting her eyes, indicating the bold-faced lie.

"Molly Wolly Doodle…" he said slowly, waiting for her to laugh. That was her favorite nickname out of all his nicknames for her.

"Julie, how are you doing these days?" he asked, looking up at her, squinting his eyes in the bright sunlight. His face was so boyish, so pinch-able.

"I'm good, thanks Matt."

He stepped toward her, and then stopped himself. It looked like he was going to hug her and then thought better of it.

"You sure look pretty, like always," he uttered quietly, so only Julie could hear him. "I guess I'll see you two later." He turned and walked off toward the door from the cafeteria, leading to the playground area, gray shorts marching back and forth with each step.

Molly looked up at her mother. "Mrs. Cooper told Mrs. Flinch that Mr. Holland has a crush on you. I heard them talking in the lavatory."

Julie laughed. "Those two are just a couple of gossips, Molly. Don't pay them any attention."

Fall Festival

Jasper Ray taped a small sign over his old wooden display table, handmade years ago to drag along with him to the flea markets around the state of North Carolina. "Jasper's Wood Works" it read in neatly printed magic marker. As Jasper pressed down on the tape to make sure it took, Buddy walked up to him with a cup of coffee in his hands, shaking his head.

"Mr. Cochran, why you shakin' your head at me like that?" he asked, noticing a subtle sarcasm to his young lawyer friend.

"Jasper, that sign could be taken the wrong way. This is a school for Christ's sake."

Jasper looked at his sign and winced. He rubbed his forehead with his right hand and stated, "Well, all these years ain't nobody never said nothin' about my sign bein' taken the wrong way."

"You need to remove the space between 'Wood' and 'Works' and have it read 'Woodworks' instead," Buddy explained, thankful for so many hours of his life spent editing his own writing and even some of his classmates' writing as a student.

He looked over at Jasper, whose face registered that he still did not quite understand what Buddy was talking about. Then he started to feel a little guilty, which quickly morphed into outright embarrassment. *What the hell is my problem?* Buddy thought, almost out loud.

Just because his mind has been consumed with the revelation that he got dumped without much warning or even a real goodbye by a girl who he was dumb enough to believe liked him – and all while he was just trying to be nice and go along with things to see where they'd lead – he was now also having to accept the fact that his sex life was, once again, dormant. But it doesn't mean he needed to take out his frustrations onto an old southern gentleman like Jasper. Buddy's ego was bruised. He needed to get over it. It wasn't like Jennifer, as a person, would be missed. Jennifer's lovin', however, would indeed be missed.

"Mr. Cochran, I don't get it. Why's my sign a problem?"

Buddy crunched his forehead up and took a sip of his coffee, a bit strong today, from the new Krispy Kreme down the road.

"Never mind. I'm just being an ass." Buddy walked around to the other side of the table where Jasper began to place out some of his wooden creations. A few brightly colored birdhouses. A carved and shellacked foot stool. Some sculpted wooden salad bowls with accompanying utensils. Real craftsmanship. The level of care that Jasper displayed in everything he did spoke volumes about the kind of man he was. It even reflected in the way he delivered the mail on his route.

Buddy scanned the cafeteria. There were about twenty other vendors setting up displays. Some tables were full of baked goods in neatly wrapped plastic bags with colored ribbons. Buddy was eyeballing a pile of brownies on the table next to Jasper's Wood Works. Woodworks. He noticed Gaynelle Flowers, whose son Clayton was a former pot smoking teenaged client of his, setting up her crocheted trivets and pot holders. He figured that if Clayton was standing there, he could be the pot holder. And that he would need to steer clear of the brownies. The idle thoughts that went through his mind during the first cup of coffee should qualify him for a writing job on "Saturday Night Live" Buddy reckoned.

And then, as if the heavens opened to reveal all its secrets not provided in the Bible...he saw her. The daily jogger. His daily jogger.

She stood off to the side, near the empty stage which hung back at the end of the cafeteria for school assemblies and plays and concerts. Buddy had never been in this school before today, but every primary school in America had one. And the blond jogger was standing next to this particular one. He felt his knees soften and his stomach clench. The coffee turned acid in his mouth and he wondered if this was that feeling – about a woman – the one feeling that has eluded him his entire life. He certainly never felt like this about Jennifer or any of the earlier young women he attempted to date. But the jogger. The blond-haired blue-eyed jogger. Standing over there in a pair of jean shorts and a red tee-shirt. A bow in her hair, like she was a reluctant cheerleader.

"Mr. Cochran, what you gawkin' at there?" Jasper's voice interrupted his moment of both panic and infatuation.

Buddy came out of his beautiful-female-in-view coma and turned to his mailman friend. "Uh, nothing. No one. Goddamn, Jasper, look. It's her!" he spat out like a middle school boy peeping at a high school girl changing her top in a locker room.

Jasper peeked around him. "Who?"

He didn't want to point, so he nodded. "Over by the stage. It's the lady who jogs by my house."

Jasper squinted. His eyes, crinkled and dusty from so many years outside, simply couldn't see that far anymore. "I can't see that far, but if you say so."

Buddy looked over again and saw her talking to a young man who appeared to be a soldier in an Army tee-shirt. A skinny little girl with brown hair stood in between them and looked up at the soldier. Is that her little girl? Is that her husband? Buddy really hoped she wasn't married. It's not like he had any balls whatsoever to say anything to her or ask her out if she was single, but he just didn't want her to be married. He didn't want any other guy to lay claim to his little daily burst of sunshine. It would ruin the fantasy he created inside of his head, considerably.

The little girl started jumping up and down in place. Her hair was cut in a bob, straight and thin, and went up and down with each hop. She wore a pair of purple shorts and a purple and white top with a monkey on it. She had on a pair of white tennis shoes and appeared to be around six or seven years old. The soldier walked away, and the jogger and little girl sat on the edge of the stage, looking around the room.

Buddy, without thinking and almost on instinct, grabbed three cellophane wrappers full of brownies, put a five-dollar bill on the table, and told the elderly lady standing there to keep the change. Then he walked over to the jogger and little girl. As he got closer, he could see that the jogger's tee-shirt had "staff" written on the front and "Frederick Morrison Elementary School" written over a picture of a blue dragon.

The little girl's legs were swinging out, one after the other, with each tennis shoe bouncing off the side of the stage. She noticed Buddy walking toward them, and they made eye contact almost immediately. Buddy, not usually good with eye contact, looked right at the little girl watching him. He could handle a kid. When he got up to them, she said, "Hey," as if they already knew each other.

"Hey yourself," Buddy said with a wily smile.

The jogger – who Buddy now figured was either a teacher or something – looked over at him. "Can I help you?" she asked.

"Well, I was hungry and thought it might be nice to bring some brownies over to this nice young lady sitting here." It sounded awful and completely rehearsed – which it wasn't – because Buddy was now working on what-the-hell-am-I-doing fumes.

"She's just had breakfast, but maybe she can have one later for a snack. Do you think you'll sell out fast?"

"Mom, just let me have it now, and I promise I won't eat it 'til later," the girl said, both legs now swinging and bouncing in unison. She had a round pale face full of freckles.

"Where did you get all those angel kisses?" Buddy asked her.

"Angel kisses?"

"Yeah, the angel kisses all over your face."

He could see the jogger grinning out of the corner of his eye. It was so hard not to start hyperventilating while talking to this little girl.

The girl smiled a huge smile, missing a front tooth. "My daddy used to call them that!"

"What? He calls your freckles angel kisses too?"

She nodded her head while beaming at him. "Yeah. He used to tell me that every night I went to bed. That an angel came and kissed my face and added more and more each night when I was sleeping."

"Well, my mother called them angel kisses too. How about that?"

Buddy sensed the jogger shifting in place.

"Hi," she said suddenly. Buddy turned toward her and felt his gaze go just past her ear – his usual coping mechanism – locked in like an instinctual response to beauty. "I think I know you."

Buddy felt his whole body tighten even more than it already was. "You do?"

Nodding, she explained, "Yeah. You're the guy always walking a big dog on Triton Hills. I run past you almost every day."

Buddy's heart, almost ready to heave through his chest, pumped fiercely.

"Um," he started.

"I'm Julie," she interrupted him, before he could pass out. "You have a beautiful dog, some kind of lab mix maybe? We cross paths almost every day. Not sure what time exactly, but it makes me think of the movie Groundhog Day."

Buddy's head was so jumbled with words and thoughts and feelings, he felt his throat closing. He became dizzy.

"Are you okay, Mister?" the freckled-faced girl asked, head cocked sideways in concern.

Buddy breathed as deeply as he could without appearing to be breathing as deeply as he could. How has he mastered that, exactly? He rarely found himself in such an overwhelming situation. He was the kind of man who stood off to the side and watched other men talk to the women he wished he could talk to.

The jogger – Julie – hopped off the stage and onto the floor. She stood in front of Buddy, her height at just about five feet five inches. She came up to his shoulders, and Buddy always felt like this was the perfect height for a woman: short enough to be protected and carried around – like a bouquet of flowers, not a cave woman – and tall enough to fill out the length of her legs. Her blond hair was straight and pulled tightly, her forehead showing no signs of age. Her skin was pale but not sickly at all, just like the little girl's skin, only she hadn't any freckles that were as prominent.

"Well, like I said, I'm Julie. This is my daughter Molly. So now when I run by you and your dog, you'll say 'hey' to me, right?"

Julie spoke and Buddy watched her mouth move, not quite hearing her clearly.

"Uh, yeah," he stammered.

Julie put out her hand. Buddy looked down at it and put his hand in hers. Her eyes squinted. "I thought you wanted to share your brownies."

Embarrassed, Buddy handed her a brownie. It had a green and yellow ribbon around the top, serving as a tie.

"What about me?" Molly asked, hopping off the stage and standing next to her mother.

Buddy smirked at her and handed her a brownie.

The three of them awkwardly stood in place, looking at each other, Buddy feeling the most out of place he has ever felt in his life. He wanted to tell Julie that he purposely walked his dog at two o'clock every day just in case she runs by. But that would've made him sound like a stalker. He wanted to tell her that he thinks about her all the time, even during the short time he attempted a relationship with Jennifer the law student. But that would've made him sound like a jerk. He wanted to tell her that he thought she was beautiful, that he hoped she was single, that he'd like to cook her supper, that he wanted to take her to the movies some time. He saw no wedding ring on her finger, the telltale sign of a committed woman. Having a little girl wasn't something he thought of in his imaginary life with the jogger, but he had always wanted a family.

Buddy was paralyzed in his thoughts. Here was this woman he has done nothing but wonder about for months – talking to him right here and now – trying to have a conversation with him...and he was on the left side of speechless. Isn't this what teenaged girls do? Plan their future lives with someone they just met?

As if on cue, Jasper walked up to the threesome. "Mr. Cochran, I was wonderin' if you could help me for a minute."

Buddy came out of his confused state. He looked at Jasper, standing in a pair of old work jeans and a long-sleeved shirt.

"Uh, yeah. Of course."

"Mr. Cochran?" Julie asked.

Buddy looked over at her.

"You gonna introduce me to your friends?" Jasper asked.

"Uh, yeah, sure. This is Julie. And Molly."

Molly put out her hand. "I'm Molly. This is my school."

Jasper smiled at her and asked, "You own a school?"

Molly laughed. "No silly, I just go here."

"My name is Mr. Ray." He pointed at his table just along the wall of the cafeteria. "You see all those wooden trinkets?"

Molly nodded her head.

"That's my table. So, I hope y'all will stop by and visit sometime today."

Molly looked up at Julie.

"Hi, Mr. Ray. My name is Julie Saint. I'm one of the teachers here. Thank you so much for participating in our Fall Festival."

Jasper shook her hand.

"And Mr. Cochran? What's your first name?" she asked, turning to Buddy, her blue eyes gleaming at him. "You haven't told us your name."

Buddy looked briefly down at his feet. "My name's Jonathan Cordova. But people call me 'Buddy.'"

"Ah," she said. "Who's Mr. Cochran?"

Jasper interjected. "OJ Simpson's lawyer. You know? The one that said, 'If it doesn't fit, you must acquit.'"

Julie looked confused.

Buddy grinned and explained. "I'm an attorney. Here in town. Jasper is my extremely talented mailman. Really, he is a wood-smith who delivers mail during the day to pay his other bills. I ah... I promised him that I'd stop by the school to see his projects and help him out if he needed it. Also, so I could buy my mother something for Christmas."

Smiling, Julie replied, "I see. Well, thank you both for coming to support our fundraiser. This is our biggest one every year, and we raise a lot of money for the PTA."

Molly, hopping in place, demanded, "You have to come dunk the Principal in a little while!"

Buddy watched her bounce. "Dunk the Principal?"

"Yeah!" Bounce, bounce, bounce. "We're in charge of the dunk tank. Come throw some balls and dunk him." Molly continued to hop.

"Okay, Molly, we will."

"Promise?"

"Yeah, I promise." Buddy wondered why this child hopped so much and found it both charming and exhausting at the same time.

"It was nice to meet you ladies," Jasper said. "I need to set up a couple of things here and Mr. Cochran's gonna help me get the chairs out of my truck."

"It was so nice to meet you," said Julie, putting her hand on top Molly's head to get the hops quieted down.

Buddy looked at her, really looked at her, for the first time. When she runs by him, she is just a flash of beauty, a mesmerizing blur of female athleticism. She gazed at him softly with her big blue eyes and a warmth took over his entire body. He was happy – really happy – in this moment.

He felt her go almost shy with him, unlike the confident and polite, but authoritative, teacher she had just been. She looked away, knowing that he sensed it. Jasper walked off and Molly hopped over toward Dallas the Dalmatian mascot from the fire department who had just waltzed in.

He watched Julie, wondering who would say something next. It was almost a tranquil stillness hanging between them. "It was really nice to meet you, Julie." Buddy spoke with more confidence than he had ever known in his life.

"Will I see you soon?" she asked, peering over at Molly talking with the big dog.

Continuing to observe her, Buddy, not thinking, blurted out, "You're not married, are you?"

Julie, suddenly shaken out of her shyness, eyeballed Buddy harshly. "Um, no. I'm not. Not anymore." She wiped her hands on her shorts and looked around the room.

"Good," Buddy said, his heart soaring. He winked at her.

Julie appeared taken aback. "Well, I. He. I'm widowed. My husband passed away."

And just like that, Buddy felt like the biggest ass who has ever walked the face of the earth. Wow. He couldn't believe it. How selfish of him. This whole time he was dreaming about this mysterious jogger and wishing he had the courage to say something to her, kind of lurking around her like a dorky prepubescent boy every day with his well-timed walks, and she was just a woman in pain. A single mother in grief.

"I'm so sorry," Buddy responded. "I'm, um, really, I'm sorry. I feel awful."

"No, it's okay. Really. You didn't know. How could you have known, right?" she asked.

Molly started hopping again, this time out of the cafeteria and over to the water fountain. Julie and Buddy watched her. Buddy was amused but treading lightly.

"She sure likes to hop," he said, breaking the tension of Julie's apparent sadness and Buddy's mortification.

"She does. She really does," Julie laughed. "Well, I need to get going. We need to help out in the art room before we take care of the dunk tank outside. I hope I'll see you again some time, Mr. Cochran."

With that, she walked off toward the water fountain, collected her daughter, and they headed down a hallway.

CHAPTER 5

February 1971 – May 1973

Second Chances

Retta Kaspar and Kenny Bellinger stood in the chambers of the Honorable Montgomery Ewing, Justice of the Peace. Retta beamed in a long, form fitting yellow dress and a full crown of baby's breath peppered inside of her raven hair swelling with bouncy curls, sewn together by her talented fellow hair dresser best friend, May Ellen Jones. May Ellen stood next to the soon-to-be Mr. and Mrs. Bellinger, bursting with joy and hope for her young widowed friend.

Lots of women were becoming husbandless by the war in Vietnam. Retta was just one of them, but out of how many, May Ellen didn't know. She was lucky. Her husband was a plumber who did his two years early on and came out of the whole thing unscathed. However cruel the war in Vietnam was to so many women left behind, it was also particularly ugly to a legion of small children. That war left little Daniel Junior fatherless.

A war widow was a sad thing, but a fatherless boy was even sadder, as far as May Ellen was concerned. A woman, especially a young and pretty one like Retta, could always find herself another husband.

But a little boy's father was his father. And there was no one else who could replace that relationship in a little boy's life.

Kenny Bellinger came back from Vietnam with a shrapnel wound in his leg. The wound was bad enough to send him home for good and get him medically discharged. But not so bad that he couldn't find a job quickly, settle himself in Killeen and fall head over heels in love with the delicate Italian beauty from New Jersey, who sometimes cut the hair of the stray Army man wandering into the hair salon on Fairmont Avenue.

It always made May Ellen laugh when the soldiers came in to Delta's Hair Salon. They all thought they were so smart, doing something nobody had thought of before. The salon was not a barber shop, but instead, it was a bona-fide beauty shop for women – hair and nails and facials and whatnot. May Ellen figured that these lonely boys of war knew exactly where to find women. And where better than in a beauty salon nestled inside of a military town?

Kenny was big and cute and friendly and smitten with Retta right off the bat. He sat down in her chair, smiled that jillion-watt grin of his, and said, "Miss Retta, darlin', I need a high and tight." But Kenny wasn't in the Army anymore. He had a job at a warehouse, or at least that's what he said, and soon enough, he charmed Retta right out onto her first date…the first date she agreed to since that dreaded visit from the Casualty Notification Officer on a Tuesday afternoon about her beloved Danny and his remains heading back on a plane.

May Ellen watched her quiet but feisty friend go from withdrawn and depressed to hopeful and in love, and while she didn't act like some women in love act around here – all goo-goo-gah-gah and touch-kissy – she was happier than she had been since she learned Danny wouldn't be coming home alive.

Kenny was good with little Buddy, who was only three years old when his father fell over there in some type of mine explosion. He seemed like he had their best interests at heart. He accepted that Retta once had a husband who she loved and a sweet little boy from that union, and to him, it was preferable to have a widowed woman over a divorced one. Men generally thought that divorced women had some undesirable fault with them…or they wouldn't be divorced. They carried ugly baggage instead of just a sad story.

He would take them to the new McDonald's for burgers and fries, and he was sure to give Buddy piggy back rides to and from the car. He was thoughtful with his gifts and compliments, and the other girls who worked in the salon wondered why they themselves weren't so lucky to have one nice man love them – let alone two – like Retta got to have.

Some days, Buddy would come into the salon with Retta because she had no sitter for him. He'd sit off to the side and color in a coloring book, quietly. He was such a well behaved young man, unlike Donna's son, who was always climbing on everything and causing a ruckus. May Ellen thought that Retta deserved her good fortune in finding Kenny: a husband and lover for her, a father and friend for Buddy…a second chance. After all, everybody deserves a second chance.

Kenny was so handsome in his dark blue suit, probably the only suit he ever owned in his life. He was a bit mysterious himself, never spoke of any kin or much of his upbringing, but they all knew he was from some place in Florida – not the nice parts, but instead the crevices that nobody really talked about or went to while on vacation. He was just another impoverished boy drafted into the Army out of a rural town, who did his grunt work as best as he could, got injured, and was given a Purple Heart and a discharge as a "thank you" from his government. That was certainly better than the "F you" he got from many of his fellow Americans. And a hell of a lot better than what Retta's Danny got: a body bag, a folded flag and his dog tag on his cold, stiff toe.

Buddy sat quietly in the Judge's big brown leather creaky chair. Judge Ewing gave him special permission to do so. He wore a white collared shirt and dark blue dress pants. His buzzed blond-brown hair was a staple of Texan boys, regardless of age. He was a thoughtful and polite tyke who would never quite know the love in which he had been created. He would never see how much his father loved his mother, other than maybe a stray photograph that captured just the right look or moment. Maybe someday he'd find an old letter. But soon, he would probably not remember anything about his father, Danny. And that was the saddest thing of all. That little boy had the gift of someone truly loving him, something so wonderful in life; and yet, at some point, he'll probably never realize that he ever had it.

After all the kind words between the Justice of the Peace and the young couple in love, the small ceremony started. Mrs. Ewing stood nearby, and along with May Ellen, served as witnesses. Buddy held the rings, just as he was told. The Judge's secretary, a fat middle-aged woman who wobbled as she walked, stood next to Mrs. Ewing, also as a witness. May Ellen figured that being a witness to civil ceremonies was probably part of her job. Then she wondered how many weddings the secretary had been a part of during her career and if she held an office pool on the couples…an over and under on whether the next marriage works out, using months as point.

"Retta Kaspar, do you take Kenneth Bellinger to be your lawfully wedded husband?" Judge Ewing asked, his bald head shining in the overhead lights of his otherwise darkened room.

"I do," Retta uttered, smiling at Kenny who beamed back at her.

"I now pronounce you man and wife," Judge Ewing announced.

Kenny and Retta kissed each other...not in the way they probably wanted to...but in a formal and sweet way, the way you should in ceremonies or in church. They embraced, and Kenny picked her up, her hair falling back in a cascade of curls, her baby's breath crown staying in place. Buddy stood thoughtfully and still with his hands in his pockets, watching his mother be a new bride, something he had never seen before, other than perhaps in pictures.

Baby Brother

Buddy sat with his stepfather in the waiting room of the big hospital. The walls were high and a mint green color, the chairs were tan and plastic, like big bowls missing an entire side. Kenny smoked a cigarette and leafed through a car magazine. He kept making strange grunting noises that bothered Buddy, but he knew better than to say anything about it. The last time he asked Kenny a question in a way that he didn't like, he got the back of a hand to his cheek. Buddy knew that he wouldn't let that happen again. When his mother asked him why his cheek was swollen, Buddy just told her that he accidentally walked into the corner of the door. Since he was a growing boy, apt to get into a little mischief now and then, that was completely plausible.

His birthday was a few days ago, and he was so happy to finally be six years old. He had three friends come over who also lived on his street. They had a cake with yellow icing. They played Pin the Tail on the Donkey. They had party hats with big blue polka dots on it and noise makers that about sent Kenny into a bad headache by the end of the afternoon. Gary gave him a Matchbox car, Freddy gave him a cap gun, (which his mother immediately took away for when he's older), and Billy gave him a GI Joe. Billy's gift was the best one by far, but Buddy knew to make a fuss about all of them equally. Being six also meant that he could start school soon and wouldn't have to go to the salon with his mother anymore or stay home with Kenny while he was off from work.

It's not like Kenny was a bad stepfather or anything like that. He was usually real nice and a lot of fun. He liked to sing songs in the shower – loud – and Buddy and his mother would laugh in the other room. Kenny was one of those people who thought he was a good singer, and the shower made him think that even more. He also liked to take Buddy with him to look at cars at the car lot place. He kept telling the man in the suit, who'd walk over from time to time, that he was, "Just looking today."

"Why are we always just looking?" Buddy got up the nerve to ask him one day.

Kenny took a drag on his cigarette and answered, "I am a man who loves cars, son. I'm always just looking. But someday, I'm gonna buy one. I'm gonna buy one for your mama, and when you're sixteen...I'm gonna buy one for you, too."

Other times, Kenny liked to play Matchbox cars with Buddy. He'd lay on the floor, like a massive boy himself, and they'd put the cars out like they were for sale in the car lot. He'd ask, "Young man, which is the prettiest car?" and Buddy would answer, "I like this blue one." Then Kenny would pick up the car that Buddy chose and tell him what kind it was, what year it was and where he last saw one.

Kenny liked to take Buddy and his mother out to a nice dinner at least once a week. He always opened the door for them and pulled out the chair for his mother. If Buddy needed a booster seat, he was always sure to ask the waitress for one. Buddy hated needing a booster seat, but he was at that in between size that five and six-year-old boys tended to be.

He kept promising to take Buddy fishing and to teach him how to catch a squirrel or a rabbit, but his mother made Kenny wait on that. "You can do all that when he's just a little bit older. Please!" she cooed at him. "He only gets to be small once and then he's all yours, Kenny."

Kenny kissed her forehead as she looked all the way up at him and responded, "Yes, Ma'am, I will wait a bit longer just for you." He winked at Buddy, indicating that he couldn't wait to show him the ropes of boyhood, just like every other father in Texas who had a son.

But the best game they'd play was truck driver. Kenny had two CB radios that he found at work. No one claimed them so his boss told him that he could keep them. Kenny would tell Buddy to go out on the back stoop with his CB radio and Kenny stayed in the kitchen with the other one.

"Breaker, breaker, one niner…this is Big Daddy…" Kenny would say into the speaker, as Buddy heard the static flow along. "I got a Grizzly Bear on the left side at exit forty-two…you copy, Good Buddy?"

"Copy that, Big Daddy," Buddy responded into the static. "Is it a Bear Trap, you think?"

They'd play that trucker game for hours, sometimes making up some of the silliest stories and situations on the side of the Texas highways involving "grizzly bears" and "mama bears" and "choke and pukes." Kenny taught him the entire phonetic alphabet. Buddy took that knowledge to school and then taught his friends.

"Why didn't you become a trucker?" Buddy asked Kenny one day after he put the CB radios into a drawer for safe keeping.

"Aw son, I could never be on the road like that and leave you and your mama all alone. I'd miss you both too much."

As Kenny and Buddy waited patiently for the new arrival in the hospital, a man in a white jacket came out and inquired, "Mr. Bellinger?"

Kenny looked up, put his cigarette out on the sole of his work boot, and replied, "Yes, Sir, that's me."

The man looked down at Buddy and then again at Kenny. "May we speak privately?"

"Uh, yeah, sure thing," Kenny answered, not quite sure what he meant by that. He looked down at Buddy. "Son, you stay here. I'll be right back. Then we can go and see your mama."

Buddy watched Kenny and the man in the white coat walk off to the side of the waiting room. Kenny stood silently, listening to what the man was saying to him, his face growing ashen and his eyes starting to sink in. He looked down at the floor and put his hands deep into his pockets, jingling the coins inside with his fingers. The man in the white coat walked away and Kenny faced the wall, his back to Buddy. Standing like that for a few minutes, his shoulders sunk, and he turned back around. Walking toward Buddy, he stated, "Son, your mama gave birth to a baby boy, but he didn't make it."

Not understanding, Buddy looked up at Kenny and asked, "What's that mean?"

"It means that there's no baby. No baby is coming home with us."

"But what happened to the baby?" Buddy felt himself starting to get upset. The tears started to come up through his legs and into his stomach and then welled up around the rims of his eyes. He had been looking forward to seeing this baby who had been growing in his mother's belly for a long time. He had even made plans on all the things he would teach the baby if it were a girl and the things he would teach the baby if it were a boy. If it was a girl, he would teach her how to color in the lines and paint by numbers. If it was a boy, he would teach him how to build a fort and catch a football.

Kenny sat down, and with a cracked voice and subdued tears, he uttered, "He was born dead and not breathing. They call it 'still-born.'" Just then, Kenny put his hands on his face, covering his eyes, and Buddy could tell he was crying.

Buddy decided then and there that he was not going to cry for his dead brother. He was going to be strong for Kenny. Kenny lost his son – his real son – and now all he had left was only a stepson. So maybe he had better be the best stepson that Kenny ever had. He stood up in front of Kenny and put his arms around him and held him tight, like his mother would do for him when he was sad about something or scared. Kenny pulled him close and sobbed into Buddy's neck. It was the only hug they had ever shared.

Retta walked slowly into the house, her body sore and aching. The rolls from her childbirth experience were buried under her shirt, and all she wanted to do was go to bed. Kenny held her bag from the hospital and set it down on the couch.

"Buddy, you go mind your mama. Help her get settled in bed so she can rest," Kenny instructed.

Buddy followed his orders, walking behind his mother and into the bedroom. She seemed to squeak as she walked, a broken emptiness with each step. Buddy wondered what it must've felt like to give birth to a dead baby. And as he turned around, he watched Kenny take the bag of baby supplies, which was full of diapers, blankets, and some new bottles that they had just purchased from the store, and put it deep into the trashcan.

Retta slowly got into bed, rolled up the covers, saying nothing to anyone. Three days later, she had still said nothing and had barely moved in the bed. In the late afternoon, Buddy got into the bed with her while Kenny went to work, and he could feel her crying on the pillow. He looked at her, her dark hair long, unkempt and messy over her face, her small frame stirring slowly, and he asked, "Mother, do you want something to eat?"

Retta opened her eyes and put her hands so that she cupped his small rounded face. Her face became stern and her dark eyes appeared almost wild as she said, "You, Daniel Junior, are my baby. You are the only baby I will ever have. You are all I have left of your father. And that makes you my everything."

Buddy didn't know what to think about what she told him, but he felt in his heart that it was very important. He was already close to his mother. Kenny sometimes said that he was "a little mama's boy." And while Buddy reckoned that it was meant to be a dig at him because of how he said it, he thought that it didn't make any sense to him that being a "mama's boy" was such bad thing. Being a "mama's boy" seemed like a right good thing to him.

Night Terrors

Kenny went through the thick green brush as quietly as he could. His boots were soaking wet from the rice paddy he walked through by accident. But his boots weren't the jungle boots that he wore in Vietnam. They were his brown work boots, the kind that announced a man's station in life: he worked a laborious job, a job where he had to use his hands and his back and was tired at the end of the day. The bottoms of his jeans were soaked as well, but the rest of him remained dry. He approached a small house in a clearing, and it started to downpour.

"The fucking monsoon season in this goddamned place!" Kenny shouted. He was trying to be quiet because he wasn't sure if he was about to be ambushed, but for some reason, it was okay to yell like that. There would be no ambush.

He kept walking toward the house that rested alone in the clearing. There was no normal vegetation surrounding it and no lights were on inside as far as he could tell. The house looked like it could be a small Cape Cod on some coastal plot of land in Maine, but Kenny knew he wasn't in Maine. He was in Vietnam. In jeans. In a monsoon.

As Kenny approached the house, he looked down at his hands. He was carrying an M16A1 rifle, but there was no magazine in the clip. He looked inside the chamber and saw no solo round in there either. It was covered in mud, and while it was raining heavily, neither his dry parts or this rifle were getting wet from the weather. Just his boots, his jean bottoms, dragging and heavy with rice paddy water.

The house looked familiar. The steps were made of rotting wood. He carefully walked up and knocked on the door. It swung open. No one seemed to be inside. It was dark. There were no shadows, almost like the house was completely empty.

Then, he saw one. A shadow moved past a doorway, quickly. It was so fast that it was nothing but a blur. Kenny's chest started to pound. What was he going to do with an unloaded rifle?

"Hello?" Kenny yelled into the void.

There was no answer. He decided to keep going forward toward where he saw the shadow. Like those dumb chicks in slasher movies walk toward the evil killer…and therefore…their own death.

His heart racing, he continued toward the open door and saw something sitting in a corner in the dark. It was a girl, but he couldn't tell how old she was. Maybe a teenager. She watched him as he crept closer to her. Her hair was black and straight and long like a show horse's mane. Her face was round and she had slanted eyes. She had a small mole near her mouth. She had to be Vietnamese.

As he got closer, he asked, "Who are you?"

She didn't answer him.

"Do you speak English?"

She glared at him like she was not scared of him at all, her stare almost frightening Kenny into an odd submission. Kenny stood still and then decided to put his rife in firing position, pointing it at the girl.

"Who are you?" he shouted at her.

"Han," she answered.

Kenny was surprised by that answer.

"You are not Han!" He knew who Han was. He remembered Han like she was in his arms yesterday. This girl looked nothing like Han. Did she? He was now…not so sure.

"Han," the girl said again.

Kenny, enraged, screamed, "You are not Han! Stop saying that name!"

"Han."

"I will shoot you, you dumb fucking bitch! Stop it!"

"Han."

"Fuck you! I will kill you! I will shoot your fucking face off right now!"

"Han."

Kenny could feel some kind of unseen presence take a hold of him. His throat became tight, like someone put their large hands on it and started to squeeze. He couldn't see anyone doing it, almost like some ghost was there just choking him, slowly…and growing stronger with each passing second. The girl in the corner disappeared, Kenny's eyes started to bulge, and then he heard coughing and choking noises. Someone was clawing at his face.

"Stop! KKKKKKennnny! Stop!"

He felt the slaps on his mouth and a fingernail scraped his cheek. He opened his eyes to find Retta underneath of him, his hands pressed firmly on her delicate throat. Her eyes were wide and terrified, her dark hair in a nest around her pillow. Horrified, Kenny let go of his wife's throat and fell back onto the floor.

That was the first night Kenny's bad dreams started. That was the first night Kenny had ever put anything other than a loving and tender hand on his wife. That was the first night Kenny started drinking something hard…something harder than a beer.

Pain

It took almost four weeks for Retta to go back to work at the salon. The childbirth was easy, much easier than Buddy had been in 1966. She was given this form of anesthesia called an epidural, where they basically knocked out the bottom half of her body for the entire birth. The only pain she had was when the labor started, but once they were settled at the hospital, the doctor came in and gave her the epidural. Retta couldn't believe how she didn't feel anything at all.

Then she started to push, the baby came out, and there were all kinds of quick but hushed moving and shuffling around the room.

No one would let her see the baby, despite hearing a nurse say, "It's a boy." She knew something was wrong, but no one would say anything concrete to her. They just sewed the tear near her vagina, cleaned her up and one of the nurses would say every few minutes, "The doctor will be back soon, hon."

Retta laid there, legs numb, head fuzzy and stomach clenched. She wasn't supposed to feel her stomach, but for some reason, she could. Maybe if they had cut her open, she wouldn't have felt that, but the pit of fear and anxiety overwhelmed her gut and there was no dulling that with any fancy schmancy anesthesia.

Eventually, the doctor came back into the room. He was an older gentleman with dark hair, graying at the temples. It was slicked back, covering a stubborn bald spot on the top. He had deep set eyes with black horn rimmed glasses, the kind that Kenny called "birth control glasses." When Retta had once asked him why he called them that, he told her that they were issued in the Army. "Those things make you so ugly that no girl wants to have sex with you," he explained.

The doctor's white coat hung low, and his sleeve touched Retta's arm as he pulled up a chair next to her. And then, when Retta peered into his face, she knew. She knew her baby was dead.

The doctor couldn't mask his sadness. She realized that he had probably been through this very scenario several times over the years with lots of young mothers just like her. But she could also tell that he was the kind of man who wore each dead baby he delivered on the many harsh creases that cut along his face.

He told Retta that her baby boy had been born already gone, that he never had a chance, the umbilical cord wrapped around his neck had strangled the life out of him before he was ever able to take a breath on his own. He was on the wrong side of the birth canal, and by the time he came out, it was too late.

"Ma'am, I know it's important for a mother to hold her baby. But I also understand that it might be too much for you to do. I will bring him back in here so you can hold him once, so you can see your baby's face," he whispered.

The birth room was quiet. Retta's body remained still, a suspension of numbing disbelief and the harsh beginnings of grief stood in the air around her like a gaseous cloud of toxins. Retta nodded.

The doctor left again and soon put a small white bundle into her arms. She held her son against her chest. His skin was cold, his face was a faint purple, and his eyes were permanently closed shut by the unrelenting brutality of that thing called "God's Will."

As she memorized the shape of his face so she could burn it into a permanent photograph within her heart, Retta started to weep. Losing Danny to some far away war was bad enough. But she didn't have to hold him and see his purple face. This baby boy was a different kind of loss. He was now an eternal unfulfilled promise, the ripened bond between she and her new husband…who now had no name or future.

It didn't happen all at once, but a couple months later, Kenny started hitting her. The first night that he had almost choked her to death, just a couple of weeks after their dead baby boy came out from her, several more weeks went by before he was violent again. The choking was while he was in a dream, "A night terror," per her mother's definition. Retta knew that. She knew that he didn't mean to hurt her and that he was not really himself in that scary moment.

Kenny cried on the floor after it happened and grabbed her like he couldn't believe what had just occurred. He apologized a million times, swearing that he had no idea what he was doing, that he thought he was somewhere in Vietnam. Retta felt horrible about it all, wondering if it was her fault somehow.

Another four weeks went by. Kenny, after coming home from Del's Bar down near the warehouse, slapped her in the face. But he was drunk and stunk of cheap whiskey. Retta knew the cheap whiskey smell from growing up in a tavern. She knew Kenny didn't mean it, that she shouldn't have been so nasty with how she asked him where he had been for so long. She should've asked nicely. He was working so hard and doing so much overtime lately and deserved to throw back with his friends after work. She had been so down and out since the hospital anyway. Poor Kenny just needed to unwind.

So, when he apologized to her the next morning and promised that he would never do it again, she hugged him tight, they kissed a nice kiss, and all was well.

Another few weeks went by, and Retta had already mastered the art of applying makeup in just the right way and in just the right amount over the bruises that would develop on her arms and face. She was especially skilled at covering the small cuts that would open from time to time on her cheek or under her eyes during a particularly bad evening.

One night, when Kenny started screaming obscenities at her and came after her with a fork, Retta locked herself into the bathroom with Kenny outside, jamming the fork into the wood of the door. After about an hour, Retta could hear him sitting next to the door crying...sobbing, really. When she decided to open the door to find out what her husband was doing, she found him rocking back and forth, his head buried in his knees. All he said was, "Retta, I don't know what is wrong with me. What's happening?" She crawled out of the bathroom on her knees and held him there on the floor as he rocked and cried.

At some point, Retta looked up and saw Buddy's little white face watching them through a crack in his bedroom door in the darkness.

Cheerios

No Name Baby Brother would have turned one-year-old today. That thought pinged into Buddy's head as he slept and forced himself to open his eyes, facing the small framed photo he had on his nightstand of his real father holding him when he was a baby. While his brother had no official name, Buddy called him Joey in his heart. He thought that was a nice name for a baby brother.

The early morning sunlight lasered through his room's sole window. He peered over at the way the rays hit into the floor, like if he dug a hole into the wooden slats, the light would continue in full strength underneath the house.

The hollering from the night before was finally over, and Buddy wasn't sure if it was okay to get up now and have a bowl of cereal in the kitchen or if he should mind his mother and, "Stay in there and don't you come out of there 'til I tell you it's alright." Because the house seemed to be quiet, he figured it would be fine to tip-toe out. He hoped that he wouldn't see anything broken on the floor, like the last time he crept out after a night of loud noises and voices and slapping sounds.

Buddy pulled his Snoopy sheets off his thin frame, revealing his new Superman Underoos. They were a gift from his grandmother up in some place called New Jersey. He had never met her, but he had seen her in pictures and talked with her on the telephone a couple of times. His mother didn't like him walking around the house in just the Underoos, so he pulled on his blue robe. It matched his stepfather's blue robe.

Creeping out of his room, Buddy made his way into the kitchen. Nothing was broken, as far as he could see. There were some empty smashed beer cans on the kitchen table and an empty brown bottle of something. Buddy smelled it and scrunched his nose. It didn't smell very good.

He looked in the living room and was able to make out the silhouette of his stepfather on the couch, a blue and red afghan covering his body. As he opened the refrigerator to get down the gallon of milk, his mother came out of her bedroom. She wore a pair of blue jeans and a striped shirt. Her long curly hair was back into a clip. She hadn't yet put on her makeup because Buddy could see the fresh cut on her left cheek. Part of her bottom lip was a little swollen too. Buddy had no idea how she would cover that over with makeup, and he could feel the rage inside of him start to build up. His mother should never have to cover up cuts and bruises. Why did she let Kenny hurt her?

"Buddy, I'm going to your brother's grave site today. Do you want to come with me?" she asked.

Buddy thought about that. The last time he went, it was Easter. Lots of people came on Easter to visit their loved ones, Buddy had noticed. There were fresh flowers everywhere. They brought a small basket of flowers with them and set it at the foot of the grave stone. Buddy wasn't reading well enough yet, but his mother read the words for him: "Beloved Baby Boy Bellinger, Born and Died May 10th, 1972, Watch Over Us." It was a tiny spot in a large field full of dead people, most of whom got to live a lot longer than "never" or "not at all" and all of whom had names.

At the gravesite, he had wondered aloud why his brother had no name, like everyone else's brother. His mother replied, "Because Kenny didn't want to name him. He figured it'd be easier that way." Then she bit her bottom lip, her eyes held low, and whispered under her breath, "Nothin's easier about this."

As he looked into his Cheerios, Buddy asked his mother, "Is Kenny coming too?"

"Don't know, son. That's up to him."

Buddy watched his mother wash a few dishes still sitting in the sink. She looked down, like she was studying something inside of the foamy water and moved slowly. He rarely said anything to her about all the fighting that went on between her and Kenny. The one time he did, she replied, "There is something wrong with him. He needs to see a doctor for his nightmares."

But Buddy didn't understand how nightmares had anything to do with sitting around and talking funny with droopy eyes or hollering at his mother who never did anything mean to anyone, or getting mad about things, silly things, and throwing bottles and plates around the house. Buddy had nightmares before and never punched his mother in the face or grabbed her arms so tight that he left bruises on them for weeks. He had bad dreams before, but he never had an urge to shove his mother across a room or pull her hair so hard that a bunch of it came out in a big clump.

As he poured himself some Cheerios and piled sugar on top, his mother peeked into the living room, where Kenny slept.

"Are you gonna wake him?" Buddy asked.

"He should be fine, now. He's slept it off."

His mother walked quietly into the room, the floor creaking, and put her small feet onto the green shag carpet. The couch was green as well, and Kenny was too tall to fit his whole body on it, so his legs went just past the end. Buddy could see his bare feet poking out past the end of the cushion. There was a brown chair next to the couch, where Kenny usually sat to watch TV. The TV was sitting on the floor on the other side of the room, and his mother had a nice bookcase with some books and these strange little statues of people that she called "Hummels."

She got on her knees next to him and rubbed his back gently. She leaned her face onto the side of his cheek, and Buddy watched her whispering to him. But he couldn't hear what she said. Kenny stirred. Then she got up and quietly walked back into the kitchen.

"Son, we're gonna go visit your brother by ourselves. Kenny doesn't feel so good." Then she walked back over to her bedroom, leaving Buddy alone in the kitchen.

He continued shoveling his cereal into his mouth, observing his pile of sugar slowly melt into the milk. As he chewed, he watched Kenny on the couch, who did not move. He ate the remaining little Cheerios that looked like the letter O in the alphabet, which also happened to be the letter of the week in Kindergarten. There was one left. He poked at it with his finger, as it bobbed in the milk.

Buddy hated when there was one O left because he always struggled to get it onto the spoon all by itself. Eventually he'd give up and drink the sugary tasting milk with the one O feeling like an errant chunk.

As Buddy put the bowl up to his mouth, he slurped the milk, bit by bit, enjoying the sweetness of his favorite morning taste. When he finally finished, he put the bowl down and looked up to find Kenny standing right in front him, the afghan hanging loosely off his body. His eyes were wild, almost like he was a frightened animal at the zoo.

"Boy," he said sharply.

Buddy was full of anxiety, afraid of what was about to happen. Kenny had never looked at him like that before.

"I am tryin' to sleep. Can you not see that? Did you not see me asleep there on the couch?"

Buddy nodded. "I saw you," he said sheepishly.

"Well if you saw me, then why in the hell are you makin' so much racket over here?"

Kenny had light brown eyes and shaggy brown hair that he had let grow out after he wooed his mother and stopped going into her salon for Army style haircuts. He was tall and big like a lumberjack, the kind that Buddy saw in pictures inside the books that Mrs. Holloway, his teacher, read to the class during Carpet Time. Like the lumberjack, Kenny's face was unshaven with lots of stubble and he stunk of sweat or beer or something bad, like a dead rat.

"I'm sorry, Kenny. I didn't know I was loud." Buddy was terrified.

Kenny grunted and sneered at him in a way that seemed almost other worldly.

"You go get ready to visit your dead brother," he snapped, spittle forming around the edge of his lips where some curious white stuff had collected.

"Are you coming with us?" Buddy asked.

Kenny didn't answer. He walked back toward the bedroom that he shared with his mother, went inside and shut the door behind him.

CHAPTER 6

October 1996 – July 1997

Bo

A long time ago, Buddy's mother informed him that getting a dog would make him immediately attractive to women and would always serve as a natural icebreaker toward further conversation.

"You are a very good looking young man, son. And those eyelashes are God's blessed gift to you. There is no need for you to be so afraid of women. They don't bite. Well, not until they know you better," his mother explained.

Buddy always figured his biggest problem was just that he could never think of anything to talk about with women. He had a lot of thoughts in his head, a lot of useless knowledge – like batting averages for the Braves and how many licks it takes to get to the Tootsie Roll inside of a Tootsie Roll Pop and the names of every song, in alphabetical order, on every album put out by Boston – but he could never understand women or the nauseatingly boring topics that he'd overhear at the courthouse and when he was in the law library at Carolina.

Most of the time, he sat there wondering why the hell anyone would care about covering their faces with just the right "tint of beige" or have baby names written on a list for babies who did not exist yet – and wouldn't – for years, or what some stupid celebrity was doing for her "fabulous birthday week in Maui" with some other stupid celebrity. A birthday is just one day. He never understood why people celebrated them longer.

His mother never celebrated his birthday after their disappearing act all those years ago. It was strange being the only boy at a birthday party in North Carolina who would never have one of his own to invite his new friends. When Joe asked his mother when her birthday was, early on, she replied, "I don't have birthdays anymore." Joe probably thought she was just being a typical woman.

Buddy always guessed that his mother wanted to forget that they ever had another set of roots somewhere else, roots still sitting there in the hard earth of Killeen, Texas, now a long ago stunted and infertile bush. Did their bush ever bloom again after their absence became permanent? He always wondered but knew better than to bring it up.

It took a long time for the crippling fears of seeing Kenny Bellinger walk up to them on the downtown streets of Welby, North Carolina to go away for good. Buddy reckoned that for a battered woman – like his mother – those fears never left entirely. He hoped Kenny was either dead or had been taken away into a mental hospital and has been sitting in there all these years in a white straight jacket – talking to no one in particular – about fancy cars and fishing and how his wife probably left him on the floor to die.

One day almost three years ago, Buddy walked by a pet store on his way to a take-out Chinese restaurant. There was a cute girl, probably in her early twenties, standing there in a page boy hat and holding a big golden mess of a dog on a long brown leather leash. There was a small wire fence in a circle next to her with another dog, some kind of Beagle mix. She had a folding table nearby with a sign on it that read Adoption Day.

As Buddy looked at the tip of her hat, which was Army green and hiding a crop of sharply cut brown hair sitting just above her shoulders and pushed neatly behind her ears, she grinned at him, her cheeks full and round, and said, "Hey."

Buddy stopped and peered down at the dog, sitting butt end on the cement sidewalk, and looking up at him with big brown eyes and his tongue hanging out in a mild pant. He reached down and pet him. "Hi boy, how are you today?" he asked the dog, whose eyes shut when Buddy's hand touched his head. The dog licked his hand, his tongue thick, wet and just on the verge of slobbering.

"He likes you," the cute girl said, trying to look Buddy in his eyes. Knowing how to manage his shyness, Buddy kept his gaze downward at the dog or on the tip of the fraying brim of her hat.

"How do you know?" Buddy asked, accepting the dog kisses and lowering himself down to the dog's eye level.

"Well, he kind of likes everyone," she admitted.

Buddy gazed right into the deep-set chestnut brown eyes of this frazzled mutt, who looked back into his eyes as well. He wondered if it were true…if dogs really were the philosophers of the soul. He heard that somewhere once, and every time he looked at a dog, he thought about that…how dogs seemed to be beyond this world and at an understanding of the human condition more than humans themselves understood it.

Isn't it strange how dogs seem to be the only animals who look at you right into your eyes? How they seem to see past your fears and insecurities and shame and secrets, and instead see you – the real you that stays hidden from the world? Finding that level of intimacy with another human being is damn near impossible. But finding it with a dog? Easy peasy.

The dog looked down briefly, panted for a second and then looked back up at Buddy. He appeared to be pleading with him.

"Is the dog for sale or something?" Buddy asked the girl, who remained still as she held the leash. She wore jeans with a hole in the left knee, a flannel shirt draped over her waist and a pair of scuffed up combat boots, as if she just got out of a Nirvana concert. If Buddy had more game, he would have asked her name, but he was distracted by this pleasant and unspoken interaction with this large dog.

"He's up for adoption," the girl said, a small twinge of hope in her voice. "I'm from Polly's Pet Rescue over in Haddleboro. I got Bo, here, out of an animal shelter over near New Bern two days before they were going to put him down for overcrowding. He's been staying with me and my daughter for now, but he needs a good permanent home."

Buddy stood up and looked down again at the brim of her hat. She was sweet. He could tell that she was probably the kind of girl who once enjoyed climbing trees and swimming in lakes.

"Really? They were going to kill him just because they're overcrowded?" Buddy never heard of such a thing before.

"Well, they try to find the owners of any strays, and when they can't, they put the animals up for adoption. But it's hard for the older ones like Bo. People want a pure-bred dog or a puppy or one who has a lot of years left in 'im. Bo is an older dog, but not too old, and he's still got lots of life to live. He is so friendly and would be a great family dog. Do you have kids?"

Buddy thought about how funny that sounded. He couldn't even get a girlfriend, let alone get someone to have kids with him.

"No. It's just me, but I always thought a dog would make a good companion. I have a lot of room for one."

"Have you ever owned a dog before?"

Buddy was thoughtful. He hadn't. When he was small, Kenny wouldn't allow it, and when he and his mother became new people altogether, there just seemed to be too many other things to be concerned with than to bother with the likes of a dog.

"No, actually, I haven't. But I'd like to, I think."

The girl continued to eye Buddy, who either looked at the hat's curve or down at Bo the lonely golden mutt.

"Do you know why he was in the shelter?" Buddy asked.

"His previous owner died and none of his kin would take Bo in. He wasn't abused or anything."

"That's awful," he uttered. "The owner dies and no one steps forward to help an old loyal boy like this? They'd rather he be put into a shelter to die?" People perplexed Buddy. "How does one adopt this dog from you?" he asked, deciding that it was time he make a spontaneous decision for himself and get this dog.

The girl smiled and seemed very pleased that this was working out. She gave the leash to Buddy and asked him to come over with her to the table. Handing him a form on a clipboard, she asked him to fill it out. "There's just a small fee to cover the dog license," she said. "He has all of his shots up to date and he's been neutered."

Buddy read through the forms quickly, knowing that it didn't matter what they said. He was getting the dog.

"If you want to donate additional money to help us continue to care for these pets in our fostering system, you can do that too. But believe me, just adopting Bo and taking him into your home for good is enough."

"Is this your job or something? Trying to get dogs adopted in front of pet stores?"

She grinned. "No, not really. I'm just a student right now, trying to finish college, and I have a part time job. But dogs who need homes...they are my passion. I do this for the Pet Rescue once a month."

As Buddy filled out the form, the girl bent down and started to rub Bo's ears. "I'm gonna miss this one," she started. "He's my favorite guest dog. He's my little girl's favorite too. But I can tell that you two will be fast and best friends."

Then the girl started to do that thing that girls do – yammer. The more she talked, the more Buddy tuned her out, the more Buddy wanted to take Bo and get the hell back home. She was real cute – actually too cute – and so she started to make him both very nervous and slightly annoyed. But then he stopped himself for a moment to consider that this was most likely a good and kind person with a big heart and maybe he shouldn't be so uptight over the fact she liked to talk too much about nothing in particular. Maybe nothing in particular wasn't such a bad conversation piece after all, since that's what most people seemed to talk about. Maybe he was missing the boat on how great talking about nothing in particular could be – with just the right girl.

Within an hour, Buddy loaded up this large, loving animal into his car. He had a set of bowls, a large dog bed pillow, a new leather leash, and a huge bag of some generic brand dog chow. As they drove back to his house, Bo stuck his head out the window and felt the wind in his face. At stop lights, women would look over at Bo and wave at Buddy. Some would smile his way as they walked down the street.

When Buddy pulled into his driveway, two little girls followed his car while on their bikes. As soon as he got out of the car and let

Bo out the passenger side, the girls dropped their bikes on the driveway and ran up to the big golden boy who was now a part of this family-oriented neighborhood.

"Mister Buddy, is this your dog?" Lilly from a few houses down shouted, hugging him tightly as if Bo were hers. Janie, the other girl, was a bit timid but put her hand out to Bo and he licked it.

"He is. His name is Bo," Buddy answered, watching this scene in front of him, a scene that he hoped to have in his own life some day: a couple of happy little girls embracing their new dog…a real family of his own…a pipe dream.

After that day at the Fall Festival, Buddy seemed to miss Julie when she would normally go on her jogs. His timing was all off. He would grab Bo and go for a short walk down the street at the usual time, but Julie would never run by. A whole week went past, and Buddy started to feel bummed out about it. Had he scared her off or something during their brief conversation at the school? It seemed to him that she was friendly and nothing was strange or fake between them. She wasn't like the law student, who Buddy decided was just another young woman out there whose mind and desires seemed to change from sunset to sunset.

Julie had a daughter, a bouncing and happy little ball of freckles, and she had a peace to her that burned deeper than most, way beyond her youthful age. He figured Julie was around the same age as he was, give or take. He wondered where she lived and if he could be so bold as to find out. Maybe he could show up with a casserole – that's what neighborly people do, right? Maybe he could find out her phone number and give her a call – and then not be able to say anything to her when she answered the phone. Maybe he could sit outside of the elementary school and wait for her and Molly to come out. No, that's creepy. Maybe he could go to the school office and pretend that he needed to give her something, a gift from Jasper perhaps, a bird house with bright colors. Maybe he could become a volunteer in the school, read to the little kids once a week, until they were able to at last bump into each other in the hallway. Maybe – just maybe – he could stop being a pathetic loser and obsessing about a woman he could never even hope to have.

A week after the Fall Festival, which was also a week since he last saw Julie, Buddy woke up and decided to go with Bo over to the state park nearby. It was the time of year when the high school kids were enjoying their Friday night football games in coats and hats, the ice cream shops weren't so busy anymore, and the pumpkin patches were offering hay rides and corn mazes and haunted houses and warm apple cider until late at night each weekend.

With his ego no longer stinging from the passive rejection by the law student, he threw on a pair of jeans and his fading Carolina Law School sweatshirt and headed out into the sunny Fall Saturday morning with his best friend. It was a nice day, feeling a lot cooler out; a slight breeze brushed his face with a touch of cold air, a welcomed feeling. He brought a tennis ball for Bo to chase...or more like...wobble toward quickly. While Bo didn't complain, Buddy figured he had some kind of arthritis or deterioration in his leg joints.

He parked his car in a parking lot, which included only one small white Dodge Neon, threw the tennis ball along the grass of the deserted park, and waited for Bo to go get it and bring it back to him. Several minutes went by, and Buddy took the ball and threw it farther into the woods along a bike path. Bo wobbled quickly over to the path, picked up the ball, and brought it back. Buddy felt the slobber on the green padding of the ball, threw it long, and watched it bounce onto the path, disappearing off to the side somewhere. And as Bo wobbled over, he, too, eventually dissolved into the brush area, his golden fur consumed by the Fall foliage.

"Bo!" Buddy yelled toward him. Bo did not come out.

"Bo! Here, boy!" he hollered again. Still nothing.

After about a minute or two, Buddy started to get concerned. Where would Bo have gone? The ball couldn't have bounced very far off the path and, while he was old, he hadn't lost his ability to smell.

As Buddy started to walk toward the path, he saw a woman come out in a slow jog with his big loveable mutt in lock step with her. The ball was in his mouth and he ran right next to her on the bike path – like the woman was his owner and they did this together every day and he wasn't in his senior dog years.

"Bo!" Buddy yelled at him, trying to get him to leave the woman alone.

He watched her in a familiar rhythm, wearing a ball cap and an electric blue athletic running outfit and jacket. She peered over and began to lead Bo toward him. As she came closer, Buddy realized who it was. Julie. Julie had been running the bike path at the park.

As she jogged toward him, she slowed down to a walking pace; and while a touch out of breath, she pulled the headphones off her ears and pressed a button on her CD player – sitting buckled to her side – to turn off her music.

"Hey, I know this dog," she said through harsh breaths. She bent over and pet Bo on the head. Bo allowed her to do so and then licked her hands.

"I'm really sorry; he doesn't usually do anything like that. He's... really kind of old and never runs anymore."

"It's okay. I'm done anyway," she said and looked up at Buddy. Her smile was bright and alive and there was nothing awkward about how she was talking with him. She treated him as a familiar face, someone she knew, not a stranger at all.

"Where have you been?" Buddy asked her, and then felt like a complete idiot. He didn't mean to say that out loud. That was supposed to be a thought that remained trapped in his head. And as it came from his mouth, he imagined his hands going out in front of the words marching out into the air and scooping them back into his throat and locking them inside of his heart.

"What do you mean?" Julie asked.

"Uh, sorry. I didn't mean that how it must've sounded," Buddy stammered. He was back to not being able to look at her eyes, looking instead at the left earphone which hung just below her neck.

"Oh, you mean my usual running route?" she stood up and took a deep breath. "I needed a measured path to practice on with no distractions, like cars and such. I want to run a half marathon and so I decided to try this trail for a while to train."

She stopped and gazed at Buddy, who could not bring himself to look back into her eyes. She moved her head to where his eyes were, putting hers in direct contact with his, widening them on purpose, forcing him to look at her.

"You're a shy one, aren't you?" she asked him.

Buddy didn't know how to respond to that.

"But you have a good wing man, here, in this big sweet dog." She petted Bo's head. Bo dropped the ball in front of her feet. Julie picked it up and threw it toward the path. Bo scurried off to get it, just like his old self and not that bionic canine he was just a few minutes ago, distance-running like a puppy.

"That'll keep him busy for a minute," Julie said. She turned toward Buddy. Buddy finally looked at her. She paused and smirked at him just a bit. Eyeing him, trying to read his signals and figuring that she understood completely, she asked him, with all the confidence of a recently elected politician, "You think you'd like to meet me for lunch later?"

All Buddy could do was stand there with a grin on the inside realizing that all along...his mother was right...Bo would help him pick up a woman. The woman. The only one he had ever truly wanted in his life. Or was Bo picking up the woman all for himself and Buddy was quietly taking over?

He wasn't sure, but he didn't care either.

Sad Stories

Julie brushed her damp hair and started the hair dryer. Molly was at her first slumber party. She spent the night at Zoe Wade's house, and there were four other girls also invited, probably keeping Linda Wade up all night with their giggling. Molly was small for her age, and some people felt like she was a little odd – who bounces like that? - but Julie was so happy that she seemed to have finally made some friends in her Second Grade class.

The brush went through the thick blond waves, drying one hunk after another. She tried to straighten it with the tip of the dryer facing down and the hair frying along on the curve of the brush. Hot air slowly went down the strands. She wanted to be cute for her lunch date because this shy man who can't look at her in her eyes has her uniquely intrigued. And she hasn't been intrigued by any man – certainly not like this – since Gabe Saint waltzed into her life years ago.

Buddy was so cute. He was tall, but not too tall, with a lean build, blondish-brown hair in a neatly cropped high and tight cut. He wasn't in the military, but he looked like he could've been or had been at one point. His face was boyish, and his eyelashes were the longest eyelashes she had ever seen. Men were not supposed to have eyelashes like that, and she was certain that women who noticed them were jealous of them. Females paid good money for the kinds of eyelashes he was lucky enough to be born with.

His eyes were a cobalt blue – not bright and shiny – but instead serene and calming, like a water color painting. She wasn't quite sure what in the world she was doing, but Julie believed that everything happens for a reason…even the bad things that aren't fair.

Molly was at her first slumber party, and she didn't need to pick her up until three o'clock. Julie wasn't sure what got into her to conjure up the gumption to ask this shy man on a…date?...but she did it, and she actually felt good about the whole thing. She put on a pair of black slacks and an off-white sweater. It was just lunch. It was just lunch with a man that she couldn't get to look directly into her eyes.

The first time she noticed him was one Tuesday afternoon while she was on her afternoon jog with Gabe's ghost. Buddy was walking on the sidewalk with his big golden dog. She was still well behind him and saw that he had a peculiar but familiar walk. Not sure what it reminded her of exactly, she found herself slowing her jog so she could try to figure it out. John Travolta in Saturday Night Fever? Patrick Swayze in Dirty Dancing? Was that a strut? She wasn't sure – but it caught her eye. It was not a stride she saw often and it did stand out.

She would notice him most days after that and watched his strut from afar, until she got up near him, and then quickly ran by. She was usually on the side of the street while he was on the sidewalk. One day, she decided she would try to see his face. So, when she saw him in the distance, instead of remaining on the side of the street, she popped up onto the sidewalk instead. It was a clear, hot afternoon...probably too hot to be jogging per the weatherman. But if Julie didn't jog, she didn't have Gabe. Gabe didn't mind the heat so much in death.

Forgetting Gabe for a brief spell, she paced herself so she would be able to get a look at this now familiar stranger, her Groundhog Day moment of late. As she came up behind him, she yelled, "On your left!" as to give him the proper running etiquette announcement when going by a pedestrian. He was startled, they locked eyes, and she saw that he was very attractive – cute, really – and probably around her age. She was sure to smile at him, and it felt nice for the first time to smile at another man...the first man after Gabe...who she saw as a real man and not just another annoying intrusion trying to finagle himself into her dead husband's shoes.

After that, Julie wondered if she would ever see him in a normal setting. He had to live nearby. She lived only about two miles from his neighborhood, so certainly they would bump into each other somewhere ordinary, like the Post Office or the Food Lion or even the mall. So, she was really surprised when she happened to bump into him at school. For some reason, she hadn't imagined that scenario.

She met Buddy later that day at Flora's Bistro, a small café in downtown Fayetteville. It was a nice sandwich place with happy décor that always made her heart feel much lighter when she walked inside. Molly was always with her when they went after church, which was just down the street. On Sundays, Flora's also had breakfast served until two o'clock in the afternoon, so it was especially popular then.

Julie walked into Flora's and found a two-person booth. Buddy walked inside with his hands deep in his pockets and his head bowing down slightly, soon after her. He grinned a wily smile when he saw her and shyly walked over to her table and sat down. He looked around and scanned the room, noticing the bright orange, purple and yellow walls.

"I haven't been in here in a long time," he declared looking at the flower pot collection sitting near the window on a shelf.

"It's cute, isn't it?" she asked.

"I suppose," Buddy responded, shifting in his seat.

They ordered sandwiches off the menu from a young waitress who babysat Molly a few times during the rare occasion Julie had an appointment or meeting that she didn't want to drag Molly into. Buddy asked the waitress if they had any grape Kool Aid. She looked perplexed and suggested he try their freshly squeezed Lemonade instead.

"So, what's your story, Mr. Cochran?" Julie asked, trying to break the ice. She was floored as to how reserved this man was. Most men who interact with her are trying to figure out how they can ask her out on a date without offending her. It seemed that when a woman is an Army widow, there's a certain unspoken rule among single men in how to deal with it. They don't want to come on too strong. They don't want to be disrespectful of the dead. But they don't want to miss out on being the one to snag the young, attractive, single blond, either. In this case, she had to ask the guy out on a date, and she also had to initiate even simple conversation with him.

"My story?"

"Yeah, your story. I'm going to assume that you're not married. You have a dog. You're a lawyer. What else?"

Buddy took a bite of his BLT. After swallowing, he answered, "Correct. I'm not married. I do have a dog. I'm a criminal defense attorney and live on Triton Hills. Have for about three years now, ever since I got out of law school."

"Are you with a firm?"

"No, I'm on my own. Other lawyers call it 'hanging a shingle.' I work out of my house." He paused. "I do hope to be able to open a more professional office someday, but for now, this works for me."

"Were you in the Army? Are you from here?"

"No," Buddy started. He would have to stop himself from time to time and remember – then forget – that he is originally from Killeen, Texas. There was always a piece of him that held onto that. There was always something inside of him that wanted to find out the rest of that unfinished story…the story that he and his mother left behind and never spoke about again. "I'm from Welby," he shared instead. "It's near Chapel Hill."

"I've been there before. Little rural country town. A few cute quaint stores," Julie said in between bites.

"Yeah, I grew up there on a large property owned by a man named Joe Horton. My mother and I were on our own when we first moved there. I was young, and so we rented a small place on his land."

"So, you're a country boy?"

Buddy nodded. "I suppose I am a country boy," he chuckled to himself. He hated country music and all the country stuff the guys he grew up around were into. Things like muddin' and dirt bikes and racing. He liked to read. He liked baseball. He liked movies. He liked politics.

"How about you? You're a teacher, and you have Molly. And Molly is always hopping around. Where is Molly, anyway?"

"She's at a slumber party," Julie answered, gazing up at Buddy. "Her first one. I have to pick her up at three."

Buddy looked at a couple filling up their sodas at the soda fountain. Then he peered down.

"And you're widowed," he started. "I'm really sorry that happened to you. And Molly, too." Buddy knew what it felt like to be raised by a widowed woman, and he knew what it felt like to not know his own father. He wanted to tell Julie this, tell her about his mother's pain and strength after his father dying in Vietnam. He wanted to tell her how he had nothing of his father…not even his name anymore. He wanted to tell her that his mother once told him that while he can't have his father's name, he could take pride and comfort in knowing that he had his father's blue eyes and long eyelashes.

"Yes, it was really hard. It's been a year and a half now, and Molly and I have adjusted. It's an odd adjustment for sure. No rulebooks or manuals. But we miss him every day. He was a good man, a good husband and father, a damn good soldier."

"So, he was in the Army then?"

Julie looked down at her plate and took a sip of her water. "He was in the Eighty-Second and, during a training exercise, his unit was participating in a jump. His parachute didn't deploy correctly. So, he pulled his reserve and it collapsed them both. He didn't pass right away. Lingered for another day in a coma. He never had a chance." Julie looked sad and thoughtful. "Or at least, that's what the Army said happened."

"Do you think they'd lie about something like that?" Buddy asked, concerned.

"Who knows? It doesn't matter anyway. Gabe is gone. And we never really got to say 'goodbye' to him. I stayed at the hospital, kept vigil by his bed. I held his hand and talked to him, like they said to do, but he never responded to me or my voice. Not even once."

Julie started to feel depressed again, and that's not what this little lunch date was supposed to be. Her chest felt heavy, and her stomach began to clench, like the monster named Grief decided to intrude on her first date and remind her that it still owned her…all of her. This deep pain came from nowhere and everywhere, whenever it wanted to be felt. And it sucked. There was no timetable or warning.

She liked this Buddy guy for some reason. Something sweet about him. He didn't try with her; he didn't pursue her or make her feel like she was single and ready to mingle. She wasn't. She was an Army widow with a little girl to raise. She loved her husband and expected to grow old with him. She never saw herself as a single woman, certainly didn't feel like a single woman, and honestly had no idea what the hell single women her age did with their time. Her life and their lives were like night and day. And for the first time, she looked down at her empty ring finger and wondered why she ever felt like she had any right to take it off. The law said she wasn't married…but she sure felt like she was.

She looked up at Buddy and noticed that he was staring back and into her eyes for the first time. He wasn't doing that weird thing he seemed to do where he looked just past her face, as if he had a lazy eye or something.

"I'm sorry. I'd really rather not talk about all that."

"It's okay, Julie. We can talk about whatever you'd like. We don't have to tell our sad stories today," Buddy said deliberately.

Julie liked how he added that "today," like he meant that there would be another time they could talk about their sad stories. She felt comfortable with him, almost like they had been friends a long time ago in childhood and had now reconnected by coincidence later in life.

The waitress came and left the bill. Buddy swiped it first. "I got this," he said, obviously raised right and not buying into the whole "Dutch Treat" concept of first dates between men and women in the Nineties. If that was what this really was.

Julie watched him fill out the credit card slip, trying to determine a tip amount.

"Fifteen percent isn't too hard to figure out, counselor," she stated flatly, trying to sound like she was kidding him.

Buddy was quiet, writing an odd amount as the tip.

"What kind of a tip is $4.71?" she asked, confused.

Buddy completed his math and looked up into Julie's big blue eyes. "I like the total to be an exact dollar amount," he explained, holding up the slip to show an even $22.00 bill total.

Later that afternoon, after Julie and Molly were back at home preparing for an evening of popcorn and a video, the phone rang. Molly answered the phone and yelled for Julie.

"Hello?" Julie said into the receiver.

"Hey, uh…this is Buddy."

After an awkward pause, with Julie thinking that he was going to continue – and then didn't – she added, "Hey, what's up?"

"Well, I was wondering what you and Molly were doing," Buddy said nervously.

"We were just going to watch a video."

"Oh, okay, then. Well, I won't bother y'all."

"No, what? What is it?"

"Well, I uh…I have some chicken here that I was going to grill. And I needed some help eating it."

Julie decided that was probably one of the more adorable things she had ever heard come out of the mouth of a grown man.

"Molly! Put on your sneakers," Julie commanded of her daughter after hanging up the phone. "We're going to have grilled chicken with Buddy and Bo."

Christmas Eve

Buddy was looking forward to this Christmas unlike any other Christmas in his entire life. Christmas growing up in Texas was exciting like it is for any kid. That is, until Kenny started to drink and beat his mother and just generally be an asshole to everyone… ruining their family. Then Christmas wasn't so much fun anymore. It was just a short break from the loud, sad, horror show that seemed to hijack his interrupted childhood.

Christmas, after arriving in North Carolina, seemed to be okay, but it took a while for Buddy and his mother to make their own new traditions for the holiday. They were living someone else's life at that point, and so they were doing someone else's traditions.

They had no family to speak of, no one to go visit, no one to come visit them, no one to send Christmas cards to…not even to the nice ladies they met in New Mexico. There was no receiving a gift in the mail, such as a dress shirt that didn't fit quite right, from Daniel Junior's Uncle Frank and Aunt Nikki. It was a strange holiday now. Just – nothing, empty, voided – but with reds and greens festively adorning the nothing, empty and voided. That took some getting used to.

When Buddy first arrived in North Carolina, he still believed in Santa Claus. Some of the kids at his new school talked about how Santa wasn't real, it was just their parents pretending, it was just another lie about the world that adults told their children. But Buddy kept it secret, like he kept a lot of secrets. He still believed.

He asked his mother, "How will Santa know where to find us if we ain't who we used to be?"

"Santa knows all, son," she replied, rubbing his hand with her finger.

"Does he know that I'm still me? Just that I have a different name and a new home?"

"I promise, Buddy, he will not forget you."

Buddy believed her and Santa did not disappoint. Years later, he learned that Joe did his mother a favor, dressed up as Santa and put the presents under the tree for her, just in case Buddy woke up in the night. Joe bought Buddy a brand new Kelly-green Schwinn from the big toy store in Durham and put a huge red bow on top of it. He decided during that very first Christmas that Joe Horton was good people and he could trust Joe being around his mother.

But this Christmas, more than twenty Christmases later, Buddy was bringing Julie and Molly to meet his mother and Joe at Christmas dinner. This Christmas, he would have a little girl in his life to buy presents for. This Christmas, he got to play up Santa Claus and accompany Julie to the mall where she proceeded to have a photo taken of Molly on Santa's lap – but only after Molly stopped hopping long enough to sit down and explain to him that she wanted Polly Pockets and a new art set for her room and a cure for cancer.

Watching the pure joy in the face of a kind and genuinely open child, like Molly, tear into a cheerily wrapped Christmas gift would be a first for Buddy. Since he had no siblings and no nieces and nephews or cousins, it would probably be the most exciting part of his entire holiday – being a witness to such a magical moment.

Buddy and Julie, with Molly in tow most of the time, started spending lots of their free time together ever since that Saturday in late October at Flora's Bistro. They would eat supper together almost every day, either at Julie's or at Buddy's and sometimes at the Bojangle's close to the highway. Julie enjoyed leaving her sweatshirts and jackets behind at Buddy's and poking fun at his assorted Kool Aid flavors resting inside several plastic jugs, which he kept lined up like soldiers in his fridge. Buddy enjoyed keeping a box of some chewy Chips Ahoy chocolate chip cookies in Julie's pantry and a container of grape Kool Aid in the back of her fridge. He hoped someday, he would be able to leave his toothbrush.

Julie let Buddy go trick-or-treating with them on Halloween. She invited him to have apple pie and vanilla ice cream with them on Thanksgiving, after they got back from feeding the homeless Thanksgiving dinner at church. They took walks with Bo, played at the park, enjoyed movies either in the theatre or videos at Julie's house. Molly read to Buddy a few times, Junie B. Jones books mostly, but she started reading the Box Car Children per Buddy's recommendation, and Buddy found himself being the new kid with a new name in a new school in a new state all over again as he listened to her read.

Buddy taught Molly how to ride her two-wheeler, something she couldn't get the hang of until he spent an entire Saturday morning, in late November, working with her. She wore a pink jacket with a tear in the elbow and a pair of jeans over her skinny legs. Her new white Nikes were bright as they sat neatly positioned on the pedals.

"Now listen," he told her in his best pep talking voice. "Moll, you got to use all that energy you have hopping around all the time and put it into balancing yourself. Once you feel it, it will be so easy to keep on going. You'll wonder why it was so hard to figure out."

He pushed her, as she sat on the bike, onto the grass. Molly sat still.

"I just don't see how the grass is gonna help," she said.

"The grass keeps the bike from moving too fast. So, it will give you confidence. Then when you have your confidence, we will move the bike onto the sidewalk, and you'll be off."

It took him a couple of hours to get Molly to the point where she was comfortable trying to ride the bike on the sidewalk. But as soon as he moved the bike onto the pavement, she hopped on and rode away to the end of the neighborhood. There was no stopping her.

When she finally came back to her house several minutes later, she parked the bike and walked up to Buddy, hugging him with the mighty strength of a small girl who just accomplished something big. It was the first time in his life that he felt like he would make a good father someday.

For the past two months, Buddy and Julie grew closer, but there had been no romance attached to anything. They were friends – but with powerful and ever-growing feelings toward each other. They didn't really talk about it except once time. And Buddy did not want to ruin the special bond they had forged so far by suggesting they kiss. Although he wanted to. He wanted it all.

He knew that if any of those things were ever going to happen, they would happen on Julie's time table. She was still grieving her loss and a single mother, which is a sacred kind of woman in this world, Buddy knew all too well. Women like that are deeply wounded but also exceptionally brave. Wounded, because they can never quite heal from losing their husbands. Brave, because they have a child to care for, so there's no feeling sorry for themselves for too long. And since he was too shy to make any kind of move on her anyway,

Julie couldn't have been in a safer situation with any other man on the planet.

But he knew that her heart was opening to him. He could tell. She was the only woman he had ever met in his life who genuinely seemed to like him – like him as a man, just as he is. Sure, there were always girls who thought he was cute, and they always had something to say about his eyelashes, but after they figured out he wasn't interested in romancing them or writing songs for them or playing irrational "read my mind" head games or bouncing around and buying them expensive gifts and expensive dinners or telling them things they just wanted to hear – even if they weren't true – they quietly disappeared. No matter how much Buddy had wanted to meet a nice girl to marry, he did not want some plastic existence meandering along the roads of North Carolina inside a Chevy Venture minivan.

Julie seemed to like that he never pressured her for anything and he'd listen to her talk about her husband. She didn't expect anything from him at all but would always invite him or accept his invitations – no strings attached. And Buddy never realized that he could simply enjoy being in the company of a woman and it have nothing to do with the possibility of – or hope for – sex.

On Christmas Eve, Julie invited him over to decorate cookies with them. Buddy and Bo showed up at the door, and Buddy brought a bottle of red wine from Duplin Winery with him. When Molly answered the door, Bo bounded inside, almost as if his youth returned like that one day he ran with Julie. Molly hugged Buddy tight and asked him if he got her a present.

"What do you think?" Buddy asked her, hugging her back.

"Well, I don't know. I think maybe you did because we're friends."

"We are."

"We're buddies."

"The best."

"Isn't that funny?" Molly asked with her hand on top of her head.

"What's funny?" Buddy asked, setting the wine bottle down on the coffee table near the front door.

"You are my buddy. And your name is Buddy."

"Well that's why my mother named me Buddy, a long, long time ago."

"Why?"

"Because of you."

"Because of me?" Molly looked confused. She started hopping in place.

"My mother must've known that someday, I would meet a girl named Molly who hops around a lot and whose daddy went to Heaven. And so, she would need a buddy," he explained.

"But I wasn't born way back then," she said, still hopping.

"No. But you and me, we've got something in common."

"What?" she asked.

Buddy walked over to the couch and sat down. Molly stopped hopping and sat on his knee.

"What do we have in common, Buddy?" Molly looked in his face, her saddle brown eyes bright and wondering.

"Well, you know how your daddy's in Heaven? Because of the Army?"

Molly nodded.

"My daddy is in Heaven because of the Army, too."

Molly started to bounce on his knee and then stopped suddenly. She considered this new information.

"Did your daddy die from a parachute? Like mine?"

Buddy pursed his lips together and said, "No, he died in a war overseas. It was a long time ago, and I was only three years old. So, I don't even remember him."

"I remember my daddy."

"Yeah, I bet you do. I bet you miss him."

"I do miss him. Do you miss yours?"

"Well, it's kind of strange, but I do. Even though I have no memories of him, I've always felt like something's been missing in my life. I suppose that it's him that's missing."

"Did he ever take you to Disney World?"

"No, he sure didn't. Never got a chance to."

"My daddy always told me that he was gonna take me to Disney World to the Magic Kingdom." Molly sighed. "But then he died."

Buddy's stomach tightened. He never knew how much he missed his own father until this very moment...just like Molly, he was nothing more than a man with a childhood full of stories that were never realized...and only because life wasn't fair.

"I hope that someday your mom will let me take you to Disney World," he blurted out in response. He and Molly were eye to eye. She smiled at him crookedly, raising her fingers onto his left cheek.

"Did your daddy look like you?" Molly asked, starting to bounce again.

"My mother says that I do. That we have the same eyes and coloring."

"I look like my daddy too. My mom has blond hair and blue eyes and I have brown hair and brown eyes and freckles. And so did my daddy."

Buddy poked her freckles. "You know, my mother calls those angel kisses."

Molly nodded yes. "You told me that before. I knew we were gonna be friends, Buddy. That time I met you in the school at the Fall Festival. Me and you, we're both children growing up without our fathers. Only you're all done growing up now. But that kind of makes us the same." She stood up and picked up the bottle of wine. "Is this for my mom?"

"It is."

"I'll bring it to her. She's upstairs still," Molly explained and then hopped into the kitchen.

Later that night, after all the sugar cookies were decorated with green and red and silver and gold colors, some smudged and messy, some too pretty to eat, and Molly had been put to bed, Julie came outside and sat next to Buddy out on the front porch steps. The air was thick with a crisp new Winter chill, and they sat wrapped underneath a quilt which Buddy had taken off the couch and put around himself. They said nothing for a few minutes and watched their breath matching along in puffs, like cigarette smoke.

"I heard you tell Molly about your father," Julie said out loud, breaking the nighttime silence. Everywhere, kids were going to bed to get ready for Santa's arrival at any time.

"Were you eavesdropping on us?" Buddy asked, looking over at this woman he knew he loved with every piece of heart.

"I was," she said, her breath with a touch of red wine still gracing the hollow of her throat.

"Yeah, well, I just thought she should know that she's not the only little kid who lost their dad."

Julie put her head on the top of Buddy's shoulder. It was one of the first times she initiated any kind of physical intimacy with him. "Tell me."

"Tell you what?"

"About your father."

"Well, there's really not much to tell. I was only three."

"How did he die?"

Buddy felt the warmth of her breath near his neck. It was so hard for him to not turn to her and kiss her. He wouldn't allow himself to do it. He just knew that if he tried, he would scare her away, and he hadn't come this far to lose his chance with the most incredible woman he could ever even hope to know.

"Vietnam," Buddy stated. "Killed in action." This was the first night since 1975 that Buddy spoke of his real father or of his real life from what felt like a lifetime ago.

Julie pulled her head up from his shoulder and faced him. Buddy turned his head slightly and could see her looking sharply at his profile. The space between them was ripe with tension.

"Would you mind if I kissed you?" she asked, like she was asking him if he wanted a cup of coffee.

Buddy grinned just a bit and said, "No, I don't mind at all."

He turned his head toward her and put his arm around her waist, pulling her into him. They shared a tender, thoughtful, restrained, yet full kiss, ripe with so many unexamined possibilities waiting to find their moment.

Julie smiled at Buddy and whispered, "That was really nice."

Buddy, satisfied, nodded and agreed.

Johnnie Cochran Law

It was cold outside, and the sky looked like it was begging God to let it drop a few inches of snow onto the Carolina Sandhills' landscape. Buddy decided that he would take Julie and Molly over to the North Carolina Zoo in Asheboro. The mother and daughter pair had been there only once before, and while Buddy had no particular interest in zoos, he thought it would be a fun activity that they could all enjoy together. It was good to get outside when it's cold – it makes you appreciate the sun's heat, and Buddy liked the way cold air felt on his face. Walking around the zoo would warm them up quickly, there would be no crowds, and the polar bear might feel at home enough to come outside and give the Winter patrons a good show. If there was a kangaroo, maybe Molly could befriend it, and they could hop around together.

As they piled into Buddy's Pontiac, a middle aged black lady walked up into the driveway. Buddy put the car in park and rolled down the window.

"Ma'am?" he asked.

"Are you the lawyer? Johnnie Cochran?" she asked looking down at Buddy crouched in the driver's seat. She appeared to be in her mid-fifties and had a set of rugged lines etched into her face, a weathered storm really. Her hair was a dyed blond, but she looked like she hadn't had a chance to brush it out yet today.

Buddy thought about that. *Johnnie Cochran. Must be a Jasper the Mailman referral.* "I am," he answered.

"Can you help my son?" she asked, the desperation evident in her voice.

Buddy looked at Julie and Molly. "One sec, let me talk to her."

He got out of the car and stood with his back to the door.

"He's a good boy, but he's gotten into some trouble. He's at the jail right now, and they think he's taken part in a killing, but he hasn't. He ain't in any gang, and he don't run around. He's scared and don't know what to do."

"Have they arrested him for anything?"

"No, but they got him in one of those rooms and the police are asking him questions. He called me when they stepped out and let him make a call. He's answering their questions, but they won't stop making him feel like he's answering wrong. He saw on one of the TV shows that he might need a lawyer if the police are asking him questions like he done something wrong when he didn't."

"How old is your son?" Buddy has heard of these things countless times. Police interrogations, using harsh tactics to get better information about crimes when they're working on a theory and fishing for evidence and testimony. They use all kinds of tactics – completely legal – to glean information. It's nothing new, but sometimes it can lead to arresting the wrong person or gaining false confessions. And to Buddy, that is not justice at all.

"Eighteen," she answered. She stopped talking and bent over, her tan puffy coat had a large hole in the left side and white stuffing was starting to come out. Her right hand covered her heart. "I'm dying. I'm dying here."

Buddy leaned over and put his hand on her back. "Ma'am, are you okay?"

Julie got out of the passenger side and trotted quickly over toward the woman. "Hon, are you okay?" she asked, rubbing her hands along the woman's back. "Can we help you sit down on the steps for just a moment?" Julie helped her walk over to Buddy's front porch.

"I'm...I'm just breathing too hard or somethin'," she stammered, a panicked look on her face. "I think I'm havin' an attack. One of those ones where you can't catch your breath." She was a pale shaded woman, and Buddy could make out lots of light freckles peppered along her cheeks.

Julie sat down next to her, and she had her left arm along her back. "Breathe in, breathe out, breathe in, breathe out," she instructed, trying to help the distraught woman calm down. "You must be beside yourself with worry."

"I am. My son is not a bad boy. He did not murder no one. I'm afraid the police is gonna try to make him confess to it. I've heard them doin' that to some of these boys before," she started speaking again, only faster. "Jesus, please help my son. Please, Jesus."

"Well, the first thing you've got to do is calm yourself down and try to breathe normally. Okay? Then you can explain to Buddy the entire situation, and I have no doubt that he can help you and your son," Julie explained. Her hair hung lightly over her navy blue coat. She wasn't wearing her gloves. Her face was bright in the sunlight, and she wore that motherly-nurturing-Kindergarten teacher face. It was serious and comforting…but cute. Buddy loved it. He loved everything about her. He watched her soothe this woman's nerves and fears all the way down to a softened tone. The woman's face became sullen but alive again.

She looked up at Buddy. "Mr. Cochran, I am really sorry to just barge in on your day like this. It's just that my friend's mailman told me about you and how you might be able to tell me what I need to do so I can help my son."

Julie looked up and squinted her eyes. "Mr. Cochran?"

Buddy smiled.

"Ma'am, what's your name?" he asked.

"Janice. Janice Wells."

"And your son?"

"His name is Roger Pearce."

"Alright. And Roger is at the station now?"

Ms. Wells nodded her head. She put her head into her hands. "He wasn't involved in no murder," she cried, barely audible.

Julie piped in. "Listen. How about me and Molly head back home so you can help out Ms. Wells and Roger." Buddy watched Julie as she rubbed Ms. Wells' back. "You are in good hands here with Mr. Cochran," Julie soothed, with the emphasis on "Mr. Cochran." "I'm going to go now but only because I don't want to be a part any lawyer-client confidentiality going on here. If you feel yourself starting to panic again, just take a deep breath in and then out and then in and out again. Okay?"

Ms. Wells nodded again. "Thank you, young lady."

Julie motioned for Molly to get out of the car. Molly hopped out quickly. Then she walked over to Buddy and glanced into his eyes. "I think you need to bail on us, counselor. But for a good reason. Your law firm, Johnnie Cochran Law, does great work for some struggling Fayetteville citizens who need someone like you in their corner." She grinned and kissed his cheek, grabbed Molly's hand, and they headed over to her car parked on the street. "Call me later!"

Buddy's heart swelled. Julie was such a good person. She wasn't demanding of him or of his time. She didn't require his constant attention. She was understanding about the nature of his job. She was kind to everyone, even perfect strangers in bad family situations who start into panic attacks in his driveway.

He still didn't know what to do about his ever-growing feelings for her and still had no courage whatsoever to make any kind of move. He wanted to kiss her, all day, and make love to her like she was the only woman in the world for him. He never thought of women like this...like there could be one perfect female made just for him. He was a rational and logical man and all that made no rational or logical sense. But this one woman...Julie...he did think of her like that. All the rational realities and rules which he had adhered over the years about men and women and love and sex and friendship and "true love" and "the one" and all that fairytale jargon and silly sophomoric pipedream language that isn't supposed to be real – it just didn't seem to apply to Julie Saint.

As Julie and Molly drove away in Julie's Neon, Buddy turned to Ms. Wells. "How about we go down to the station and see if we can help Roger."

Spelunking

It was a Sunday evening and the southern Winter contained a certain level of warmth to it for a change. They got a break from the bitter cold this past weekend, and it was nice to spend the day together outdoors in just a sweatshirt and jeans. Molly rode her bike along the bike path at the park, while Julie and Buddy walked Bo. There were a few ducks out along the pond hoping for some generous humans with food scraps, so Molly got to feed them some chunks of stale bread.

She fell asleep on the living room couch watching Nickelodeon, and Bo sat guard over her from the floor beneath. It was dark outside, and Julie and Buddy sat in her back yard on the small patio housing a two-person bistro set under the flood lights. She held a Diet Coke can in her hand, and Buddy took a sip of his red wine. He hadn't been a wine drinker before meeting Julie, but he found that he liked a couple of the ones she made him try. He was now down to only a couple of flavors of Kool Aid in his fridge. He admitted to Julie that she was helping him be a "beverage grown up."

They sat in stillness for a while, watching the stars dot the sky. Julie enjoyed moments like that. She felt so in tune with Buddy at this point, even in their silence...and that, to her, meant that they had reached a certain level of emotional intimacy that was no longer easy to deny. For months, she spent so much time with him, slowly spilling her secrets, confiding in him her sad stories, sharing her deep pain and real fears about losing her husband and wondering what her life would hold without him. Buddy was so thoughtful and understanding toward her. He was patient and sweet. He never told her how she was supposed to feel or how she needed to get over Gabe and move on. He never treated her like some wounded bird who couldn't figure it out herself, either. He was respectful. Always. She knew that he was in love with her – she could just tell. And she was afraid – terrified actually – that she had fallen in love with him, too.

It was hard for her to know what to do about it. The truth was that she was already basically dating him, without any pointed romance or further discussion about the status of their relationship. Molly adored him and always wanted them to do things together. Julie wondered what held her back. She couldn't use Molly as an excuse, and because of how she knew she felt about Buddy, she couldn't use Gabe as one either. She loved this guy. That didn't change her love for Gabe at all. Gabe was just gone, and their love would always be a part of who she is going forward in her life. Gabe would've wanted her to find love again.

But there was something about Buddy that remained hidden from her, and she wasn't quite able to put her finger on it. She had spent time with his mother and her boyfriend Joe several times now. She felt like they really liked her. She could tell that Buddy was extremely close with his mother, a regular mama's boy, but not in a bad way. She knew that Buddy went to Carolina and that his father had died in Vietnam. But the rest of him – he was a mystery, really. He was elusive about his wider life, and she felt like she needed to know more than he had been willing to share with her.

"You hold many secrets, Johnnie Cochran," Julie said out of the blue. "You're like an undiscovered cave just full of them…and now that I've found this cave, I want to go spelunking."

Buddy was surprised by this. He never felt like he came across as a man who had a bunch of secrets. Even though he was.

"Why do you say that?" he asked.

"I can just tell. We talk about so many things, but mostly, they're my things. And I'd like to think that it's because I'm a girl and girls talk about themselves all the time. But I don't think it's that at all."

Buddy sat back and folded his arms. "And so that means I'm full of secrets? Because I don't talk about myself as much as you do?"

"That's not all of it. You're just guarded, and it's not only because you're a man or because you're shy. I can tell the difference. You guard your innermost thoughts. Sometimes I think you want to tell me more about the things you keep hidden from everybody."

Buddy laughed inside. Yeah, he wants to tell her how much he loves her. He wants to tell her that meeting her and Molly has been the greatest thing that has ever happened to him in his entire life. He wants to tell her that she is the most wonderful woman he has ever known. Maybe those were the secrets she wanted him to tell her. Maybe she just wanted him to confess his feelings once and for all. Say it out loud. Or maybe not. Maybe Julie was as smart and as perceptive as he always figured she was.

"Well, you got me," Buddy said, matter of fact. A serious look came over his face. He took a deep sip out of his wine glass. Julie's eyes got brighter in the lights. She pulled her arms out of her sweatshirt sleeves and put them against her chest, making her sleeves armless.

"Spill," she demanded.

"No."

"Come on. You know all my stories. I've told you everything there is to know about me. You know every single solitary thought I've had, experience I've gone through, scar I've endured...complexity. It's only fair."

"Not gonna happen. I can't."

"Why not? You don't trust me?" she asked, eyeballing him across the table.

Buddy looked down at his feet. "If I tell you, I'd have to kill you," he said, almost in a whisper.

Buddy felt a little buzzed. He wanted to tell her everything about himself. He wanted to give her the lowdown: he was someone else entirely, his mother was someone else entirely, they have been on the run for well over twenty years. But he knew he couldn't do it. At least, not fully. It was too big of a secret and too many years had gone by now. If he told her the truth about himself, he would be risking everything he had built with her and Molly, and he'd be risking his own mother's safety and welfare and maybe even legal situation. He had no idea what ever really happened to Kenny Bellinger, and now that he was grown and a lawyer on top of that, he didn't want to know.

"Where were you born?" Julie asked. "You've never told me where you're really from. I know you grew up in Welby. I know your father died in Vietnam. Where were you and your mother when he died?"

Buddy sighed. "Fort Hood, Texas," he uttered. "I was born in that Army hospital there. But then my father died, and I guess we had to leave."

Julie wrapped her arms around her torso, starting to get cold but feeling like she was making progress in getting to the bottom of a few answers to her questions. "Where is your kin from? Your grandparents? Where are Loretta's people? Your father's people?"

"Why do you care so much? It's really not important."

"Well, you know all about my people. I've told you everything. My mother, my father, Gabe, his parents, my hometown in Texas, my short stint at A&M, my elopement, my estrangement. I feel like I'm just on the cusp of really knowing you, Buddy, but every time I try to scratch this surface, you just got nothin' for me. I think it's odd is all. I think there's more to your story than your father dying in Vietnam and you and your mother ending up in Welby in Joe's barn apartment. You don't talk about any family, grandparents, why your mother has some kind of North Eastern accent, even though you say you're from North Carolina."

Buddy shuffled his shoes and took the last swig of his wine. He set the glass down and looked over at his Julie. How he wanted to tell her everything about himself. He thought he had, really…at least the important things. She knew him. She knew who he really was inside. Just not this one small piece of himself, the only thing he couldn't give her. Just not this one bit of his history that had to remain sealed forever. Some secrets were better left buried.

Realizing that she was not going to get anywhere further on this issue, Julie slid her arms back into her sleeves. She stood up, seeing that she was rattling his chain a little bit and didn't mean to do that to him. She walked over and hugged him.

"I'm sorry, Buddy. I don't mean to be so pushy. You don't have to tell me anything you don't want to tell me. I understand," she breathed out in the night with her head buried in his chest.

"It's not that, Julie. I promise. It's not that I'm keeping secrets from you or don't want you to know me or anything like that. I do. And I think you do know me. More than anyone ever has before. I don't know why me telling you some of the darker and sadder stuff of my past would make you know me more or better than you already do. It wouldn't." He stood straight and stretched his legs; his voice started to get animated and direct. "You don't want to know about that shit, Julie. No one does. Some things aren't meant to be talked about. Some things aren't meant to be shared. I'm just not a big talker. It doesn't change anything. It doesn't change how close we are right now to each other or how close we can be in the future. Not to me, it doesn't." His voice started to trail off, and he held his face up to the darkness.

Julie watched his face tilted up, with its boyish features and those long eyelashes glimmering in the moonlight. She again wrapped her arms around his middle, looking up into his eyes, and he held her back and gazed down at her face with a sense of fear lingering between them.

"You're right," she said, tiptoeing up and kissing his cheek. She went back down on her heels. Buddy leaned down and pulled her into himself and gently kissed her lips, which told her every secret passion he held for her in his heart.

St. Patrick's Day

Julie sat with her legs criss-cross-applesauce on the floor of her living room. She wore a pair of denim crop pants, a Kelly-green and white striped long-sleeved shirt and two long beaded necklaces with small smiling shamrocks along every few beads in a line. She had a green leprechaun hat on top of her blond hair, which stuck straight out of the bottom. A glass of red wine, half empty – or half full, depending on your personality – sat on the cream colored, newly cleaned carpet, which just screamed for a big red stain to happen to it. She stared at the wine glass and wondered how much more wine she needed inside of her to have the courage to tell Buddy how she was feeling…to tell him the truth.

Buddy rested across from her with his back against the couch. His legs spread out straight ahead, his feet were bare, and his heart was open. He, too, still wore his own leprechaun hat on top of his head, a remnant of their evening meal: a "pot o' gold pot roast" for him, a corned beef sandwich for Julie, and good ol' chicken tenders and fries off the kid's menu for Molly at Sully's Irish Restaurant over near Post.

Julie claimed Irish ancestry, so that meant Molly did too. They both were adamant about celebrating St. Patrick's Day because it was their birthright, and Buddy found it amusing that Julie had an entire box dedicated to Irish items stuffed in her storage closet, like some people have a box for Easter or Halloween decorations.

Buddy, however, walked around with a Hispanic last name and no real clear idea about his ancestry. According to his mother, people just didn't pay that much attention to such things after all the immigrants started inter-marrying. It happened a lot where she was from because it was a busy, transient military town during the draft years in New Jersey. Girls from town found husbands in basic training at Fort Dix who were on their way to somewhere else. That was how his mother had met his father. He knew that his grandmother was part Italian, but there was no confirmation on what his grandfather was. Also, Italian? Polish? Lithuanian? French Canadian? He knew nothing about his natural father, other than his name and death. He didn't even know where Daniel Kaspar, Senior came from.

So, Buddy would just tell people he was a Hispanic man who spoke no Spanish. And when Hispanic people would start talking to him about Hispanic things, Buddy had to laugh along or pretend like he knew what the hell they were talking about.

But St. Patrick's Day in the United States was for everyone. Everyone gets to be Irish for the day. He and Julie and Molly looked like every other little Irish-American or just simply American family out having an Irish evening after having an Irish day.

It was late, and Molly was long asleep. Buddy spent just about every waking moment with Julie and Molly for several months now. If he wasn't working or taking care of errands or small jobs for his mother and Joe, he was with the two of them. Then at the end of the day, he would go home to go to bed. Or they would go home to go to bed. And other than the one nice kiss they shared on Christmas Eve while sitting on the porch steps, and that other kiss he gave to her a couple of weeks ago in Julie's backyard, that was as close physically that they had been.

The two sat silent. Buddy shut his eyes. Then he opened them.

"Julie," he said, quietly.

Julie continued to stare at her wine glass.

There was tension between them, but it was the good kind. Not quite sexual tension, but something more profound. It was the type that could be easily broken with one kind word or a brief warm smile or a simple kiss.

"Hey," Buddy said. Again, quietly.

Julie continued to look at her wine glass. She was motionless and was starting to feel the effects of this second glass.

"Julie, I want to tell you something," Buddy uttered, a little louder.

She peered up at him. Her eyes were filled with tears just begging to drop from the rims of their sockets. Buddy watched her, not quite sure what to make of her sadness. He hadn't seen Julie cry yet, in all this time together, but he feared he was about to. And now he was also afraid of what she was going to say to him. His gut tightened like a fist ready to react to a punch. His heart started to beat faster. *No, please, no…*he thought, expecting the worst.

Buddy rose to his knees. He moved a bit closer to her and, as she watched him, she blurted out, "I'm in love with you. I love you, Mr. Cochran."

The fist inside of him unraveled. His gut relaxed. He was so full of fear in just that brief passage of time. He was certain she was going to tell him that she didn't want to see him anymore or she was moving away or she was going to go out with that arrogant gym teacher.

But no. She loved him. It was the last thing he thought she would say tonight.

Buddy sat back on his heels in disbelief. Julie's face was bright through the dimly lit room, and the tears rushed down her face. It was not the kind of crying that a woman does to make a guy feel bad for her. It was the kind that came during a profound moment. She watched his face closely, and Buddy was dumbfounded.

"Say something, you fucking idiot!" Julie shouted at him.

She swiped the back of her hand across her cheeks and wiped some of the tears. Buddy was in unchartered territory. In his thirty-one years, no woman has ever said these words to him. No woman has ever said anything like this to him – through tears – filled with emotion that he wasn't sure quite how to handle.

Buddy's emotions were always in check. He had them inside, but they were fully managed at all times. Seeing this incredible woman, who he has been in love with for months now, express such a heartfelt and meaningful confession, meant more to him than he would be capable of ever telling her in response. It was a game changer for their relationship. But still, everything between them also felt the same – only now fortified and backed by a militia.

They shared a gaze, frozen in time. Neither turned away. Buddy held it as long as he could. He never wanted to forget what she looked like right here in her living room on the floor in tears while wearing a stupid green leprechaun hat. He never wanted to lose this feeling he had inside of him, this closeness, a promise, a symphony of music that played in perfect simpatico and in all the right places. This was better and stronger than any kiss or any touch or any sexual encounter they could have.

After some time had passed, Julie asked him, "So, what do you think about that?"

Buddy was shy. He was no good at this. He was better at the silent exchange than he was verbalizing his feelings. Insecure and overwhelmed, he looked down at the floor like a little boy who got caught stealing a cookie.

"Julie, I love you too." He looked up briefly and then back down again. "I've loved you since the first day you ran by me."

Julie got up on her knees and lunged at him and into his arms. Her knee hit the glass of wine with all its deep red contents pouring onto her cream carpet. No one cared. Buddy held her tight, thin runner's body like he had always wanted to, with a man's strength but also with a tenderness that spoke of what he held for her in his heart.

He kissed her like he dreamt of kissing her someday...fully, completely, like a long-awaited buffet table spread out with all his favorite foods.

Gay Day

Buddy, Julie, and Molly pulled onto the long, well-manicured and happily designed highway leading into "The Most Magical Place on Earth." It was a hot and humid Central Florida Saturday in early June, school had just released for the summer in North Carolina, and the trio were taking a week to see Mickey and Minnie and Goofy and the whole gang. Buddy and Molly had never been to Disney World. Julie went two times as a girl, but it was a long time ago.

Before he died, Gabe had been making plans to take them to Disney for vacation when he could get leave from his unit. But then those plans...along with the trajectory of their little Army family's lives...blew straight into an alternate universe where there was no Disney, no leave, no vacation, and no clear future.

Parking the car, and then jumping onto a tram with hordes of other patrons ready to start their Disney adventures, Buddy noticed that most of the people walking along the edges of the parking lot or riding on the tram were wearing red tee-shirts. He, too, was wearing a red shirt, but instead of feeling like he was part of some secret red shirt club, he felt like he was an uninvited guest, crashing a wild party that he had no idea was occurring around him.

He turned to Julie, who was curiously looking around herself, obviously noticing the same loud phenomenon. Molly sat in between them, a white visor with glitter spread across the front of it, spelling out her name and resting on her head...completely oblivious. Her eyes were as big as saucers, filled with anticipation and excitement of meeting the characters, going on Space Mountain, and sitting on the sidewalk for the three o'clock parade with a turkey leg in hand.

Julie leaned over Molly's head and whispered to Buddy, "Oh my God!"

Buddy looked at her, questioning with the slow heightening of his eyebrows.

"It's Gay Day!" she said just a tad louder, trying not to draw attention to herself or anyone else sitting around her.

Buddy was now officially confused. Gay Day? What's that?

As the tram made its way through the throngs of red shirted men, with a few women here and there sprinkled into the mix, Buddy started to read the printed backs of the many red tee-shirts as they glided by them: "Gay Days Disney 1997," "Seattle Gay Pride," "Play the Gay Away at Disney 1996," "Out and Proud at Disney," and "Making Magic at the Most Magical Place." Many red shirts had nothing written on the backs, but some of the men wearing them were holding hands or had their arms around each other like they were romantically entangled.

Buddy looked down at his own red shirt. Then, like a slap to the back of his head, he got it. Here he was…a heterosexual male, on vacation with his fiancé and stepdaughter, wearing a red shirt on Gay Day at the Magic Kingdom. He was not only in on the wink, but he was also the joke.

Julie was giggling quietly to herself, as Molly noticed the Magic Kingdom castle peeking up over the trees and beckoning them from the distance with all its sparkle. She started hopping, furiously. "There it is! There it is! There's the castle!" she shouted, so happy and excited to finally be at Disney World.

They stood before the crowds and took in the incredible site before them, a moving tide of gay people dressed in red, with a few unsuspecting other-colored shirts out there. Others – like Buddy – who did not get the memo about the first Saturday in June in Orlando. Buddy peered over at Julie, who was laughing uncontrollably at this point.

"Do you think we should leave?" he asked her, not quite sure what to do.

"Leave?" Molly shouted out. "Why? We just got here! The castle is right there!" Her hopping was in sync with Julie's laughter, and Buddy knew that he would forever be the butt of this peculiar joke…a coincidence…the kind of funny family vacation story that would be the highlight of their Disney World memories for years to come, retold at church picnics and neighborhood barbecues, saved in a computer file for later viewing on a rainy Friday night.

Buddy knew that they wouldn't be able to leave now that Molly had seen the castle, but he didn't want to be part of a Gay Pride Parade with a fairly sheltered little girl who just wanted to meet Belle and Mickey and go on Space Mountain. He was a little annoyed. Why wouldn't the travel agent tell him that the days they booked for the Magic Kingdom included Gay Day? And why had he never heard of this before? Then, thinking about it further, he realized that the travel agent refunded him $500 the week before their trip for no known reason, her mutterings about an overcharge error.

"It's not a big deal, Buddy. I read about this before once in a newspaper article. One of the big homosexual publications sponsors Gay Day, but it's not like an official Disney event. Honestly, it's probably just a group of people, like any other group of people, who want to have a nice day at Disney."

Buddy took in the red flood of people in front of him and watched Molly hop up and down in her sneakers. He saw a few others like them – other nuclear families taking their little kids to Disney – their eyes darting around.

"Come on, Buddy, the castle is right there!" Julie yelled. "What are we waiting for?" She pulled Molly's hand, and they started speed-walking, joining in with all the red shirts on their special day at the Magic Kingdom.

"Julie, do you think this is a good idea?" he asked her, jogging up next to them, not quite sure how he would handle explaining certain things to Molly if they came up. Did Molly even know what 'gay' meant? he wondered. While Buddy had no problem with gay people specifically, he always heard that gay pride events were full of nudity and debauchery. As much as he felt that all human beings should be free to be who they are, he didn't want Molly to be exposed to people stripping off their clothes and making out in public and groping each other.

"Sure. It will be fun. Seriously, Buddy, it's Disney World. Not some late-night bath house. Gay people have families too. What do you think they're going to do? Act like they're in some sleazy night club? They just want to go on the rides and get their pictures taken with Mickey Mouse, just like anybody else."

"I guess..." he said, again looking down at his red shirt. "Okay, let's go."

As they approached the Magic Kingdom castle, he pulled out his camera and took a photo of Julie and Molly posing like rap stars from the Eighties. Julie had her long shiny hair in a ponytail and wore a light-yellow tank top and jean shorts. She was his. She was going to marry him soon, and they would be a real family. Going to Disney was just one of those family things that you're supposed to do.

Off to the side, there was a man in a "Jeff Gordon 24" ball cap and a red tank top. His arms were thick with tattoos. His hands were resting on top of a blue and white polka-dotted stroller, and a woman sat next to him, helping a little boy clean up his mouth from a chocolate doughnut. The two men nodded at each other.

"Looks like you and me picked the wrong day to wear a red shirt," the tattooed father said to Buddy.

"Yeah," he answered back, trying not to start laughing at their mutually awkward situation. "Looks that way."

Waiting in line for the Aladdin Magic Carpet ride, gay couples and groups of friends were everywhere. Buddy did not see anyone behaving in a non-family friendly way. He was pleasantly surprised at that good fortune because he had no idea what he would do if all the gay stereotypes played out in front of Molly.

"Have you ever been on this ride?" a young blond man, who appeared to be college-aged, asked Molly as he looked down at her. "I like that visor you're wearing. Did you make it yourself?"

"Thank you! Yes, I made it in school," she replied, her hopping starting to pick up steam again.

"I've been on this ride two times, and it's so scary. But you look brave to me," he said to her, winking.

Julie asked him where he was from, and as he answered "New York," a small plane flew overhead with an advertisement reading, "Club Pickle in Downtown Orlando! Hot fun all night!" Buddy hoped Molly wouldn't look up and read it. She loved pickles – it was a borderline obsession with her. She would want to know why she couldn't go to a place called "Club Pickle," and Buddy did not have a prepared answer for such a question.

A few hours later, as the three of them made their way around the park, they happened upon Space Mountain. Molly had been talking about it nonstop since Buddy made the plans to take them all to Disney. She was so excited to go on the "scariest roller coaster there" because several kids she knew in school had been on it already with their own families. She hopped over to the wooden Mickey Mouse with his big gloved hand stretched out, designating the approved height for riders, and Buddy suddenly realized that Molly wasn't going to be able to go on Space Mountain. She might be entering the Third Grade in August, but she was one of the smallest kids in her class. She was flat-out too short for this ride.

Standing as straight and as tall as she could possibly stretch herself underneath Mickey's big white hand, she still came up as too short – by like a half inch. Buddy couldn't believe it. All this excitement, all this anticipation for weeks, and the poor kid was not going to be able to go on the one ride she wanted.

"I'm sorry, Pudge, but they're not gonna let you get on," Julie tried to explain. "You're not tall enough."

Molly's face was obviously upset, and while she wasn't the kind of kid to whine or cry because she couldn't get her way, she was clearly disappointed. One half inch. Ridiculous!

"It's a safety thing. If you're too short…" Julie continued and then stopped as she watched Buddy walk over to a gay couple sitting on a bench.

"Hey," Buddy said to the two men. They both wore nondescript red shirts and Philadelphia Phillies ball caps. If Buddy didn't know that it was Gay Day, he would've thought they were brothers headed to Veteran's Stadium for a ball game in Philadelphia. Hell, maybe they were brothers. Wearing red shirts.

"Hey yourself," the man on the left replied. He looked to be in his forties, a bit overweight and sweating profusely from his forehead and underneath his armpits. There were wet patches outlining his gut.

"I was wondering if you guys were done with your bottled water," Buddy said, eyeballing the two empty bottles on the bench next to them.

"Uh, yeah, I guess so," he answered, handing the bottles to Buddy, who proceeded to take off the caps.

"Are you the Disney garbage man, sweetie?" the sweaty man asked.

"No, just trying to finagle a way to get my kid onto Space Mountain," he explained, tossing the two bottles into the trashcan and pocketing the bottle caps. "Thanks."

Buddy, Julie, and Molly stood in the long line for Space Mountain. After an hour, they approached the end, and Buddy could make out the Disney worker holding the height measuring stick for questionably sized youngsters. He bent down and had Molly pull off her sneakers. Sticking the bottle caps into the bottoms of each one, he helped her slip them back on so her heels were resting on top of the improvised height enhancers.

"Now stand up your tallest, like before." Yup. That'll do it. She'll be tall enough now.

She stood up, legs stretched to their max and whispered, "Buddy, this isn't real comfortable. I don't know if I can walk like this."

"It's okay; I'll carry you," he said, picking her up into his arms and holding her like she was just another little girl at Disney, tired from walking and standing in line all day.

As they finally got up to the measuring stick, Buddy put Molly down in front of it; she stood tall and made height by a quarter inch.

Fireworks

Julie handed Molly a Fourth of July tee-shirt that she bought from a new store downtown near her church. It was blue with glittery white and red stars plastered across the front. Molly yanked off her dirty tank top and pulled the new one over her head. Bo started licking her bare legs.

"Poor boy, I wish you could come see the fireworks with us," she cooed at Bo, petting the top of his head.

"He's afraid of them," Buddy hollered over from his office, a strange echo accompanying it. "If he hears neighbors setting them off tonight, he'll start howling and hide under the bed."

"But he's too big to be scared."

"Yeah. A big baby."

Molly hugged his neck and gazed into his big brown eyes. She always thought that it was neat how Bo never looked away from her. They could have a staring contest, and she would lose every time. When Buddy and her mom get married next week, she wanted Bo to be there, too. He was a part of their new family just as much as she was, and he might feel a little weird to be living in another house.

She sat back on a box resting along Buddy's living room floor and next to other boxes ready to be carried to the pickup truck outside. It had been a tiring day with all the back-and-forth between houses, moving Buddy's things into her house and making space for all of it. But they were almost done. He didn't have a whole lot of stuff for an adult, but his office was the worst of it. Books and papers and files and big fancy furniture that his mother bought for him when he became a lawyer a long time ago.

Buddy's friend James from Welby came to help move him, along with Grandpa Joe. Mr. Ray the mailman stopped by but couldn't help because his back was giving him problems. He gave us a plate of cookies. He was sad to lose Buddy on his postal route but promised to stay in touch.

Bo followed Molly to the box and continued to lick her legs.

"Mom, do you know why Bo does this?" she asked Julie, who sat on the floor closing an old fruit box full of Buddy's CDs. The zipping noise of the tape slapped along the opening and her mom's hand smoothed it down to keep it from popping up.

"Well, your legs are sweaty, so maybe it's the salt."

Molly wrinkled her nose at the thought of that. Salty legs. Like meat. Bo was being loving but gross. She supposed that was the very definition of dogs: loving and gross.

"Why are you taping that shut? We're just carrying it a few miles away in James' pickup truck." Molly was always told that she was too smart for her own good.

"Because I don't want his CDs to break. They need to be protected from the other boxes."

"But if we drive slow, then nothing should fall."

"Well, there's no promises on that when we go over that new God-forsaken speed bump in our neighborhood."

Later that evening, her family met with one of her mom's friends from work and her family at the Fort Bragg Fourth of July celebration. There was an open field on Post, full of locals and military families, food trucks, games, Army equipment and vehicle displays, and some country music band on a stage. They were singing a bunch of songs Molly had never heard before. Soldiers were stationed all around the outside of the field area in their starched camouflaged uniforms, probably sweating to death from the sweltering summertime North Carolina humidity. Some of them looked so scary with their straight mad faces and big arms. Molly wondered if any of them knew her daddy before he died.

As the Golden Knights Parachute Team appeared in the sky and fluttered neatly to the ground after doing a few stunts with red, white, and blue colors while in the air, Molly's heart rose into her throat, and she held her breath and shut her eyes. Would one of their parachutes fail? Would one of them fall like a rock to the ground? Would someone die? Would someone leave behind a wife and a little girl?

Suddenly, Molly felt Buddy's hand grab onto hers, and when the Golden Knights landed, he squeezed it tight three times to let her know that all was well with those brave men falling from the sky.

When it finally got dark enough, her mom lined up their blanket next to her friend's family, and they all sat down together to wait for the fireworks show to begin. The heat, along with all the moving from earlier in the day, were taking its toll on Molly. She wanted to stay awake for the fireworks but was starting to get worried about making it because she was so sleepy. Crawling in between Buddy's outstretched legs as he sat comfortably on the blanket next to her mom, she leaned back onto him, her head resting on his chest, her eyes slowly closing. A few minutes later, she was startled right out of her sleep to the sound of loud, happy, and patriotic band music coming from behind them, followed by big explosions of American colors in the nighttime sky.

The next morning, when she woke up and came down to have some cereal, Buddy showed her the local newspaper, which had been delivered early that morning. Right there on the front page was a picture of Buddy sitting on the blanket, with her sitting in between his legs, looking up at the fireworks show at Fort Bragg. The caption read, "Father and daughter enjoy the fireworks at Fort Bragg's annual 4th of July celebration."

Buddy winked at her. *Father and daughter*, Molly thought to herself.

CHAPTER 7

March - April 1975

Delta's Hair Salon

Retta's fingers were brushing through Mrs. Sanders' thick and slightly overgrown salt and pepper hair. She had been complaining about her "good-for-nothin'-dumb-ass son" who "knocked up a teenager" named Sally. Sally "got knocked up on purpose because she needed to keep herself a man somehow and get out of her house where her mama's good-for-nothin' perverted boyfriend was tryin' to get with Sally because Sally's mama was goin' through the change and not puttin' out like she used to."

Mrs. Sanders was not happy about becoming a grand-mama when she was "barely forty" herself and the last thing she wanted was "to have to raise some damn kid" when she was "done raisin' damn kids."

Whenever Retta did Mrs. Sanders' hair, she always got a mouthful of colorful stories involving her husband, her husband's sister, her mama, her dumb-ass son, and of course, her perfect daughter. The perfect daughter's stories were always colorful because she was a nineteen-year-old who had won some kind of local pageant a few years ago and was destined to be "goin' places." Retta thought of the perfect daughter as the kind of girl who knew she had her mother's heart above all others, so she took advantage of that with the hopes of getting out of Killeen, Texas someday – maybe on top of a white horse ridden by an older politician or a Texas Ranger or an oil tycoon or a professional baseball player. The perfect daughter was going to capitalize on her beauty and have the kind of life Mrs. Sanders always thought she should've had herself but never found.

All this time Mrs. Sanders had come into Delta's Hair Salon for Retta's hair and makeup skills – and sometimes Marlene's skills if Retta was out sick again – and she never asked Retta about her life. She never asked about little Buddy or big Kenny or her people or her South Jersey accent. She never asked about where she learned how to do hair and makeup, if she had any siblings or why she was always covered in strange bruises and cuts and missed so much work for illness. She never asked Retta why her hands started to shake uncontrollably one day as she washed her hair in the sink, and she never concerned herself with the time Retta did not come into work for three whole weeks...mysteriously.

Mrs. Sanders was a self-absorbed, bitter, and lonely woman, and Retta would rue the day she ended up like that. It didn't matter to her what kind of cockamamie horseshit that life was throwing her way, she would never allow herself to become the kind of selfish white trash who sat in salon chairs and ran their mouths about the sordid details of their lives and the lives of their families...and never once caring about the young mother wearing down her fingers every day, trying desperately to make her pretty, just so she could make the rent payment for the month. She would pay attention to the people she met on her walks of life. She would notice when they were gone for a while. She would ask after their children. She would say something about their accident-prone nature. She would ask if they were doing okay.

Eyeing May Ellen's empty salon chair as her fingers quickly moved through Mrs. Sanders' hair, Retta noticed that the drawer in May Ellen's spot was slightly opened. She would need to mosey over there and close it shut, so no one would notice the pistol May Ellen kept in there for safe keeping. Retta liked knowing there was a pistol inside of that small drawer – just in case she ever decided to take it home. Just in case she got punched one time too many. Just in case she felt like she needed to defend herself and her son…once and for all.

Today, she was sporting a new gash near her eye and was not able to cover it very well this morning, no matter what tricks she tried. However, the gash was nothing compared to what she inflicted upon Kenny, all by herself.

Kenny had been out of work since Christmas due to a dust up at the warehouse. He and Bob McGinley got into it for the third round, and this time, Kenny sent Bob to the hospital with a broken jaw and an immediate future that included drinking his food through a straw.

He was still drunk from the night before and had been warned several times about showing up to work intoxicated. His supervisor, Hollis Foster, knew that something hadn't been right with Kenny for a long time, something to do with the war…like maybe he was dealing with shell shock. Some of the vets who served in the Infantry came back from war and had a bad case of shell shock, according to Hollis. But he couldn't allow the drunken behavior and the fist fights to continue in his warehouse. He had a business to run. And since Kenny couldn't clean up his act after second chance and second chance, Hollis fired him on the spot, just a few days before

Christmas. It was probably one of the worst times for a man to lose his job when he has a family to provide for.

Kenny had been drinking some kind of homemade whiskey while in the living room, and Retta was cleaning little hairs, from buzzing Buddy's head earlier, off the bathroom sink. Buddy was outside playing with a neighbor boy, and it would turn dark soon. As she bent over to pick up the cleaning rag she accidently dropped, Kenny stumbled into the bathroom, catching her by surprise. He grabbed her by the waist with his strong, calloused hands and proceeded to pull up the back of her skirt with such force, she screamed in horror. While she took the slaps and punches and the occasional throw-down, he had never forced himself on her sexually – he never raped her.

Kenny knew that Retta wanted nothing to do with him when he'd been drinking. She had been balancing this battered-but-concerned wife act for so long now, all with the hopes that Kenny would come out of this mental fog which had a firm hold on him, and instead become the man she thought she married: the thoughtful, hard-working, attentive, and good, solid person.

But this man? She didn't know how much longer she could last like this, just waiting and hoping he'd get some help and get better. She knew he wasn't a bad man, that he didn't mean the things he did to her. She knew it was something deep and scarring, something that plagued him, something he saw or experienced in Vietnam. The night terrors, the screams, the many times she found him, dripping in sweat, shaking on the floor and sobbing "I didn't save her" or "Wake up Han!" The time he cried for his best friend Teddy, who died in an explosion while they were on a weekend pass. The time she found him sitting on the bathroom floor, banging the back of his head on the toilet and yelling, "Make it stop! Make it stop! Make it stop!" She knew. It was a darkness that was choking the life out of him every single day, turning him into a monster. But it was a monster who might kill her.

Retta would soothe him, hold him, and after a while, he would be alright. His tears were real. His pain was genuine. She helped him through it. He'd be sweet again, eventually, but he would never talk about the war to her, and he never explained who "Han" was.

She begged him to go to the veteran's office to see if he could get a medical or mental test. He went one time, but since the lady there wanted to put him on some medicine, Kenny told her that he would do without instead. He wasn't taking any drugs that would destroy his brain and make him feel sick. He would find a way to manage his madness himself. But apparently, he had no problem drinking alcohol to excess and drowning in his pain – and then taking his torment out on her.

Retta found the strength to put down her foot on certain things, and Kenny seemed to respect a few of them. Sex with her when he had been drinking was one of her no-nos. And so far, Kenny never crossed that line in the sand, and certainly not with any kind of force. Not that he wanted to often anyway. The story about the alcohol ruining a man's sex drive was true. At least for Kenny it was.

Shocked and horrified, especially because she feared Buddy would walk in on the sight of his stepfather attacking his mother like this, as if he hadn't seen or heard enough over the past few years, Retta writhed and wailed and started to pump her thin and sharp elbows against Kenny's waist and stomach. He fumbled and fell backwards onto the floor, and Retta ran away from him and into the kitchen. Kenny, furious, got up off the floor and went after her, grabbing her skirt by its bottom and tearing it down the side. Retta picked up a butcher knife, which sat in the sink, waiting to be wiped off from lunch earlier.

She stood there in an offensive posture, almost like if someone walked in on them, they would've thought she was the crazy one. Her bony hand, white with every vein standing at attention through the skin, grasped the converted weapon with a strength unknown to her before. Her face tight, her dark chocolate brown eyes almost glazed over in a rage reserved for wounded animals in the wild, protecting themselves from the stronger predator.

Kenny crept toward her.

"Give me the damn knife, girl," he seethed. "What you think you're gonna do with that thing?"

Retta did not want to lose her edge in this moment. She felt stronger than she had ever felt in her life. The adrenaline was pumping; she believed that if he came one step closer, she would bury the knife in his chest, leave him dying on the floor, and never look back. If anything, that would solve his wartime suffering for good. He would be free of it. And so would she and her son.

"Retta, give me the knife."

She felt her eye throbbing and tasted blood near the edges of her mouth. There was a cut somewhere on her face, a bad one. She didn't recall hitting her face on anything, but she reckoned it could've been against the sink when she first tried to get away from him.

"Get the hell away from me, Kenny, or so help me God, I will sink this mother fucking thing into you!" she shouted.

Kenny's eyes were droopy, and his words were slurring. His face was haggard, and the handsome lumberjack look he carried on his frame when she first met him, was long gone. He looked pathetic now, almost like a man given in to defeat, the energy having leaked out of his body, day after day, like an old wrinkled birthday balloon.

"Retta, please just give me the knife. I don't want you to hurt yourself with that thing. Look at you. You're bleeding by your eye. We need to clean you up." He seemed almost concerned with her well-being and had somehow managed to morph into a piece of the Kenny she knew was still in there somewhere. If he could just get some help. If he would just talk to someone. Talk to her, even.

"If you ever touch me again, if you even lay one drunken hand on me again, I swear to God in Heaven, and I swear on my husband's grave and our son's grave...I will kill you. And then I will take my son, and we will leave you here dead on the floor in this house. And no one will ever find you." She was firm. Her voice, unshaking, resolute.

Kenny felt his body tremble, his mind suddenly calming down like a set of slowing ripples in the lake after a boat goes by. He knew that she meant it.

Mama's Boy

Buddy sat on his bed in his pajamas. His blue blanket and Snoopy sheets were crumpled at the foot, and the lamp on his nightstand was dim. The light bulb would be going out soon.

Earlier, he was outside playing with his friend Gary. They had brought Gary's huge Matchbox car collection down to the dirt pile area in his backyard. Gary was good at constructing roads and inventing quarries, and Buddy was good at coming up with stories for them to play out with the cars.

First, he wanted them to be cops, like on TV. Then he wanted them to be the bad guys being chased by the cops. Playing bad guys was more fun because there were so many ways they could elude the pursuits. The quarry was deep and had a couple of construction trucks inside of it, so it looked real. There was only one cop car left because Gary lost the others, so he wanted to turn the red Chevelle into a second cop car. The boys had to do a lot of pretending to make the stories work. Buddy agreed but insisted that since the cop was in charge, he was allowed to drive whatever kind of car he wanted while on the job.

His jeans were filthy, his jacket was covered in mud, and he was afraid to go back home without being cleaned off first. Kenny would holler at him for tracking dirt into the house, and he might even slap him if he got mad enough. He used to get spankings, but his mother told Kenny that he was too old for those now.

For a long time, Kenny had been hitting his mother. It wasn't every day, as far as Buddy knew, but it was often enough that he felt like there was a quiet madness building inside of him and making is stomach feel sour all the time. He wasn't quite sure what to do with the feelings and sickness anymore, and he had started picking at his fingernails 'til they bled.

Buddy was a calm boy, the kind of kid who rarely got upset about anything. He was "cool headed" according to his teacher, and so she always had him be the student who helped the kids who needed extra assistance with their word problems or had him escort the new student around the school whenever there was one who moved to town and came into his class. Buddy was the kind of boy who was responsible and hardworking, well read, and respectful to authority. But this anger about Kenny was changing him into something else altogether.

The first time he saw Kenny losing his mind, it scared him to death. He heard all the shouting and his mother's crying and some banging noises. Then he began seeing his mother's face change. It would have cuts on it from time to time, and she would cover herself in makeup and wear her big sunglasses like that lady in the movie singing "Moon River." Her arms and neck sometimes had bruises on them. She was always a thin mother, but she looked even thinner, and he rarely saw her eat anything.

Buddy never asked her about any of it because he knew what it was, and he didn't want to upset her more than she was already. His mother wasn't the kind of woman who talked about her problems with other people, like Gary's mother who complained about every little thing she didn't like to anyone who would listen. Buddy's mother endured problems; she made do with life's messes. She never complained.

One time, when he was in his room, his mother shouted, "I am out of here! I can't take it anymore!" Buddy's heart flipped, and for a moment, he felt like he was happy. He thought to himself, *Finally! No more of this! No more Kenny being so mean and no more being scared!*

But she didn't leave.

Another time, Buddy overheard her on the phone talking to his Uncle Frank. "No, I just can't, Frank. He needs help. This is not his fault. There is something wrong from the war – something happened to him over there. I know he loves me. I know he loves Buddy. I know he doesn't mean it."

Buddy couldn't understand what could've happened in the war that would cause a man to hit his wife. He figured the worst thing that could happen to a man in war is what happened to his own father... die so badly that only parts of you come back in a bag to be buried in a coffin. Kenny only had a shrapnel injury as far as Buddy knew, and that never kept him from doing anything he wanted to do.

He reckoned that Kenny was just a son of a bitch. A mean son of a bitch. And he didn't care about him or his mother at all. Kenny probably even killed his brother while the baby was still inside of his mother just because he's a son of a bitch. And Buddy figured that how he felt about Kenny…was what hate felt like. He had never hated anyone before in his life. Until now.

Just then, Buddy was torn from his thoughts as his mother came into his room and laid down on the bed next to him. She was always so pretty, even when she didn't need to be. At home cleaning, going for a walk outside, running to the store for a carton of milk, cooking dinner – she always looked like she was heading out somewhere important to see someone even more important. Tonight, her dark curls were hanging down, and her makeup seemed fresh. She was wearing a different skirt than she wore earlier, but the shirt was the same. Her thin arms flopped gently over her head, and she took up half the bed.

"Son, are you gonna go to sleep soon?" she asked, her eyes looking up at the popcorn ceiling.

"I don't know…I guess so," Buddy said, using his finger to trace the outline of Snoopy's doghouse on his sheets.

She sighed.

"What's wrong?" he asked.

"Just tired, son. Real tired, is all." She moved her arm and covered her eyes. "I wish I knew what to do."

They never discussed what went on in their home, and they never talked about Kenny's hollering and drinking. Buddy knew what she meant, even though she didn't outright say it. Instead, he figured that this was his moment to say what was on his mind.

He began to whisper, "There's nothin' you can do but get us out of here. He's a son of a bitch, and I don't like him anymore. He's not a nice man, mother."

Retta rolled onto her stomach and buried her face in Buddy's pillow. "But he is, Buddy. That's the problem. You don't know him like I know him. There is something wrong with him…and it needs to get fixed…and I just know that he will be himself again. I still see the real him from time to time so I know he's in there, somewhere, underneath whatever crazy things are mixed up in his head." She started sobbing. "He was really good to us before. Something's just broken in him."

Buddy rubbed his mother's head. She was such a good woman, a good person, who always saw the best in others. He guessed she must be right – that Kenny is broken. But she couldn't fix him. And if she tried much longer, Kenny might break her too. He only wished she could see that for herself.

"You know son, I told you once before that you are my whole life?"

Buddy nodded.

"As long as I have you, I think I can stand just about anything in this world. Even Kenny Bellinger's nightmares and beatings and drinking."

That made Buddy boil up inside. She shouldn't have to stand Kenny's beatings and drinking at all. But he knew he could never run away and leave her here alone with the likes of his stepfather.

Earlier in the evening, after the boys were done playing Matchbox outside, Buddy went inside of Gary's bathroom to try to wipe off some of the dirt on his clothes before going home. He spotted Gary's father sitting on his bed in the room across from the bathroom. His bare feet were off the side of the bed, and he wore green shorts and a blue crew neck sweatshirt. He had red hair, the kind of red that's really the just color orange and makes a grown man look like he is still a little kid – at least on top of his head. He was holding a pistol and rubbing it with a small rag. There was some solution on the rag because the smell was strong as it came through the doorway. Then he saw Gary's father stand up and slip the pistol into the drawer next to the bed.

Kenny didn't own a pistol or a rifle like lots of folks around here did, and Buddy had only ever seen them on TV or in movies or the one at Gary's house. But he felt good knowing that if he ever needed a gun, there was one not too far away. If his mother wouldn't protect herself, or couldn't protect herself, maybe it was his job to protect her instead. Even though he had no idea how to use one, he figured that it wouldn't be too terribly hard to learn. Maybe Gary's father would teach him.

Han

Kenny sat in a large leather chair at St. Paul's Episcopal Church across from the Reverend Phillip Jenkins, whose oblong bald head full of age spots, sour facial expression, and horn-rimmed glasses made him look like a bespectacled penis. At least, that was how he would later describe the man's appearance to Retta.

The sun shone through the tinted window behind him, casting a shadow on his mahogany desk. For the past few weeks, Kenny met with the Reverend, who was recommended to him by his former boss, Hollis, at the warehouse.

One afternoon, Hollis called on Kenny – unannounced – out of concern for his wellbeing. He visited him while Retta was at work and Buddy was at school and told him that if he confessed his sins to the Reverend, the sins would remain in confidence. The Reverend would keep it private and guide him down a spiritual path and directly toward the open arms of God's love. He would help Kenny heal from his war problems, and then he'd be able to stop his drinking, go back to work, regain his strength, and take care of his family again.

Because Kenny had been so touched by the fact that Hollis cared enough about him to come by and talk with him about his troubles, he reckoned he owed it to the man to go to this "Man of God" (who really did look like a penis with glasses) with his burdens. After all, they were overwhelming him at this point. The drinking sure hadn't solved anything, and he knew he was going to lose Retta forever if he couldn't get his act together. Not only that, but he loved her. He didn't want to hit her anymore. He didn't want to make her cry anymore.

Kenny tried to explain to the Reverend what had been going on with him and how he had been hurting his wife and family, even though he knew he didn't want to.

"Are you afraid that you'll hurt her worse than you have? Meaning, do you think you will hit her or choke her to the point where she'd need to be hospitalized?" Reverend Jenkins asked, as if he were talking about how to properly bread fried chicken.

"Yeah," Kenny responded. "Sometimes, when I'm drunk, the dumbest things just set me off. And I get mad and can't stop being mad until I break something or hurt something. It's like the anger, and then what I do with it…just lets me release something ugly inside of me. Like a bunch of bad air is let out. Then after it's all over, I feel better."

He shuffled his feet, took a deep breath and continued. "Other times, I don't even know I'm doing anything and can't remember what I just did. I don't remember a damn thing. Nothing! But Retta'll be on the floor crying, hiding under something, and then I'll see that I musta clocked her," he explained and then stopped. His voice started to quiver. "I don't mean to. And I know she knows that. But it's like I can't control anything when it happens. Like something…

maybe a demon or an evil spirit…comes into my body and takes it over and doesn't leave until I fight it out of me."

The Reverend leaned back in his chair and ran his finger slowly across the shadow on his desk.

"Do you think you're ready to tell me about Han today?" he asked deliberately.

The last time he asked Kenny to explain Han, he lost him. Kenny started to cry like a child. In all his years serving God in this capacity, he had never seen anything quite like Kenny's struggle. Even the grown men whom he had counseled through their wives' deaths or the deaths of children or their own war stories, didn't sob like Kenny Bellinger had about this Han person.

Kenny put his head in his big hands. And with a heavy heart and all the courage he could manage, he began to tell the story about Han.

He had seen death in combat, avoided his own several times, and saw fellow soldiers suffer loss of limbs. He saw genuine poverty in the streets of the villages and in pockets of Saigon. He took some shrapnel to his own leg during an ambush. He thought he was going to die that day. Kenny had been through a lot…just like lots of the other guys over there. No one came back the same. There was no way they could, really. And anyone who said the war didn't affect them were either liars or lacking any kind of conscience.

But no matter what carnage he had witnessed and experienced firsthand as a soldier, he was certain that there was only one thing that had obliterated a part of his soul. And he didn't know just deeply Han's story haunted him these years later…until he lost his baby boy in the quiet comfort of his wife's womb.

It was during the second day in Saigon, when he and his best Army pal, Teddy Edwards from Biloxi, Mississippi, were in the city on a three-day pass. It was August 1969, and he remembered falling onto the street because he had a little too much of the local beer at a popular GI hangout. Kenny and Teddy finally got to have sex with some bar girls the day before, which had been way overdue. They ate some of the local cuisine, which was a lot better than they thought it would be. They wore normal clothes, like tan slacks and buttoned up collared shirts and white sneakers. Their haircuts and tall, lean bodies screamed "American GI." This was the first time they had both been allowed to put the war and all they'd been through while in country out of their heads…and attempt to be two young men in the prime of their lives just enjoying a day out on the town. Even if it couldn't be in New York or Paris and had to be in Saigon.

Teddy helped Kenny up off the ground. The streets were full of people milling about during their day. Some were on foot, some riding bikes, some on scooters, some in pedi-cabs. Street vendors in conical hats hocking their fruits and vegetables and baked goods and wares were sprawled about. Whenever they'd see Kenny and Teddy, they figured there was some American money to be made. All Americans had money, after all. Certainly, more than the humble folks sitting in Saigon and wading in the rice paddies on the countryside.

As they walked upon a small shop full of beautiful linens and hand crafted bags, a young Vietnamese girl, who looked about twelve or thirteen, sat patiently and clearly in charge of the items. She was delicate – like all the women in Vietnam were – slight and thin with black shiny hair and slanted eyes and flawless olive toned skin. She wore a white dress and traditional sandals. As Kenny looked around the busy streets, it was apparent to him that God took a mold for "Vietnamese female" and pressed a "repeat" button a million times before dropping them all into this dusty and overpopulated city.

There was nothing that stood out about this girl on this day and in this place. She looked just like the rest of them.

Kenny felt the linens through his fingers and thought about how his little sister might like one for her trailer. A souvenir from his war days. But then he remembered his sister ran off with some asshole from Tampa. Maybe he'd buy it anyway and give it to her if he ever saw her again.

"Do you speak English?" he asked the girl who was watching them intently.

She yelled, "No boom-boom."

He was sober enough to know what the hell she just said. No matter how desperate he was for some action, he was not interested in action with little girls. He was no pervert.

He grabbed what he thought was a scarf. "How much?"

"Fie dollar."

Kenny was surprised by that. Five dollars for a piece of cloth? He knew the deal. These street vendors were like street vendors everywhere. Suggest a ridiculous price for something cheap and hope that the sucker will go for it. Or haggle. Either way, the vendors would make their money.

"Five dollars?" Kenny laughed out loud. He felt bad because the girl was obviously very young and was probably instructed to take advantage of any soldiers on leave. She stood up and handed Kenny a bag. It was soft and hand sewn with bright colors and small stitching.

"For lady?" she asked him. "Fie dollar. Number one." Her voice was high-pitched and still sounded like a small child, almost cartoonish.

Before Kenny could answer, there was an excruciatingly loud noise, his ears were deafened, and his body flew up and over the curb on the street, landing hard next to the girl and her table. There was smoke everywhere, and slowly, as his hearing returned, he could hear all the screaming…the kind of screaming that you don't even know exists until it happens.

People were running and sirens were blaring and the girl's head lay next to his chest. She wasn't moving. Teddy was nowhere to be seen. Kenny couldn't move, almost like he was pinned down by something large, but he wasn't able to see anything keeping him in place. Except for the girl's head and body.

Kenny tried to sit up. He looked down at the tiny human being, limp and crumpled on him. Her eyes were open, and she stared into his own, full of fear and pleading. As he moved her head slightly to the side, he saw she had no right arm below her elbow and there was something sharp jutting out of the side of her head. His eyes were wild, welling up and filling with tears like a stopped-up bathtub. He quickly came to understand what had happened to her. Her lips were plump and a shade just below ruby. She had a pin prick sized mole near her mouth. Just a young girl. Somebody's daughter.

Starting to panic, his heart racing, Kenny held on to her tightly. He didn't know what to do. Should I go for help? Should I look for Teddy? Should I just flee and leave her here? She was dying anyway. What if another bomb went off, and this time, instead of it just missing me, I lose my arm and take something to the head?

Kenny knew the deal in Vietnam. He was an American in Saigon during an unpopular war. No one would help him, that was for sure.

The girl started to speak with a slight gurgle to her voice. "Han," she said.

Kenny soothed, "It's gonna be okay. I'm gonna take you to the hospital." He was overcome with emotion, engulfed with fear, operating only on instincts. He had never felt so overwhelmed before, bordering on helpless. Protect. Help. He started crying, almost a panicked cry, tears finally making their escape from his eyes, a primal kind of stress triggered aloud inside of him. All this time in Vietnam, all the carnage and atrocities he's seen…and this was the first time he cried. This was the first time he moved with desperation.

"GI," she said.

"Yes," Kenny blurted. "I'm a GI."

"Han," she said again.

"What's Han? What's that mean?" he shouted at her, still panicked.

With her left hand, she brought it up to her chest. She pointed at herself. "Han." Then she softly touched Kenny's face, right along his left cheek. "GI."

Kenny, now losing himself in an uncontrollable sob, yelled, his voice cracking, "Your name? Your name is Han?"

He held her closer, knowing deep down inside of himself that she was going to die and that there was nothing he would be able to do for her. He should just run and try to find Teddy and get the hell out of this place. But he would not allow himself to leave her behind. And he had no idea why. She became still and looked to be at peace. In their mutual silence, there were sirens and the echoes of chaos all around them.

He pointed at her chest and said "Han." Then he pointed at his own chest and uttered, "Kenny."

Han smiled slightly right at the corners of her mouth. "Kenny," she repeated.

"Han, I'm going to get you to a hospital, okay?"

Kenny rose to his knees while lifting along with himself the petite girl's body. She couldn't have been much more than seventy-five pounds. She groaned but was likely in shock and could not feel a thing. There was blood coming from the side of her head, but unlike most head wounds, it was a slow flowing wound, as if the piece of metal sticking out kept it from gushing, serving as a dam of life for the moment. Her arm, now mangled and in two pieces, needed a tourniquet. Kenny grabbed one of the beautiful linen pieces that she had been trying to sell to him for five fucking dollars only minutes ago, and wrapped it tightly above the wound, just as he learned in Basic Training.

He grabbed another piece of linen and tried to stop the bleeding from her head. Her white dress was sopping wet and full of her own blood. Kenny had plenty of it on him, too, but it appeared for now that he was spared any real injuries. Screams and blowing horns were all around him, the smoke was beginning to dissipate, and Teddy was nowhere to be found. A few minutes ago, he was happy and drunk. But right now, he was as awake and as in control as he could possibly be…as if he never had a drink in his life. His senses were heightened in a way that he only ever experienced in combat. Something took over. Something surreal…but focused and strong. He could lead a charge up a hill. He could take a medical school entrance exam. He could perform any number of songs with a guitar on a stage. His confidence soared in this moment, and he believed – just for a moment – that it would save little Han from her early death.

Carrying Han in his arms, he started to jog down the street and toward somewhere that would lead him to the closest hospital or to some medics tending to other casualties. People were running about, frantic, chaotic, and confused. Kenny saw a man in the street with his head half blown off, a woman in a deep red and orange traditional Vietnamese getup picking up the pieces of the other half, trying to affix the brain matter to his missing side. She was strangely calm about it – like in a slow-motion video – almost as if she were Jackie Kennedy picking up the pieces of the President's skull in the back of that convertible in Dallas several years ago.

A stray dog was barking and a pedi-cab was on its side with a wheel blown off, the driver pinned underneath by his legs. One of the food vendors had a huge gaping hole in the side of its wagon with food strewn everywhere, falling over and onto the street. Kenny continued to run amid the noises and the shrieks of an unconventional wartime in a populous city. Everyone always talked about how the fighting was in the bush. Not much was said about the bombs from Charlie hiding out in the city – using the civilians as shields – blowing up the places which gave refuge to the easy money of American GIs helping the South Vietnamese economy.

As tears streamed down his nose, Kenny looked down at Han. Life was draining from her face; her stare was vacant.

"Han! I'm taking you to a doctor! I'm taking you!" Kenny shouted at her.

She blinked. "danh từ," she said, her mouth dry and voice gurgling.

Kenny didn't know Vietnamese. He had no idea what she just said. Trotting along with her flopping body in his arms, his heart was pounding. If he could just get her to a doctor, he could save her. Her wounds were bad, but they could be fixed. She was too young for this nightmare, too young for this kind of brutality by her own people. Her softness and willingness to trust him in this brief catastrophic moment had moved something inside of his heart unlike anything that life had shown him so far. All the harshness of his upbringing and the sadness of his family's own poverty and the challenges of combat made him tougher than most; but this girl, this simple hard working innocent child on the streets in this God forsaken place, touched him in a space he had no idea resided inside.

As he neared a meat wagon on the side of the road, he saw a medic helping a lady sit down on the side walk. "Help! Help me, please!" he screamed as he ran as fast as his big long legs would take him. Han moved her head slightly to the side, like she wanted to see the side show going on around her. He brought her to the short Vietnamese man who immediately reacted to the emergency brought to him. He pointed to an empty stretcher lying off to the side.

Kenny gently put Han down on the ragged stretcher. It looked like it had been lifted from the Army at some point in its history – olive drab green and with US stamped on the side in black ink.

Han's almost lifeless body was devoid of form. Kenny leaned over her, peering down into her coal black eyes. His hulking American frame dwarfed Han even more that it had before. "Han, they're gonna help you," he whispered, trying to calm his own nerves.

Han moved her good arm and pointed to Kenny's chest. "Cảm ơn lắm," she said.

With tears, he hollered, frustrated, "I don't know what that means…what does that mean?"

She whispered, "cảm ơn lắm."

The medic left the lady on the curb and came over to tend to Han. Another medic ran by, helping a man by his arms who appeared to be bleeding profusely from his ear.

"What does that mean?" Kenny shouted again. He wanted to know. He wanted to understand what she was saying to him.

The medic spoke in rapid Vietnamese, and Kenny felt like he was now an outsider to this rescue. Han's face watched him, and her mouth moved slightly into a half smile. "Cảm ơn lắm, Kenny," she uttered slowly in broken speech. His heart filled up when she said his name. Maybe she had a chance. Maybe in all this horrible haze, one good thing would happen. Maybe instead of being a part of killing another Vietnamese person, he might be a part of saving one.

Han reached for Kenny's hand and held it. She wrapped her tiny fingers around his huge thumb. "Cảm ơn lắm, Kenny," she said one more time and then closed her eyes forever.

PART II

"we were together—all else has long
been forgotten by me,"

—Walt Whitman, *Leaves of Grass*

CHAPTER 8

June – November 1998

Gabrielle

Loretta and Joe sat in the waiting room of the maternity ward at Harper Hospital with nine-year-old Molly Saint. Molly sat on a chair with her legs swinging back and forth, drawing a picture of a rather detailed elephant breaking free from an evil circus master underneath a colorful big top in her sketch pad. A pink helium balloon, which read "Welcome home baby girl" over a brown teddy bear, sat at her feet. Molly's brown hair fell way beyond her shoulders, and her tank top straps barely covered her shoulders, which were peppered with some large, some small freckles.

A nurse wearing light blue scrubs walked by, whispered something to an old man sitting alone next to a vending machine, and then walked back down the hallway leading to the birthing rooms. Just then, Buddy came around the corner. He was wearing black shorts and a green and black striped collared shirt with "Mid Pines" written over the left side of his chest. His face was freshly shaven and his blond-brown hair neatly trimmed, the hairline beginning to show its recession. He was smiling – without actually smiling – that odd phenomenon which seemed to describe Buddy's entire personality best. However, this time, it was all shown through his eyes. The cobalt color in his irises was brighter, and his eyelashes seemed even longer than usual. Instead of the tell-tale pregnancy glow, men who became fathers of baby girls seemed to get an eye color glow.

Buddy walked up to Molly and hugged her tightly. He kissed her forehead. "Do you want to meet your baby sister now?" he asked.

Molly, having at last outgrown her hopping phase, jumped up and down only once. "Yes!" she shouted.

Loretta and Joe were beaming. They were so excited for the arrival of this new member of their family. Loretta had been so happy to have Molly as her granddaughter when Buddy and Julie got married, but this new little life resting in a plastic hospital bassinette inside of a nursery just feet away, was a feeling she couldn't put into words. Over the years, other women would tell her that there was just something different about becoming a grandparent. It was its own special experience that you can't understand until it happens to you. Well, she understood it now.

Buddy escorted his family back to where Julie and the new baby sat in a huge hospital bed. Molly walked in, hopped onto the bed and looked at the small bundle wrapped in a white blanket. The baby was wearing a small pink hat on her otherwise peach-fuzz bald head. Julie rested back on pillows and wore a hospital gown. Her blond hair, messy and in serious need of a brush, fell scattered down her back. She held her baby like the delicate new being and precious life she was. She would protect her as she had protected Molly. Her heart was full.

"Is she sleeping, Mom?" Molly asked, not allowing herself to touch her new sister. She was in awe of how teeny-tiny she was.

"Yes, she is," Julie answered, smiling down at her. "And look at those eyelashes. She sure didn't get those things from me!" She looked over at Buddy, who was blushing, a lifetime of eyelash-related bashfulness.

"What did you guys decide to name her?" Loretta asked, watching the pure joy emanate from the only woman who ever held her son's heart.

Buddy stood at the foot of the bed. "We decided to name her Gabrielle. Gabrielle Loretta."

Loretta started to cry. Joe pulled her into himself.

"Do you want to hold her?" Julie asked Loretta.

Loretta, trying to maintain her composure, walked over to Julie, who handed to her Loretta's firstborn grandchild. She pulled Gabrielle up into both arms and looked down at her scrunched up little face. Honest people say that newborn babies look like featherless chickens. But grandparents think that honesty is over-rated. They don't see a featherless chicken. Instead, they see another beautiful branch of their own personal legacy, reaching up into the sun to breathe.

Joe and his first wife never had children. She had been saddled with an unfortunate and tragic cancer when she was only nineteen years old, forcing her to choose between losing her uterus or dying young. She chose childlessness and not dying, which brought with it its own particular suffering, underneath the surface, for the rest of her shortened life.

When Joe married her, he understood that he would never have a child of his own. And that was okay with him because he loved his wife dearly. Then she got sick again in her thirties and passed away despite her bold choice. It wasn't until after Buddy and Loretta moved onto his property a few years later, Joe felt for the first time in his life that he genuinely felt the pain of something he never realized he endured...the loss of something he never had...his own child.

Buddy was not his son. He knew that. But Buddy coming into his life gave him a small piece of fatherhood, and he knew that he indeed loved him like a son. In his own way, he helped raise him. And now Buddy gave Joe not only that feeling but also the experience of being a grandfather, something he would never otherwise know without first Molly, and now, Gabrielle. Family is blood and family is bond. Sometimes you get both and sometimes you get just one...but one isn't any less than the other.

"Will you call her Gabby?" Loretta asked.

"Yes, we think so," Julie replied.

Several weeks ago, when Buddy and Julie were lying in bed and talking about baby names, Julie held a book full of them. She read through meanings and origins and spellings and a list of famous people who had them. As they shared with each other what different names meant to them, they came across the name "Gabrielle." Buddy, who had been silent during most of Julie's name-related musings, said suddenly, "That's it."

Julie, a bit surprised, asked him, "You don't think that's weird?"

Buddy was on his back, shirtless and in his tighty-whiteys. He looked up at the ceiling. "Not at all. It's perfect, actually. A name should mean something. Something strong, something powerful, and it should have depth. It connects us all in some ethereal way." He rolled onto his side, put his head along Julie's massive baby bump, and then his hand on top. "And you know what I normally think about words like 'ethereal.'"

Julie laughed. She knew.

"Gabrielle means 'God's strength.' And it means just a little bit more than that in this house," Buddy added.

Julie put her hand on Buddy's hair, running her fingers through the thinning rows. "I guess…" she started.

"Gabe is Molly's father. Without him, I would never know either of you, never have either of you as my life now. Gabe didn't leave his family because he's an asshole. He left because an accident, while serving his country, took him away. He was an honorable man. I feel like we have some kind of bond."

Julie was a little taken back with this confession from her sweet husband. She never heard him speak like this about Gabe. She had no idea that he felt anything this profound toward him. In fact, other than the few times she talked about Gabe earlier in their relationship, Buddy never discussed anything related to him before.

He continued. "Gabe trusted you with his daughter. You trust me with his daughter. I have taken over for him because he can't do the rest of this…the rest of the fathering. And it sucks because life is not always fair to good people. I know how that feels. But now it's on me to finish what Gabe couldn't, to do right by him as a man who loves you and Molly. I have taken on his daughter as my own – and I have taken his wife as my own – kind of picking up where he left off. And now we are going to have our own baby, a sister for Molly." He paused and put his hands on his forehead. "It's just important to me that Molly understands that she matters just as much as this baby. I am just as much her father as this baby's father. And I want Molly to feel like no one has forgotten her real father either, just because he can't be here anymore."

Julie laid still, digesting all that Buddy shared with her. She didn't think that she could possibly love Jonathan Cordova any more than she already did. But here it was. More love. More admiration. More appreciation for the fact that this wonderful, humble, thoughtful man was brought into her life, into her daughter's life. There was no fanfare and no fireworks, no mind-blowing crazy story that they shared around fire pits on Friday nights. It was just two lonely people with some ugly life scars who found each other, became friends, and then fell in love. It wasn't the kind of love that knocks you into the street, only to fizzle out when the passion fades. It was the kind of love that lasts and stands the test of time, the kind of love where passion simmers within the lining of what they shared. She knew right then without one single doubt in her mind that no matter what life threw at her, as long as she had Buddy, she would always be alright.

"Can I hold Gabrielle?" Molly asked, waiting to sit down in the chair near her mother's bed.

Loretta walked over to her, and as Molly backed herself up, Loretta placed Gabby into Molly's arms. Molly held up Gabby's tiny head in the crook of her elbow, her rosebud mouth moved slightly in a sucking motion. As she slept, her eyes twitched a bit. Molly put her index finger on Gabby's forehead and rubbed it gently.

"She's so light, so tiny," Molly whispered.

"Just over six pounds," Julie reported.

Loretta laughed. "That is a small baby! Buddy was over nine pounds if you can believe that."

Buddy looked over at Joe. Joe winked at him. Life was pretty damn good.

Hiking

Molly picked up her new lime green backpack and slid it onto her back. It was stuffed with a water bottle, sunscreen, a parka, a hat, twenty chewy oatmeal bars and a pack of Swedish Fish. Buddy closed the trunk of his car, threw his backpack over his shoulder and walked up to Molly who was waiting on him. She was excited. She had never gone hiking before.

Buddy announced to her a week ago that at least once a month, he wanted to take her on a nice hike in one of the North Carolina State Parks. This morning, they woke up early and drove two hours and a half hours to Hanging Rock State Park for their first outing. It would be about a six-mile hike if they completed the whole thing, which was a good haul for a nine-year-old girl with no experience.

Julie and Gabby were left at home. Gabby was still sleeping a lot, had on-demand nursing needs, and Julie needed to work on some of her Back to School cutting and pasting for her classroom.

It was end-of-summer warm – but not too warm – up in the higher elevation, and Buddy wanted to be sure that the two of them started this new monthly bonding tradition before Molly started to become too serious in a sport or activity like so many of the other kids seemed to do these days. She had been playing recreational soccer for the past year and was surprisingly good at it.

Buddy had pegged her to become a distance runner like her mother, but when Molly brought home a flyer from school and asked to be signed up for a soccer team, Buddy figured it would give her something active to do to help with her above average energy needs. Plus, being a part of a team would help her make friends.

Molly was a nice girl with a big soft heart, but other kids thought she was a little on the weird side because she was a lot smarter than everyone else and appeared to live in her own world at times. Soccer was the magic pill, rather than something like Ritalin, that cured Molly of the constant hopping. And because she was the fastest player on the soccer team and scored the most goals, everyone wanted to be her friend.

They started out at the foot of the trail, taking in the pin-pointed map on the park display board. There were signs indicating where to hike and some photos of the different plants and critters and birds that nature-loving hikers might encounter while walking along the trails. Buddy wore a pair of cargo shorts and a tee shirt along with a new pair of boots he bought from an outdoors store.

"Ready?" he asked Molly.

"Ready!"

They started to hike, and within two minutes, Molly said she wanted to eat one of her oatmeal bars. She stopped, pulled one out, took off the wrapper and shoved the small treat into her mouth.

"So, tell me. Are you ready to take on the Fourth Grade?" Buddy asked. School was starting on Monday.

"Yeah. I'm excited about it. Kara and Kelcey from my team are gonna be in my class and Mom said that I'm really gonna like Mrs. Schell as my teacher."

"Which ones are Kara and Kelcey?"

"Kara's the one who always plays defense. She's the big one with blond hair. And Kelcey was the goalie."

"Ahh, I remember now. Kara takes people out," Buddy laughed, recalling how during one of the games, a girl on the opposite team literally bounced off Kara as she stood in the box like an oak tree. The parents on the sidelines were laughing. Even the parents from the other team were laughing.

"Yeah. She's so big. She should play football with the boys instead," Molly said, putting one Carolina blue Nike in front of the other.

"I liked playing soccer when I was younger…when I was in college. We would play pick-up soccer just for fun outside the dorms. I wish that I could've played when I was your age. Maybe I would've been good at it like you are."

"How come you didn't play when you were my age?"

"No teams, I guess. I don't know. I don't really remember a whole lot about when I was your age. A lot of it is a blur," Buddy admitted, realizing for the first time that he had specific memories of being nine and not one of them had anything to do with a normal boyhood activity, like playing on a team or riding a bike or going to school or having an ice cream cone on a hot summer night.

"Wow, is that what happens when you get old? You can't remember anything?"

"Hey now. I'm old but not that old."

"Okay. So, do you remember anything, anything at all from when you were nine? Like even one memory?"

Buddy thought about it some more. He saw himself sitting on an old dusty couch next to his mother somewhere, deep inside of someone's dark house. He was wearing a pair of shorts and had a big scab on his left knee. He didn't remember how he got it. The scab was still dark purple and black but bright pink around the edges and starting to itch a lot. He spent the time sitting on that couch picking at it until it started to bleed again. There was an older woman in a big dress which sat on her like a tent. She had fat rolls coming off her arms, a long dark braid in her hair, and she was sitting in a chair across from them. She was nice.

He saw himself sitting on a train, watching a lot of empty brown spaces go by in the window. The seat was a dark green and had a hole in the cushion. He put his finger inside of it and made the hole bigger by picking at the foam stuffing inside. His mother slapped his hand and told him to stop. He remembered having to get up from his seat to use the bathroom, and when he got inside, he could see that someone had vomited in the toilet. So, he peed onto the vomit.

But the most vivid memory in Buddy's head from when he was nine-years-old was the day he and his mother were sitting at a bus stop. It was early in the morning, fairly cold, and they were all alone. No one else was there, or seemed to be anywhere nearby, and he recalled feeling scared and anxious. He held a paper bag that said "Safeway" in his arms, which housed two shirts, two pairs of pants, two pairs of underwear, a pair of socks, a copy of The Boxcar Children, and a toothbrush.

A lady pulled up in a big gray car. She had dark curly hair just like his mother and wore a whole lot of makeup on her face.

"Hey, y'all. Are you Loretta?" she asked while chewing some gum.

His mother stood up from her spot. She was frail and wore a pair of jeans and a long brown coat. Leaning her head down to the window, she replied, "I am. Are you Mary Stuart?"

"I'm Dixie, her sister. Mary Stuart sent me. Y'all get in, and I'll take you to her." She popped her gum.

His mother, starting to become accustomed to being called, "Loretta," got into the front seat, and Buddy slid into the back. His nerves were a little calmer now; he was taking his cues from his mother's body language. Dixie drove them for quite a while, and Buddy watched all the greens, yellows, oranges, and reds go by. He was sure he had never seen anything like it before, except in a picture book at the library. He saw plowed fields and piles of yellow brush and open blue skies and big green tractors.

When they arrived into the heart of a small town, passing by a gas station and a small grocery store, Dixie pulled her car into a short gravel driveway and walked them onto a huge porch, stretching all around the front and sides of the entire house. It had a two-person swing sitting off to the side.

Dixie opened the screen door and yelled inside. "Mary Stuart? It's me!" Then she turned to them and smiled, "Come on in."

Buddy and his mother walked inside. Immediately, a rather round, bubbly, big toothed woman with curly dark hair and ruby red lips, wearing an equally red shirt, walked out of the kitchen. She wobbled over to them like they were long lost family members. "Oh my, I'm so happy y'all are here! You made it! Bless your heart, what a trip y'all musta had!"

She hugged his mother tight, like she could press all one hundred pounds of her completely into her bosom, making his mother disappear altogether. She grabbed Buddy like he was her nephew from far away, hugging him just as tight. She pulled away and put her fingers under his chin.

"Dear boy, you're just lovely. Like a blossom. My Lord in Heaven, look at those eyelashes Jesus gave to you! How lucky you are! You know how many ladies pay good money for such things?" She took a deep breath and then sighed. "You and your mama, I'm so happy to finally meet y'all both." Then she leaned down and kissed his forehead, no doubt leaving a large red lipstick stain behind.

Buddy had never met anyone quite like Mary Stuart before. She talked funny and was real loud and everything was such a big deal… but in a good way. She made big exaggerated sighs when she talked about the goings-on in the town that day, and her hands were always moving. She fed them a big lunch, a full meal with cornbread and mashed potatoes and fresh green beans and fried chicken she made herself just that morning. They even had something called Brunswick Stew that she got from the Methodist Church ladies' ministry covered dish the day before. She let them use her bathroom to clean up from all the days they spent on trains and busses to get there…all the way to Welby, North Carolina.

When they were done cleaning up, and Buddy's hair was still a bit damp, she drove them several miles away along country roads to a large piece of farmland, which had an older looking farmhouse, some small rustic shacks, and a barn with a one-bedroom apartment on the top of it. Mary Stuart pointed up at its perch. It had steps all up the side that led to a small white door. "That'll be all yours. It's not much, but it'll do for now, 'til you get yourself all settled somewhere more permanent."

A large, weathered middle-aged man came out of the barn wearing a pair of jeans, a flannel shirt and a John Deere ball cap. His thick brown hair came out of the bottom. His face was wide and friendly, and he had small creases near his eyes when he smiled at them. Sticking his hand out, he shook his mother's hand and said, "Ma'am, my name is Joe Horton. Y'all are welcome to stay here as long as you'd like." And Buddy knew that he meant it.

As Buddy and Molly walked along the trail, Molly was as quiet as a church mouse, listening to him tell her this mountain of information. She took in this story about her stepfather's past, a story she had never heard before, a story that Buddy had never even once shared with Julie. Molly figured that there was a lot more to this story, but either Buddy didn't remember it or Buddy wasn't interested in telling her.

"So, is that when Nana and Grandpa Joe started to be boyfriend and girlfriend?" she asked suddenly, breaking the extended silence between them.

"No, they didn't become boyfriend and girlfriend until a long time later," he explained.

"Do you know where you lived before you got to Grandpa Joe's? Where you came from?" she asked.

"I lived in Texas, but really, I don't remember a whole lot about it. It was a long time ago."

"How come you don't ask Nana about it? I bet she'll remember."

Buddy thought about how he and his mother never spoke of the past, how they never discussed his stepfather Kenny or his real father or where they used to live or the handful of memories he held onto when they fled. They never discussed their real names or their real family or even the bus and train rides all the way out to North Carolina from some place dry and plain and brown. But he knew that whatever they left behind was bad and something his mother had no desire to ever address again. And that fact had never changed in all the years they'd been gone.

When Retta Bellinger became Loretta Cordova, and when Daniel Kaspar Junior became Jonathan Cordova, it was as if they had been born again, never to recall their real names and real lives and real selves. They became new people in every way, only he was reborn at nine years old, and his mother was reborn at twenty-nine.

"Not sure, kiddo. Nana doesn't like to talk about those years. So, we don't. And it's okay. I've had a great life since coming to North Carolina, especially a couple of years ago when I met you and your mom."

"My grandparents live in Texas. That's where my mom is from," Molly offered.

"Yeah, I know."

"Wouldn't it be neat if you lived in the same town as my mom and just didn't know it? Like maybe you were in school together or had the same dentist."

"Ha," Buddy said. "That would be neat. But I doubt it. Texas is a big place. One of the biggest in the whole country."

"My mom doesn't talk to my grandparents, so I don't really know them at all," Molly said, sounding sad. "Never even met them except when I was really little. And I don't remember it."

"Did you ever meet your father's parents?" he asked. He knew that Gabe's mother was dead and his father wasn't a part of the picture.

"When I was a baby, I met my grandmother. She was real sick at the time so I think it was when she was about to die. But I don't remember that either. There's a picture though. Me, my grandmother in a red toboggan hat and my daddy…all together."

"Life's been a little tough on you, shorty," Buddy said to Molly, who seemed to be handling the six miles of rough terrain with no problem. They stopped and sat down for a few minutes, drinking some water and sharing some Swedish Fish.

"I guess so. But I think life is tough for everyone."

"You think?"

"Yeah. Some have it worse than I do."

"Like who?"

"Well, there's a boy who was in my class last year whose dad has cancer, and they say he's gonna die soon…and a girl in Mrs. Holloway's class who has some other kind of cancer. She's always having to miss school for doctors and told me that the treatments made her real sick. Like, she throws up a lot and can't eat anything cold."

Buddy thought about how fortunate he had been to have exactly what he had as a boy. Molly was right. As bad as it was, it could've always be worse.

Molly continued, "So instead of just seeing the sad things in my life, I try to see how lucky I am. I have my mom and you and Bo and now Gabby. Nana and Grandpa Joe. My friends in school and my soccer team. The biggest thing is that I know that I'm loved," she explained, showing more of life's wisdom within her pinky finger than most people have in their whole bodies for their entire lives.

Soccer Dad

Somehow, Buddy got roped into being a coach for Molly's soccer team. It wasn't one of those situations where the coach held a parent meeting and asked for a volunteer to help him with coaching the team. It was more like a sudden and direct: "Here, take over, I got overlapping games today with my oldest son's team." So then, Buddy was left standing on the sideline with a huge mesh sack of soccer balls, some flat orange cones, and a blank white dry-erase clipboard.

Molly was just beside herself with excitement to have him as her coach. Buddy was less than enthused about it, because while he played some pick-up games in college with his friends, he was like most American men and modern day fathers who get thrown into serving as their kids' soccer coach – not real up on the rules and strategies and game play and training needs. He knew that the team who scored the most goals…wins. You can't use your hands. That was really the extent of his soccer knowledge.

Molly sat on his left knee dressed in her yellow jersey and black shorts as they both looked over the clipboard's starting lineup for the Saturday morning opener.

"I think you need to put Hailey and Allison on defense to start, rather than Kara. Kara has been doggin' it in practice," Molly explained.

"Yeah, but I like Allison better on the wing. I think she does better up there than on defense. Kara can't really play anywhere else, and I think today, we'll only have one sub because of some birthday party that the twins are going to."

Buddy couldn't understand modern-day sports programs. When he played baseball as a boy in Welby, you would be cut from the team for missing practices; and if you missed a game, you'd be cut and then also tarred and feathered in the center of town. Missing a game for a birthday party? That just didn't make any sense to him. But that was the way it was in the late Nineties, so Buddy rolled with it, like he rolled with everything else in life he didn't understand.

"I guess you're right," Molly agreed. "You know…I get it if you feel like I shouldn't start all the time. Because of favoritism or something."

"You're the best player on the team, Molly. I don't think the other parents would look at you starting the game as favoritism. They'd look at it as smart. Plus, judging from some of the comments I've heard in practice, they want to win more than most of the girls even care to."

"But they might get mad. I don't want any of the parents to yell at you."

Buddy smiled, put his hand around her neck, and pushed her forehead to his forehead. "Don't worry about me. I can handle the parents. You just do what you do best, and it won't matter if we only have one sub today," he said encouragingly, and then kissed her freckled nose.

Julie walked in with Gabby. Gabby was dressed all snug inside of a full teal colored onesie with small white bows adorning her Michelin man legs. It was a warm day, so she probably didn't need anything more than that. She fixed Gabby inside of the car seat carrier as Gabby batted at the small plastic toys hanging from the top, alternating swings with a baby smile that melted everyone's heart.

"We're ready to go!" Julie declared, outright giddy to be getting out of the house and into the sunshine for an entire afternoon. This was exactly the kind of thing she always saw herself doing one day: going to a soccer game with a man she loves to watch her kid play a game she knew absolutely nothing about. Normal mom. The simplicity of that.

To Julie, it was the unremarkable stuff of everyday life which formed the glue running into the cracks of her heart, forcing together all the jagged pieces, which consisted of the otherwise remarkable stuff of life meant to break you. It's the unremarkable moments that made you whole again. Buddy's tighty-whiteys left on the floor was her glue. Bo's golden hair all over the furniture was her glue. The formula stains Gabby would leave on her left shoulder while trying to burp after a feeding her was her glue. Washing the grass stains out of Molly's uniform was her glue. Running with Gabe's ghost along the side of the street was her glue.

Julie knew she'd never need another thing in her life to make her feel as whole and at peace as she did in this one single moment. And to think there were many days that she couldn't even get out of bed. To think there were days when she couldn't stop crying. To think there were moments where she believed she'd be better off dead than living another day on this earth.

They loaded up into the Pontiac and headed over to the designated parks and recreation field. When they arrived, it was difficult to find parking, but soon enough, Buddy squeezed into a spot next to a minivan with its hatch open. Five small boys sat inside the back, wearing gray and black soccer uniforms, sipping on Capri Sun juice boxes.

Walking over to the field, Buddy carried the team kit and tried desperately to look like someone who knew what the hell he was doing. His mother and Joe were waiting for them next to a large tree in their red and white striped beach chairs. When Loretta saw them approaching, she got up, hugged Molly, and immediately asked to hold her grandbaby. Knowing better than to mess with Loretta when she was intent on something, Julie gladly unclipped Gabby from her seat and handed her over like a baked loaf of bread. As Loretta gazed down at her precious baby girl, her dark curls fell into Gabby's face just a smidge. Gabby squealed at the light and tickling feeling on her cheek.

When the game started, the Cordova-Horton clan sat unified in a straight line along the sideline across from the teams. The Stars' parents were across the field from the Stars' team and the Hurricanes' parents across from the Hurricanes' team.

Molly scored her first goal for the Hurricanes within the first three minutes of the match. Buddy stood quietly on the sideline, trying not to allow himself to get too worked up about anything that happened on the field. Normally, sports were the only thing that managed to get him worked up. But he kept whispering to himself these are little girls…this is just a rec league…don't be that guy… to be sure that he did not turn into that psycho alter ego who took over his body during an Atlanta Braves or a Carolina Panthers game.

"Why can't Molly just stay up by the goal and that big girl in the back kick it over everyone's heads to her?" Joe asked out loud. Observant. Realistic.

One of the fathers, a short and fat stubby looking man in a Yankees ball cap and a white golf shirt with the Pinehurst Putterboy logo answered, "They can't do that because it's off sides."

"What's off sides?" Loretta asked.

"It's when the first player on offense gets past the last defender without having the ball or being in receipt of the ball," he explained.

"But you can't…unless you somehow go past the goalie," Joe said.

"The goalie don't count," the man replied, and then assumed a posture of authority on all matters of soccer. "See, Number Seven on our team can't go past their last defender unless she beats her with the ball. The only way Number Seven cannot be off sides on a pass is if she's running – and not yet past the last defender – when the player on her team is kicking it to her."

Joe looked around and then grunted. Loretta laughed. "Well, I reckon I'm too old or too simple minded for this sport. That's awful confusing," he opined.

Yankees Hat agreed with Joe.

After Molly scored three more goals, and the Hurricanes were winning four to nothing, Buddy pulled her from the game. But then the Stars finally got a break and scored…and then another break and scored again. So, Buddy decided to put Molly back in the game.

"Listen, I need you to score one more for cushion, and then I'm gonna put you on defense for the rest of the game, okay?" Buddy explained to her.

"Can I score from defense?" she asked.

"Well, don't try to. Just don't let them score anymore."

"Number Four is the only one who has wheels," Molly stated glancing out over the field, observing every little thing that a seasoned adult fan of soccer would see.

Buddy laughed. "Wheels, huh?"

Molly was a marvel. Everything she did on the soccer field seemed to be at a different level than everyone else. She worked hard, played hard and thought hard. She was the player who was also the strategist. Buddy almost felt like he could leave her in charge of the entire game, and it would still turn out just fine for the Hurricanes.

After the game ended, they headed over to the Dairy Queen for some ice cream to celebrate the McDaid's Gravel Hurricanes sound butt whoopin' of the Dr. Horrace Orthodontics' Stars.

CHAPTER 9

September - October 1982

First Case

Buddy drove up to the County Courthouse in Joe's rust orange Chevy pickup, parked it across the street and walked inside. His best friend, James White, was sitting outside of the room holding Traffic Court, wondering what to do next. He was biting his fingernails, which were no doubt disgusting since he got out of auto shop class early to get to Court in time. Buddy was sure that James did not wash his hands before leaving.

"Man, I'm glad you're here," James uttered, watching Buddy walk toward him.

"Why are you sitting out here? You need to go inside because if they call your case, and you're not there to answer, you can get in all kinds of trouble," Buddy explained.

James handed him the summons and Buddy looked it over. "The State of North Carolina versus James T. White," he read aloud. If Buddy didn't know this was a speeding ticket, he would've thought that James murdered some family in the dead of night…right in their beds. He handed it back.

The boys walked inside of Courtroom One. It was the only courtroom in the whole place, so the fact that it had a number made Buddy chuckle to himself.

James held his summons tightly in the palm of his hands. It was only a speeding ticket, but if James' father found out about it, he would be in more trouble than he cared to think about. Mr. White was the Pastor of the First Baptist Church of Welby, and his children – all seven of them: Matthew, Mark, Luke, John, James, Paul and Lee Ann - were not allowed to get tickets or summonses or citations or anything indicating that they were…indeed…average American human teenagers. If they did any law-breaking whatsoever, then the Lord Himself would show up and strike them dead. Or, at least that's what Pastor White told them, and that's what they believed – even at sixteen years old.

While Buddy was not under the impression that the Lord cared to strike dead mostly well behaved teenagers over minor traffic tickets, he was afraid his good friend was going to suffer from a panic attack. So, he got excused from class early to help him out. Buddy was known for being resourceful and having a keen way of handling the kinds of situations that got anyone else worked up into a tizzy.

Judge Hauser, who won his sixth term last year, and who doubled as a fireman part time, sat on the bench. He watched Buddy and James, through his coke bottle thick glasses, walk inside and sit down. James was not represented because he could not afford a lawyer on his own, and the last thing he wanted to do was have his father find out about it if he tried to pay for representation. Word got around in a small town. Buddy informed him that he didn't need a lawyer for something like this. All he needed to do was ask for a Prayer for Judgment Continued. Since this was his first offense, and he had no driving record to speak of, maybe Judge Hauser would give him a mulligan. After all, being a Preacher's Kid must come in handy sometimes, especially among the God-fearing judges in this county. Of course, being the Preacher's Kid could also backfire.

After twenty minutes, the Clerk called James' case, and James stood with Buddy behind him.

"Mr. White, do you have representation?" Judge Hauser asked.

"No sir," he answered, too quietly.

"Have you spoken with the DA?"

James felt confused, so he turned his head and looked at Buddy. The District Attorney, who was just an assistant and appeared to be about a day out of law school, stood at the other table.

"Uh, no? I don't think so," he stammered.

"No, you haven't spoken with the DA," Buddy whispered.

"No," James stated more confidently.

"Your Honor, the State has not had the opportunity to talk with Mr. White about his options yet," the Assistant DA said.

"Okay, I'll allow you to confer briefly," he said.

The Assistant DA walked over to James, who was shaking at this point. Buddy couldn't imagine how bad off James would be if he had been charged with a real crime.

"I'll offer you a PJC," the young lawyer said to James, whose eyes started to bug out. "It's the best deal you'll get for a first-time speeding ticket. We won't dismiss it, not even for the Preacher's Kid. Otherwise, we'll go to trial and you'll lose and then face all penalties for losing your speeding ticket case. Which can be pretty harsh."

Buddy walked in between them and looked at James. "It's a Prayer for Judgment Continued," he started, "like I told you. You should take it and then drive like your Memaw for the next five years."

"Who are you?" the Assistant DA asked.

"Sorry, sir, I'm James' friend. He was just real nervous to come in alone and so I told him I'd come with him."

"Are you trying to advise him?"

"Well, yeah, I'm his friend. That's what friends do."

"How old are you?"

Judge Hauser interrupted. "What's going on? Did you give your offer, Mr. Stiles?"

"Yes, Your Honor. Mr. White is still deciding."

"But it's not fair. I wasn't speeding, and I don't see how the cop can say that I was when I wasn't," James whispered, starting to get upset.

"Look. Unfortunately, in Traffic Court, it's your word against the cop's and, well, the Court tends to side with the cops," Buddy explained. "Am I right?" he asked the lawyer, whose suit was a size too small around his middle and the bottoms of his pants rose about an inch above his dress shoes.

The Assistant DA nodded. "He's right."

"Just take it. It's a gift. Otherwise, you'll be back here fighting a losing battle and then your father will find out," Buddy whispered, trying to convince his friend.

"Mr. White, who is that with you?" Judge Hauser called from the bench.

Buddy felt his stomach twitch and straightened himself up tall. "Your Honor, my name is Jonathan Cordova, and I'm James' friend."

"Are you advising him?" Judge Hauser asked pointedly.

"Yes sir, I am, but just as his friend. I'm not a lawyer or anything."

"Mr. White, where is your father? Did he not want to come to Court with you today?"

"No sir, he don't know about all of this. I'm trying to deal with this matter myself – like a man," James answered, his knees about to give out – like a girl.

"Have you made a decision concerning the DA's offer? We don't have all day."

James looked at Buddy and then back at the Judge.

Buddy whispered, "Just take the PJC and be done with it. I'm tellin' ya, if you go to trial, you'll lose and then it will be so much worse."

James nodded. "Okay," he said to the Assistant DA.

Several minutes later, as Buddy slid back into Joe's truck to drive home and get started on his research paper on President Teddy Roosevelt for his American History class, the lawyer from inside the courtroom approached him.

"Are you a law student?" he asked.

Buddy peered out the crack in his window. "No. I'm still in high school."

The young man ran his hand through his thick light brown hair, moving his poorly cut bangs to one side, trying to make himself look older and more professional. "Well, you should really think about going to law school someday," he added and then walked away with his black leather briefcase bouncing off his leg, headed toward the DA's office, which sat just a block away from the Courthouse.

Right to Die

Kenny Bellinger's emaciated body, now at one hundred and twenty-six pounds, remained in a persistent vegetative state and lay dormant in a state-run long term health care facility in Bell County, Texas. He had no brain activity. He was fed through a tube. He was kept alive by machines.

No one ever came to lay claim to Kenny's care after he had been found shot and in a coma on his kitchen floor. His wife Retta and stepson Daniel vanished off the face of the earth. No one who knew them: Retta's best friend and co-workers, neighbors, young Daniel's friends, or Retta's family members had any clue what happened to them. Retta's brother and wife were never contacted by either of them. Retta's mother sat in New Jersey, waiting and hoping that one day her daughter would call her on the phone. But she never did. And neither did anyone else. The police talked with everybody they could find about Retta, her son, and the Bellinger marriage.

Kenny's sister never responded to correspondence or phone calls to her house, or what authorities thought was her house. No one knew the names of his parents or whether they were alive. His family was odd - scattered to the wind like a dead dandelion, as if his whole childhood had been nothing but an All-American blur. But that was the way it was with poor nobodies from no place. His younger brother had been killed in Vietnam – that had been verified by the Army. There was no human alive who cared one lick about the current state of being that was Kenny Bellinger. Except for one.

Hollis Foster was once Kenny's supervisor at a warehouse in Killeen. He liked Kenny a lot, both as a worker and as a friend, even when he could tell that he had a bad case of shell shock on a count of the war. He knew Kenny's drinking and poor behavior, which had escalated into violence and deteriorated over a long period of time, was a result of something that was beyond his control. He needed some help. Lots of the boys who came back from Vietnam needed some help.

Hollis was a devout Christian who believed that every earthly problem had a spiritual answer. He found that his Reverend was very encouraging and helpful to him during his trials, which included some shell shock of his own in World War II, the death of his lovely wife, and then the never-ending battle with the bottle. He wanted to get Kenny into the local AA, which was made up of a small group of men who met at his church and confronted their drinking head on through twelve steps and a lifetime of accountability. It strengthened his faith in God and the power of friendship and his resolve to conquer the demon drink. It was bad enough Hollis had to fire the young man when he crossed the line one too many times, but he had no choice. At the time, it became his mission to help Kenny not lose his family, too.

Since he convinced Kenny to go talk with his Reverend a few times, he was certain he'd be able to get him to start coming to the meetings as well. When he went to talk with Kenny about how things were going in his meetings and to invite him to AA, he found the front door unlocked and partially open, and Kenny lying near death on the floor.

Hollis ran through the small home and yelled for Kenny's tiny wife, Retta, and the young boy, Daniel, but they were nowhere to be found. He called the ambulance and the police, and ever since that day, he operated on a theory: Retta Bellinger got sick of her husband being drunk and unemployed and then beating on her and being a low life son of a bitch, so she took matters into her own hands and disappeared. While he understood that it must've been hard getting beat on, she shouldn't have shot him and left him for dead. That was just plain wrong. He deserved to go to jail, maybe, or he deserved to have her divorce him...but killing him? Hollis did not think that was right. Thou shall not kill.

For more than seven years, he wondered what happened to her and her boy and where they went to. And for seven years, he felt like Kenny needed at least one person in his corner. Maybe he'd never get justice, and then again, maybe he got what he deserved, but he was a good man once who served his country and worked hard to support a family. Now he lay like a hunk of broccoli under florescent lights on a slab – and no one in Texas or in the entire United States cared.

There was some kind of movement afoot about a person in Kenny's condition having a "right to die." Some young lady up north was living in the same kind of situation – alive in a bed for years but not really living at all – and her parents had been fighting the doctors to let her die. The doctors believe they are supposed to do everything they can to prolong her life, even it's a life hooked up to machines and lying on a mattress under some blankets. Her parents were fighting for her to be free from her suffering.

No one was around to fight for Kenny. There were no lawsuits in his name, no parents or family members visiting or holding his hand, no newspaper articles about his plight, and no one to lead his cause. Hollis felt like maybe he should be the one to do it. He should be the one to speak for Kenny Bellinger in some small way.

While he had no legal standing to file any lawsuits for his right to die or had any kind of Power of Attorney, he could pester the police about finding Kenny's wife, make some phone calls, and write his Congressman. He could come and see him sometimes, maybe talk to him awhile. Who knows? Maybe Kenny would wake up one day.

The Trouble with Girls

Buddy combed through his thin dirty blond hair and then smoothed it over with his hands. He looked at his watch. Time to go pick up Ginny Tart for their date.

A few weeks ago, he got up the nerve to ask Ginny to the Homecoming Dance. Ginny was a cute girl from a well-to-do family nearby. Her father owned three gas stations, which also had small markets and fast food grills inside of them. The burgers were tasty and very popular. People would drive all the way from Raleigh and Greensboro just to have one. Her father asked him to come work for one of the markets closest to Welby, and Buddy was still thinking about it. He liked his job at Joe's feed store but figured maybe it was better to impress Ginny's father, just in case things went well in their new courtship.

Ginny was studious, well behaved, traditional, and not loud and wild like some of the girls in school. While Buddy liked some of those wild girls, and wouldn't mind making out with some of them, they scared the bejesus out of him. Ginny wanted to go to Duke to study biology and had hopes of becoming a cancer researcher. Not many girls at Welby High School were that ambitious beyond getting their MRS degree and then having lots of babies, so Buddy found Ginny to be intriguing, certainly more intriguing than anyone else in his class.

She had strawberry blond hair, green eyes and long legs that were usually covered with appropriate length skirts or Bermuda shorts. She attended Pastor White's Baptist church, sang in the choir, and tutored kids enrolled in the After School Program at the elementary school. She was well bred and polite and had recently broken up with Rhett Butler Bailey, after about a year of going steady, over the past summer. The rumor in school was that Rhett Butler met a girl from Australia at Wrightsville Beach and messed around with her quite a bit behind Ginny's back. It all sounded a little too much like the movie Grease to Buddy, but he figured something like that could happen in real life, too. Only without all the singing and dancing.

Buddy liked Ginny because she was not just cute but also very smart. She could carry on in a real conversation about things that matter – things like politics, economics, books, the law, history. She thought Buddy was cute, too, and liked how he talked about his own ambitions that didn't include playing outfield for the Braves or becoming manager of Joe's feed store someday. He had bigger goals than the small town of Welby.

While Buddy wasn't from the same economic class, was maybe even a blond haired Mexican or something…with a name like Cordova…a bit of an outsider, and did not seem to be like all the flirty boys at school, Ginny saw in him a nice, polite boy with great earning potential.

Pulling up to Ginny's house in Joe's truck, Buddy eyed Mrs. Tart standing out in front of the porch with her Polaroid camera. Mr. Tart was, thankfully, nowhere to be found. When Ginny came outside, she was dressed in a beautiful, long royal blue dress, which did not show any cleavage and did not reveal much of anything else, either. While Buddy hoped to see something a bit more substantial, just like any red blooded American male, he was basically satisfied that she agreed to go to the dance with him at all. Ginny was pretty, but she wasn't too pretty. The ones who were too pretty were the girls who made his hands sweat and thought he didn't speak.

Mrs. Tart took some photos of them together, and they went off to the dance, where Pauline Hanes was later crowned Homecoming Queen and James' older brother John was crowned Homecoming King. Ginny mostly hung around her girlfriends throughout the night, dancing with Buddy just a handful of times during the slow songs, and Buddy stood around with James and his date. He thought they had a good time. Rhett Butler was there with a Freshman, and Buddy watched Ginny glancing over at them from time to time and then whispering something to her friends.

After the dance, he and Ginny had permission to go to a party held in a barn at a popular football player's family farm. The barn was known to have parties from time to time, but Buddy had never been to one before. There was a keg and some old beaten up couches sitting among bales of hay. A huge boom box with even bigger speakers sat propped up on a shelf near where there should be horses. "Celebration" by Kool and the Gang was blasting into the straw speckled nighttime air, and soon the place was filled up with teenagers still in their Sunday finest – all too nice for a barn.

Ginny started drinking beer from the keg, which surprised Buddy. He held a cup of beer himself, but after tasting it, realized he didn't like the taste, so he just kept it in his hand in order to look the part. After about an hour of watching Ginny drink paper cups of beer and dance with her girlfriends, Buddy checked his watch. It was almost her curfew, and the last thing he wanted do was bring her home late.

Ginny, obviously intoxicated, did not want to go home, but she reluctantly agreed. She knew that Buddy was right. She couldn't break curfew or else her parents would never let her come to another party…until she was thirty! When they arrived at Ginny's house, the porch light was on, as was the living room light. Her parents were upstairs. Mrs. Tart left a note on the couch that read: "Hope you 2 had a nice time. There are cookies in the kitchen."

Buddy was relieved that he would not be confronted with the reality that he brought Ginny home – on time – drunk. She went into the kitchen and got them each a cookie and then sat on the couch with her bare feet on the edges and her knees up to her chest. Buddy sat down next to her. She stuck the cookie in her mouth and motioned for him to come closer. Buddy was confused but realized that she wanted him to take a bite of the cookie while it was sticking out of her mouth. *That's a little gross*, he thought to himself. They hadn't even kissed yet, and Buddy wasn't the most experienced at kissing, let alone eating cookies straight out of girls' mouths.

He went in closer to her face and brushed her straight hair, which fell over her cheek, out of the way. He put his teeth on the half of the cookie sticking out toward him and bit down on it. She pulled the rest of the cookie into her mouth, then moved forward and started kissing Buddy. Buddy was a bit disgusted by the cookie crumb exchange going on between them, but he wanted to kiss her, and he could feel quite a boner developing underneath his dress slacks.

He adjusted his position next to her, and they started kissing heavy. Ginny put his arms around her waist. After several minutes of making out, Buddy's hands remained firmly on Ginny's waist. Sensing that he was afraid to move his hands, Ginny moved them to the front of her breasts. He felt himself become terribly overwhelmed with everything that was going on.

Buddy wished so badly that they were somewhere else, anywhere else – a private bedroom someplace far away or even inside the bed of Joe's truck would be better than this. They were kissing each other like new young lovers, but Buddy did not want to be disrespectful of Ginny or her parents in any way by going for second base – or third – or God, forbid a Home Run – on her family's couch! And while her parents and little sisters were right upstairs!

With his hands paralyzed on top of her B-cup sized breasts and resting on the fabric of her Homecoming Dance dress, Buddy decided that he should just keep them there until she moved them again. And then as if on cue, she moved his hands up underneath of her dress, and that was when Buddy decided to put a stop to everything.

"What's wrong?" Ginny cooed, her eyes barely opened and her face leaning into his.

Buddy was borderline speechless and trying to stop himself from breathing too heavily. He felt like he had just run a five-minute mile. The pop-up underneath of his fly was not going down at all, and he was afraid of what he might do next…either too much or nothing at all.

"Ginny, I'm sorry. Nothin's wrong, I just don't feel right doing this on your couch with your parents upstairs."

Ginny's face was in a dream-like state. "It's okay," she whispered. "I really want you to. I like you, and you're so cute." She started to move his hand up her thigh and then put her hand on his covered, but evident, erection.

Buddy pulled back and put his hands over his face. He was beet-red and felt scared, excited, and humiliated all at once. His head started sweating. "Ginny, I respect you and your family too much to do this here. Your parents are trusting me to act like an honorable man."

She scoffed. "You're kiddin' me, right? You don't want what's being offered?"

"I do, I really do. Can we maybe…I don't know…maybe go on another date, only somewhere by ourselves? Then I won't feel so strange."

Ginny sat back into the couch and pulled her dress down around her legs. "Are you a virgin or something?" she snapped at him, taking a deep breath and then standing up. She ran her hands through her hair and blurted, "It's okay, Buddy. I understand. You must be a virgin. I'm sorry about all this. It must be the beer that done it to me. I don't normally act so damn forward."

Embarrassed, Buddy stood up and kissed her cheek. "I better go, Ginny. Can I call you tomorrow?"

Ginny laughed. "It is tomorrow, dummy."

As Buddy slid into the driver's seat of Joe's truck out front of Ginny's house, he felt mortified. He had basically frozen up in his first and only actual moment of a sexual opportunity with a cute girl. He blew it. He wanted her but was so conflicted about not quite knowing what to do with her…and then also not wanting to take advantage of a girl who had too much alcohol in her. Not to mention in her family's living room, where they all no doubt watched The Love Boat together on Saturday nights.

Buddy drove back home to the small apartment he and his mother shared on Joe's land and prayed his boner would be long gone by the time he walked in.

When Monday rolled around, Ginny Tart wasn't speaking to him anymore and had told anyone who would listen that Buddy Cordova was too scared to try do anything with a girl. He was a virgin.

That reputation stayed with him until he left for Carolina two years later and got to start all over.

Unrequited Love

Joe's hands were hurting. Old man sore. He spent the day messing around in his deceased wife's beloved flower beds, which sat in front of his home, because he wanted to catch a glimpse of his sweet tenant Loretta Cordova now and again. He cleaned out a bunch of the dead summer flowers that he had neglected for too long, cleared several rows of new dark soil purchased from Hedrick's Hardware, and started to plant some bulbs he bought from the Garden Club's charity sale last week. It was time to put them into their winter niches, so it's not like he was just lingering around outside for no good reason. But he could have waited another couple of weeks before all this digging, and now he was afraid that he'd be stuck in bed for two weeks instead for overdoing it.

Loretta was off from work. She never went in on Mondays. The new ladies' hair salon she worked for over in Graham seemed to think that no one wanted to get their hair done on a Monday, so it was closed. Joe thought maybe he would knock on her door a little later and ask her if she'd give him a trim. He probably didn't need one quite yet, but it was one of the few good excuses he'd have in his back pocket to bother her on her day off.

He ran his hands into the loose ground and cursed himself for not wearing gloves. He knew he was not a young man anymore and that his body didn't work as well as it used to. He found himself with an aching back and pains in his legs that weren't there a year ago. Joe missed having a wife. He missed having a woman next to him in the mornings. He missed feeling loved. He missed making love. But he knew, more than anything, that he was deeply in love with this mysterious raven haired beauty who showed up in his driveway long ago with nothing but a paper bag and a little boy.

Mary Stuart Caldwell from his church had called on him one Sunday after service and asked him if he would mind hosting a homeless young mother and her child for a few months. He had an empty apartment on his land for a few years, and there were times when missionaries visiting the church or guests of neighbors would use it. He never minded. He was glad to help and open his home to his church, his neighbors, and his friends.

"I know that it's an awful lot to ask, but I would feel good knowing that they are safe on your property and that you'd be close by if there were a problem," Mary Stuart explained, when she approached him in 1975.

"Who are they?" Joe asked her, a bit confused about the odd request.

"They are just two of God's children who have hit hard times and they got nobody to help them, no kin to speak of. If I must, I will have them stay at my house until they're on their feet. But then I thought about how nice it would be for them to have some privacy, really a small place of their own, but with caring church folks nearby who can help them if they ever need it."

"Well, I guess it would be alright, Mary Stuart. But just for a few months. I don't mind helping someone in need, but I'm not sure about puttin' up strangers for an indefinite time-period," he decided.

A few months had now grown into seven years, and Joe was just as smitten with that magical woman since the day she arrived. Loretta was a lot younger than he was, but she seemed, in a lot of ways, more like a peer. He heard the ladies refer to that quality in a person as "an old soul." That was Loretta.

At times, they would have wonderful, thoughtful and revealing conversations on his front porch during cool evenings, and he felt like they were much closer in age. She looked young, but there seemed to have been an awful lot of hard living that aged her on the edges a bit faster than many of the women in Welby. She seemed to be way beyond her mid-thirties in years.

Loretta walked down the steps of the apartment on the chilly Fall afternoon. She wore a pair of blue jeans and a gray crew neck sweatshirt that he gave to her once during a rare snowstorm. She had never returned it. He recalled his heart flipping like a school boy when she accepted it and then kept it for herself. A piece of him, in the form of an old beat up sweatshirt, was now resting upon her; and every time he saw her in it, he hoped she could feel the love he had for her wrapped around her torso, like a secret, intimate hug.

She walked over to him in her normal rapid pace. "Hey," she said, approaching him.

Startled, Joe turned toward her and stood. He felt dizzy, only it was not the kind of dizzy that a man feels around a woman who melts him. He felt dizzy like something was wrong. As his body fell over onto its side, and he landed hard on top of all his handiwork, the last thing he remembered before everything went black was Loretta's hands on his forehead and then his face, her mouth near his chin, her breath near his ear and the comforting and beautiful dreams he quickly fell into.

He woke up in an ambulance, Loretta sitting at his feet. He could make out her curly dark hair resting on her shoulder and the nervous, strained look she carried on her face.

"Mr. Horton, we're taking you to the hospital in Chapel Hill, okay?" a young man in a crisp navy blue uniform spoke at him in slow, deliberate language.

Loretta looked over at Joe and then moved to be closer to his face. She peered into his crusty eyes and kissed his forehead and then his lips. "Damn it Joe Horton, don't you ever do that to me again. If you do, I will kill you myself!"

Joe tried to smile at her. He had no idea what had happened and why he passed out, but he knew that if Loretta Cordova had been the last thing he saw and the last thing he felt touching him in his small and quaint life, it would've been a great way to die.

CHAPTER 10

February - May 2001

The Rainbow Bridge

Molly's heart was racing and she was trying to get a hold on the tears falling, unfettered onto her freckled cheeks. She picked up the phone on the kitchen wall and called her mom, who was down at the church helping set up for the Keenagers' Valentine's Dinner-Dance. A local band, The Experience, specializing in Big Band and Swing music, was practicing its era-based melodies for the dancing portion of that night. Molly could hear the loud swaggy sounds in the background of her panicked phone call.

"Molly, I can't quite hear what you're saying. What's the matter? Tell me slow and loud," she shouted over the music, cupping her ear to the church's kitchen phone.

"It's Bo," Molly sobbed through the receiver. "He's not moving. He's just sitting there like a football on the floor."

"Where's Buddy?"

"He's with Bo, talking to him, trying to get him to move. But something's wrong." Molly's tears continued streaming, her fears mounting, her stomach clenching. Something was seriously wrong with Bo.

She watched Buddy try to move him slightly on his side, but Bo cried out. That scared Buddy enough. He went and found a blanket and said, direct and calm, "Molly, I need you to go next door and ask Mrs. Holiday if she can come sit with Gabby. We need to take Bo to the Vet. Right now."

Molly told her mother what was going on, and Julie hung up the phone, grabbed her purse from the church kitchen, and left the Glenn Miller tunes blaring behind her in all their glory.

Mrs. Holiday walked into the front door, her eyes wild with concern. Buddy and Molly carefully rolled Bo on the blanket, the old boy yelping out in pain. Buddy picked him up, cradling him in his arms. Molly held open the door to the backseat of the car and crawled inside with her old pal. As Buddy drove off, she buckled her seatbelt and bent over him, fresh tears falling onto his puffy golden head, petting his ears, and whispering, "I love you Bo. I love you, old boy. Don't leave us."

Julie pulled into the parking lot and jogged inside the Vet Emergency reception area. She found Molly sitting silently, her shoulders slumped over, all alone. No one else was in the reception area. *Lucky us*, she thought to herself. Soon, the Vet, a crisp, petite, platinum blond doctor named Dr. Leesa Leatherstike, came out from behind double doors and asked Julie and Molly to come back to a room. As they walked in, they saw Buddy sitting motionless with Bo's head resting up on his lap. His face said it all.

"It's called stomach bloat," Dr. Leatherstike explained. "It happens sometimes and comes on very quickly with no warning. But unfortunately, in Bo's case, his stomach has twisted as well. That adds an extra complication. Mostly due to his age."

"What does that mean?" Julie asked.

"It means that the only way to fix it is through surgery. And Bo here is already passed what we expect dogs of his mix and size to live. We can do the surgery, but it is likely that he won't survive it. Or if he does, the recovery period would be difficult enough to make his quality of life so bad that he'd be suffering."

Julie looked down at Buddy, who had his forehead up against Bo's head. Bo laid there, still and clearly in distress. The kindhearted but world-weary criminal defense lawyer looked up at Julie with sad and desperate tears glazing over his eyes. She and Molly watched, for the first time, this grown man they both adored, cry a real cry.

"I will do whatever you want me to do," Dr. Leatherstike added. "But remember, regardless of your decision…Bo has had a great, long life. And that's because of all of you and the love and home you gave to him." She stopped and sighed. "Our pets do not live long enough. And when it's their time, they take a piece of our hearts with them."

"What do you want to do?" Buddy asked Julie, his face full of angst. He was stuck in that curious kind of moment when you know what has to be done but not wanting to follow through with it, or not being sure you can. "I'm not euthanizing this dog without your say so. You have to agree."

Molly cried out, "What does that mean?"

"I'll leave you all alone for a bit to let you talk among yourselves," the Vet said and excused herself, her blond ponytail bobbing along the back of her lab coat as she walked away.

Molly's sobs grew louder. "What does that mean?" she asked again. But she knew the answer.

Julie pulled her brokenhearted daughter into her side and held her closely. She rubbed her hair with the tips of her fingers. "It means it's Bo's time. We're going to have to say 'goodbye' to him. He's suffering and it's not likely that he'll ever get well again."

Molly pulled away from her mom and bent down over Bo, putting her head along the middle of his furry body. She hugged him. Bo groaned. All three of them cried.

Several minutes later, Dr. Leatherstike came in with a syringe, and as big, loveable Bo shut his eyes one final time, Molly and Buddy held his head close to them and whispered to him that they loved him, that he had been the best boy, and to wait for them at the Rainbow Bridge.

Julie looked at her wrist watch. It was 4:23 PM on Saturday, February 10th, 2001.

Life, Interrupted

The rain swelled in true "April Showers Bring May Flowers" fashion. Julie Cordova gazed out the window of her kitchen while wearing her favorite black and neon green running outfit, the one Buddy bought her for their first anniversary. There were pink and white blossoms, wet but cheerful, sitting on the trees in her front yard. They looked like they just had a good cry after a sappy Hallmark Hall of Fame movie on a Saturday night.

Julie had been training all Fall and Winter long for a full marathon – her first one – and next Saturday was the big day up in Raleigh. Buddy, Molly, Gabby, and even Loretta and Joe would be there to cheer her on. Thankfully, Buddy and Molly did not have a soccer game to contend with until Sunday, all the way in Wilmington. But this was something Julie needed to do for herself. Sometimes a mom needs to remind herself that she is still allowed to follow her own dreams from time to time. She felt it was important that her daughters saw that for themselves.

Her well-worn running shoes were aching for a break in the rain so she could get in a smooth eight miles. Buddy took Molly and Gabby to a neighbor friend's birthday party at Chuck E. Cheese – Dear God, that man deserved a medal for that! - so she could do her training in relative peace.

Soon, the rain stopped and Julie headed out. Eight miles. That was it. As Julie took stride, with some early Nineties Garth Brooks crooning into her ears, she hit each step with perfectly timed momentum, creeping along the side streets, eventually making her way down to Triton Hills, just as she did for years. Only Gabe didn't run with her anymore. He let her run alone now.

He kept a piece of her heart beating by filling in the creases along all the scar tissue with his love and his memory, now a regular part of her every breath. Now, she ran with her wife and mother thoughts and the new life she had been able to build without him…with Buddy. And it was a good one. A great one. One to be proud of, one to sink her soul into, and one to grow old with. Gabe would've been both happy for her and proud of her for moving on…for living… really living.

As Garth's twang rang out through her ears, and he belted out one of her favorites from 1992, Julie's feet kept hold in a solid pace and form, her eyes fixed just in front of her on the wet paved road. She never heard the swerving gray Buick driven by the eighty-year-old retired Army officer who had just left his granddaughter's house nearby. She never felt the impact of the car as it struck her. She never knew that the brief flash of sunlight that darted through the parting clouds would illuminate the last waking breath she took on Earth.

Officer Dan Smelcher was a rookie with the Fayetteville Police Department, after having served in the Army for six years as an MP. He approached the Chuck E. Cheese, which was bursting, as usual, with rowdy kids on a typical Saturday afternoon. Birthday parties, exhausted parents, divorced fathers not knowing what to do with their kids on their every other weekend visitation schedule, and a few teenagers who had put together a Skee-ball tournament, all joined the chorus of youthful voices carrying the pizzas and cakes to long, packed tables.

The neighbor who saw Julie get hit by the Buick told Officer Smelcher that her husband and two children went to Chuck E. Cheese for a neighbor girl's birthday party. She was distraught and requested to ride along in the ambulance with Julie. But the paramedics told Officer Smelcher that Julie was probably bleeding internally, and they weren't sure if she was going to make it. She was unconscious, had to be revived once already, and they needed to get her to the hospital immediately, just in case there was any chance of saving her. It was best if the neighbor helped the police find Mr. Cordova and get him to the hospital instead.

As Buddy stood outside of the ball pit, where Gabby was attempting to climb out, he saw the party host point a policeman toward him and his heart about fell out of his chest. He knew that something bad had happened. Something real bad. The worst kind of bad.

Something had happened to his Julie.

Molly was in the arcade playing Ms. Pacman, and she had no idea about the scene unfolding near the ball pit.

"Mr. Cordova?" Officer Smelcher asked.

Buddy stood paralyzed with fear. *Just say it. Just fucking say what you have to say,* he thought to himself.

"Sir, your wife, Julie. Um, you need to come to Harper Hospital. She's been in an accident," he explained.

As if on cue, some invisible being must have come into his body, taking charge of his ability to function like an adult man. Buddy moved toward his toddler girl Gabby, herself a rotund ball of blond hair and fat cheeks, and picked her up out of the ball pit. His mind in a fog, his body robotic, he walked slowly over to the arcade, put his hand on Molly's bony back, and they walked out of the restaurant to their minivan, following Officer Smelcher to a place where his wife – his beautiful, loving, kind, perfect wife – lay dying in an operating room.

Awkward Introductions

With the worst pit in his stomach he had ever endured, Buddy picked up the phone and dialed a San Antonio, Texas area code. It rang three times. A woman's voice answered.

"Hello?"

"Uh. Hello. Is this Mrs. McVicar?" he asked, an almost insurmountable lump lodged in his throat.

"Yes," she replied.

"Hi. My name is Jonathan Cordova, and I'm your daughter's husband," he started.

There was a long pause on the other end of the line, something much larger than a pregnant pause. Buddy could feel the resentment, the unresolved pain and frustration that happens sometimes between two stubborn women…especially a mother and a daughter.

The estrangement between Julie and her parents was real. It was probably more between her and her mother than her and her father, but from what Julie told him, her father was one of those husbands who just did whatever his wife wanted him to do. Even if it included not talking to their own daughter. Buddy reckoned that her father was just a coward who had made his bed a long time ago, and now thought he was too old to do much about it without losing all his money and the life he worked for. So, he just did what his wife said and behaved however she wanted. It was easier that way.

Buddy saw lots of men like that in his law practice – men who took the easy way out by caving into their difficult women. Or, maybe these men just loved their women, plain and simple, and thought they were just making them happy. That was true, sometimes, too. They chose their battles and decided that most weren't worth fighting over. But your daughter?

Buddy understood that Julie and her mother were always at odds, especially when she hit her teenaged years. Julie had her own mind, her own goals, her own dreams, and they didn't include the ones that her mother had plotted out on a map and planned for her. Julie did not want to become a doctor, no matter how good she was at chemistry and biology. She did not want to apply to an Ivy League school. She did not want to compete in pageants, even though she had the right figure and the right hair color. She did not want to go out with the most eligible bachelor in San Antonio, the very one who pursued her as a seventeen-year-old in high school, no matter how good looking or how wealthy he was. Instead, Julie did what she wanted, and she was disgusted with her mother's head games and guilt trips and manipulative nature.

Against her mother's wishes, she enrolled at Texas A&M, and because her mother refused to help put her through college as payback for her defiance, or as her mother called it – "natural consequences" – Julie earned a partial academic scholarship and took out student loans all on her own.

And then really against her mother's wishes, she left Texas A&M half way through her Sophomore year because she met – and then married in a whirlwind weekend – a young enlisted soldier on leave visiting a friend in College Station. His name was Gabe Saint.

"Yes, I'm sorry. I didn't realize Julie remarried," Mrs. McVicar responded.

Buddy drew in a deep breath. "Mrs. McVicar, I am calling because I need to tell you something. Is Mr. McVicar with you?"

He could hear the air go out of the phone lines between them.

"Tell me," she said, directly, her voice taking on a different tone, the kind that explained to Buddy exactly what Julie was talking about when she referred to her mother as "Queen Bitch." But Buddy also sensed there was more to her tone than that. Mrs. McVicar probably knew that something horrible had happened to Julie. Just because a mother hasn't spoken to her daughter in several years, doesn't mean that the natural bond put there by God Himself was gone, too. It doesn't mean that she had lost hope that their relationship could be restored someday.

Buddy's voice wavered, and the lump in his throat almost took over his ability to speak entirely. "Julie. She, um." He stopped.

His voice became hoarse and he was overcome with emotion. "She was in an accident. Yesterday. She passed away. She didn't make it." When Buddy spoke those last few words, he started to cry, his voice unforgiving. She didn't make it. The tears which he had managed to hold back while performing all these death-related tasks so far, escaped his eyes and down the sides of his nose. He caught them with the back of his hand.

There was a long silence on the other end of the line, and Buddy knew that no matter what bad blood had been between Julie and her mother for the last twenty years, every mother loves her daughter and every mother expects her daughter to outlive her. Mothers don't expect their children to die without ever having had made their peace. There is always tomorrow, right?

Until there isn't.

When Buddy got off the phone with Mrs. McVicar, he felt like he checked off one more horrible box on his To-Do List From Hell. He told Molly, check. He told his mother and Joe, check. He told Julie's parents, check.

He had a lot more phone calls to make and things to do, all things he never imagined even during the darkest of random thoughts that passed through his mind from time to time. Julie dying just before her thirty-third birthday was not something that was supposed to happen. They were supposed to raise their girls together, grow old together.

The next day, Connors Funeral Home sent over the funeral director to go over the arrangements with Buddy. Julie would be buried in Memorial Gardens, near downtown. Since Gabe was buried in Arlington, that removed the otherwise strange conflict Buddy would have about where to bury Julie. Since she considered Fayetteville home now, and he did as well, this would be where her final resting place would be. Not in Texas, no matter what her mother demanded. And he was prepared for that fight if it happened.

Because Julie was so young, she did not have a Will or even a Power of Attorney. She didn't even have a document that specified the care of Molly or designated Molly's guardianship should she die or be incapacitated. Young people simply did not think about stuff like that. Buddy planned to adopt Molly, but they just hadn't gotten around to it yet. There was always time, right?

Until there isn't.

Buddy wasn't a family law attorney, but he knew enough to know that legally, Molly was now an orphan. So, the first thing he needed to do, as soon as the first part of this soul-crushing experience was done, was head to the Cumberland County Courthouse to petition for custody of Molly. He needed to be able to have legal standing for all aspects of her care, and the last thing he wanted was for some social worker to step in and make a mess for them all.

Tammy Jo McVicar

Julie's wake and funeral were desperately sad affairs. Other than perhaps the death of a small child, the untimely and accidental death of a young mother in the prime of her life is the very definition of a true tragedy. While Buddy knew that life was not fair… for anyone, really…and that suffering does not discriminate among "good" people and "bad" people, that piece of rational knowledge did not mitigate his own pain and grief whatsoever. It doesn't matter if you were young, beautiful, a mother, a teacher, a kind and loving soul, a good and caring person who worked hard for her entire life. Death comes for everyone and it is never pretty, never fair, and never quite expected.

Tammy Jo and Jed McVicar were a well-to-do couple from San Antonio, Texas. Jed had a successful career in real estate development and recently retired to work on his golf handicap and exercise his left arm with a glass of draft beer at the clubhouse after each round. Tammy Jo was a big personality with her own successful real estate brokerage firm. The two of them together were quite the power couple, although Jed came across as the quiet and stoic type, who was known to answer tough questions with appropriate-length grunts.

As soon as Buddy met Tammy Jo, he could see why Julie felt like she needed to break away and be her own woman, somewhere else… far away. It would be difficult to be the daughter of a woman who was clearly used to being the center of attention, was always demanding things of others to fit however she wanted it to work out for her, and came across like she believed she owned everything by virtue of the fact that she worked hard for it and wanted it. It was as if "Girl Power" and the "American Dream" were on steroids and all packaged into one high maintenance woman…Tammy Jo McVicar.

There was a simmering anger under her appearance, almost a big chip on her shoulder, like she felt that she should be the one running this awful macabre show. Buddy was not one for family confrontations, so he remained polite and cordial all times, not wanting to make any waves, especially when all he really wanted to do was crawl into bed and cry like a baby.

"Dear Molly, darlin', I'm so happy to finally see you again. It's been so long. The last time I saw you, you had about two whole words in your vocabulary! I'm so sorry that our reunion has be like this," she cried, pulling Molly into her bosom like any grandmother would do even under the best of circumstances.

Molly hugged her back. She was quiet and shy but knew that this woman was her mother's mother. And she was certain that her grandmother loved her, no matter what happened within her family long ago. Julie would always read her the cards that would come in the mail each birthday and would allow her to keep the small gifts. Molly was allowed to write a Thank You note to her grandparents. But that was it. One gift at her birthday. One gift at Christmas.

Jed held Molly tightly. He cried. Buddy could see that there was a lot more to Jed McVicar than just being a "Yes Man" for his wife. His heart was broken, and a lifetime of regret was firmly encamped across his face.

"Molly, I've missed you for your whole life," he whispered through the tears making their way down his cheeks. He had Gabby sit on his lap, like grandfathers do, and bounced her up and down. Gabby giggled. He read her Are You There, Baby Bear? three times, just like Gabby wanted. He sat on the floor with both girls and watched Disney's Beauty and the Beast for the first time in his life.

Tammy Jo and Buddy sat in the kitchen holding their respective coffee mugs full of cold coffee, where she proceeded to tell him about the difficult and complicated relationship she had with her daughter, his wife.

"Julie was a good girl. She never gave me any trouble until she was older, like most teenaged girls give their mothers trouble," she explained. "You just wait 'til those girls hit puberty, I tell ya. You just don't know until it happens to you." Her hair was blond and routinely professionally manicured. She was about thirty-pounds overweight, but Buddy could see that Julie looked an awful lot like her mother.

She held her mug in between highly polished mauve colored fingernails. "I loved my daughter, Jonathan. I loved her so much. But I was not going to give my approval of her choices when I did not – in fact – approve. Nowadays, all parents do is give their blessing to their child's every whim, running here and there for them, going to ridiculous extremes for them, poo-pooing every bad decision they make, bailing them out and excusing everything, enabling their poor behavior. Trying to be their friend when they're supposed to be their parent. I took a stand. And I kept it." She breathed in deeply and continued, "I hoped that Julie would come around when she had her own child, maybe see how hard it is to be a mother, maybe be able to put herself in my shoes."

Tammy Jo wiped a tear off her right eye socket and quieted her voice into a dulled sadness. "Lots of my friends told me that that's what happens with daughters who grow up. They start to appreciate their mothers' sacrifices and the difficult choices they had to make as women. And I think she would've gotten there eventually and then would've wanted to mend fences with me. But she wasn't there yet, and she was too stubborn for her own good." Some more tears streamed down her face, taking a shred of mascara with them. "And now she's gone," she uttered through her pain.

Buddy sighed to himself. Tammy Jo might have felt that she was right…but at what cost? Stubborn is as stubborn does, and she had been just as stubborn as she claimed her daughter to be. It was always interesting to Buddy how people could point out the behavior in others that they hated…but were never able to see the exact same behavior in themselves.

"Well, I can tell you that no matter what happened between the two of you, she was the most wonderful woman, wife and mother I knew. She was the only woman I've ever loved in my entire life." Buddy wore his suffering on his face but kept his emotions in check. He found that state-of-being Pink Floyd called "comfortably numb."

Tammy Jo sighed again. "I hate that we never reconciled, believe me. It bothered me every day that passed by. But when she married that soldier after barely knowing him…and dropped out of college to do it…I was devastated that she'd do that to me. To herself. No wedding, not even an introduction! Everyone back home thought she had gotten herself knocked up!"

Buddy couldn't understand women in general, but this kind of thinking pattern was completely out of this world within his own mind. While it isn't necessarily the smartest thing to do when you're only twenty years old…to drop out of school to run off to Vegas and marry someone you just met…it certainly wasn't a reason to stop speaking to your young adult child.

"But it had nothing to do with you, Mrs. McVicar. She was just a young woman in love."

"It was stupid. To marry some lower enlisted soldier who made peanuts for a living and who was gonna go off to fight in wars and maybe die and leave her widowed and all alone. To throw away your future for a weekend infatuation. To act like you're the star of some poorly-written romance novel."

"She didn't throw away her future. She just did things differently. It didn't have some perfectly straight path is all. I mean, look at what she did with her life. She was a mother, a well-respected and admired Kindergarten teacher, a regular volunteer at the veteran's hospital. And she and Gabe, from what she told me, were a happily married couple."

"The only good thing about that whole mess is Molly. That man ended up breaking her heart, just like I knew he would."

Buddy was perplexed. "But he died. In an accident. He died serving his country. He didn't go willingly. It could've been a random car accident, just like Julie's. And don't you think there's honor in that? Dying in the service of your country? A part of him that Julie loved was the part who sacrificed for something larger than himself."

"I'm sorry, Jonathan, but I do not find honor in dying by putting yourself in harm's way when you have a wife and child. Jumping out of planes is far too risky. If you want to live like that, then fine. But don't add a wife and child to the mix, knowing that one false move and they're on their own having to fend for themselves." Tammy Jo's voice was quite solidified on this matter. She was not viewing what Gabe Saint did for a living as anything but selfish.

He admitted to himself that he'd never heard that kind of perspective on our American heroes before; it gave him pause. Buddy lived in a town full of flag-waving, so this was quite a revelation to him. There were Americans, hell – Texans! – who felt this way about married soldiers serving our country.

Buddy could tell that Tammy Jo was an opinionated, strong-willed and feisty woman who took no shit from anyone. He saw that in Julie as well, but it was done with a certain elegance, humility and grace. Julie had mastered that "strong woman" label but did so in a way that did not make people piss their pants. Tammy Jo obviously scared people. She was a bull in a china shop. She was probably so successful with her real estate business because her clients were too scared to not do everything she said, exactly how she said it. Like everyone else, except for Julie, they got in lock-step with her directives. He sensed that she wasn't a bad person and had good intentions, but she was a "my way or the highway" kind of person.

Buddy got take-out Chinese for everyone in the early evening, and the McVicars left to spend the night in their hotel. They made plans to come to see the girls again the next day before they caught a plane back to San Antonio. Since Buddy knew he had to deal with a delicate situation, he convinced his mother and Joe to go home after the funeral and reception and indicated that he'd be in touch after the McVicars left.

Later that evening, Tammy Jo got out of the shower, changed into a nightgown and watched her husband switch between the news and sports on the hotel cable TV. She decided in that moment that while she may have lost her daughter forever, she was not going to lose her granddaughters. She was not going to go back to Texas without an agreement that these children know their grandparents.

Transitions

Loretta spent the day after Julie's funeral cleaning out the apartment above the barn on Joe's property. She had so many memories in that small home she had shared with Buddy for so long, and now it was time to allow them to make room for a new young person. Joe decided to rent out the apartment to a young man who was attending Carolina as an undergraduate, and he asked Loretta to get it ready for him.

She packed up the handful of things that were hers, things she never got around to moving into Joe's house. Buddy's things were long gone, but as she pulled a box out of the bedroom closet, she came across one of his drawings from art class, something he drew soon after they arrived in Welby many years ago.

Buddy had been quiet, more than ever, for several months after they fled from Texas and Kenny's tirades. When they arrived in North Carolina and moved their handful of items into Joe's apartment back in the Fall of 1975, she enrolled the newly-christened "Jonathan Cordova" (no middle name) into Welby Elementary School. It took him a while to adjust, at least emotionally, to his new life, new name, and new surroundings. He had to give up his father's name, but she told him that he could still go by "Buddy." That wouldn't hurt anyone or give them away in the least, and it allowed the boy to maintain at least one small piece of himself from his past life.

Buddy was no artist. Most parents "ooh" and "ahh" over their children's artwork, even when it's terrible. Even when you can tell that the child has not one lick of talent whatsoever. When Loretta tried to "ooh" and "ahh" over Buddy's horrible drawing, he looked up at her cockeyed and deadpanned, "Mother, this sucks. I can't draw. No need to be lying about it. We have to lie enough as it is." Honest nine-year-old boy strikes again.

The drawing was what appeared to be a tractor in what appeared to be a field of plowed cornstalks. Probably something he noticed somewhere on his way out to North Carolina. God knows they passed by and through enough fields on that trip across the country. There was a stick figure wearing a hat and another stick figure with long black hair. She was never quite sure what this scene was supposed to be, and maybe she had read into things too much simply because she was a woman. But what she did notice was in the bottom right-hand corner. Buddy wrote the initials "DKJ." And after that, any drawings she saw or school papers that came home, he scribbled, "Jonathan Cordova" or "JC" instead.

Maybe he saw that final scene somewhere through the eyes of a boy named Daniel, and then at some point, he accepted that the lens through which he saw his life from that point on would be through the eyes of a new boy named Jonathan.

After he drew that picture and seemed to have accepted his new identity, Loretta found him standing in the bathroom on a Saturday morning with a pair of scissors held up to his eyes. The sight caught her off-guard.

"Buddy, what in the world are you doing?" she gently snapped, afraid to scare him and then make him jump and gouge himself in the eye with the scissors.

He stood still and she could see him slowly closing the blades with a doctor's precision. "Shhhh. I'm trying not to stab myself in the eye."

"Buddy, put those down. What in the heck are you doing to yourself?"

He pulled the scissors away from his face and informed her, "I'm trimming my eyelashes."

Loretta knew that those eyelashes were one thing that made her sweet boy stand out from all the rest. They were his daddy's eyelashes, a rare gift from the God of Genetics. "Why in the world would you ever cut your eyelashes?"

He glanced over at her and stated, "Because they belong to some person named Daniel Kaspar Junior."

Thankfully, after that one time, Buddy never cut his eyelashes again. But that image of him trimming away that special feature tore her heart in two. She didn't want him to think that shredding his name meant that he had to shred himself, too.

Loretta met Julie's parents for the first time at the wake and was quite impressed with the outgoing and not-at-all shy Tammy Jo McVicar. She tried to put herself in Tammy Jo's shoes – that of a grieving mother who never got to reconcile with her now-deceased daughter. And she would never be able to make that right. She couldn't imagine being estranged from her child like that, but the older she got, the more she knew that life was never really that cut and dried or black and white.

While she understood that Julie did not speak to her parents and they hadn't seen Molly in several years – and Gabby at all for that matter – she was sure that Julie had her reasons. And that a lot of times, miscommunication or misunderstandings mixed with stubbornness has a way of making some situations worse than they needed to be. All it takes is one person to give the other a break or one person to admit they're wrong and apologize.

Tammy Jo had been friendly with her and asked a lot of questions. She asked where she was originally from (New Jersey), where Buddy's father was (dead), how she met Joe (landlord), how long she lived in North Carolina (a long ass time), had she ever been to Texas (yes). The Texas answer was tricky for her because the truth was that she spent over a decade in Texas. But she needed to keep it strictly Vietnam War-years related. Last thing she needed was having her Texan past exposed, at least any part of a tie to one Kenny Bellinger.

"I love how hair dressers always have the best hair themselves," Tammy Jo bubbled out in conversation. "You know how they say that the cobbler's kids have no shoes? That mentality don't seem to apply to hairdressers and dentists," she explained. "Hair dressers have the best hair and dentists have the best teeth, as do their children."

"So do plastic surgeons. Did you ever notice how plastic surgeons are not only gorgeous but their wives are too?" Loretta shared her own observation.

"You're right. I didn't think about that one! But yes, yes, you are absolutely right. I know two plastic surgeons and they are both very handsome…too handsome almost. And their wives? Wow. Beautiful women. Flawless."

"Well, you have to advertise your work. You can't be cuttin' and coloring women's hair while looking like you go to a men's barbershop for your own maintenance."

Tammy Jo asked a lot of questions about Molly: how Molly was doing in school, how she was so surprised to learn that she was a soccer player, if she ever asked about her grandparents in Texas. She didn't seem quite as interested in Gabby, which seemed a little odd to Loretta. After all, Gabby was her grandchild too. Gabby was her blood too. Of course, she knew nothing of Gabby until a few days ago.

Molly was the grandchild she knew she had and, for eleven years, pined for that missing piece of her heart. Loretta tried to empathize but couldn't. She had no idea what it must've felt like to know you have a grandchild out there and be basically barred from her life – just because you were a little difficult or complex or mouthy about your opinions. Maybe Julie had been too hard on her mother.

If only all of life's problems could be solved in the mind of a woman as she worked around a house, completing chores. She supposed that most women cleaning and doing laundry on this day that Loretta stripped the queen-sized bed in the bedroom, vacuumed the carpet, made sure the bathroom had a good once-over. She couldn't remember the last time someone used the bathroom in this place. She wiped down the kitchenette and mopped the floors. She dusted the furniture and tested the TV out, just to be sure it still worked. The young man was moving in the next day, and she wanted it to look as fresh and inviting as it was for her the day she and Buddy moved in. The place had been good to them. More than good to them. That place gave them life again.

Unsolved in America

Tammy Jo sat down on her plush beige couch and picked up the remote control to the TV. She was looking forward to an early evening in after a painful two weeks, having to bury her daughter without any resolution to their issues, having to say goodbye to those precious grandchildren who she has never had the opportunity to spend any real time with, and having to be nice and friendly to a bunch of people she did not know at all. She found herself to be surprisingly fond of Jonathan and thought he seemed like a good man, but he was just a low rent criminal defense lawyer working out of his house in an ugly military town that had too many bars and strip joints and pawn shops. She would have had more respect for him as a professional if he was a judge or a prosecutor or worked in some private firm making real money.

The fact that his nickname was "Buddy" was also annoying. He didn't fit the stereotype of a guy with that name. Any "Buddy" she ever knew was big and heavy and sat his ass on a tractor, chewing a toothpick or a pack of Skoal. Buddy was no name for a grown man trying to be taken seriously in a court of law.

His mother Loretta appeared to be a nice enough lady and that Joe she was with was handsome and charming. Deadly combination when a good rural southern drawl was thrown into the mix.

But those grandbabies. Those were hers too. And Julie had kept them from her all these years, especially Molly. That was just plain unfair. She had never been abusive or had a pill popping addiction or a drinking problem like so many other mothers out there she knew. She worked hard her whole life and helped provide for her daughter and set a proper example of a modern woman who had it all…because she earned it all. Own your own business, make your own money, demand respect from those around you, and look good all times. Study at good schools, take advantage of your privileges, reach your potential, make your own way, but do so with style. Then when you meet Mr. Right, you can choose him…because you don't need him. You can marry for love instead of for security. You do not have to submit to anyone or fill some predestined chauvinistic role in life.

She tried so hard to impart her values to her daughter, and what was her thanks for all her efforts? Tossed aside for some random low life Julie met on a weekend. It was unfathomable. And to keep her from her grandchildren? Now that was cruel and unusual punishment.

Before she and Jed left North Carolina to go back to Texas, she talked with Jonathan about possibly allowing Molly to come down to their home for Spring Break so they could get to know her. And if that went well, maybe both girls could come visit for a while over the Summer. These were innocent enough requests, and Jonathan agreed to think about it and talk with Molly to see how she felt about the idea.

Well, to her, that was ridiculous. He should simply tell her that she was going to spend some time with her grandparents, and that's the end of it. No need to ask an eleven-year-old girl's permission! That was what was wrong with modern parenting. Too much "talking it over" and allowing children to make major decisions for themselves when they don't know anything.

As Tammy Jo turned on one of her favorite true crime TV shows, her guilty pleasure called Unsolved in America, she sank down into the couch and pulled her brown and light blue afghan quilt over her legs. She was beat. Physically and emotionally exhausted. All she wanted to do was lie like a piece of raw steak on the couch all night long and not be bothered with her grief and regret and the anxiety peppering her otherwise tough interior.

"Next on Unsolved in America, a cold case out of Killeen, Texas from May 1975," the regular narrator spoke in his deep, well-trained baritone radio voice. Tammy Jo loved the cases from Texas because she could always remember hearing about them when she was younger. In an alternate universe, she was a police detective, a hard-nosed bossy female in a pressed dark blue pants suit and pumps wearing latex gloves and handling questionable firearms with chalk outlines on the floor around her. She was a ballistics specialist and a blood spatter expert and a DNA forensic witness.

"In 1975, the country was still recovering from its Vietnam War years and no place was spared that challenge…especially Army posts like Fort Hood….home to the United States Army's lauded First Cavalry Division. Corporal Kenneth Bellinger was a Purple Heart recipient, having been medically discharged due to his war time injuries during his service in Vietnam. Not long after his release from the Army, he settled down in Killeen with his new bride, a young war widow named Retta Kaspar and her young son Daniel. Daniel went by the family nickname Buddy." Tammy Jo winced. Not another Buddy.

"On May 16th, after a former co-worker and friend named Hollis Foster stopped by to visit the family, he found the front door unlocked and Kenneth Bellinger crumpled on the floor of his kitchen, unresponsive and covered in blood. Finding a faint pulse, Hollis called the ambulance."

The narrator's voice added a certain dramatic flair to about every third word, Tammy Jo decided. It made otherwise boring sentences sound so much more intriguing. She often did things like that while watching this show, pick apart the storytelling and figure out which side the producers were trying to highlight in the best light to the audience. So far, on this Killeen case, she wasn't too sure.

"Mr. Bellinger had been shot in the chest and head, and his wife and stepson were nowhere to be found. There was no forced entry, and nothing was missing from the house except for Retta, Buddy and the family's 1970 Duster."

"Hmmm, that's an odd coincidence," Tammy Jo said out loud to herself. Retta and Buddy. Buddy's mother's name was Loretta.

As the faux TV detective persona started to take over, Tammy Jo found herself doing some mental math in her head. 1975. Buddy was thirty-five. Or abouts. Loretta? No idea. Her Joe was older than she was – that was obvious. Maybe she was fifty. Probably older if Buddy was thirty-five. Who knows? Tammy Jo was never very good at identifying a woman's correct age. Good Lord, stop with this rabbit trail and enjoy the show, Tammy Jo.

The episode cut to an interview of an elderly man, a former detective on the case. "We learned, after speaking with Mrs. Bellinger's co-workers, that the Bellingers had a volatile marriage."

"Retta would come into work at the salon many times with bruises and cuts that were not due to accidents. We all knew that Kenny was beating her. But no one did nothin' about it. I tried to talk to her one time, but she told me to mind my own business," a woman, who appeared to be around sixty years old and three hundred pounds explained. The name "Marlene Jackson" popped up on the screen as she sat back in a large chair.

"The family was not known to own a gun, so if Retta shot him, the gun had to have been brought into the house," the detective explained. "No gun was found at the crime scene, but the ballistics showed that it was a handgun. A neighbor had reported his handgun missing a couple of days after Mr. Bellinger was found. But our office wasn't able to match that gun with the bullets taken from Mr. Bellinger's body during surgery."

Tammy Jo faintly remembered this story when it first happened. She was a young mother at the time, working part time doing title searches for an old, nasty lawyer who smelled like cheap cigars and would always hit on her, inviting her out to dinner and to lawyer social functions. Jed was big time by then and Tammy Jo had a few extra hours on her hands to do normal things like read the paper. It was just a short article in the news about a man found shot near Fort Hood and a wife and son missing. She never thought about it again because no one wrote about it again. People got shot and disappeared all the time, especially in military towns or in places close to the border.

After several interviews with the elderly police detective and the man who found Mr. Bellinger in his house, photos of Retta Bellinger and Buddy Kaspar were displayed prominently on the screen with a phone number serving as a tip line set up by the show.

The narrator summed up the show's theory: "It's believed that Retta and her son Buddy found a way into obscurity and may be living under assumed names. For many years, there were rumors of women's organizations and societies throughout the United States hiding battered women and their children fleeing abusive husbands. However, there's been no concrete proof of such groups. In 1975, Retta Bellinger was a hair dresser in a small salon. She might still be a hair dresser in a salon today."

Then they showed photos of age progression. "This is a likeness of what Retta Bellinger would look like in 2001, at fifty-four years old." Tammy Jo almost choked on her tongue at the sight of the woman. Then came a photo of Daniel Kaspar, Junior. It was, without a doubt in her mind, Julie's husband Jonathan at thirty-five years old, sans the hair style. The age progressed photo had brown hair grown out with a neat part on the side. Jonathan had a high and tight haircut with lighter hair. But the face. The jawline. The shape of the eyes. The eyelashes. Retta. Buddy. Loretta. Buddy.

And then it hit Tammy Jo like a bolt of lightning. Buddy was thirty-five years old. Loretta was a fifty-something year old hair dresser. They had lived in Texas a long time ago. And those photos looked a helluva lot like the Loretta and Buddy living quietly up in North Carolina.

She started hyperventilating. *There is no way that this is happening right now.*

Tammy Jo's heart raced and her thoughts became jumbled in her head. She knew that she had missed her calling by not becoming a police detective. And now she was going to reckon all of it with a twenty-six-year old cold case out of Killeen, Texas.

"No, this cannot be possible!" Tammy Jo yelled at the huge green plant in the corner, which appeared to want to respond to her.

Jed walked into the room. "What can't be possible?"

"Julie's husband!" she stood up and shouted into a high pitch.

"What about him?"

"He's not him! He's not Jonathan!"

Jed put his hands on his hips and cocked his head. "What in the hell are you talkin' about TJ?"

"Buddy…er…Jonathan! He's not really Jonathan! He's that boy right there!" she hollered, almost in a full-blown panic attack, pointing to the photo of a young Daniel Kaspar, Junior on the television. He was a boy with a buzz cut and a sweet round face and long eyelashes, wearing a yellow collared shirt and holding a small American flag at a parade.

"Call Phil! Call him right now!" Tammy Jo yelled at her husband who stood at the foot of the TV, watching the show, his face remaining in a contorted mass of confusion.

"Call Phil, why?"

"I want him to put an investigator on those people. And I want to know my rights."

Jed stood silently in front of the TV with his eyes fixed on the sad old story in front of him. A Vietnam veteran who wasted away in a state facility for almost ten years, until finally succumbing to his mortal wounds. A woman who got away with shooting him and leaving him for dead. A mother and son who disappeared and remained on the run for twenty-six years. Surely, this was Tammy Jo being her usual over-the-top crazy self, right? Anything to make a mountaintop out of a simple coincidence? Anything to make a stink and be the center of attention?

"You want to know what rights?" he shouted over at her as he heard her fumbling around in the study in the next room.

"I want to know my rights about Molly. We are her grandparents and that fraud of a man ain't her father. I want to know if we can make him give us our granddaughter, the only thing we have left of our own daughter."

And with that, Tammy Jo stormed out of the study and picked up the phone in the kitchen, dialing furiously.

"You've reached the Law Offices of Phillip Crenshaw," the young female voice stated in an answering machine greeting on the other end of the line.

When the beep beeped, Tammy Jo blurted into the phone, "This is Tammy Jo McVicar! I need to speak with Phil as soon as possible, please. This is urgent! Please have him call me immediately after getting this message."

Soda Cans

Loretta washed her hands slowly in the sink, observing the older gentleman who just waltzed into the reception area. Most of the folks who walked into this salon were young coeds at Carolina... and the occasional boyfriend in desperate need of trim, per the coed's opinion.

Loretta worked at Tar Heel Hair and Nails for almost ten years and found it to be like a second home...or a third or a fourth...she lost count of her homes by this point. She was the Salon Mom or the

Den Mother to all the stylists and estheticians, some young mothers and some simply young and single.

There was much more money to be made on Franklin Street in Chapel Hill than in the rural small town of Welby. The privileged college students who attended this upscale state school seemed to have a lot of disposable income, which was odd to Loretta, and the girls who came into the salon spared no dollar on good hair and a fine French manicure or pedicure and foot massage.

"May I help you?" Liz, the receptionist, asked the man. He was large, broad shouldered, and had a head full of gray hair. He wore a long dark coat, unbuttoned due to the unseasonably warm day outside.

"Yes, ma'am, I'd like to get a trim, please. Do you take walk-ins?" he asked. Loretta noticed his accent was deep South, almost Cajun.

"Loretta?" she called over. "Do you have time for a men's trim?"

Loretta eyed the man peering back over at her. He was completely out of place in this salon and on this street and this time of day. Something inside of her squeezed slightly – a twinge of what exactly, she didn't know. She hadn't had a feeling like that in a long, long time. Dread? Awkwardness? Suspicion? She had no idea.

Something was off, though.

"Sure do," she replied and patted her chair on the back.

The man walked over and sat down. She put a huge teal colored plastic cape over him to catch any stray hairs from collecting on his coat. His hair wasn't very long and didn't appear to need much of a trim to her, so she asked him what he was looking for.

"I'd like a military style cut," he answered. "What do they call it?"

"A high and tight."

"Yes, a high and tight will do me just fine."

"My son wears a high and tight, and I find it to be very attractive on most men."

Loretta thought that a high and tight on a man his size, who appeared to be well into his sixties, probably looked stupid…mostly because his face was too fat and his skin was too haggard. But she wasn't one to judge male hair styles too harshly – unless they had those fake blond spiked tips on the top. That was just a dumb hairstyle on a man. She liked haircuts that looked traditional and not too trendy.

"So where are you from, sir?" she asked him, trying to make him feel comfortable with hair dresser lady chit-chat. "You sound Cajun to me."

"I grew up in Louisiana."

"How long have you lived up here?"

"Oh, I don't live up here," he replied. "I'm visiting my daughter at UNC," he stated proudly. "She's a senior."

"Would you like a Coke? Or wine? We like to offer our guests something to drink," Loretta explained, briefly taking a sip of her own Diet Coke sitting on the counter in front of them.

"A Coke would be good."

Loretta handed him a cold can from the mini fridge next to her station.

"You must be so proud," Loretta continued, indeed knowing what it felt like to have a child graduate from that fine institution… twice.

Loretta felt much more at ease now; this man was out of place in this salon, but he was just a daddy in town. "What's she studying?"

"Well, she is completing her degree in social work. I think she's going to apply to AmeriCorps when she's done."

"What's AmeriCorps?"

"It's like the Peace Corps, only in the United States instead of foreign countries. The young people get assigned to low income regions of the United States for a year. Or two. It's a great experience for them. Makes them appreciate what they have and where they come from, I think," he continued.

"Wow, that is wonderful. I've never heard of that before. I guess it must be like how Legal Aid is for lawyers?" she asked.

"Something like that, I'm sure."

"My son is a lawyer, and he works with low income people needing representation in court. I have always been so proud of him and how he gets to do what he loves but is also helping people at the same time. Do you know that movie with Gregory Peck? The one where he represents a black man accused of rape back in the 1940s or 1950s or something? I think it takes place in Alabama or Georgia?"

"Of course! That's 'To Kill a Mockingbird.' Classic film. And book for that matter," he responded.

"Well, that's what my son is like to me. He's like Gregory Peck in that movie. He goes in and tries to help the people who have nothing to offer him, righting wrongs and finding justice or just trying to get the best deal for someone down on his luck. I bet he would take chickens for payment from some of his clients...if his neighbors wouldn't have a fit about it."

The man laughed. "Now that's a right good attorney right there," he said. "Don't hear about those kinds of lawyers much these days. All I ever hear about are the money grubbing ones on Wall Street or the politicians who make them all look bad with their behavior." He took a sip of his Coke. "Your son sounds like a good fit for my daughter. Is he married?"

Loretta got quiet. Here she was, yammering on like a woman without a care in the world, bragging on her son like he was a teenaged football player who was just crowned Homecoming King, instead of the responsible, hardworking, broken-hearted and devastated adult man that he is.

Her gut sank. Her poor boy. So many years of being alone, finding Mrs. Right, and then losing her so quickly, so tragically, and all for nothing. She knew that Buddy would never be all alone, thank God. He was a father and had two little girls to raise. But being all alone and then being lonely – the kind of lonely that is only reconciled by the presence of the love of your life – are two entirely different things.

"Well, he was," Loretta said, quietly through a sadness that cut through the man's thick patch of gray hair. "He is recently widowed." Or was it widowered? Who knows?

All Loretta knew was that just like her, long ago, her son lost the centerpiece of his very heart. One day he woke up married and in love. The next day, he woke up widowed…but still in love. And he could do nothing about any of it.

"Oh, I'm real sorry," the man groaned. "I am so sorry."

"Yes, it was a horrible accident. She was run down by an elderly man who lost control of his car." Loretta's voice changed. "I always hated how she ran along the side of the road and with headphones in her ears…for that very reason. It's just not safe!"

"Do they have children?" he asked, quieting his voice.

"Yes, and that's the biggest part of the tragedy. They have two girls, one eleven and the other is just a toddler. It's so awful. That baby will probably not even remember her own mother."

The man's face drew down, the folds sagged lower. He had probably heard plenty of sad stories in his lifetime, and this one was another to add to the pile. He folded his hands in his lap on top of the cape and watched Loretta in the mirror as she worked behind him.

Sometimes stories are so sad, there's not a whole lot to say in response. The silence itself was enough to say it all.

Loretta clipped and cut and shaped his big head into a look that was slightly less ridiculous than she originally imagined. She took off his cape and shook the hairs out onto the salon's floor, which had been recently swept. Taylor, the Tar Heel varsity basketball cheerleader walked into the reception area, her platinum blond locks needing a touch up. She was Loretta's next appointment. Liz checked the man out on the computer, ran his credit card through the reader, and handed him the receipt. He signed it and then walked back over to Loretta.

"Ma'am, may I have your business card?" he asked.

Loretta looked perplexed, and she felt her gut flare up again, but only for a second. Why in the world was her sixth sense making such a rare appearance today after being in hibernation for so long?

"I want to give it to my daughter, in case she needs a good hairdresser for her graduation," he explained further.

Loretta grinned at him and handed him a business card.

"Loretta Cordova," he bellowed out loud reading off the card. Then glancing at her, he put his hand out and continued, "Nice to meet you. I'm real sorry to hear about your son's wife and that awful loss."

"Thank you, Mister..."

"Coughlin," he replied. "Lex Coughlin." Holding his almost finished can of Coke, he asked, "Are you done with that can of Diet Coke?"

"No, not yet, sir. Why?" Loretta asked.

"Well, I'd like to take it with me for my daughter's recycling project. She's running a recycling program for her sorority and asked me to grab any extra aluminum cans I could while I was out and about today. I have almost a full box of them in my car," he stated. "You know these liberal do-gooder kids here in Chapel Hill…always trying to save the Earth and hug a tree and all that."

"Yes, they are," Loretta agreed. "I'm not done with this one yet, though.

"Oh, alright then," he responded. "Well, you take care now," he said and walked out of the salon and back onto Franklin Street.

A few minutes later, Loretta walked back to her station from the back to replace some color supplies. As she went to grab her Diet Coke to take a sip before starting on Taylor's color, she realized it was gone.

"What happened to my Diet Coke? I swore I left it right here," she asked, hoping Taylor would have an answer. Taylor just shrugged and flipped through the latest issue of People Magazine.

A Day of Reckoning (Part One)

Buddy dropped Gabby off at her babysitter's house so he could get some work done in the peace and quiet. It's a little tough at times to tend to a toddler, and keeping Gabby out of mischief appeared to be a full-time job lately. Buddy realized, after stopping Gabby just in time from pouring the entire box of laundry detergent onto the kitchen floor, that her babysitter was probably not paid enough.

Just because the love of your life dies doesn't mean that your cases stop needing attention and the calendar call stops bellowing out your court-appointed clients' names and the bills stop needing to be paid on time. It was good for him to work anyway; it kept his mind occupied for a few hours and from dwelling on his immeasurable loss and the deep pit residing within his stomach, which was not letting up at all, even after five weeks.

Molly finally went back to school after a solid week home full of crying and watching a lot of videos in the living room. If Bo had still been alive, he would've been good about helping them through all of this. He would've sat with Molly, a constant companion, the guardian of and witness to her pain…like dogs do. But after Bo had to be put down, he and Julie decided they'd wait a while before adopting a new dog. Maybe now a new dog was just what the doctor should order for the devastated Cordova family.

As he started picking through the folders containing the cases that needed more immediate attention, there was a sharp knock on the door.

"Hi. Are you Jonathan Cordova?" the young, fresh faced sheriff's deputy asked.

"Yes," Buddy answered, puzzled. He wasn't expecting a deputy today and had no idea why one would come otherwise. The deputy handed him a large envelope. "You've been served."

When Buddy went into his house and opened it, he saw something that blew his mind into next Tuesday. It was a copy of a petition to the Court, submitted by a family law attorney in Fayetteville, for full custody of Molly Saint, a minor child. And it was filed on behalf of Jedidiah and Tammy Jo McVicar of San Antonio, Texas, maternal grandparents.

Buddy felt his stomach lurch. Running into the bathroom, he threw up the contents of his breakfast and probably his dinner from the night before.

About thirty minutes after the deputy dropped off the envelope, Gaynelle Flowers knocked on Buddy's door. Buddy let her inside, and she found her way to his couch in the living room.

He was still feeling ill after receiving the paperwork informing him that he could possibly lose custody of Molly to her grandparents.

This thought never entered his mind. Ever. And he was a lawyer for Christ's sake! He always thought of every possible legal angle in every possible legal situation! He was in between shock and horror with the desperate pang of grief hanging over everything that happened…and then came the overwhelming sensation of fear and dread. What would he tell Molly?

After some brief small talk about how well her son was doing at the community college in the general education program and in his job at the new Applebee's, which opened near the mall, she began to tell him an interesting and puzzling story.

"Well, a few weeks ago, I was mending a hem on my mother's favorite pants. And this strange man came to my door. He was real big. Well, not big like fat…more like large. Yes, the word 'large' is best to describe his size. If that makes any sense." She looked down at her fingernails, and Buddy started to squirm.

"Does this have something to do with you needing my help?" Buddy asked.

"No, it's not that. There was just…this man…at my door. And he told me that he was looking for a lawyer…you know, one that was 'affordable'…no offense, Buddy…"

Buddy waved her off. He knew what "affordable" meant. A cheap lawyer. A lawyer for poor people.

"Anyway, he asked me if I ever used you before…that he heard you were affordable and good."

"I don't get why that's so strange. People ask for lawyer referrals all the time," Buddy stated coolly. He was feeling even worse than before, and the last thing he wanted right now was one of Gaynelle's stories that he didn't have time for. He knew he was too nice or something. People just felt like they could tell him their stupid stories. Like he had nothing better to do.

"No, it wasn't like that. I just got an awful feeling from him. Nobody knows that I called you in to help my son way back when he was in trouble. So why would this random person show up at my door of all places asking me about you when nobody really knows anything about it?"

"Well somebody knows about it. Maybe your son told him?"

"I don't think so. He was humiliated. He don't talk about his troubles with the law."

Buddy sat back in the cushion. He wanted to go into the fetal position and fall asleep. The gnawing feeling of the pit in his stomach just stayed put, a permanent parasitic resident since that rainy day he stood shell-shocked in the Chuck E. Cheese.

"Okay, so why are you telling me about this now if he showed up a while ago?" he asked her.

"Well, at first I thought it was strange but didn't think much more of it. Until I watched the news about that Scott case you got goin' on. Look, I don't know what other cases you're workin' on right now, but I know you have the Scott one because the news lady asked you a question in the courthouse and everybody around my street talks about it all the time. No offense, but some of the ladies in my knitting circle don't know how you can defend someone who is obviously a murderer. But then some of the other ladies think he's innocent because no one that good looking could be a murderer. But then I remind them of Ted Bundy." Gaynelle stopped and rubbed her hands together. "But anyway, after I saw it on the news, I got to thinking about that large man. He just came across like he was diggin' around about something. Like maybe he was a PI or workin' for somebody trying to fish for information on you and the case you're working on." Gaynelle put her elbows to her knees as she leaned over. Then she whispered, like someone else could be listening in on them in the house. "I watch Law and Order, and I know what a PI looks like and their tactics. I'm just tellin' you that he's out there, and he's trying to spoil your case."

Buddy wanted to throw up his hands in defeat. Another Sherlock Fucking Holmes TV detective trying to investigate something. Those damn shows have done nothing but make the jury pool tainted with citizens who believe they know everything and are trained investigators.

"I'm just sayin' Buddy. I think that son of a bitch you're defending is guilty as sin, and I hope he rots in prison for the rest of his life. But I like you as a person, so I'm just tellin' you as a favor that the man was suspicious."

"Ms. Flowers, thank you for the heads-up. I think it's all good, though. My cases are all good, so you don't need to worry about snooping PIs and the prosecution trying to get one over on me." He stood up and started to lead her to the door. "Believe it or not, most of the time, we don't have a whole lot of personality driven drama going on between the prosecution and defense sides. It makes for good TV, but really, most cases are boring in real life."

"But Buddy, I'm telling ya, there was something about that man just telling me he was out to get you!"

"I promise. I'll be fine, Ms. Flowers. I am taking good care of my cases, so don't you worry about them. Okay?" He opened the door, and she followed him out on the porch.

"Alright, Buddy. I know you think I'm just a crazy old woman with too much time on her hands, but if that man wasn't a PI, then I will get my hair dyed purple next week!" she declared.

"Okay, Ms. Flowers. Thank you for your concern. I do appreciate it."

Buddy walked back into his quiet and empty house and decided to go pick up Gabby from her babysitter's house a bit early so he could wait for Molly to get home from school. He had no idea how to tell her about what's happened, but he knew that he had to. And soon.

Orphan

Molly put Gabby's socks over the top of her small pink feet. Then she picked up her white and purple flower print shirt and pulled it over her small head.

"Want Elmo," Gabby said in her toddler gibberish.

"You can have Elmo after I get you dressed," Molly said with the authority of a mother who has a proper feeding, sleeping, and diaper changing color coordinated schedule posted on a refrigerator.

"Want Elmo!" Gabby shouted.

The fluffy red Elmo sat across the room in a heap on Gabby's new bed. He had a huge smile, and it was difficult not to be happy inside when you looked at him. Molly liked the Elmo when Buddy found him, smiling and gesturing all that joy at them from behind his cardboard prison at the Toys R Us this past December. It laughed when it was tickled. However, Molly found herself hating the Elmo by New Year's Day because Gabby tickled it and tickled it until Buddy would have to take it and hide the toy away in a cabinet, giving them all a break.

Just before her mom died, her parents bought Gabby a "big girl bed." It was really a twin-sized bed, the same size Molly had in her room. They saw no point in buying one of those stupid small toddler beds, which would just last maybe a year anyway. If Gabby needed to be out of her crib, then she was ready to sleep in a normal bed. They added small gates to the sides to keep her from falling out at night.

"No, Gabby. You need to be dressed first."

Gabby started giving her big sister a hard time, but Molly didn't mind. She loved her baby sister and would do anything for her. She wanted to give her the Elmo, but she knew that Gabby had to first learn that there was a time and place for everything. First, get dressed. Then, Elmo. Then, breakfast.

Molly worked hard to push Gabby's pants over her squirming, chubby legs. Her own grief was now back in full force, reversing itself from a lingering dull aching pain, since Buddy's talk with her.

Yesterday, when she went to school, she felt better than she had in any of the weeks since her mom died. The constant hole in her gut, which ate not only any food she managed to get down but also any more tears she thought she had inside her, began to dissipate just a little. And then Buddy told her the news: her grandparents wanted her to come live with them. In Texas.

Molly couldn't understand why in the world they would want to take her away from her family. She couldn't understand why they would want to separate her from Buddy, who has raised her for the past five years…as well as her baby sister, who was still so small and had no mommy and needed her to be there to show her the ropes. She couldn't comprehend why they would want a young girl to come and live in their home, a girl they did not know, a girl who wouldn't mind visiting or getting to know them…but also a girl who did not want to go live there. They were essentially strangers to her.

She knew that her mom and her grandmother had some falling out many years ago. But move away from North Carolina? The only place she really remembered living? Away from her friends, her school, her soccer team and her dad and sister? It just made no sense why a couple of old people in Texas would think this was what was best for her, especially after she just lost her mom – the only person in her life who had always been by her side.

Yesterday, when she got home from school, Buddy tried to explain it to her like she was just an eleven-year-old girl learning about the laws of the land in Social Studies class. He stood in the living room with his hands in his pockets and his eyes shut, trying to keep himself from crying. But she wasn't fooled. His lip was quivering.

Molly sat on the couch with her hands and arms around her knees. Her backpack was on the floor, and Gabby was taking a nap.

"Moll, under the law, you are an orphan. Your father is dead. Your mother is dead. I never legally adopted you. That makes you technically and legally orphaned," he explained, his voice breaking into cracks, the kind that sound like you're going to burst into tears at any moment. "I just hate myself for not adopting you. I don't know why I didn't insist on it right off the bat, as soon as your mom and I got married. It's not even that big a deal to do because your real father is deceased. It's not like how in some cases the real father is still alive somewhere…and still has rights…"

Buddy looked down at the floor at the juice spot in the carpet as his voice trailed off. He put his hands through his hair, and Molly could see that his face was overcome with the guilt and pain of what his failure to act might cost him. And cost Gabby. And cost her.

Molly watched him closely. She wasn't allowing herself to cry… yet…although she was scared to death of what this all meant for her. She knew she was just a kid, and sometimes grownups will make her do things she doesn't think make any sense just because she is a kid and they are the grownups.

Buddy stood tall, clearly drained of energy, and Molly could feel herself hurting all over again. Only this time, it was for him. Buddy loved her. They were father and daughter, no matter what the stupid laws say. No matter what science says. The only steps at their house were the ones that led to the door inside. And inside was a family. A sad family...a small family...but a family nonetheless.

She had no idea that she was considered an orphan. Orphans were kids with no parents, like in the movie Annie. They were kids who lived in a big unkempt old house with peeling lead paint on the walls and were forced to clean floors and no one would bring them home to live with them because they were too old to love once they got around eight years old. Orphans were babies in foreign hospitals, screaming in cribs, their fists clenched in the air, their cries ignored, where their mothers dumped them because they were poor and had no one to help them.

Orphans were alone. They had no one.

How can she possibly be an orphan when she has a dad? Sure, her "real father," whatever that even meant, has been gone for half of her life. He loved her, and she loved him...but he died and was never coming back. Buddy is now her dad. He became her dad when her mom married him and made it all official.

But to Molly, he became her dad long before that day. Like the time when he taught her how to ride the two-wheeler and the time he took her to the beach to see the USS North Carolina Battleship and the time he brought her to Welby to show her where he grew up and the time he took her to Chapel Hill so she could get a haircut by his mom, Loretta. Buddy became her dad when he carried her up the stairs and put her to bed while he was babysitting when her mom went to a late meeting at the library. Buddy thought she was asleep, but she wasn't. She just wanted him to carry her and put her into bed, like how her daddy used to before he died. He became her dad when he sat on the floor and let her brush his hair...and he became her dad when he helped her prepare for her math test.

After he married her mom, he proved he was her dad when he went to Kerr Drug and bought her some maxi-pads when she first got her period in the bathroom at the Long John Silver's. He proved it when he listened to her read Harry Potter and the Sorcerer's Stone until late at night, long after she was supposed to be asleep. And he proved he was her dad when she told him about her day and talked about the crush she had on Tyler Grey when she started the school year. He proved he was her dad when he set her up her own bank account and put $100.00 in it as her "starter savings." He proved he was her dad every single day he worked hard to provide for her, her mom, and her baby sister…and how he led a life of integrity with everything he did.

As Gabby ran across the bedroom to finally claim her Elmo, Molly laid back on the mauve carpeting of Gabby's small girly room, still very much set up like a nursery, except for the "big girl bed" along the wall. The backs of her legs felt good resting on the cool strands beneath. Her mind continued to race. What in the world was she going to do if the people at the courthouse made her go live all the way in Texas?

Tears started streaming down her cheeks, covering the time-lightened childhood freckles, thick with the unknown angst of a young life turned upside-down. Gabby hopped over to her and laid down alongside of her big sister. She held Elmo up in the air, then put one of his tiny red hands in Molly's hand and the other tiny red hand in her own hand…an imaginary happy friend suspended between sisters.

CHAPTER 11

June – September 2001

A Day of Reckoning (Part Two)

Buddy stood outside of Courtroom 5B at the Cumberland County Courthouse as the Respondent, rather than the Attorney of Record. He was never a litigant or a defendant or anything…really… other than the lawyer representing the litigant or defendant. Not even a speeding ticket. While Family Law was not something he had ever dabbled in, he learned an awful lot of it over the past month.

Tammy Jo and Jed were suing for custody of Molly because they were her maternal grandparents. Their petition was allowed on the legal grounds that Molly was an orphan and they were her maternal grandparents. They were her "next of kin" and had the "legal standing" to claim the right to raise her. It was "in the best interest of the minor child" to be raised by her biological maternal grandparents, according to the legal documents they filed with the Court.

Buddy's lawyer, Lisa Marion-Wisnewski, a Fayetteville Family Law attorney he found after asking his local Bar for a referral, believed that Buddy had a pretty good case for custody of Molly himself.

"Look. They have a case. They have legal standing more than you do. The key here will be 'in the best interest of the child.' And honestly, it will be very hard for them to convince the Judge that two older people who live several states away, who haven't even set eyes on Molly for years before their daughter's death, would be better for her than you would be," Lisa explained during a phone call before the Temporary Custody Hearing. "Ordering a minor child out of state in a custody matter is not common, even if it's to go to the child's own legal parent. Judges do not like doing it. But this…this is tricky…and you just never know."

"I know that all makes sense. But sometimes with the courts, blood is thicker than common sense."

Buddy was ill with his nerves. Being in a constant state of anxiety, after weeks and weeks of abject grief, cost him close to twenty pounds, which he didn't really need to lose in the first place. He had been fortunate enough to win his first emergency hearing for temporary custody of Molly while he fought it out with the McVicars. The Judge felt that removing Molly from her home and putting her in foster care while this battle went on would be traumatic for her, considering she had just lost her mother. Well ain't that nice of the Court to think of traumatizing a child further… Buddy had thought to himself when he received word, temporarily relieving him of his latest nightmare.

"You have raised her since you and Julie were married. You were acting in every way as a father. You have her younger sister, who is her blood relation. Believe it or not, Gabby might be your blood-is-thicker-than-water chance here."

Buddy held the phone tightly to his ear and knew in his rational mind that everything Lisa said was correct. He had a case. He had temporary custody right now. "Possession is nine-tenths of the law" does ring true sometimes.

And then there was the matter of what Molly would want. Molly was not little anymore. She was still very young, young enough not to be able to make a legal choice for herself, but maybe the Judge would want to know what she wanted. It was one consideration the Judge could make out of all the others.

Buddy knew what she wanted. She wanted to be with him and her sister. But regardless of how much he knew all these things, how much sense it made that she stays in her home and with her sister and stepfather – no matter the biology – there was that gnawing feeling of dread covering his entire insides.

Julie had been right about her mother Tammy Jo. She was a selfish fucking bitch.

Molly was at the county day camp, Gabby was with her babysitter, and Buddy stood, several pounds lighter, in a dark blue suit and tie. It was just a hearing, not a trial, and he knew that there would be a big push to mediation. The Court would rather families decide their own fates instead of having a judge do it for them. However, this case was unique. This case had no precedent, really...not that he could find in his research, anyway. Sure, grandparents have sued for custody before, but usually it was because the mother was a drug addict, and the father was in jail, or some nonsense like that. This was different.

Buddy had even thought of alternate responses to the custody petition. He thought of having Gabby countersuing for custody, through a Guardian ad Litem or even using himself as her Guardian. Everything he thought of, though, did not shake the reality that he was in a fight for Molly. Nothing about this would be cut and dried.

Molly would have to be evaluated by a psychologist, she had already been appointed a Guardian ad Litem to represent her interests, and she would have to live with whatever the Judge decided. No matter what happened, yet another piece of her innocence would be stolen. And this time, by her own grandparents who claimed to love her.

Click, click, click, Buddy heard the heels approaching him. He turned to see Tammy Jo, also known as The Bitch from Hell, and her trusty coward of a man sidekick, Jed. Rather than fall victim to the rage boiling just under the surface, he turned back around so he wouldn't have to look at them. They were the only ones waiting outside of the room.

As the tension in the air began to ripen with intensity, Tammy Jo stated sharply, "Jonathan, I would like to speak with you privately."

Buddy and Tammy Jo walked outside of the Courthouse and stood near the flagpoles, which held the American flag, the North Carolina flag, and a Confederate flag. Tammy Jo wore a dark skirt, an off-white blouse and a blue blazer. Her blond hair was styled into a sensible bun. She looked like an overweight flight attendant.

"I know you think that I'm being selfish, and God knows my daughter must've said a lot of cruel and untrue things about me through the years, but I love that little girl and have been kept from her for almost her entire life. I don't expect you to understand what it's like to have your own daughter reject your kind of love, but it is a daily torment I wish on no one," Tammy Jo started, her voice becoming stronger as she spoke.

Buddy couldn't look at her. It made him ill to even think of what kind of a woman does this to a little girl in the name of love. "Keep telling yourself that you're doing it for the right reasons. Whatever makes you sleep at night," was all he could get out of himself.

Then he felt it…the terror. It came on all of a sudden, as if a guillotine appeared out of nowhere and Tammy Jo was the executioner wearing a black mask. The tension between them disappeared, and instead of a stalemate waiting for a judge to parcel it out, it was a checkmate… with Tammy Jo holding the right chess piece.

And all Buddy could do was watch as everything came crashing down upon him at once.

"I know who you really are," she said sharply, her hard Texas twang cutting through him like a butcher knife.

Buddy's heart held tight. He turned toward her and looked straight into her face.

"Your name is Daniel Kaspar Junior, and your mother – who is nothin' but a murderer on the run – is Retta Bellinger." She paused to give Buddy a moment to take that in. "Her real name sounds like a goddamn 1930s fugitive gangster! You two – a mother and son Bonnie and Clyde. A Lifetime movie just waiting to be made!" Her mouth turned into a smirk, her lipstick riding a side wave into her glory.

What is this kind of moment called? Buddy thought to himself. *A day of reckoning?*

This was the day he had always wondered about…would it catch up with him or not. And now, it was here. Right here, right now, in Fayetteville, North Carolina…more than twenty-six years later than that day in 1975 when their lives, as Bellingers from Killen, Texas, were over.

The Good Lie

Buddy did not know how to tell his mother that Tammy Jo and Jed had uncovered their life's big …but good…lie. They held onto it like how people in charge of things hold onto information that every-one wants – like assholes who think they're better than everyone else. Knowledge is power…he who holds the information has all the power…blah blah blah.

It was a good lie. Some lies just are. And what had been going on in their small two-bedroom rental for far too long, years ago in Killeen, Texas, was a tragedy in the making every single day…until it was an actual tragedy in one way or the other.

His mother did what mothers are supposed to do: protect their children, even if it means putting their own lives in harm's way. With few exceptions, any mother Buddy ever knew was wired to be like that. And Tammy Jo must have been the exception.

Lisa sat next to him at the conference table as they waited for the McVicars and their lawyer to come in. The mediator, a good ol' southern gentleman with white hair and wearing a seersucker suit, sat at the head of the table. Buddy had a decision to make and he wasn't sure what to do. The McVicars had him. They had his mother. And why they hadn't gone to the authorities with their information was still a mystery to him.

The conversation before their hearing, where Judge Starks ordered them to mediation, was still a surreal moment in Buddy's mind. Tammy Jo told him about the TV show that tipped her off, about the PI she had her lawyer hired to investigate his mother, about all the poking around the PI did to find out if he and his mother were indeed this missing mother-son duo from Killeen. She told him about how his stepfather Kenny had died – a wasted skeleton of a man – several years later from when they had left him covered in blood in his own home, how his mother was now responsible for his death, how if he just let them have Molly with no more fights in Court, she'd keep this information to herself and let them be the liars they are.

She told him that she'd leave Gabby alone and wouldn't come after her but wanted visitation rights with her. She explained her reasons for wanting Molly, this piece of her daughter, her second chance to get things right…and no matter how much the regret and grief seeped through her words, no matter how empty he knew he wanted them to be, Buddy felt nothing but contempt toward her.

She lost her little girl…twice. Now she wanted to take his little girl to absolve her own guilt, shame, and misery. He knew that one thing was the root of all this.

Using his mother as her winning poker chip was just Tammy Jo's way of ensuring she wins. Because Tammy Jo McVicar always wins…except in the ways that really mattered.

It was hard for Buddy to separate his rational self from his emotional self in this situation. He knew that most healthy human beings make their important and serious decisions somewhat rooted in both. However, he also felt like the blackmail Tammy Jo was conducting on him was at a level of gross unfairness. But, he supposed, if you have an edge over someone in Court, you're wise to use it. He knew that for sure in his small low rent law practice. But now he was put into a position where he had to choose between his daughter or his mother. And that was not fair.

But it was mostly unfair because of the reality of the situation. Tammy Jo, while she did have an awful lot of accurate information, did not have the most relevant and correct piece of the puzzle. She did not have the truth.

The McVicars walked into the conference room, and their lawyer was not too far behind them. The mediator began talking, but Buddy's mind was not absorbing anything he was saying. He couldn't contain his anxiety over what was going to happen to Molly and his fears about what could happen to his mother if Tammy Jo played her Ace. He wanted Molly to be with him and Gabby, exactly where she belonged.

But he didn't want his mother carted off, some kind of fugitive from the law…like one of those hippies from the Sixties who blew up cars in protest over the Vietnam War, who were now quiet middle aged women in suburban homes with husbands and children and PTA meetings, and then were found out and dragged in front of the cameras to at last atone for their sinful youth.

A part of Buddy, the competitor in him, wanted to call Tammy Jo on her bluff. Maybe even get her charged with extortion. But he wasn't playing poker. He was playing with Molly and his mother, two of the most important chips in his life. There was a reason why Julie did not speak to her parents. There was a reason why they were estranged. While Buddy thought maybe Julie was too stubborn for her own good, he knew now that her reasons were valid. Tammy Jo might think she was in the right – and maybe she was – but the way she went about things was not. It was cruel and almost sadistic. And Buddy was neither of those things.

"So, where are we?" the McVicars' lawyer asked. He was a short, stout balding man in a dark suit that looked like it needed some tailoring. Buddy never saw him before within his legal circles, but that was nothing new. The law was both a small world and a big world, depending on what's going on and where you lived in the state.

Buddy looked across the table, steely eyed. He did everything he could to suppress his anger and not allow any of it to show on his face. Years of controlling his emotions had served him well in his simple career and perhaps saved him an awful lot of extra heartache and drama. But he did want them both to know that he is not going to cower to their pathetic demands.

"My client will agree to a school appropriate visitation schedule," Lisa stated.

Tammy Jo looked right at Buddy, almost through his face. It surprised him that certain expressions and movements she exhibited resembled Julie's right down to the small crease that would form in the middle of her forehead. How could his beautiful, free loving, happy wife possibly come from this bossy self-absorbed monster?

Jed kept his eyes averted – he couldn't look at anyone. He just sat there, expected to be the dutiful husband, shelling out the checks for his wife's orders and whims. Her mouth twitched. She leaned over and whispered something to her lawyer.

"Look. Molly has been raised by Mr. Cordova in a father and daughter relationship since she was seven years old. He has her sister, who is Molly's biological half-sister but still her sister…unless we are going to start defining what is and what is not a proper legal sister," Lisa continued.

"This isn't about her sister. It's about what is in Molly's best interest," the lawyer said, leaning back into his chair.

"Yes, I know that. One piece of what is in Molly's best interest includes living with her only blood relation sister."

"These are her grandparents. They are her blood. Mr. Cordova has absolutely no rights to her in accordance with the statutes. He is not her blood relative."

"Well, first of all, that's not true. A stepfather does have standing in custody cases. Secondly, Gabrielle Cordova is Molly's blood relation. She has her own kind of standing and right to her."

"A toddler has no standing in this case, Ms. Marion-Wisnewski. There is certainly no precedent involving a toddler having standing or having a say in custody of another minor child, so it's probably wise to keep that out of your argument," short baldy stated flatly.

"The point here is that Molly's maternal blood relation grandparents have standing. They certainly have standing over a non-blood relation stepfather, who couldn't even be bothered to adopt her when it would have been appropriate to do so."

Buddy almost jumped out of the chair. The gall of this asshole to say such a thing to him. Even if he was right. Even if Buddy wasn't already beating himself up every single day over not having gone and taken that final step to make Molly his. If only he had done that, none of this would be happening.

"Mr. Cordova and Molly have been in a normal, loving, caring and respectful father-daughter relationship for more than four years. He helped her mother raise her after her biological father passed away. He has been her soccer coach, has attended all Parent-Teacher conferences, taken her to doctor's appointments, and signed off on her important papers as her father," Lisa began explaining, listing off all the ways in which Buddy served as a parent in an official capacity.

But there was more to it than that.

Being a father wasn't just signing off on a spelling test that came home and going to listen to a teacher tell him what he already knew about Molly. Being a father is who he is within everything he did, every action he took, each thought that ran through his mind. What's for dinner? Well, tonight I think we'll go with Chinese because the other day Molly said she was hankering for some General Tso's. Should I mow the lawn today or wait until tomorrow? Well, I promised the girls that I'd take them to park after the workday ends, so I guess I'll mow tomorrow. The corner of that table looks real sharp. I better put something over that in case one of the girls runs into it so they don't get hurt.

Just a few weeks ago, Buddy was scrubbing Gabby's orange vomit out of the carpet. And now, here he was in a gut-wrenching custody case, having to prove that driving a kid to school on time and providing a roof over her head is enough. There were other men out there, the actual blood kin, who beat their kids or disappeared and left them to poverty and single mothers trying to pay the bills, and the ones who made all kinds of money working all the time, never bothering to ask their own kids how they're doing…and yet those are fathers.

But here he was, doing all the stuff you just do from your heart because you love your children, alongside of the obligatory responsibilities that come with parenting, and it's being questioned, it's being picked apart, it's being challenged, and it might not be enough for him to keep his own kid in her home.

As he sat there listening to both lawyers going back and forth about what makes a father and what is in the best interest of a child, his stomach remained in a clenched state, to the point where it was almost unbearable. All the love he had for Molly and her mother might not matter to these people or to Judge Starks, and that was hard to imagine. Buddy thought, *You've done everything right, and still...you're not enough.*

"May I speak?" Tammy Jo interjected at some point. "I have something to say."

She said it loudly enough to cause everyone to stop speaking and look at her. She realized that she may have spoken too loudly for the size of this conference room, but in typical Tammy Jo style, she justified it in her mind. She had something to say, damn it. So, people needed to listen.

Buddy looked up at her and waited. He waited for what she was going to say, how she was going to say it, and what it would mean for him and his mother and poor Molly. The air was thick with that unknown quantity, something that felt heavy and icky and even ugly. Buddy never was the kind of man who acted on impulse, so he figured in this case, he'd let Tammy Jo take the lead…and he would figure out how to react. What was she going to say? What would she do?

Either she was going to out him from his twenty-six-year old hiding place and sound like a mature, rational human being who conducted a thorough investigation and solved an old mystery for the state of Texas…or she was going to start spouting off nonsense and sound like a crazy person. Please be the latter.

"Go ahead, Mrs. McVicar," her attorney groaned, probably not realizing what he was allowing. It appeared to Buddy that the guy's inner voice was telling him that he needed to keep this woman on a leash, that she was her own worst enemy at times, that just by opening her mouth in a sensitive case like this, she might ruin the entire thing.

Tammy Jo took a deep breath.

"Jonathan Cordova is not who he says he is," she stated firmly. And with that, the heavens parted and Mrs. McVicar showed, what she believed to be, her winning hand. She was not bluffing. At all.

Classical Music

A Texas criminal defense attorney by the name of Merle Patchett sat inside of the county prosecutor's office in a large government building, which carried that constant hum of an overworked copy machine in the background. There were still too many trees being killed in the pursuit of justice, no matter the technological advances by the year 2001.

Known as "Patchett the Hatchet," Merle was the best criminal lawyer in Eastern Texas that Joe Horton could find, and then retain, for five-thousand dollars. After visiting with Loretta in North Carolina, Merle believed the woman had a sound claim for self-defense, especially due to the police recorded interviews with those who knew her, as well as with those who knew Kenneth Bellinger.

However, there was still the pesky issue of convincing the District Attorney to either give her a lenient plea deal on the crimes she most likely committed in her escape and evasion or let her off the hook altogether due to lack of evidence. The Good Lord knows the woman paid enough of a price – her entire identity – for anything she ever did wrong in her life. But Texas prosecutors were their own breed of "tough on crime," and it was up to him to convince the man that he would have done the same thing if he were in Loretta's shoes.

Not only did they not have enough evidence to charge and then convict Loretta – who was apparently born and baptized "Retta Sofia Scarpelli" – with murder, or really any kind of lesser offenses, Merle figured that the DA might try to charge her with all the small offenses associated with her disappearing act, including falsifying official government documents and theft of a firearm and obstruction of justice. She was not out of the woods by any stretch of the imagination.

Meanwhile, Buddy sat in the lobby of the Bell County government building, waiting to learn what was going to happen with his mother. He promised her that he would wait on what Patchett the Hatchet could work out with the DA. If was acceptable to him, he would honor her request to keep quiet about what he knew to be true.

"The only reason I'm going along with this is because of my fight for Molly," Buddy had declared to her, his voice heavy with fear and anxiety. He was not the kind of man to lie – except for this one huge thing that he has lied about almost his whole life.

"If you lose Molly because of what happened in 1975, I would never be able to forgive myself," Loretta cried though her tears. "The whole damn thing was my fault. You are not responsible for any of that mess. You were just a little boy!"

"But the police do not have the truth, Mother. They don't have the right information. All they have is what some crack pot PI thinks he found out, and none of it proves anything except that we're still alive and living under different identities. For all they know, which ain't much, some angry guy who Kenny pissed off during one his drunken rages could've come in the house and popped him."

"You are not to tell them the truth! You are not! I forbid it. So help me God, if you do, I will tell them you are lying just to save me. And they will believe it. Everyone knows that a boy will do anything to save his mother!" Loretta stood in her own kitchen, sobbing, Joe standing near her, ready to catch her if she fell over.

Buddy found himself wondering what Joe must've been thinking about everything going on. Then it occurred to him that Joe probably figured everything out years ago.

No one just shows up out of the blue onto your property, coming from nowhere with nothing but a paper bag and an enduring mystery. He likely determined that there was an ugly story behind the pretty face of young Loretta Cordova and her shy and studious son. But to him, it didn't really matter what that story was. All people carried a past, whether it's displayed out in the sunshine for all to see and celebrate…or buried in the silent echoes of their souls.

As Patchett the Hatchet waited for the District Attorney to share his thoughts about the alleged crimes of a twenty-eight-year old battered mother, based on 1975 Texas law, a young woman in a business suit stormed in the office. The door flew open, and the force knocked over a glass vase resting on a small table.

"Dang, Melissa, what in the world?" the District Attorney yelled out loud, dropping his files onto the desk.

"You need to come. We're all watching it in the break room. Two planes have flown into the Twin Towers, and the buildings are on fire. The news is saying we are under attack by terrorists!"

Patchett the Hatchet and the District Attorney stood up and followed the young woman into the break room, which housed a refrigerator, a microwave, a bulletin board with employee news from Human Resources, and an old TV hoisting rabbit ears and sitting up on a stand. Seventeen prosecutors, legal assistants, investigators and administrative personnel stood in awe and horror at the national tragedy unfolding in New York City.

Buddy remained seated in the lobby on a stained tan leather seat, stomach in knots, waiting for his mother's boisterous and borderline obnoxious attorney, while listening to the chirpy classical music coming from the receptionist's bright pink CD player. He heard her scream, "Oh my God!" and watched her run from her desk and through the doors to where Patchett the Hatchet was discussing the Bellingers' dark past.

Nine Holes

"C'mon, c'mon, c'mon," Jed said out loud, probably the only time the man was ever animated about anything. The tiny white dimpled ball, carrying a small black number four on it, flew through the air at a speed too fast for non-golfers to even notice where it eventually landed.

"Damn, that thing is gone," Dale, Jed's long time golfing partner exclaimed as he leaned on the off-white golf cart with the green CWCC crest on the front. "Well hit. Must be the longest one you hit for quite a while. That's a real beaut."

"Yes, sir, it's about damn time. Been playing like ass for so many weeks, I was considering taking a break until all that custody mess is done with."

"Well, you got a lot going on. That kind of thing can be right emotional for people. When my daughter was in court with her ex over their kids, she lost about twenty pounds just in stress alone."

Jed stood back and tapped the head of his Taylormade driver on the tee marker twice, pulled his gray Crest Wood Country Club cap down over his forehead and walked toward his friend who was stepping inside the golf cart.

"It's tiring. I wish it was all over with," he admitted, climbing into shotgun position, as Dale drove along the cart path toward the fairway where their golf balls rested comfortably on perfect patches of turf. "TJ is just out of her mind about everything. She's crazier than ever. And that's saying something. Doing things like decorating the spare bedroom in all of Julie's old stuff that she had stored in the attic and meeting with a palm reader. A palm reader! She's even trying to make us eat healthy all the time and bringing that sushi business into the house. And I'm afraid of what it's all doing to Molly. I mean, can you imagine what she must be thinking?"

"You think Molly would be better off living with that guy?"

Jed sat back in the chair cushion and folded his arms. "There's nothing wrong with him. He's a good man; I can just tell. He loved my daughter, and he does nothing but good for people who need his help. He has a respectable career and is obviously real close to Molly.

And the whole way TJ went about bringing that man's messy history to light was just plain ugly."

Jed began rubbing his chin with his left index finger and his voice lowered. "Cordova was just a little boy when his mother took him on the run. None of that had anything to do with him, and hell, if she was being beat up, like she claims, then she did nothing wrong in my book. That asshole deserved what he got. No man should be hittin' on a woman like that. And she's a tiny thing, too!"

Jed paused again and stood up, adjusting his belt on his pants. His voice got a bit louder. "And no matter how many times TJ says it out loud – 'that it's the best thing for Molly – coming to live here with us'…well, that just don't make it true."

"Why did she push so hard?" Dale asked, pulling the cart up to his ball resting in a crop of grass near a tree. He climbed out, grabbed his eight iron out of his bag, and took a couple practice swings.

"Because she wants what she wants. That's TJ. Stubborn as a mule her whole life. She thinks having Molly around will bring Julie back somehow. But it won't. It's only gonna hurt that little girl, not to mention that darlin' baby grandchild of mine, and traumatize them both more than they already are." He sighed. "I'm an old man. I've worked my whole life. I love my granddaughter, but I don't really want to be raising another child if I don't have to…if she's fine where she is. Grandparents are supposed to step in when there's no one to do the job. Cordova is perfectly capable."

Jed looked up into the sky, like he was searching for a sign. "And that's what Julie would've wanted, I have no doubt."

Dale stood next to his ball and chipped it onto the far side of the green. "Goddamn it, that's gonna be a par at best. I thought I'd get me a birdie with such a great tee shot."

They drove up to Jed's ball, where he quickly chipped it up onto the green and about two inches from the pin.

"Somethin's gotta change," he said. "I don't know quite how to go about it, but all this pullin' on that little girl and trying to take her away from those folks up there...when she's already lost so much..." his voice trailed off.

"Well, judging from that chip, it looks like your golf game might be changing...for the better, anyway."

After they finished up with the Ninth hole, Jed and Dale walked into the clubhouse for a beer. Through the glass window, Jed noticed several men with a plethora of colored golf shirts, seated around the bar. All of them had their attention firmly on the TV behind the lines of liquor bottles. Light music was being pumped into the background of the patio area, which held several empty tables and chairs. Normally, the patio was jammed with people, but it was early yet and the lunch crowd hadn't showed up: golfers finishing up, wives waiting for their husbands, ladies lunching.

Jed noticed something was slightly off about the scene inside the clubhouse. As Dale wiped his shoes on the brush mat outside of the door, Jed walked in, looked up at the television and could see smoke rising from the Twin Towers in the New York skyline.

Time literally stood still, and Jed McVicar could not move any farther along the carpeted room floor.

Social Studies

Molly filled in the letter B on her last multiple choice question of her first full test in Seventh Grade Social Studies. Mr. Davies sat up in front of the classroom and started collecting a small pile of tests on the right-hand corner of his desk. Kaitlin Finney stood up, flung her long blond hair over her shoulder, and then carried her test up to him, walking with a confidence that Molly craved in areas of her life other than on the soccer field. She wished she had that long blond hair too. Her mother had blond hair, and while she loved her father and missed him dearly, she wished she had been gifted by God to be a tall and clear skinned blond instead of a skinny fully freckled girl with straight mousy brown hair and bony elbows and knobby knees.

The boys in her class seemed to like the girls who looked like Kaitlin instead of the girls who looked like Molly…except for the boys who played with Pokemon cards and read graphic novels on the concrete barrier near the carpool lane outside. Those boys liked the girls like Molly.

Someone knocked on Mr. Davies' door. He slowly rose from his chair as the simultaneous cadence of heads flew up from their testing induced quiet. He cracked the door open, mumbling ensued, and he closed it.

"Class, I have to step out for a moment. Please continue to take your test and do not speak or… Can I trust you all?" he asked. The students just sat there rather dumbfounded. *That was kind of a stupid question*, Molly thought to herself. *Of course, he can't trust a bunch of Seventh graders taking a test with no adult supervision.* But Mr. Davies didn't wait around for an answer. He just walked out the door. And he didn't come back for almost twenty minutes.

Molly watched her classmates as several talked quietly among themselves after about five minutes of silence. A few kept to themselves, like Molly did. As she waited for her teacher to come back, she fell into her head again, into all the chaos surrounding her young life.

At first, it took a good three weeks for Molly to grasp everything that was happening and her role in it. The Guardian ad Litem assigned to her case was a nice lady name Cate DeLuca. When she wasn't Guardian ad Litem-ing, she worked in a lawyer's office transcribing videotaped depositions part time. She told Molly, when she first met her, that transcribing testimony was awfully boring, but it paid the bills. She enjoyed being a Guardian ad Litem because it kept her involved with her real passion – helping the children who existed in the in-between and in the cracks of society – kids in an unfortunate bind not of their own making.

Kids like Molly.

When she met with Cate to discuss Buddy, her little sister, her life, and her own wishes, Molly shared with Cate her own feelings: she wanted to know her grandparents and wouldn't mind visiting them from time to time, but she didn't want to live with them. She told Cate that she wanted to live with Buddy and her baby sister in Fayetteville and remain with her friends and her school and her soccer team.

When the Temporary Custody Hearing came up on the calendar, Cate reported to the Judge, who presided over the case, that Molly wanted to stay where she was…with her stepfather. Then there would be a mediation session to see if a deal could be worked out, rather than go to a custody trial. But before they could make any headway in the mediation, there was a whole big blow up about Buddy not really being Buddy, and his mother not really being named Loretta and some man down in Texas who died a long time ago because Loretta shot him and ran away.

Buddy explained to her what he could but swore that even though he was born with the name "Daniel Kaspar Junior," he was still the same person she has always known. He never lied to her – he just kept certain secrets to himself to protect his mother. So, Cate explained to Molly that the final custody wouldn't be determined until they had a mediation or a trial. And she had no idea how this new mess would play into it all.

Since it was all so confusing to Molly, Cate just promised her that she would keep fighting for what Molly wanted.

At first, when Buddy and her grandparents went to Court for the Temporary Custody Hearing, to talk about where she would stay until the mediation or custody trial, the Judge ruled that Molly could stay in Buddy's custody temporarily, until final custody was decided. Then later, when her grandparents' lawyer tried to get custody because of what they discovered about Buddy, Judge Starks thankfully let his original Order stand…that all the sordid business down in Texas with his mother Loretta had nothing to do with him and his fitness as a temporary guardian for her.

Molly would never forget that day.

She came home from school and walked toward the front door with more anxiety wailing around inside of her than she ever recalled experiencing before. Somehow, she got through the day okay, and somehow, she made it off the bus without falling down the steps from the lightheadedness that dogged her. She could see the front door cracked open and so she knew Buddy was back from the Courthouse. She was so scared to go inside, to find out what went on, to know the truth about what would happen to her for the near future and then maybe for the rest of her childhood.

Buddy had warned her that he could lose. He warned her that he wasn't sure what would happen, which way it would go, especially with all the crazy stuff about his mother and their life before they came to North Carolina. He said he wouldn't lie to her just to make her feel better. He wouldn't give her false hope. He would treat her like a young lady because it was also her life being decided for her. He promised that if he lost this first round, he wouldn't give up on keeping her home for good. He would keep fighting through the custody trial, and if he lost that, he'd keep on appealing until he won. That no matter what happened with his own mother, he would never stop fighting for her so she could stay home, where she belonged.

Molly had slowly opened the door, her stomach in knots, revealing Cate and Buddy standing in the doorway between the kitchen and the living room. They were talking. Cate wore a form fitting business suit, and her wild black and gray hair looked like it needed a good brushing. But it always looked like that. And when Buddy turned his head toward Molly, she knew. She knew that she could stay. At least for now. The first round went to Buddy.

Buddy's full smile – something that came out only once in a while – was huge. She could see his teeth. Buddy was one of those people who rarely showed happiness or joy in the form of a full tooth smile. But today, there was one. Molly ran toward him, and the floodgates opened. She cried months' worth of suppressed tears as she jumped into his arms. He held her tightly, full of fear that if he let her go, the Judge might change his mind and make her leave their home.

No words needed to be said between them. It was one of the happiest moments of her twelve years, even though she knew deep down inside that it wasn't the end of it. At least it was a win. One small win. But in Molly's mind, it was the most hope she felt within her entire frame since the day she learned that her mother went for a run and would never come back.

Cate rubbed her back with the tips of her fingers and said gently, "Congratulations to you both. It's okay to breathe now." Molly's head stayed firmly in the crook of Buddy's neck until he put her down on the couch like she was still a small child.

As Molly came out of her one recent happy memory and looked over at the ever-rising giggling and laughter going on between Kaitlin and the boys in the classroom, Mr. Davies opened the door and pushed a TV on a stand inside the classroom.

"Class, please…everyone…go back to your seats." He plugged in the TV and tuned the channel to the news. "Everyone, listen. There is something happening that you all need to know about." His voice was desperate, almost like he was scared. "History. Now. You're going to witness history today right on this television. A horrible history. Every day for the rest of your life, you will remember this day, this moment, this classroom, who's sitting next to you and how you will feel."

The class went completely silent. Even though they were basically just a bunch of self-absorbed, drama obsessed, videogame playing Seventh graders, telling them that they would be a witness to history was an awfully big way to grab their full attention.

"Planes have flown into the World Trade Center in New York. The news is saying that they believe it's a terrorist attack," he announced, almost like he was out of breath and entering into a panic. "There is another plane that's flown into the Pentagon in Washington DC, and they're saying that there's another plane out there that no one has contact with…maybe…headed for the Capitol."

Molly sat back in the hard and uncomfortable chair that adorned public school classrooms across America. The students sat still and upright in their seats, quiet and serious, young minds fully engaged with their teacher.

The news finally came up onto the screen with live video and split screens, and as Molly and her fellow classmates watched devastation and carnage and smoke and fast speaking pretty people on the news who seemed flummoxed and baffled, even though they had been trained to talk through tragedies, she knew that no matter what happened in her case with Buddy and her grandparents, the world would never be the same again.

As she took all of this in, the sadness and magnitude of this day, Molly had a moment of clarity…the kind that usually only happens in the midst of a crisis. She knew that she needed to – against Buddy's wishes and without his permission – tell her grandparents her own feelings about everything. She needed to confront them in her own way.

Life was too hard and too short to be anything but honest with the people in your family and with the people who say they love you.

CHAPTER 12

September 12th, 2001 – March 2002

Grassy Knolls

Buddy stood at the bottom of the small grassy knoll, thinking about the JFK assassination. He wasn't yet born when that national tragedy occurred; however, as a boy, he recalled an afternoon when he was very young, at work with his mother in Delta's Hair Salon in Killeen. He sat on the floor in a corner coloring...inside the lines... of a large dog in a coloring book. Kenny bought him a fresh pack of crayons from the new drugstore near their house, and he was using a new brown one – its tip sharp and ready. He tried to stay within the lines but went outside a little bit along the dog's floppy ear.

All the ladies were talking about where they were when President Kennedy was shot by that crazy Communist with three names. They all kept referring to a "grassy knoll." And, ever since that day, whenever he saw a grassy knoll, he thought about those ladies and their expressive stories...their own memories from Texas in 1963.

"I was cuttin' hair in my daddy's place when it happened!" his mother's best friend May Ellen shared with her friends that day. "My friend Martha asked me to cut the back of her hair so she could look like the girl on Mickey Mouse Club. My daddy had a tall stool in his office. So, I took Martha in there and started cutting her hair with a pair of scissors I found in his desk drawer. Then we could hear people in the hardware store gettin' loud and the TV volume being turned up. Martha got up with only half her hair cut off, and we watched everything in shock. My daddy was wearing his white work apron and crying right there in the store! I don't think he even cried when my mama died!"

"I was in school sitting next to Bobby Walton. I went to the private school. Bobby was so dreamy, and I had the biggest crush on him. I don't remember the class we were in at the time. In fact, I forgot everything else that was going on whenever I was around that boy. But not on that day! We were trying to sneak a piece of bubble gum in our mouths without getting caught when the school secretary came in the room to tell us about President Kennedy," another hairdresser named Donna told everyone. "My most vivid memory was a quiet girl in the class who always kept to herself...well, she started bawling like a baby...like the President was kin to her!"

"I was shopping with my mama. She let me skip school that day. We were trying to find a dress for a birthday party. I remember walking by the department store window, and there was a crowd building up inside of it near the television sales area. All the TVs were on and showing the same thing. Mama and I went inside and watched Walter Cronkite for a long time. My mama cried like a black person...what's it they call that kind of crying?...wailing?" one of the customers shared.

Buddy listened to the ladies that afternoon long ago and took in everything they said about President Kennedy's assassination. It was something he had not been witness to, something that sounded like a cartoon on a Saturday morning involving talking animals instead or a scary storybook that he would only find at Gary's house...because

Gary's mother was a little on the dark side. Someone so important getting shot in his car in broad daylight was unheard of back then, as far as he knew. And now, as he stood in front of yet another grassy knoll in Texas, he found himself a newly minted witness to a national tragedy of his own generation. He would always know where he was and what he was doing on the day the Twin Towers fell.

This was the spot that the nice gentleman in the Veterans' Cemetery office directed him. Buddy's legs stretched out as he walked among the small gravesites, the white tooth shaped hunks of cement informing the living that they were in the dead's garden now.

Buddy always thought it was weird what humans do. Bury each other. Put each other under the ground to rot away. And then erect simple or elaborate monuments above it.

Approaching a small flat marker, which also held a small American flag sticking out of the ground, he read:

Kenneth Bellinger
CPL
US Army
Vietnam
JUL 26 1945
SEP 2 1982
A good man

Apparently, a man who had tried to help Kenny with his drinking and his mental problems paid to have him buried in the Veterans' Cemetery near Killeen after he died. He was the one who found Kenny on the floor – very much alive – back in 1975. The paramedics worked hard to save his life, but because he had gone too long without oxygen to his brain, Kenny remained in a vegetative state for years. No one ever claimed responsibility over his medical care, and the man felt so badly about everything that he decided to look after Kenny in the hospital from time to time. The man died in 1994, but before he passed, he asked that a letter be given to the police detective who had been assigned to Kenny's case.

When all the files of Kenny's cold case were reopened upon the revelations of Tammy Jo McVicar in that North Carolina courthouse conference room on a sunny day in 2001, that letter was unearthed at last. And Patchett the Hatchet handed it over to Buddy privately, out of his mother's presence. It was dated September 11th, 1982.

Dear Buddy,

You didn't know me real well, if you remember me at all, but I met you a couple times when you were just a little boy. I know by now you are almost grown, and I hope that wherever you are, you're happy. Your stepfather Kenny would've wanted that for you and your mama too.

I'm writing this letter because I want you to know about the man your mama shot. I'm sure she did it because he was going to hurt her or even you. And I'm sure he wanted her to shoot him, too. Your stepfather was suffering for a long time with a disease in his mind and he didn't feel like there was much of a way out of his suffering except for alcohol.

By the time that I found him on the floor, he was almost gone. After what I saw happen to him afterward that in the hospital, I probably should've left him there to die in that house. It would've been more humane.

He'd done some bad things, I know. He hurt your mama something fierce and kept her living in fear for a long time. He put all his pain onto both of you, and he could've killed your mama, I'm sure. But I want you to know that something happened to Kenny that also happened to a lot of the boys who went over to Vietnam. It took a while for it to surface in Kenny after he got back, but he was slowly losing his mind and taking you and your mama down with him. And I know that was bad.

Kenny was a good man before that started happening. He worked for me, and I could always rely on him. He worked hard, always did extra and was a good friend to everybody who met him. He loved fast cars and wanted so bad to afford a nice car for you one day when you were old enough to drive. He loved your mama so much that he talked about her all the time and how she made him feel. Only men who are truly in love do that. And he loved you too. Like you were his first born son. He said you both made him want to be a better man.

I remember him telling me at the warehouse how he had met this dark haired beauty and her good little boy, who she called Buddy. He always called you his "Good Buddy." He was so happy when he became a stepfather to you because you and your mama gave him something he always wanted – a family. He never had much of a family when he was a boy. And I know that you might not feel like this is true, but Kenny meant to do right by you and your mama for the rest of his life.

I don't know where it all went wrong for Kenny, but somewhere along the way, maybe around the time when your mama lost the baby, he started slipping away from all of us. He changed completely. I've seen it happen to so many good men here in this town after Vietnam, and lots of the boys ended up losing their families because of it. Some call it "shell shock" and the doctors are now calling it "Post Traumatic Stress Disorder."

I don't know about all the fancy names of things that doctors talk about, but I do know that I had suffered from some of that myself years ago – until I found the Lord who helped me heal.

I'm telling you all this because I want you to know that your stepfather was a very sick man who needed the kind of help that only doctors or God could give him. But he never got it in time. He wasn't a bad man. He wasn't evil. He wanted to do right. And he loved his family.

I hope when you read this, you'll be old enough to understand that life can be just a cruel and dark place at times, and no matter how much good you do and how hard you try and how much you love, sometimes a man is just broken and cannot find his way back to wholeness.

When Kenny finally passed away, I wanted him buried proper because no family claimed him, and I felt that he deserved a resting place among his brothers. I paid for him to be buried at Fairfield Veterans Park with the rest of the men interred there, some who died on foreign soil, in defense of freedom. Kenny may have died in a hospital, a shell of the man he once was, but the best part of him – the part you and your mama saw for a while - died in Vietnam right along with your real father.

I wish you and your mama well, Good Buddy.

Sincerely,
Hollis Foster

Buddy folded the letter back into its years-long deep creases and stuffed it back into the envelope. Putting it into his pants pocket, he walked closer to Kenny's gravestone, bent down, and allowed his fingers to trace over the etched stone. He sat down on the neatly manicured grass which covered his remains hidden deep down and underneath the ground.

As hardened memories of those last few years of living with the likes of Kenny Bellinger and his anger and drinking and destruction began to take over Buddy's emotions, he let himself feel it…really feel it…for the first time in his entire life. He allowed himself to weep over those lost years, years that were taken from him as a boy. And he wept over the years that Kenny lost, too, years he never had to get the help he so desperately needed, years he spent as a shadow, a wasted soul never to see the light of day again. As a boy, he grew to hate him for what he did to his family. As a man, he realized that life's not always so black and white.

"I'm sorry, Kenny," he said softly at the cold white stone, which stared back at him in eternal silence. And then as if there was a wrinkle in the space beyond life and death, he swore he heard a faraway but familiar voice whisper, "That's a ten-four, Good Buddy."

Scrapbooking

Tammy Jo sat on Julie's old double sized bed, which was primarily used for any out-of-town guests who happened to need a place to stay. It was raining outside, and she felt the quiet wrapped around her unlike most mornings since Julie's passing. The rest of the world was watching the day after and the day after that of the September 11th attacks on all the news channels, and Tammy Jo just could not watch it anymore. She hadn't slept in two days. It took until nighttime, but she finally got word that her niece Randi, who worked for a marketing company in Manhattan, was safe and had escaped the North Tower in time.

Life was weighing heavily on her, and as she wiped another tear from her eye, she gazed down at the large box, which sat open on the floor with a pile of scrapbooks inside. Tammy Jo reached down and picked out her favorite one, a large book with a leather-bound cover and "Julie Marie McVicar" inscribed on the outside in gold italic print.

When she was a young mother and Julie was just a toddler, a friend, who was also in the same boat, got her into the art of scrapbooking. At first, she found it tedious because she wasn't the most creative woman in the world. But then, she found that she truly enjoyed it. Immensely. It calmed her down, made her incessant worrying more of a dull buzz in the background of her heart. She could live with it after cutting paper and pasting it into pretty pages of stories. The madness in her heart became less paralyzing.

Scrapbooking made her take her time, slow down, work at a delicate pace, take in the details of her daughter as she grew up, notice the little things. Even when she started working and building her company when Julie was much older, it was scrapbooking that kept her grounded and sane. Some mothers read a lot of books or sewed or knitted or joined a gym for their space and peace. Tammy Jo would disappear into her box of photographs and scraps of paper and specialized photo tape that didn't yellow over time.

She'd take the photos of her daughter throughout the years and paste them onto nice pages, adorning them with colored paper and embellishments and funny captions, until she completed an entire book. She finished about four of them during Julie's childhood and figured she'd continue doing them as Julie went through college and got married and had a career and her own children. Then she'd start scrapbooks for her grandchildren. But that didn't happen. Instead, the scrapbooks, just like her entire relationship with her daughter, simply stopped in time.

As she flipped through the pages of Julie's photographed childhood, her blond hair wild in the sunshine, her smile as bright as the future she could've had, her joy spreading throughout each captured moment, as she waded in a kiddie pool and ran through the sprinkler and chased her father around the backyard on a warm summer evening. She was a fun child, so full of life and laughter, and each photo brought back those early years of motherhood – the exact feelings and smells and thoughts that make up that crippling disease called "nostalgia."

Why did nostalgia only seem to include these bright and sunny times? Was it our brain's way to temper the pain of the general suffering of real life in real time? Why did nostalgia insist on only going back to those years, the ones where motherhood appeared to be the happiest and most fulfilling? To a time when a mother didn't feel like such a failure at everything she did for her child? When youth was not just with the young…but also remained within the hearts and minds of the mothers who held a child she loved more than anything…and that child loved her back the same?

She was hard on Julie when she got older because she knew that girl could've had whatever kind of life she wanted if she applied herself. Then Julie did the dumbest thing, the stupidest thing, the very thing that young women have done throughout all of time…fall head over heels in love and then surrender herself to a man long before she ever got to do a damn thing for herself. Her entire identity. Lost in a man. Yet again. Progress for modern women ultimately went straight back into the toilet.

And because she was the mother, she was the only one who would do anything or say something to her daughter about her poor choices. Fathers just go to work, come home…and then if they have enough energy…might say a few words. They only observe the hard things…and at a good distance. Fathers do their own thing, and let the mothers do all the dirty work. Fathers are only perfect in the eyes of their baby girls because they don't ever have to utter a harsh word or speak the ugly truth. Fathers can disappear to have a beer with their golf buddies after being gone all day and then just swoop into the house with a rose or a ten-dollar bill and be the greatest parent who ever lived. If mothers did that, they'd be classified as "selfish" and "neglectful."

Life was nothing but a double standard for mothers. Being a father was easy. Mothers carry the weight of their daughters' tears and failures and heartbreaks and shame. And fathers? Fathers carry their daughters' hearts. And they don't have to do much of anything at all to have them…other than give their girls a hug from time to time…or a buy them a new dress. At least, this was how Tammy Jo McVicar saw it. Her father was no different than her own husband.

Ever since she lost her daughter for good, Tammy Jo wallowed in the pool of regret. She should've done this, she should've done that, she wished she had done this, she wished she had done that. But it was a waste of her time. There was no righting the wrongs with Julie. There was no reconciliation between them to be had.

God only gives us so many chances to get things right in life. At some point, there are no more chances left. Julie had run out of time to get things right with her mother. And her Tammy Jo had run out of time to get things right with Julie.

But there was still time to get things right with Molly. She had not lost Molly. Julie's untimely and tragic death gave her the window she needed to be able to touch her granddaughter again. She would be damned if she ruined this gift from God…or maybe even a gift from Julie herself…with her own hard-worn stubbornness.

Tammy Jo started to cry years' worth of tears, the kind that hide behind a tough exterior and a big fat mouth, the ones that don't come out until the moment they really need to, an empty reservoir outside of her body waiting to be filled with all its pain. Her tears built up like an impenetrable fortress since the day Julie packed her car, drove off to Texas A&M and never came home again. And now that wall was coming down.

When was the last time that incredible girl set foot in this room? she thought to herself as she glanced around its pastel walls and shelving full of childhood knick-knacks like Precious Moments figurines and Raggedy Ann and Andy dolls. It had to have been in early August 1986, soon after she went out with her girlfriends to see Top Gun.

Julie packed up her clothes and everything she could stuff into her maroon Datsun 200SX, hugged her father tight and kissed her cat Muffin goodbye. The last memory Tammy Jo had of Julie at this house – her home – was her blond ponytail bobbing up and down as she walked along the driveway toward her future. And Tammy Jo watched from the bathroom window on the second floor.

This all could be Molly's now. Molly could have this room, this room all full of her mother's things and her mother's memories. Molly could have what Julie rejected – all the love and adoration in the world from her own mother who loved her more than anything in the whole world.

Molly could have a fresh start in a new place, a safe place, a place away from that sad town in North Carolina, the very place that stole both of her parents right from underneath of her. But she knew in her heart that Molly didn't want these things. At least, not the way Tammy Jo wanted her to want them.

Mail

Jed looked outside at the rain pummeling the window, his sleep deprived mind in stitches, and took another swig of his coffee. As he watched the mail truck drive by his house, at its normal time, he was reminded once again that life goes on. Just because his beautiful daughter died in an accident, and just because the country is in the immediate aftermath of one of the worst days in its entire history, doesn't mean that the mailman gets to stay home. The mail still needs to be delivered. People still need to go to work. The children still need to go to school. The sun still rises and sets.

No golf yesterday, no golf today, probably no golf tomorrow. It's just rain, rain, rain right now.

Jogging outside and dodging raindrops like an ambushed soldier dodging bullets, he grabbed the mail from the mailbox. When he got back inside and stood at his desk, he rifled through the stack of post and came across one with a young person's handwriting adorning an envelope. The letter was address to "Mr. and Mrs. McVicar" and was postmarked Fayetteville, North Carolina.

Dear Grandma and Grandpa,

I hope that you both are doing well down in Texas. It was real nice to spend time with you while you were up here for my mom's wake and funeral. I wish it had been a better time, though. I wish it had been at a time when my mom was still alive. Then we could've had a barbecue out back and then played a game of Yahtzee inside when it got too dark. I'm pretty good at Yahtzee, but my mom told me that Grandpa was the best at it when she was a little girl.

I'm writing you this letter because I want to tell you about what I think and what I want for my own life. My dad Buddy doesn't know I'm writing this letter and might be mad at me for doing it if he found out. So please don't tell him because he doesn't need to be more upset about everything going on than he already is. He wants me to try to stay away from all of this as much as possible and let the adults work it all out. But because I'm 12 years old now, and not really some little kid like Gabby, and this is supposed to be all about what's best for me, I think maybe I should be able to have a say and tell everyone what I think. So here goes.

Buddy, my dad, is a great dad. I don't care what his real name was when he was a little boy. And I want to stay with him and my little sister. They both need me and I need them, too. We are a team and have been since I was 7 years old.

When my mom died, it felt so much worse than when my real father died. When my real father died, I was still small, and I can remember being real sad and crying about my daddy, but it wasn't the same as with my mom. Probably because I was so little at the time and it was so long ago. But when my mom died, I don't think that I can describe just how much that hurts all the time. I can't believe she's gone. I still think that she's just out running like usual and will be back soon. Most of the time, I don't even know what I'm doing. I know that it's just a part of grief. My school counselor told me about all the stages of grief and so I understand all that.

My little sister isn't going to remember my mom at all. It's going to be my job to help raise her and be there for her every day. But it's also my job to carry my mom's memory for her. It's going to be my job to show Gabby who my mom was because I am the only person even more than Buddy who knew her the best.

My mom was a great mom, the best mom in the world. She took care of me all by herself after my daddy died, and then she chose the best new father for me that she could ever find. She gave me a baby sister too.

My dad Buddy is everything that a dad should be. I love him. And I just don't feel like I can leave him all alone now. Someday, I'll grow up and will need to leave him like all kids leave their parents for college. But now is not the right time. He has lost so much already.

I'm sorry that you guys and my mom didn't get to work out your problems before she died, but I hope you understand that I want to stay with my family here in North Carolina. I do want to know you better, though, and I hope that you'd want me and Gabby and even Buddy to come down there and visit sometimes. Maybe we could spend Christmas together or go to Disney World. I bet that Buddy would love for you to visit us here, too.

If all the stuff that's happened in New York can happen to anyone, then we should be trying to live each day like we love each other. We don't have a big family. All we have are each other. So, can't we stop fighting over me and where I live and Buddy's mom and instead maybe see that it doesn't have to be some contest about who is blood related and real family and who belongs where.

I belong with my dad Buddy and my little sister. That is what's best for me. But what's also best for me is that my grandparents are a part of my life, just like every other kid gets to have their grandparents.

Anyway, I'm sorry that I don't want to move down there and live with you. But I love my dad and my sister too much to leave them. I hope you understand and that we can still always be a part of each other's lives. Because I love you.

Sincerely, your granddaughter,
Molly Saint

Jed McVicar dropped the handwritten letter onto the kitchen counter, put his hands to his face and started to cry. He knew – like he knew the whole time this had been going on – what needed to happen.

Buddy sat on the floor of Gabby's room trying to separate her laundry into colors and whites. The whites pile was much smaller than the colors, mostly full of tiny under shirts. How does a kid go through so many tiny pieces of clothing in one day? He recalled running the washer and dryer a little more than usual when Molly was in soccer season; however, a toddler gives the weekly uniform demands of an athlete a run for their money.

"Hey, Buddy! It's for you," Molly hollered from the kitchen, snapping him out of his mind's laundry musings. Realizing right then and there that he was so out of it that he hadn't even heard the phone ring, Buddy got up and stretched his hamstrings. How many calls had he missed today? From clients, even?

He left the chore of the hour on the carpet and walked to the kitchen to find Molly standing with the receiver in her hand. With a Pringle chip inside her mouth, she shoved the phone into his hand and said, "it's Miss Wisnewski."

Buddy cringed. No one wants to hear from their lawyer, unexpectedly, while in the middle of an ugly and emotionally charged case…it usually meant bad news. He put the phone up to his ear and took a deep breath.

"Hey, Lisa, how's it going?"

And as Buddy listened intently to his lawyer excitedly explain to him that the McVicars wanted to withdraw their petition for custody of Molly, he could feel the hairs on his neck and forearms begin to stand at attention. Goosebumps took over the fabric of his skin and his heart rate began to rise. They had a guardian angel after all.

Visiting Day

Buddy, Molly, and Gabby waited at a picnic table outside the Trudeau Correctional Facility for Women in Becton, North Carolina, a minimum-security prison, where Retta Bellinger was given yet another identity…Inmate Number 476329. She had one more month left to serve on her active prison sentence and then she'd be on parole for three years.

Since the Bell County, Texas District Attorney decided not to charge her with any criminal offenses, due to lack of evidence that she had committed any crimes in Texas, the Cumberland County District Attorney in North Carolina, who had been waiting on Bell County's decision, felt that Retta Bellinger, AKA Loretta Cordova, should have to suffer some legal consequence for the crimes she committed while living in North Carolina in the years since her arrival in the Fall of 1975.

Apparently, hiding in fear of your life and having to give up your entire identity and ties to all friends and family was not enough of a consequence in the Prosecutor's mind. So, nine months of prison in a minimum-security facility, where she could bake cookies and make crafts with a few white-collar criminals and downtrodden women with drug problems, and then three years of probation, sent enough of a message to the electorate in Fayetteville about his "compassionately tough on crime" campaign slogan. That was the best deal Loretta could get worked out with the District Attorney, even with her own son serving as her defense attorney.

Loretta pled guilty to Forgery, a Class G Felony, and was extremely fortunate to be given the sentence she received. The DA could have charged her with the lesser offense of Possession of Fraudulent Identification, a Misdemeanor, but felt like that was too lenient. However, she had a sympathetic judge who signed the plea deal and gave her a short speech during her sentencing hearing: "Mrs. Bellinger, today you begin the last leg of carrying that traumatic burden on your back. Keep your eyes forward, your head up, and before you know it, you will be set free from all of it. No more running and hiding from the past."

Joe was in tears as she was escorted away by the Sheriff's deputy, and Molly held his hand tightly. "She's going to be okay, Grandpa Joe," she whispered to him.

Joe squeezed her hand, knowing Molly was probably right. She had been through so much for so long that a short prison sentence at a place nicknamed "Camp Cakewalk" might feel a bit like a vacation.

"I'm gonna miss her, Molly," he whispered back. But he also knew that in nine months' time, not only would his beautiful Loretta be free from a literal prison, but she would be free from a prison of her own making...she would finally, at long last, agree to marry him.

Loretta walked out to the visiting area, and Gabby toddled over to her grandmother with her arms stretched out. The weekly visits made the time go by faster, and Loretta was grateful for that. So was Buddy. The guilt he carried because he was unable to get her a zero-prison time deal, weighed on him unlike anything else.

Everyone hugged Loretta and sat down on the bench. Women in tan jumpsuits and wearing prison issue sweatshirts walked around a dirt track on this rather mild early February afternoon. Several children were at the other picnic benches, some visiting their mothers who were at Camp Cakewalk for similar types of offenses and some for lesser drug crimes. However, the most interesting prisoner was a famous author who was found guilty of insider trading several months ago, serving ten months at Trudeau right alongside Loretta. The author was sitting on a bench talking to a young man, her adult son, per her cellmate Katherine.

"Son," Loretta reminded Buddy, who always looked defeated when he arrived to visit his mother. "You got me the best deal you could. If that rich author couldn't get out of her crimes, then I had no chance getting off scot-free for twenty-five years' worth of fraudulent living."

Buddy knew she was right. "Some things shouldn't be crimes, Mother. Protecting your child should not be a crime. You never defrauded anyone. You paid your bills – on time – and kept all your contracts. It just pisses me off because no one was actually victimized by what you did in North Carolina."

"It's okay, Buddy. You might be right in a way, but the law is the law, and I broke it for good reasons. And as a lawyer, you know how it is…it doesn't matter if it was for good reasons."

She held Gabby on her lap and bounced her up and down a bit, humming the Lone Ranger theme song to the bouncing. Molly and Buddy sat across from her and watched her black hair flop around, starting to fill in with some pesky grays here and there, no longer such easy access to quality hair care products.

They talked about the famous author and how she was handling laundry duty this week. Buddy guessed that the author would have one hell of a new book completed by the end of her prison stint. They discussed what was going on in the world, how Molly was handling the Seventh Grade, and if she was ready for her soccer tournament in Richmond next weekend.

Loretta's spirits were higher than last weekend because she knew that her time in this place was coming to an end. She would be so happy to go home again, to be back with her sweet Joe, to resume her life...but she was also a little apprehensive. There was this awkward pause in her daily existence which would need to be explained in detail to the wonderful law abiding citizens in Welby who had long considered her one of their own.

After their hour was up, Buddy stood with Gabby on his hip.

"Son, are you alright today?" Loretta asked him, grabbing his hand. It had been almost a whole year without Julie. So many of the "firsts" had gone by...except for the first anniversary of her death.

"Still day-to-day, Mother. Most days are still tough. But I'll get there. I've got no choice, really," he winced, squeezing her hand.

Loretta pulled Molly into a full embrace, the going on thirteen-year-old girl now even with her in height. Kissing her on the forehead, as she said her goodbye to her family, she pulled back and looked Molly into her big brown eyes. "I can't wait," was all she said. Molly knew exactly what she meant and hugged her back with an extra tight squeeze.

Flags

The country seemed like it was just in a consistent state of mourning, mixed with a collective simmering anger. After September 11th, eventually, people got on with their lives…like people do. They went back to work each day and buying stuff they don't need and going on vacations they couldn't afford. Spending money became the rallying cry of American patriotism.

Every day, there was something that reminded Buddy of September 11th. Sure, he knew no one personally who died in the World Trade Center or in a field in Pennsylvania or in the Pentagon. But there were whispers of war and terrorism and Osama Bin Laden and al Qaida and "boots on the ground" and Iraq and Afghanistan… and no whispers are louder than when whispered within the confines of a military town.

The Airborne Museum was a place that Buddy had always planned to take Molly. Her father was a paratrooper, and he died from jumping out of a C-130 aircraft. The history of the Airborne was located inside of the facility, and he wanted Molly to understand the kinds of risks her father took for freedom.

Inside Buddy's mind, when passing by this place, the Army cadence, "C-130 rolling on the strip, Airborne Ranger on a one-way trip…" played on a cassette tape loop throughout his mind from all his years overhearing it on and around Post. As he, Molly and Gabby made their way out of the parking lot and onto the sidewalk toward the sea of American flags standing united in an open field, his heart held tight.

Buddy always knew that he would've made a good soldier had he enlisted or pursued a commission as an officer. His family, whether biological or assumed, were all parts or products of military service:

his father in Vietnam, his mother's father in World War II, his mother's brother during Vietnam, Joe Horton served four years in the Navy, and then Kenny. Buddy always felt like he was missing out, but other than registering for the Selective Service when he was eighteen, Loretta made him swear he'd never go in, never take an oath to "support and defend the Constitution of the United States."

"I know that there's something special about being a soldier, Buddy, but you just can't do it. It's another opportunity for us to be found out," she explained to him years ago, when he was a teenaged boy leafing through a pamphlet given to him by a recruiter who had visited the high school. "Besides, I lost your father and even your stepfather to war, and I cannot bear to lose you."

So, Buddy found another way to support and defend the Constitution of the United States. People always wondered why he left law school in Chapel Hill and decided to settle by himself in Fayetteville.

So many folks who lived there were either native for generations or affiliated in some way with the military. It wasn't the sort of place that a young single man simply transplanted himself and turned into a home. It was transient. There were seedy and impoverished areas, like in most military towns, and a hustle and bustle in certain parts that made you wonder if it ever stood still. But he felt himself drawn to it…enough to go there and set up a life of his own. And it led him to Julie. It led him to Molly. He found his home for the first time in his life.

Gabby held three small American flags in her chubby fist. There was a slight breeze outside, a bus load of elderly people coming out of the entrance of the museum door, and a set of biker-less Harley Davidsons with POW/MIA stickers and American flags lining the parking lot next to the sidewalk.

"Can I have one of the flags?" Molly asked her little sister who stopped along the first row and looked up at her daddy. She gave one of the flags to Molly.

Molly placed her flag into the ground, adding it to the many already standing at attention. "This flag is for my daddy, Sergeant Gabriel Saint."

Gabby watched her big sister kneeling on the ground in front of the flag. She bent down and stuck the other two flags into the ground next to Gabe's. Molly turned toward Buddy, looked up at him, and then she put her hand to her eyes to shield them from the sun.

"One is for your daddy, Daniel Kaspar Senior," she stated. "Who's the other one for? Grandpa Joe?"

Buddy took a deep breath…let it out…and replied, "No. It's for my stepfather, Kenny Bellinger."

Molly eyed him for an extended beat, and then turned back around, adjusting the flags so they were an equal amount of space apart from each other.

Official

A large red velvet sheet cake with "Congratulations Molly" written on it in red icing from the Food Lion bakery, sat undisturbed on the dining room table in the Cordova home. It was a Friday evening in late March, and friends and neighbors would start to fill up the kitchen and living room soon.

Jed and Tammy Jo McVicar flew in from Texas in the morning and should be arriving at any minute from their hotel. Some of Molly's teammates and classmates were coming over. Cate DeLuca, her Guardian ad Litem, and a couple of her teachers, some of whom were friends with her mother, were coming as well. Several neighbors promised they would be there. Even Jasper Ray, the mailman, said he would stop by with a special gift, handmade in his shed. He loved to tell Molly that if it hadn't been for him, she never would have met Buddy.

Buddy and Loretta stood in the kitchen setting up the chafing dishes, paper plates and utensils, waiting for the caterer to arrive with the hot food. It would be Molly's favorite: General Tso's chicken, white rice, fried rice and egg rolls. They would also have a nugget platter from Chick-Fil-A just because that was Gabby's favorite, and Molly wanted her little sister to be as happy as she was on this special day.

Joe was out at the store looking for a new knife to cut the cake. He accidentally broke the handle when pulling it from the drawer and dropping it onto the floor.

Gabby sat on the couch quietly, watching Blue's Clues and holding her Tickle Me Elmo.

Molly stood alone in her bedroom, flooded with her racing thoughts and so much happiness swelling in her heart. So happy that she couldn't remember the last time it felt so full.

She looked straight into her dresser mirror, which was accented with small photos of Mia Hamm, Brandi Chastain, Abby Wambach, Cindy Parlow and several world class female soccer players. She had a photo of the 1999 World Cup women's team stuck to the top of her mirror, and then there was the rogue David Beckham photo with a small heart sketched next to his foot. A few soccer tournament medals draped along the top, hanging down, a reminder of small successes on the pitch. A simple neon green brush sat on top of the dresser, alongside a jewelry box holding her mother's special pinky ring and two mother-daughter necklaces she wore around her neck. She would give one of them to Gabby someday when she was older.

Instead of the usual ponytail she sported on most days, her straight brown hair fell well past her shoulders. Instead of a pair of jeans, a tee shirt and her soccer team's warm-up jacket that she wore to school most of the time, she wore a plain pastel pink and white dress, which came down to the bottom of her knees. Her feet remained bare.

A new gold necklace with a pearl white locket hung down on her chest. It was a gift from Buddy. He gave it to her earlier today outside the courtroom when the Judge made everything official.

Peering down, she opened the locket and looked inside. "To my daughter," said the engraving on the left side. On the right side, there was a small photo of the two of them sitting on the grass at the Fourth of July fireworks at Fort Bragg, Molly sitting between his outstretched legs, during their first summer together. It was the same one that had been in the newspaper. Molly wondered how he got the photo so small that it could fit inside the locket.

She faced herself in the mirror again and took a deep breath.

"Molly Saint Cordova," she said out loud to herself. "Hello. My name is Molly Saint Cordova. So nice to meet you."

EPILOGUE

May 15th, 1975

Buddy could hear the nightmarish screaming coming from the kitchen, the clanging from a pot or a pan or an unbreakable dish – was there even such a thing? – and his mother's cries were the worst he had ever heard before. In the darkness, he sprinted from the side alley and wondered out loud to all the people huddled in their small houses around him, *Can't anyone else hear her screaming?* But no one seemed to. Or if they did, they kept to themselves and did not want to be involved in the Bellinger house's usual mayhem.

It was the first time in his young life that Buddy learned people who allowed evil to go on and did nothing about it were just as bad as the ones perpetrating the evil.

It was a breezy May night, cooled off significantly from the impending summer warm weather that had engulfed the town earlier in the day. The end of school was nearing, and the children were getting antsier than usual by the final bell. Buddy wasn't one of them, though. He wanted to be in school all the time. Being in school meant no Kenny to tip-toe around all day. Could there be such a thing as school all year long?

Buddy quickly ran across the short concrete slab serving as a patio in the patch of grass, which doubled as a backyard. He slid open the back door to the small rented house his family called home for several years and found the deafening moans and desperate pleas to outshine the hollering and wailing noises by Kenny's madness.

Buddy glided across the shag green carpeting, and in the faint light of the oven, he could see Kenny…with his hulking body over his mother…bang her head onto the floor of the kitchen, as she held her arms over her face and cried.

"You better stop! Stop it now!" Buddy screamed into the violent shadow in front of him.

Through her cries, he heard his mother yell, "Son, go! Get help!"

Kenny was in such a rage-fueled tirade, Buddy could not understand what he was shouting or saying. His words were unintelligible. His voice was strained. His anger consumed him; he seemed possessed by a demon like in that scary movie The Exorcist that he watched with Gary's family at the movies without his parents' permission. And as he pictured the many deep cuts in that little girl Regan's face as she spewed her vitriol at the Priest, housing the devil inside of her body, Buddy decided once and for all that his stepfather was not going to hurt his mother anymore. This was the last time.

He put his hand underneath his tee-shirt and felt the tip of the cold metal barrel resting in his belt loop. The cowboys on the western TV shows did it this way. So did the cops who wore no uniforms and forgot their holsters back in the car. So did the bad guys in the nice suits and sharp hats in the fancy black cars.

As he ran into the kitchen, he saw Kenny stand up, his mother lying on the floor in her underwear and still wearing the shirt she had on from the morning. Her arms and hands were covering the sides of her head and face. Her knees were up into her chest and her bare feet held firmly on the floor. Kenny started to step toward Buddy.

Retta Bellinger screamed out loud a shrill unlike any other he heard before, as they both watched Kenny fall backward and then into a heap onto the floor next to her. Completely overwhelmed with horror and shock of the ringing intensity coming from Buddy's way, Retta became engulfed with panic and fear about what was happening in front of her. She quickly scooted herself off to the side near the kitchen sink and then got onto her knees in tears. Buddy inched into the kitchen toward his mother, who then fell back into a ball, her arms wrapping around her thin bare legs…her body rocking back and forth.

Kenny was quiet. He was completely still and did not move. There were no sounds coming from him at all. His chest did not rise or fall. He was nothing but a large mass clumped onto the floor, shot cold in his place.

After a few minutes, which felt like a few hours, Retta remained frozen, crouching in her assumed spot on the floor. Buddy stood next to her, almost in a trance, and as she looked up at her son's face and found his beautiful eyelashes lingering in the moonlight as it shone through the small living room window, she knew deep down inside that her little boy was not a little boy anymore. He was a grown man now.

As Retta slowly managed to gather her head and calm her racing heart and control the unrelenting sobs as they hiccupped from the hollow of her throat and into the air, she realized that whatever hell they endured these past few years was now over…and a new hell was starting…the moment someone found Kenny Bellinger dead on their kitchen floor.

"Buddy!" she yelled at him, trying to wake him up. "Buddy! Son!" she started to shake him lightly, her hands wrapped around his small arms. Her cries were controlled, but she could feel herself holding off the panic inside. "What have you done?" she whispered.

There was no answer from her good boy, the quiet and thoughtful son she had raised so far. Buddy remained in a statue-like position as if he were like Lot's wife in the Bible, a frozen pillar of salt.

A gun sat on the floor at Buddy's feet. Retta had never seen the gun before and had no idea where it came from. Kenny did not have a gun. She did not have one. She knew May Ellen kept one in her drawer in the salon, and God knows she thought of stealing it once or twice...did Buddy steal May Ellen's gun? She had no idea but knew that regardless of where it came from, she had to get rid of it. She had to protect her son.

Soon enough, Retta found herself changing her shirt and pulling a skirt over her legs and shoes on her feet and hiding her stash in her bra and tossing some blankets and her paralyzed baby boy on the Duster's back seat. She grabbed her purse and cigarettes off the kitchen counter, closed the front door behind her, jumped into the car, put it into drive and drove west.

The end.

Author's Note and Acknowledgements

I started writing this novel while I was editing my first novel, *Scout's Honor*, and long before I knew my husband Eric was terminally ill. From the very beginning, Buddy Cordova was inspired by him and his selfless act of becoming our daughter Abigail's stepfather back in 1995. It was written for him, and ultimately, finished just in time for him. It was the last book Eric ever read.

I had the desire to tell a heartwarming story about a good, solid man who took on the responsibility of raising another man's child. But because of what happened to my husband and my family, the book's purpose grew into so much more. There are all kinds of step and surrogate fathers who come into our lives and take on this most important role. And none of it has anything to do with blood. It's about integrity, character, and ultimately…love.

Throughout the story, I tried to weave in pockets of hope for my husband. For us. Julie was always supposed to be a widow, and little did I know that I was, in some way, slowly turning into parts of this character. This book became Eric's novel, with fictionalized pieces of our own family, a morsel of his legacy – for not only him – but for our daughters and for anyone who ever knew him or cared about him. It became a way to keep a part of him alive.

Good Buddy is brush-stroked with some of the best of Eric's personality, his integrity, long eyelashes, blue eyes, military high and tight haircut (when I first met him), some of his quirks – like walking with his hands in his pockets, the way he always handled tipping in restaurants, awkward shyness around attractive women…with his endearing wily smile, and lots of inside jokes. Molly is a fusion of our daughters. When I first met Eric, he indeed had jugs of different flavors of Kool Aid in his refrigerator. And "Gay Days at Disney" hilariously happened to us in the summer of 2002.

I have a mountain of photos and a lifetime of thoughts, memories, regrets, joys, sorrows – just like every other family. But ours have ended, turned off like a broken faucet, never to be fixed. However, writing fiction allows me to create a few more. Writing – and then publishing *Good Budd*y – was really the only way that I could make a part of Eric live forever in my own fashion. He deserved so much better than what life handed him in his last year here. I hope readers are touched by this story, the characters I've created to tell it and will get a glimpse into a damn good man who inspired it all…through one significant act of love.

Thank you to my husband Eric and all the other incredible step and surrogate fathers and grandfathers out there who make the choice to love children who do not carry your DNA. Men like my brother Jon, my father-in-law John, my Uncle Glenn, and my brother-in-law Andrew. You are all a gift to your wives, their children – which are

YOUR children too, your grandchildren, extended family, and society at large.

Thank you to my resilient, intelligent, compassionate, and beautiful daughters, Abigail Raelene and Allison Leigh, who have been there to hold up their mother during her darkest days. Thank you both for being my strongest allies in our mutual hardships and grief, for shining a light on my mangled path and for reminding me that my life still has a purpose despite losing almost everything I had worked for…all at once. Thank you to my doxies, Stretch and Slinky, who have provided me with more snuggling and comfort than I've deserved.

Thank you to Mom, Jon, Ginger, John, Judy, Kristin, Celeste, Andrew, Zach, Micaela, Chase, Samantha, Sean, Jenny, Lorrie, Dan, Mel, Jo, Tom, Tanya, Melanie, Mikkel, Doug, Joanne, Rich, Lisa, Maureen, Tami, Lyle, Todd, Monica, Martha, Ken, Krystal, Jon, Suzanne, Chad, Hemed, Anne, Scott, Marcie, the Working Moms Exile Group, Chapell, Kelly, Caroline, Laura, Dana, Hailey, Louis, colleagues of the NCCJCP, my former neighbors who checked on me, the (loosely assembled) Pittsboro/Chapel Hill Widows group, Colleen, Danielle, and Harry & Anthony.

Thank you to the USMA Class of '91 (especially the I-Beam), USMA AOG, West Point Memorial Affairs, Eric's colleagues at SAS Institute, Eric's clients from Carolina Small Business Solutions, Eric's golf pals at the Chapel Ridge and Preserve Golf clubs, Zach Johnson, the Kraft family, Dr. Coler and the nursing staff at Swedish Hospital in Seattle; Dr. Carlson, Cat, Dr. Park, and the nursing staff at UNC Lineberger Cancer Hospital; UNC Hospice Chaplain Gail Ritter and nursing staff; Abundance NC, Spark of Life, Transitions Life Care

Grief Center, Triangle Skydiving, and the amazing women at the Hope for Widows Foundation.

Thank you to my editor and cover designer Dionne Abouelela of HappyWritingCo and my fellow indie authors within the PNP family, the Third Wednesday Open Mic'ers at Lucky Tree, Anchala Studios, and the throng of other talented writers – near and far – I've met since beginning this author endeavor in 2014.

Thanks to all my readers for your continued support of my writing. Stories are born from those we love. I hope you enjoyed this one…it is the book of my heart.

Good night, E. I will love you and carry you forever. "Love you too."

> *"I know my family cares about me and loves me despite whatever flaws and shortcomings I might have. In the end, that's enough for me. As I said before, everything I've done in the last 20+ years has been for them anyway."*
>
> *– Eric John DeJong, Journal entry 5/29/2016*

Other Published Works by Dori Ann Dupré

Short Stories:

"See You in September" – *The Collection: Flash Fiction for Flash Memory* by Anne Anthony and Cathleen O'Connor, PHD

"Yellow" – *On Life and Living*, Pen Name Publishing Charity Anthology, VOL I.

"Water Island" – *From Words to Water, Pen Name Publishing Charity Anthology*, VOl II.

"The Win" – *Miscreants, Murderers & Thieves* by Samuel W. Reed

Novels:

Scout's Honor

2016 Readers' Favorite International Book Awards Bronze Medal – Southern Fiction

2017 Eric Hoffer Book Awards - Finalist

In Haddleboro, North Carolina, Scout Webb is a 14 year old kind and spirited small town southern girl and a tomboy much like her namesake, the young narrator from her mother's favorite book. With both her name and her Christian faith deeply woven into the fabric of her identity, Scout always felt like she had a lot to live up to and was the kind of girl who made her parents proud.

It's August 1983, and Scout is playing on a summer baseball team with Charlie Porter, her best friend since Kindergarten. More than anything, she is looking forward to her last few weeks at Camp Judah, a Christian camp near the Catawba River. She can't wait to see her big crush "Brother Doug," the thirty-two year old camp lifeguard who has watched her grow up each summer since she was seven years old. But after a fateful few days and one catastrophic event during her last day at the camp, Scout was changed forever.

Written through multiple narrators over the course of twenty years, this story follows Scout's personal struggles as a freshman away at college in Raleigh and later as an overworked single mother approaching middle age, where she is forced to confront the causes of her own quiet suffering, the consequences of her actions and why even the eternal love and devotion of just one true friend can't save her.

A story of a self, lost...a self, loathed...and a self, rediscovered... it examines the harsh and cruel ways in which otherwise well-intentioned and decent people treat each other...even those they claim to love, but even more so...ultimately, how we treat our own selves.

Reviews for Scout's Honor

"*Scout's Honor* thoroughly engages us from the moment we first meet the engaging Scout Webb, a sort of female Holden Caulfield whose lifelong struggles with love make a compelling read and teach us much. First-time novelist Dori Ann Dupré does a terrific job telling her story through an array of interesting characters while demonstrating a keen eye for detail and a true gift for exploring the joys, heartbreaks, complexities and deep truths of human relationships. *Scout's Honor* will capture your heart."

~ Mark Ethridge, author of *Grievances* and *Fallout*, screen writer for *Deadline*, and two-time Pulitzer Prize for Public Service recipient as managing editor with the *Charlotte Observer*

"Dori Ann Dupré crafted this tale that followed the life of Scout Webb, quite delicately. Her use of first person narrative of the main characters drove the story and revealed all the coming of age, humor, heart-break and often horrendously real situations in such a unique way. Each voice was captured well and you could feel each of their triumphs or pains as they were unfolding. I commend her choices to give us this story in this way. This is a bold debut and you will feel the gambit of emotions as you turn the pages."

~ Mike Hansen, author of *When Life Hands You a Lemon*

"Dori Ann Dupré is one of those authors who write so well you forget you're reading. She brings you into the story, and you become invested in the characters and their stories. You are angry with the antagonists, but you understand them too. You know where they went wrong, but you still care for them, just as you have done with people in your real life who have stumbled."

~ Scott Thompson, author of *Eight Days*

"Dori Ann Dupré has written a wonderful debut novel about a character named Scout – after the character in her mother's favorite book *To Kill a Mockingbird*. The book covers Scout's life with all of its joy and pain, mistakes and successes. She is a real multi-dimensional character and I found myself thinking about her even after the last page of the book was read.... I loved this novel and it was hard to believe that it was this author's first novel. I look forward to her next novels and predict some great books in the future from her."

~ Susan Roberts, reviewer for *Girl Who Reads Book Blog*

About the Author

Dori is the author of the two-time international award winning debut novel, *Scout's Honor.* She has several published short stories, poems, and articles; serves as a contributing blogger to the Hope for Widows Foundation, and is the founder of the Grieve the Write Way grief writing workshops. Dori is the proud mother of two daughters, works full time in the legal field, is a veteran of the United States Army, and resides in Raleigh, North Carolina. *Good Buddy* is her second novel.

www.DoriAnnDupre.com

Follow Dori on social media:
Twitter @DoriAnnDupre
Facebook @DoriAnnDupreLLC
Instagram @doridj

EJD Press

Raleigh, North Carolina